RITUAL

LOLA TAYLOR

Elijah Johnson never thought he'd see one, let alone both, of his brothers again. If only it were a happy reunion, but that bullshit was usually reserved for fairy tales and soap operas. One brother is lukewarm and civil; the other wants to knock his block off. Not that Elijah can blame them. He's feeling pretty rotten about the state of their relationship, and is starting to question whether staying away was the right choice…

Verika Tate—whoops, "Johnson"—is growing into her powers at an alarming rate, but she's not about to tell her mate that. He has enough on his plate as is, namely dealing with his own insecurities about magic while his brothers try convincing him to join them on an epic quest to defeat the witch he fears more than death itself.

As Verika and Elijah struggle to deal with their inner demons, the strength of their bond will be tested—especially as Mistress Black draws closer, determined to convert Verika over to her side and use her to destroy everything in her path.

Can true love survive in a world wrought with war and treachery?

The climactic ending to the Blood Moon Rising series.

Cover designed by Kitten of Deranged Doctor Design
Interior design and formatting by Champagne Formats
Copy edited by Faith of The Atwater Group
Proofread by Susie of Red Adept Editing
Indigo Dreamer Press logo designed by Indi99o of 99designs
Author photograph by Sara Rogers Photography

INDIGO
DREAMER PRESS

www.lolataylorbooks.com
www.indigodreamerpress.com

ISBN: 0-9835131-8-X
ISBN-13: 978-0-9835131-8-6

For more information, please visit
www.lolataylorbooks.com

CHAPTER ONE

ELIJAH TOOK A SIP OF THE LUKEWARM SOUP, WINCING AS pain threaded along his jaw. Nik had left a nice-sized knot there. He'd be lucky if he could chew right for a week.

He smiled a little. *Hits like a Johnson, all right.* Looked like Elijah's instruction on fighting techniques wasn't completely lost on his younger brother.

The two of them used to spar and wrestle in their backyard when they were kids. Elijah even got it in his head to open up a neighborhood fight club and charge spectators money. He set up all the matches himself, even made a ring out of some rope and old gym mats he'd found in a Dumpster. His "concessions" had consisted of microwavable popcorn and beer from their father's stash. For a thirteen-year-old, the money had been pretty good. The fight club lasted about a year before other kids' parents caught on and all but broke down their door, cussing and yelling at their dad. He'd beaten Elijah hard that night. Which was fine by him. At least he hadn't gone after Nik or little Gage.

Verika sat beside him at the small dinette set in their private suite. The place was luxurious, with five-hundred-count this and designer-brand that. He'd half-expected Nik's taste to drift toward the Walmart or Goodwill chic, but hell, people's tastes changed.

He had changed. He'd always been a hard man, speaking more with his fists than his mouth. But there was a weight to him now that had settled in the creases on his forehead, the hollows of his eyes. That was another thing—his eyes had lost their luster. Mischief once sparkled there—Nik never had taken the damn world seriously—but now there was a deadness, a worry to them that troubled Elijah.

Verika clenched and flexed her fingers—a nervous habit, he'd noted. Worry wrinkled her lovely features, those green eyes of hers bright as she looked at his jaw. "Do you want me to heal it?"

His heart skipped a beat with fear, which he shoved back down.

Verika's eyes widened. She swallowed hard and looked down, staring at the half-eaten soup.

Shit. He hadn't been quick enough to hide his reaction. Yeah, he was still scared of magic, but he hated himself for it because of her. Dealing with his personal demons would take a whole lotta therapy and a whole lotta time. He accepted that. Didn't mean he liked it. For her sake, he wanted to be fixed now, to let some spell wash away all his fears. But he knew there wasn't a snowstorm-in-hell's chance of that happening.

He grasped her hand and squeezed. "I'm so—"

"Shssh." She pressed a finger to his lips and shook her head, those red curls he loved so much bouncing around. A smile lit her face. "Don't be. You have nothing to be sorry for. I shouldn't have pressed you. I'm the one who should be sorry."

"Bullshit." He grabbed the back of her head and pulled her close to kiss her forehead. "You're amazing."

A pretty blush colored her cheeks. He'd never get tired of making her blush, of hearing how her heart sped up ever so slightly every time he touched her.

Glad to know he wasn't alone in that respect. His own heart tickled his chest with a fluttering thrill whenever he caressed her. A warm glow overtook him each time he looked at her, somewhat overshadowing any lingering fear he had about magic.

Or her ability to wield it.

His throat tightened slightly, and he cursed, letting his hands drop from her face. Fuck it all. He wasn't about to let some trauma determine how he felt about his mate. Clearly, fate wanted him to get over his old wounds, to heal and move forward with his life. Otherwise, why make his mate the very creature he was terrified of?

Though it was a bitch to clutch the spoon because his hand hurt so much—hey, clobbering people was hard work—Elijah hurried up and ate the rest of the soup. It was good. The chef here was almost as good as Mistress Black's had been.

He shuddered. That bitch had a taste for good food and had hired only the best chefs. Sometimes, she'd fly in cooks from California, New York—all over, really. He swore some of the meals he'd eaten had cost more than the shitty little house he and his brothers had grown up in. He just knew it was a whole lotta money, which he'd never seen much of. Not legally, anyway. Not until he'd decided to turn over a new leaf. And look where that'd gotten him.

Maybe he should reconsider this whole "law-abiding citizen" act. After all, the only reason he'd met Verika was because he'd been caught trying to buy some illegal papers to get out of the States. Maybe his penchant for breaking the law was actually a *good* thing.

But he knew in his heart of hearts, his honest, law-obeying mate—who, hello, was a freaking cop— wouldn't see it that way.

Verika watched him in silence while he finished eating. The worry never left her eyes.

"I'm fine," he said—er, mumbled. Moving his jaw hurt, but he was used to it. He'd been busted up worse. Actually, he'd suspected Nik had taken it easy on him.

Which meant there might be a ray of hope he could fix things with him.

The thought made his heart speed up, he wanted it so badly.

A family. *His* family.

Yes, he was determined to create another one with Verika. Maybe even have pups someday, if she was up to it. They hadn't gotten that far yet, though he sure as hell hoped she was all right with it. She hadn't mentioned being on birth control, and they'd made love under the stars a few times now on their way here. They'd been responsible,

4

used condoms. But still… accidents happened.

If he had pups, he wanted—needed—his brothers to be involved in their lives. To tell them embarrassing stories about their old man when he was a kid. To look after them and Verika should anything happen to him.

Ever since they'd mated, he'd had this ominous feeling hanging over his head. As if all this happiness was a dream that was going to be ripped away by Mistress Black when she found him. And considering Verika hadn't had any luck yet lifting the brand that bound him to Mistress Black, he knew it was only a matter of time before that happened.

"Elijah?" A warm hand rested on his arm. "Are you all right? You've been drumming your fingers harder and harder…and you've bent the spoon."

"Huh?" He looked down. Sure enough, the metal spoon was now crooked, courtesy of his thumb. And his fingertips actually hurt from tapping them on the table. "Sorry." He bent the spoon back into shape before he set it down in the empty bowl and pushed it aside. "I get like that when I'm thinking."

"They must not have been good thoughts."

He smiled, hoping it reached his eyes so it would hide the shadow of fear there. "Some were good. I was thinking of us."

"Oh?"

"Yep." He pulled her onto his lap, her back to his chest, and pushed aside her hair so he could kiss her neck. He loved the spot just below her ear. It always made her shiver when he planted his lips there. "I was thinking about how damn sexy you look naked."

She snorted and gave him a playful shove. "Scoundrel. What would my parents think, knowing I've been traipsing the countryside alone with a man I'm not married to?"

He stiffened. "Are they that upti—er—traditional?" His "Johnson bluntness" was something he was trying hard to work on, too. Gage always had been the most considerate and tactful speaker of the three of them. Most of the time, whatever flew out of Nik's and Elijah's mouths was the first thing on their minds. Sometimes to the detriment of whomever they were speaking to. Verika was still very fond of her adoptive parents, despite her father pointing a gun at Elijah and all but running him out of their house. And for her sake, Elijah was damn well going to make an effort to try not to insult them.

Verika winced. "Dad is, for sure. He grew up in a very strict, conservative military family who were devout Christians. Mom is a Christian, too, but I think her parents weren't quite as strict as Dad's. I think that's why she has a bit of a hidden wild side."

Elijah thought back to when he'd stepped out of the shower and Mrs. Tate's gaze had swept his very naked body down and up again without shame. "Yeah, I kind of got that vibe."

Verika groaned and covered her face with her hands. "Don't remind me of the shower debacle. That was mortifying." One of the weird quirks of their mate-bond was that they could share mental images with each other. A few memories had leaked into Verika's mind and vice versa, the shower scene being one of them. Elijah knew it wasn't an uncommon quirk, especially if one or both parties had some magical ability.

"Come on." Elijah kissed her hands. "You have to admit it was funny as hell."

"Nothing about my mother seeing you butt-naked and *liking it* will ever be funny to me." With the mood officially killed, she stood and stretched her arms above her head. A yawn followed. "We should get to bed. It's nearly dawn."

He'd figured as much, even without looking at his watch. The light behind the curtains was growing brighter.

After they'd both showered and crawled into bed—holy fuck, it was nice to sleep on a mattress that didn't feel as though it were made of straw—it took Elijah another half hour to finally pass out. His brain kept working, turning over every worry and finding no way of resolving them.

Getting rid of his Blood Magic mark.

Overcoming his fear of magic.

Overcoming his anxiety around Verika when she went all badass Black Witch on people.

Patching things up between him and his brothers.

Killing Mistress Black.

Saving the Underworld and, hell, probably the whole world in the process.

Damn.

When his brain couldn't think anymore—because let's admit it, saving the world is damn exhausting—he at last succumbed to sleep.

And immediately wished he hadn't when he saw who waited for him inside the cage of his nightmares.

CHAPTER TWO

SHE WAS BOTH BEAUTIFUL AND TERRIFYING, AND MADE him feel small and frail despite how petite she was. Her elegant body lounged on the chaise, those long, pale legs partly covered in draped scarlet silk. The inky dress flowed over her body, hugging every curve and leaving little to the imagination.

To think he'd once found her beauty irresistible made him want to vomit.

The room was Persian elegance: Ornate lamps of turquoise- and amber-colored glass held twinkling tea lights. Intricately woven tapestries and rugs. Velvet, tasseled pillows of rich jewel tones piled near the chaise.

Mistress Black always had possessed a flair for the exotic.

She looked up at him beneath thick, dark lashes. Those ruby lips of hers parted into a warm smile. Her dark hair hung partly over her shoulder, drawing attention to the plump breasts she had no problem displaying. Her eyes raked him down and up, and he suddenly felt naked despite his pants and shirt.

Mistress Black pursed her lips. With a snap of her fingers, his clothes vanished, and balmy air rushed in to kiss his bared skin.

He resisted the urge to turn around or cover himself from her slimy gaze. He would spite her violation of his privacy with defiance. His chin held high, he set his jaw and stared back at her without blinking as she took him in.

"That's better." Her gaze lingered on his broad, chiseled chest before it lifted to his face. "I've missed the view."

"Well, now you've seen it. Give me back my clothes."

"So demanding, not to mention rude. I thought I taught you better manners than that, my pet."

"I'm not your fucking pet."

She laughed. "Of course you are. You always will be, Elijah, for you bear my mark."

As soon as she spoke about it, the seal flared brilliant red. He hissed and gritted his teeth against the pain. It felt as if someone had taken a brand to his back and pressed it against his skin.

When his knees didn't buckle, Mistress Black's smile vanished, replaced by an icy glare. Her eyes flashed crimson, two pinpricks of fire among a too-perfect face.

The pain intensified. A thousand fiery hooks dug into his flesh, setting his bloodstream to boiling. He roared; his back arched as his knees started to buckle. Righting himself, he forced his legs to hold. His chest heaved with the effort of withstanding the pain, and he glared right back at the bitch of a witch before him.

He chuckled. "That all you got? You're losing your touch."

Bracing himself for her to lash out, he blinked in surprise when the pain disappeared, as did the fury and fire in her eyes. She gazed at him placidly, the remnants of a saturnine smile on her lips. In a blink, his clothes were back.

He staggered backward at the ozone-like stench of magic, terror catapulting his heart into his throat.

"Still afraid of magic, are we? That must be a problem in the bedroom." She rose and walked over to the short, elegant table a few feet away. Kneeling on one of the plush pillows, she poured a drink from a crystal tankard that had materialized out of thin air.

He grew tenser as he stared at the tankard.

It's not real.

His palms felt clammy.

"Sit." A soft command from a master to her pet.

When he didn't move, she arched a brow. "What are you waiting for?"

"You didn't say please."

A slow smile spread on those full lips. "Please," she purred, stretching the word out.

Her sinful voice oozed over his skin like oil, making him shudder. He could try to wake himself up, get the fuck out of here before—

"Actually, you can't," she said.

He startled. "Excuse me?"

"I'm inside your head, remember?" She tapped her temple with a scarlet nail for emphasis. "I can hear your

10

thoughts. In this dream world, I am your ruler. You won't be leaving until I say you can go. I suggest you sit down so we may discuss some business."

Not seeing that he had much of a choice, he forced himself to walk over to the table and sit. The pillow was comfortable—damn comfortable, if he was honest—but he sat as if he had a stick shoved up his ass.

Ready to move, prepared to defend himself if need be. In another lifetime, he might have appreciated Mistress Black's penchant for the unpredictable. It had made her exciting, fun.

What a goddamned idiot he had been.

Live and learn…or die, in this case. Maybe. Probably. Inevitably.

She hummed to herself as she poured a second glass, some sorrowful tune he didn't recognize. The lyrics most likely contained something about killing puppies or screwing people over. Those sorts of things gave her the warm fuzzies.

"Let me see," she murmured, setting the glass in front of him and tapping a nail against her pouty bottom lip. "You prefer your wine dry."

Before he could answer, she waved a hand over his glass. "Shiraz." She lifted her glass and smelled it. Her eyes fluttered closed in pleasure. "It's supposed to have Persian roots, or so I'm told. I know you'll appreciate the flavor."

He didn't want any of her damn wine.

When he didn't move to drink, her knuckles turned white around the glass, which had cracked beneath her grip.

Fine, fine. To spare the glass's life... Lifting the glass, he sniffed. The rich aroma of smoke, spices, and fruit drifted to his nose, sharp and sweet at once. Call him intrigued. Taking a sip of the red liquid, he let the wine swirl over his tongue, washing his palate in the colorful flavors of blackberry, cloves, thyme, oak, and smoke. "It's good," he admitted.

"Isn't it, though? It goes great with gouda cheese, in my opinion." She pushed forward a little silver platter of perfectly cut cheese squares he hadn't noticed before.

"You didn't bring me here for a wine-and-cheese party."

"No, I suppose I didn't. That's one of the things I like about you. No bullshit. You like to get right to the point."

He raised a brow, a silent "get on with it."

Pursing her lips, she tempered her glare. "I was wondering when you're coming home."

He laughed. "That's easy to answer—never."

"But you'll have to come home sometime. What are you going to do about the infection?"

"*Infection?*"

"Oh, well, it might not have been long enough for it to set in. You haven't been feeling nauseous lately? Sudden wooziness, insomnia, fevers, and fits? That sort of stuff?"

He'd felt under the weather while he and Verika were on the road, but he had dismissed it as a bug.

"So you have felt something," Mistress Black mused, pressing her palms flat to the table and leaning forward. "Probably thought nothing of it, too, knowing you. But let me warn you, Elijah—the longer you're away from me, the worse your condition will get."

"What the hell are you talking about?"

She held a hand over her heart. Red light flickered beneath her fingertips, outlining a brand that matched the symbol inked upon his back. "I'm talking about our Blood Bond. The tie between our souls."

"I have nothing in common with you."

"Oh, but don't you? You and I are just alike. Two sides of the same coin, as they say." Her voice lowered to a whisper. Her steady, black gaze bored into his eyes, as if she could see down into his core. "You're just as broken, your heart just as black. We understand each other on a primal level. Few people on this earth ever experience that."

"Bullshit." He shot to his feet, staggered away from the table as spots fired before his eyes. Horror made his heart hammer. It had to be a lie—a filthy, disgusting lie. Anything that came out of that woman's mouth generally was. She thrived on others' misery. "There is no bond between us. It's just a mark, nothing more. And somehow, some way, no matter what it takes, I'm going to break it."

She threw her head back and laughed. "Oh, Elijah. I never tire of hearing your passion for defying me. It's refreshing." She sighed and stood, a single, fluid motion. Like a snake uncoiling before preparing to strike. "Here's the deal, pet. That bond ensures you'll return to me. There is no way for you to break it."

"But you can."

She smiled. "Perhaps. For a price."

Of course. "And what would that be?"

"I'll break your mark if you bring me Verika."

The sweet, smoky aftertaste of the wine turned to ash on his tongue. It took him a moment to find his voice. "Why do you want her?"

"Because she's my daughter."

Time stopped. Like, literally, freaking stopped.

He thought of Verika, of the goodness shining through her gaze, the kindness in her gestures. There was no resemblance to the creature before him. No, the witch before him was so cold, cruel, and twisted, she might as well have been a demon. Though no physical resemblance lay there, he also knew Mistress Black was using a borrowed body.

What did her true form look like? Would she have hair of fire, or eyes the color of spring grass?

Mistress Black and Verika's magical affinity was the only thing they had in common. Black Magic was a rare gift, as was White. Both were also usually hereditary.

Though everything in him screamed that there was no way in hell this thing had spawned his sweet Verika, he couldn't deny the potential truth laced in those three words.

She's my daughter.

Verika had few good memories of her mother. Some weird details stood out—like how she'd earned her unique name—but most of her childhood was hazy. The spell that had been used to bind her powers had also impacted her memories, she'd assumed. It had come up during one of their late-night, fireside conversations.

Still, Mistress Black had to be delusional. Or screwing with him.

But...what if?

The witch and the wolf stared at each other. The tension thickened until it made the air damn near unbreathable. "That's impossible," he finally whispered.

"It is, actually. I just wanted to see the look on your face."

Fucking bitch.

Snarling, he lunged, fangs bared, claws extended. Her pale throat looked like a great place to put them.

Before he'd drawn close, she flicked her hand in a careless gesture. His body launched off the floor, thrown backward by an invisible force that felt like an oversized baseball bat had smacked him along his front side. He landed on the chaise, toppling it over, and sprawled out onto the carpeted floor.

Groaning, he sat up. His ribs hurt, most likely bruised.

Could she fuck up his real body by hurting him in a dream? Seemed like the kind of thing she'd find a way to do. He wouldn't put it beyond the scope of her vast power.

"When will you ever learn? I suppose that wicked scar stretching across your abdomen didn't teach you anything."

Although it looked cool as shit, that scar was a reminder of the day he'd gotten it into his head to attack her while her back was turned. It had been shortly after she'd hypnotized him to make him think he was hunting down the wolf who'd turned him and his brothers, and instead found himself dripping in the blood of an innocent White Witch when Mistress Black had lifted the hypnosis. Enraged hadn't come close to describing how he'd felt.

He'd never despised anyone more in his life than he

did her. Needing to let the anger and sorrow out somehow before it ruptured inside him, he'd gone after her.

And had found a blade embedded in his stomach. "Let this be a warning to you—never sneak up on a witch. Especially one as dangerous as me."

She easily could have gutted him. Maybe that had been the point all along, to get her to kill him to end his misery and disgust at what he'd just done to that poor girl.

But she hadn't. Instead, she'd lanced the blade across his abs, cutting deep but not too deep. Scoring his skin with yet another mark of her dominance, much like a wolf marking her territory.

Her property.

Elijah started to rise with a grunt when she placed a stiletto-clad foot on his chest and pressed down. The tiny heel dug into his sternum, but he refused to wince. Staring up at her, he bore her weight with a clenched jaw.

"Stubborn to the bitter end, Elijah?" She propped a hand up on her hip and gazed down at him, her dark eyes glittering. "You're saying you would rather meet a miserable end than reunite me with my kin?"

"What do you mean, 'your kin'?"

"Promise you won't bite?"

A growl was his response. Seemed good enough for her, because a moment later she lifted her foot and the stabbing pain in his chest subsided. Coughing, he rose to his feet as she sauntered away to pour herself another glass of wine, those hips making the crimson fabric of her dress swish and sway.

Mistress Black took a gulp of her wine, not looking at

him. Her eyes lingered on the wall, a faraway look on her face. "Verika may not be my daughter, but we are of the same blood. She's descended from me."

"How do you know this?"

"Like calls to like," she sang, tearing her gaze off the wall with a blink and smiling at him. "I just know."

More mystical bullshit, most likely. She was toying with him. Had to be.

But what if she wasn't? What if his precious Verika truly was related to the most terrible witch the Underworld had ever seen?

He'd allow himself to contemplate that later. Right now, he needed all his senses sharp, in case this monster tried anything.

Like killing him in his sleep, literally. Though that seemed a bit far-fetched. If she were going to kill him, he'd already be dead. Killing was something she wasted no time with. Once she'd made up her mind to do away with someone, she got right to it, by any means necessary.

Not to mention there was the Blood Mark. She couldn't very well kill him without removing it first, or she'd risk harming herself in the process.

He suddenly appreciated the mark more. Pain in his ass though it was, it could very well be the only thing keeping him alive right now. A bargaining chip, to be used at a later time perhaps, when he'd pored over every possible way to best exploit it.

More on that later.

Focus.

"What do you want with Verika?" he asked.

Mistress Black swished the wine in her glass for a beat, took a delicate sip, and then set it down. "To help her. To guide and shepherd her. Her power is vast. Too great for one person to figure out on her own. When I first came into my powers…what I endured…" She shuddered. "I won't subject another Black Witch to that."

"So you expect me to believe you're doing this out of kindness?"

"You know me better than that." A cunning smile. "There are other chips at play."

"Such as?"

"A good player knows never to reveal her hand."

"As it were…" he murmured. "And if I refuse to give her up?"

"It won't matter. She'll find me, one way or another. Oh, wipe that doubtful look off your face. You really think a wolf—an outlaw, might I add—with nothing to his name except a list of people who want to put a knife in his back can make someone like her happy? One of the most powerful witches the world has ever seen?"

He shifted his weight. Yeah, he knew he had little to offer Verika, but he'd never had it spelled out so bluntly.

"Her powers will grow," Mistress Black said in a quiet voice that seemed to boom with power, despite its volume. She took a step closer, and then another and another as she spoke. Those wicked eyes of hers held his, a dark promise of things to come. "She'll have so much power, she'll struggle to know what to do with all of it. She won't know how to contain and master it. No one will understand her. The world will loathe her, as it has been known to do since the dawn of time to those blessed with the Dark Gift. She'll need me because no one else in the world will get her like I do. And when she's ready, I'll be waiting." She stood before him now, head tilted back to stare up into his eyes. A triumphant smile had already wriggled its way onto her lips.

Cocky bitch. She thought she'd already won.

"I'll never let you take her," Elijah promised.

Mistress Black leaned forward, her lips an inch away from his. "You won't have a choice."

With the warmth of her breath caressing his skin, she suddenly wheeled about and walked away. "I'll give you some time to think on it. If you ever need to find me, just touch your Blood Mark, close your eyes, and think of me. I'll hear you and answer." She picked up her glass of wine and curled up on the chaise. "But don't take too long to decide, my dear. I hear the effects of the Blood Mark are most unpleasant, once the sickness is in full swing. Adieu."

With a snap of her fingers, the floor opened up beneath Elijah, and he tumbled into darkness.

Downward he went, turning head over heel into endless night while Mistress Black's chuckle echoed all around in the frigid air.

The stink of magic clung to his nostrils, coating his throat and choking him. He clutched at his neck, drowning on the scent of magic. Every horrible thing he'd been forced to do, or that had been done to him, crashed through his mind's eye.

Hell. This had to be hell.

Serpentine bodies moved through the darkness, slithering and hissing as they watched him fall with eyes of burning hellfire. Purple lightning crackled along their bodies.

Magic. They were made of Black Magic, just like those serpents Verika had summoned back at her parents' place.

Fear spiking, he Shifted his hands into paws, his sharp claws poised to shred flesh.

One of the snakes lunged for him, much faster than it should have given its enormous body. Its jaws opened wide. Elijah looked straight down into its throat and lashed out. His claws found purchase, shredding through scales, muscles, tendons.

The snake roared in fury, screaming as its twin hissed, and encircled him as he fell. Elijah cursed, his feet and hands unable to find something to grab to stop his descent. The darkness was an open pit, ready to swallow him whole. Black blood and gore dripped from his claws, splattering onto his face as he tumbled.

The snakes suddenly joined and morphed into a young woman, a White Witch, her white gown stained with blood. The fabric had been shredded, as had the flesh beneath. With tearful eyes, she begged Elijah to spare her.

"Please…please, don't kill me…"

His claws abruptly changed back to fingernails as shock jolted the wolf right out of him. He stared, shaking his head. "No…no, I didn't mean to…"

The fear fell off her face, turning to cold malice. "Yes, you did. You enjoyed killing me."

"No!" he shouted. "It's not true! I'm not a murderer! She made me do it!"

"Liar."

"No… No, get back!"

"Liar." The girl drew closer. Her face had changed into that of Mistress Black's.

"Liar."

The face morphed again. Verika now stood before him, eyes glowing green, hair lifting around her face in a cloud of crimson. Her power snapped and crackled around her body. A dark voice chuckled, and perfectly manicured hands curled around Verika's shoulders. Mistress Black peeked from behind Verika, whom she clasped like a doll.

A possession.

"Told you so," she whispered, smiling.

Elijah reached for Verika, swimming through the darkness. Mistress Black pulled her farther away.

Verika! he cried out through their bond.

Things swam in the darkness, nipping at him, leaving small bloody wounds on any piece of exposed flesh.

Verika!

The creatures hissed, struck. Their wispy bodies slithered around him faster, thicker, as they worked up a frenzy. The air stank of magic—and death.

He gasped for air, choked on the reek of rotting flesh and decaying bones. God, he couldn't breathe. He was drowning.

Sweet sunlight broke through the darkness, warming him and chasing the writhing shadows away. They hissed, recoiling as a rush of spring air enveloped him, slowing his fall. His chest heaved as the thick tartness of magic cleared his throat, and he was able to breathe again. The darkness around him gave way to brilliant sunshine and a sky so blue it almost hurt to look at it.

He landed on a bed of grass beneath a massive oak. Its shade dappled his face; the supple leaves rustled in the gentle breeze.

A soft hand with delicate, feminine fingers stroked his cheek. "Sleep, beloved. I'll keep the darkness at bay."

A wave of drowsiness hit him, ushering him under. He started to smile. Ah, there it was—relief. A feeling of complete and utter safety washed over him, and his tensed, battle-ready body at last relaxed.

As his eyelids fluttered shut, he caught a glimpse of red hair and sparkling green eyes filled with eternal love.

CHAPTER THREE

VERIKA HAD BEEN AWAKE FOR THE PAST HOUR AND A half, as soon as she'd felt her mate's terror. She hadn't told him about that side effect of their bond—that she could feel not only his thoughts, but also his emotions while both waking and dreaming. If he knew, she was positive he would never fall asleep again.

When she'd first stirred, his skin had been awash in a cool sheen of sweat. His fingers were curved and twitching, as if he were in his wolf form and lashing out at some unseen monster. The instant she saw him in pain, trapped in a nightmare where she couldn't reach him, she'd summoned a simple healing spell to help soothe him. A lot of massage therapists she knew who dabbled in the magical arts also used this very same spell to help their clients relax. She'd closed her eyes and imagined his face, imagined a gentle land of sloping green hills kissed by sunshine. In the dream, she'd summoned a soft breeze to whisk his worries and fears away, had stroked his face lovingly until he'd at last fallen asleep.

The touch of dark magic in the dream bothered her. It would have slipped her notice if she hadn't felt it tug at her own magic.

Mistress Black had been there, inside her mate's head. The possessive urge to rip her to shreds, to claw her beautiful face apart, surged up inside her as her inner wolf growled. The closer she drew to her first Change, the more wolf-like traits she displayed. Among them, catching herself staring at the swelling moon, a sharper sense of smell, hearing things from far away, much farther than the human ear could hear. It was frightening at first, she had to admit. Now, she'd overcome the scary stage and was on to the curious phase. She wondered what all she could do with her new form, if she would retain any of her magical abilities.

And whether or not she could use said abilities to track down Mistress Black and end her before something terrible happened.

Whatever had pulled at her own magic in the dream faded away. Unable to locate the source, Verika opened her eyes in the real world with a sigh of disappointment.

She glanced at her mate—and smiled. Her shoulders relaxed when she saw her mate now lying at peace, a blissful smile on his face. Sometimes she would sit and watch him, struck speechless by the gorgeous man who was destined to be hers. How kind fate had been indeed.

Her eyes roved over the hills and slopes of his chest, crowned in a patch of dark hair between his pecs. Though lax, his thick arms were corded with muscles honed from years of fighting. Scars crisscrossed his flesh, the wickedest of which slashed over his abdomen. She'd wondered where he'd gotten it, had even asked about some of the others. Brawling, mostly, or "getting some sense knocked into him," he'd said.

But he had yet to tell her about that large scar across his abdomen, the one that looked as though it had cut so deep he should have been dead.

A shiver raced over her flesh, and she rubbed her arms. How close had Elijah come to greeting Death that day? How many more times would they face down the Grim Reaper before they were allowed to be together?

If they were allowed.

No. She wouldn't allow herself to think such thoughts. Doing so meant giving up hope, and no way in hell was she doing that. Not now, not ever. It was the only thing she had to hold on to, the thing that kept her going. That, and Elijah's love.

Rising and squinting at the sunlight pouring in through the windows, she flicked her wrist. The gauze curtains instantly thickened, shutting out any hint of light and darkening the room.

At least Elijah wouldn't wake now. Truth was, he was probably so exhausted that the light wouldn't have been a problem. But it had concerned her, and she couldn't quite let go of the need to fuss over her mate.

And, if she were honest, she'd admit she'd grown rather fond of the darkness these past few weeks. And it wasn't just because her inner wolf was growing stronger. She'd always been drawn to the night, even as a child. For all its pretty colors and warmth, a trickle of sunlight couldn't hold a candle to the frosty beauty of a star-swept sky awash in soft, silvery moonlight. Night had always seemed more peaceful to her—and her powers had felt stronger. Especially now that her Dark Gift had awakened, seemingly restless after years of suppression.

But why now, after all these years?

She nibbled her lip as she wandered over to the bathroom to draw herself a hot bath. It wasn't that her powers were out of control. Not yet. Though if they kept growing at the pace they were, she feared she may someday be unable to contain them.

And then who—or what—would she turn into?

Casting aside her silk nightgown, she lowered herself into the steaming water, sinking lower and lower until it rose to her chin. The warmth burned and prickled at first, her skin was so cold. Tiny ripples raced across the water's surface as her body trembled, fighting to warm itself. Within a few minutes, her muscles unwound and the surface stilled.

Yet the chill—the fear she'd tried so desperately to suppress—remained rooted in her bones.

Every witch had grown up with "ghost stories," tales of blood and death swapped over pillow fights and flashlights at slumber parties. Most spoke of the worst of their kind, those dark women and men who'd been granted powers from the devil himself. Or so the legends said.

They destroyed towns, burned families alive in their homes while their screams and pleas filled the smoky air. Devoured children and fashioned necklaces out of their bones.

Verika stared at the murky water. A deadweight settled in her chest.

There was no such thing as a good Black Witch or Warlock. That's what everyone said, what everyone believed because they'd been taught it from a young age and had probably never questioned those beliefs because they'd never met a Black Witch or Warlock. She'd met plenty of witches and warlocks of the other magical houses, and especially being a cop—or rather, ex- cop—she knew all too well that the soul of the magic depended on the heart of the user. There had been plenty of Blue, and even White, Witches and Warlocks who were as corrupt as they came. Even the gentler houses weren't immune to defilement.

"You always have choices," Satine had told her. "The choice to be good or to be bad. All you have to do is decide."

Decide. Such a simple thing to do, and yet it held so much weight. A single choice could determine your entire future. But what Verika had wondered as she'd gorged herself on the pain and suffering of Gerard, the man who'd killed her mentor in cold blood, was whether she was really so different from him.

She'd enjoyed it, killing him. Or rather, her magic had, but weren't she and her powers becoming one and the same? Every night, she could feel her magic's inky threads lazily weaving their way throughout her blood, bonding with her. Making her feel stronger, in body, mind, and soul. Her endurance, she'd noted during their woodland treks, had grown exponentially. Unnaturally so. Or rather, supernaturally. Eyesight, taste, and sound had also sharpened, though she couldn't be sure whether that was due to her impending Change or another magical enhancement.

She knew witches and warlocks changed when coming into their powers. With deep longing, she'd watched her childhood friends receive their gifts, come into their own, and couldn't wait until it was at last her turn.

But she waited and waited. Day by day, that burning hope to belong to her tribe diminished, growing smaller and smaller until she almost couldn't remember what she'd been excited for, save for the bitter taste of disappointment that reminded her she was different.

Oh, how right and wrong she'd been.

Leaning forward, she stared at her reflection in the pool, at the green eyes so full of light and goodness. Elegant, mystical markings inked her neck, back, and shoulders, curving gracefully down onto her chest, where they stopped just above her breasts. Indigo whorls and delicate crescent moons accented the Celtic knots, vines, and roses scattered over her torso. Her body had changed so much. Getting out of the office had done her physique good. Her arms and legs seemed more defined, and she swore her waistline had shrunk.

She smirked. The secret to weight loss? Running for your life. She could imagine the infomercial now: "Nothing gets you in shape like having a death threat hanging over your head!" Cue a thumbs-up flash and an overly enthusiastic grin.

Yeah, that would probably be one fitness plan she'd never be able to sell mainstream.

Bad ideas aside, *she* had changed even more. She'd sworn never to date another werewolf, and here she was mated to one.

One who made her want to be the best damn witch, and woman, she could be.

She knew she was good, deep, deep down—but not completely. No one was. People were varying shades of gray, some darker than others.

You always have choices.

"I choose to be good," she whispered to herself. "No matter what, I'll keep running toward the light."

She wasn't sure who she was promising: herself or Satine. Either way, promises held power. Resolve. She needed that, needed the surety of that commitment burning in her soul if things went wrong.

Which, she had a feeling, was going to happen eventually, given the circumstances.

After lounging in the bathtub until her skin pruned, she toweled off and threw on a black silk robe she'd found in the enormous closet. She was almost afraid to put it on. The label bore the logo of some designer she'd never heard of, but it sounded fancy. The robe was thick and finely sewn, with small pockets on the front, and buttery soft. Her skin practically purred with satisfaction as the expensive material brushed over it. The cost of that single bathrobe—a freaking bathrobe, for crying out loud!—probably cost more than her entire wardrobe put together.

Still…it was nice to wear something so pricey. Probably one of the few chances she'd get in her life to indulge in a little finery.

Threading her fingers through her hair to untangle it, she patted off the excess water, letting it hang freely over her shoulder to air dry. She'd never been fond of hair dryers. They always seemed to make her hair extra frizzy, and God knew she could use all the help she could get taming it.

After brushing her teeth and applying a silky, jasmine-scented moisturizer to her face that she'd found in the cabinet, she padded out to the bedroom, when a soft knock came at the door.

Careful not to make a sound to disturb her mate, who still slumbered with a smile on his face, she opened the door—

And went rigid all over.

Alara Crescent blinked, but other than that there was no other sign of surprise on her lovely face.

The two women stared at each other, the silence heavy.

Alara recovered first. "Hello." The word sounded strained. Cold. As if all her pretty manners had kicked in and made her attempt to be polite.

"Hello," Verika answered quietly.

More silence.

Alara's eyes flitted past her and flicked toward the bed. "Gage is on his way. He should be here within an hour. I was coming to wake you up, but I see you're already awake." A pointed look to Elijah.

"I'll wake him up soon," Verika promised, crossing her arms. Under that woman's imperial stare, she felt naked.

Alara didn't respond, instead assessing Verika with a critical eye. As if sizing her up. She'd seen that look before, usually when one werewolf came across another.

"Was there something I could help you with?" Verika at last asked when the silence became uncomfortable.

Alara pursed her lips. "I don't sense it."

"What?"

"Your magic…it's gone silent." The subtle shudder didn't escape Verika's notice. "Is hiding your signature another one of your powers?"

Truthfully, she hadn't even realized she'd been doing anything. Which made her giddy as hell. For weeks now, she'd been focusing on masking her and Elijah's signatures, so as to better stay hidden from other paranormals. And, namely, to stay under Mistress Black's radar. At first, it had been hard to focus on hiding a part of herself. But with practice, it had gotten easier. Apparently to the point where Verika didn't much have to concentrate on it.

"I've been practicing," she said lamely. She prayed her ineptitude at making conversation didn't show too badly.

"So I see." Alara sighed and put her hands on her hips. "Look, we should talk. When you get dressed, come find me. I'll be in the garden out back. There's a pea gravel pathway off the veranda. At the fork, take a left. You'll come across a stone angel."

Giving an awkward but tight smile, Alara turned and left Verika in the doorway.

We should talk.

Oh God. Verika didn't need to be psychic to know what about. She was Alara's mate's ex-girlfriend, after all. Plus, her magic was one of the most feared in the land. Alara probably thought she was evil; maybe she'd even try to go Buffy on her.

Your imagination is running away with you again.

Shaking her head free of such nonsense, she shut the door, raided the closet, and two minutes later emerged wearing black leggings, a black, long-sleeved tunic top, and…her mud-spattered, run-down boots. Realizing they were going to be in the woods for a while, she'd bought them from an outlet-mall store soon as she had the chance. Though once sleek and shiny, they were now coated in a thin layer of mud.

No matter. An easy fix.

With a snap of her fingers, the mud vanished.

"Where are you going?"

Verika turned to see her mate rising from the bed with a yawn. "Gage will be here within the hour, presumably to see us," she said. *To see you.*

Nervous energy crackled through their bond. On instinct, she sent soothing energy back to calm her mate. "Alara asked me to meet her in the garden to talk."

"You sure that's a good idea?"

"I think staying here and ignoring her invitation would be worse." Kissing him, she left him to get ready, regrettably declining his offer for a joint shower, and made her way downstairs.

The house was huge but not overly complicated in layout. She wandered until she'd found the back of the house, and said veranda Alara had spoken of, well aware of the fact eyes watched her warily and people went out of their way to avoid directly crossing paths with her. A maid spotted her, gasped, and scurried off in the opposite direction as fast as her feet would carry her. Never in her life would Verika think she'd instill that kind of terror in people. It would almost be comical, had it not been a grim reminder of how terrible her power could be.

Two guards were posted at the doors that led to the veranda. Neither made to stop her as she swept past, though she felt their inner wolves' hackles rise.

And the wolf spirit inside her growled back.

She shoved it down. She'd heard from werewolf friends that "the inner beast" could be a little dominant at times. Some people gave in to it altogether, shifting and never returning to their human forms. Which, Verika thought, didn't sound so damn bad right now. A drama-free life... oh, if only. If the most she had to worry about were fleas, she'd just about take it.

Keep dreaming, girl.

She thought she had an advantage to keeping her inner wolf in check, considering she was used to dealing with her powers. Well, at least for the past month. When she'd been a dabbler, a clever little witch who happened to be good at spells, curses, you name it, she hadn't had to worry much about power supervision. Now, with this darkness inside her swirling, changing, and growing, every day was a constant battle to keep it in check.

Sunlight hit her face as she stepped out onto the pea gravel pathway Alara had spoken of. The gravel was a nice beige color that complemented the vibrant brick-red tiles of the veranda flooring. The air was perfumed with the sharp musk of roses and the sweeter tones of lavender. The air had that cool crispness to it that she'd always loved about fall. Unfortunately, it also had a smattering of dust, thanks to the surrounding forest, the trees of which had begun to shuck their leaves. Her nose started to tingle.

Verika admired the garden as she walked. It was immaculately kept, with tall hedgerows dotted in petite white flowers lining the path. At the fork, Verika took a left as instructed, and she found herself in a rose garden. White, yellow, red, pink, burgundy, blue, orange…the full blossoms danced in the chilly fall breeze, reminding her of home and her mother's love for flowers.

A pang of homesickness went through her. It had crossed her mind more than once that she might not ever get to hug her mother or father again before this all played out.

Don't think like that. You'll make it. You all will.

At least, she hoped so. Prayed so.

After a few winding turns of lovely rose, lavender, and baby's breath flower beds, the stone angel came into view. Centered in a courtyard of pearly tiles, the angel looked down on the earth with a benevolent smile, her long hair flowing over enormous tucked-in wings. Her dress looked like that of a goddess, flowing to the pool of water at her feet and disappearing beneath the gentle waves of the fountain. Three pea gravel paths adjoined the courtyard, leading off to different flower gardens, it looked like.

The courtyard itself was surrounded in lilies: wild, tall blossoms of vibrant orange and pink that rose to Verika's hips. Pastel-colored pink and white water lilies floated in the fountain. Which, she noted upon inspection, was filled with koi; their orange, white, and black scales shimmered in the sunshine speckling the water.

"Peaceful, isn't it?"

Verika jumped and whirled. A little yelp flew out of her mouth. She'd been so focused on the beauty around her that she hadn't felt Alara's signature until now.

Reckless. What if it had been the enemy?

Silently chastising herself, she smiled sheepishly at Alara as heat crept into her cheeks. "Yeah, it's pretty, um, private. And quiet. Like your own little secret garden."

Alara sat on a wide stone bench adjacent from the fountain. She patted the seat next to her.

"It is," Alara said as Verika stiffly walked over and sat down, keeping a good foot between them. "I come here often when I need to think. Or be alone. Usually with a journal in tow." She smiled softly.

Verika hesitantly smiled back, fidgeting with her hands on her lap. "I don't blame you. It's nice." She winced. Why was it that everything that came out of her mouth sounded lame? At least where the werewolf princess was concerned.

A moment of silence passed, filled with the music of the babbling fountain. "I don't expect us to be best friends," Alara said at last, eyes fixed on the angel. "But I want us to at least make an attempt at liking each other. Our mates will need our strength. And if we're quarreling over things that happened in the past, we can't give them our full support for the battle that is to come."

Verika's lips turned up slightly. "You remind me of Elijah. He likes to get right to the point."

Alara barked a laugh. "Probably because I've been

hanging out with Nik for too long. I never used to be so blunt." She blinked suddenly. The laughter died on her face as she looked at Verika in question.

"It's okay." Verika waved her hands. "I don't mind you talking about him. Believe me, one Johnson is plenty enough for me to handle."

Alara's lips cracked a smile, her shoulders relaxing, and she looked again at the fountain. "I never thought I would find a love so pure as this," she said quietly, as if afraid to speak about it for fear it would vanish. "I always thought my father would marry me off to some nobleman for power, money, influence, whatever suited him best, the mate-bond be damned. To have found Nik... I still can't believe how lucky I am."

Verika smiled. "He needs someone like you. Someone strong yet patient. I can already tell you're rubbing off on him. He seems more stable. In the office while he was questioning us, I could tell by the way he looked at you how much you mean to him. You steady him."

Alara's eyes turned shiny. Blinking, she quickly looked away, though her nails dug into the bench. "I'm...sorry I was so cold to you." A long sigh. "I knew how much you meant to him—still mean to him—and it intimidated me. Like I could never measure up, somehow."

Verika was about to insist that was ridiculous, but instead said, "If it's any consolation, you're pretty intimidating yourself."

"How so?"

"Well, you have this whole princess thing working for you. You're poised, regal. Things that look goofy on me, even when I'm trying."

Alara pursed her lips. "I suppose that's one thing that hasn't worn off in my time away from court. Poise was something my mother and etiquette instructors drilled into me from the time I was old enough to walk."

Verika tensed. Uh-oh. Was it a sore subject? Crap. She was having a hard time reading this woman.

Talking about anything princessy makes Alara a dour wolf—got it. Add that to the list of topics to avoid.

She didn't mind having to take extra care with her words. She was used to having to tiptoe around specific topics with certain people at work. Some people didn't mind opening up about things, but others were more sensitive. Clearly, Alara didn't think fondly of her time at court.

Or of her family, it seemed.

Verika inwardly frowned. What kind of a family life did Alara have growing up? Something told her they didn't have many—if any—family nights, where everyone would get together and play board games or charades. She imagined cold, imperial parents who saw not a little girl but an heir to carry on their legacy, to ensure power remained within their line. It made her sad to think someone could grow up with such a distant family when Verika's childhood had been filled with memories of baking cookies with her mother, watching football with her father, and magic lessons spent with the ever-patient Satine.

Verika winced, thinking about her.

"What's wrong?" Alara asked, watching her carefully.

Double-crap. She hadn't realized she'd outwardly

winced. Alara had a way of frazzling her—and making her feel like a clumsy country bumpkin. She was so cultured, refined. And Verika was, well, not. "My mentor was murdered," she blurted.

Alara's eyes widened in shock.

"It was by a werewolf," Verika went on quickly. "A man named Gerard."

Verika swore the other wolf's spine snapped straight, and she stopped breathing altogether. "Where did you see him?"

"In Florida." Verika leaned back slightly as Alara leaned in. "He kidnapped my parents and tried to kill Elijah."

"What happened to him?"

Uh-oh. Now it was her turn for a topic she wanted to avoid.

When it became clear Alara wasn't going to drop it, she simply told the truth. Filled with dread that Alara would look upon her with loathing for the murderer she was, Verika braced herself.

"I killed him," she whispered.

A dark, lovely smile seeped across Alara's mouth as she gazed at Verika with cold satisfaction. "Verika, I believe you just became my favorite witch."

CHAPTER FOUR

ELIJAH STARED AT THE BRAND IN THE BATHROOM mirror. A tattoo artist would have been drooling over it. Whorls and knots and writing too small for him to read wove in and out of the design, looking like a coiled serpent.

A masterpiece made of blood and magic.

Even he had to admit—it looked cool as shit. Coupled with all the scars marring his body, the brand definitely brought up his badassness on the Badass Meter. But the way it shimmered faintly in the light, the subtle heat it put off…

Shit.

Elijah dove for the toilet in time to hurl his guts. Of which there wasn't much left to hurl, considering he'd spent the past fifteen minutes since Verika had been gone doing just that.

Groaning, he flushed the spittle and sat up on wobbly knees.

Magic, magic, magic…

Swearing, he went to the sink and splashed cold water on his flushed face. He'd noticed the subtle rise in his temperature when he'd woken up, an ache settling into his muscles that heralded an oncoming fever.

You're just exhausted. There's no such bullshit "brand infection" or whatever the hell she called it.

He prayed Mistress Black was staying true to form and just screwing with him. The body aches could easily be from overexertion while hauling ass across the nation to find his brothers. The low-grade fever could be some bug he picked up from one of the shitholes they'd stayed in along the way.

He cringed. One of the inns, some run-down roach motel in the Middle-of-Nowhere, America, had more insects staying at it than people. He could smell the filth a mile away, and had tried convincing Verika to reconsider the forest. At least the bugs belonged there.

But she'd insisted on sleeping in a bed at least one night, and so in the roach motel they went. He swore things were still crawling on him, climbing into places they didn't need to be. Infecting him with God-knew-what.

So help him, he swore never again to subject himself, or his mate, to that kind of bullshit.

Glaring at himself in the mirror, he growled, "Come on, you ragged son of a bitch. You're not sick—or scared of magic. Stop being such a pussy and suck it up."

His spine straightened. Nothing like a little tough-love self-talk to get a wolf going.

He opted for a shower, turned the heat high, let the

steam billow and build. He practically purred as the luxurious soaps and shampoos cleansed his body. Hot damn, it was nice to stay somewhere decent. More than decent—downright five-star-worthy accommodations.

The manor screamed "old money." All the expensive furnishings and high-end knickknacks weren't just the work of a handful of wolves—it had taken a few generations of packs living here to acquire this kind of moolah.

For a second, jealousy flared in Elijah's chest. He'd chased money, had lost everything he had on some crack dream that hadn't panned out. Dive in first, ask business questions later. Like how to actually run a business, for starters. And what a legitimate business actually looks like.

One juicy idea in particular had caught his eye a few years ago, promising him thousands of dollars a month if he would only do "this one simple thing." The bills had been piling up, due in part to his inability to say no to his drug addictions. But rehab hadn't sounded like much fun, and he was so wretched back then he preferred the dream world the drugs created over harsh reality.

At any rate, the phrase "thousands of dollars a month" made him salivate. The website he'd found the bogus offer on hadn't looked very professional, but hey, he wasn't one to judge. Maybe they were a start-up and had limited funds. Which, in hindsight, meant they weren't even making those thousands of dollars with their own business. Lesson learned? Don't be so goddamn gullible, especially when you were desperate. Maybe then he wouldn't have blown his savings and maxed out his credit cards to make some scam artist in some remote part of the world rich.

Of course, it wasn't 'til later on, after he was stealing chicken from the food buffet at the grocery store so he wouldn't have to make a pit stop by the Dumpster drive-thru, that he discovered he was just another victim of a "get rich quick" scheme. But at that point in his life, he'd been so desperate for cash, so eager to have some funding for that next fix, that he'd tried and done just about anything to get it.

Which was probably why he ignored all the warning bells when Mistress Black had crashed into his life.

Mistress Black had the art of entrepreneurship all figured out. Fanning herself with one-hundred-dollar bills and handing out fifties as if they were candy, she'd easily been able to back up her promise to make him "wealthy beyond imagination." What he hadn't realized when he'd taken up her offer to come live with her was that he'd literally just sold his soul to the devil wearing Jimmy Choo and Valentino.

He'd just gotten out of jail—again. The police down at the local station had even gotten a name plaque for him made out of cardboard and Sharpie and had posted it outside his cell. "His" cell, because he practically lived there. Looting, stealing, fraud…they were all drugs to him, as potent as any smack he could find on the streets.

Get that next high, so he could feel alive, feel free, feel something other than regret for abandoning his brothers and resenting the lifestyle change becoming a werewolf had brought upon him. Stay doped up so he could ignore his quickly growing pile of problems.

Mistress Black had been an epic high. Sure, early on

he'd convinced himself it was love, that she was his one and only and all that.

He snorted. His lovesick pup self hadn't even known what real love was. What he'd felt for Mistress Black was foreign and shallow compared to the depth of emotion he felt for Verika. He thanked God every day she'd come into his life. It scared him to think where he'd have ended up if she hadn't.

Probably six feet under, by an unmarked gravestone. If he was lucky enough to get one of those.

A quiet knock came at the suite door as he was stepping out of the shower and toweling off. A moment later, the door opened. Sensing his mate's signature, he smiled mischievously and set down the pants he'd been about to pull on.

"Elijah?" came Verika's soft voice from the other room.

"In here," he called, grinning. "Still trying to be polite, I see. You know I don't mind you walking in on me."

"What can I say? Old habits die hard." She stopped in the doorway when she saw him, her eyes slowly raking over his body in a hungry way that made him harden.

He reciprocated the favor. Damn, did she look sexy. The outfit was a bit snug. Didn't surprise him the spare clothes in the closet were made to fit slimmer bodies. Most she-wolves he knew were lean and muscular. Before meeting Mistress Black, he'd bedded a few of them, especially when the moon was full and his werewolf instincts were at their peak. But Verika's curves and the softness of her skin were the first things he'd noticed when he'd touched her.

The curves and texture of her skin were not breakable

but…nice. Feminine. Delicate.

Addicting.

And the more he touched those curves, the more he craved her.

His eyes rested on the thin material that covered her breasts. *Those* he'd especially come to appreciate, though every inch of her was beautiful. The tunic—wasn't that what they called those things that looked like too-long T-shirts?—had a low neckline that immediately had him giving the designer props.

"My face is up here, you know," she chided playfully, though her own eyes remained locked on his sex.

"Could say the same to you," he purred as he walked closer. He let the towel fall out of his grip and raised both hands to her hips. He heard her heart speed up and her breath catch as he leaned in to kiss her.

Verika couldn't think. Couldn't breathe, couldn't move.

Elijah's arresting touch had her pinned to the spot, her eyes lowering to his parted lips as he leaned in. Her eyes fluttered shut as their mouths touched, and he coaxed her lips open. His tongue slipped into her mouth, raking along hers and making her groan. She leaned into him as he deepened the kiss, guiding her to the bathroom countertop. Grabbing her rear, he gently lifted her up so she sat on it, her legs straddling him.

His erection rubbed against her sex through the soft cotton leggings, making her core burn that much hotter.

When she'd walked in and seen him naked, the sudden

need to mate with him had become unbearable. Even with their Blood Moon over, Elijah had said she might be a bit, well, hornier than usual.

Boy, had that been an understatement.

Her breath quickened as he broke the kiss to trail those sinful lips down her throat and onto her breasts. "Elijah," she breathed, digging her nails into his biceps. Every inch of him was a weapon, a beautiful, scarred force of nature that made her pulse race and her breath tremble.

He paused just long enough with his barrage of kisses to give her a breathless, "Yeah?"

"I—we—Gage will be here soon."

"But he's not here yet."

Damn good point.

He didn't wait for an answer or another protest. Gripping the hem of her shirt, he pulled it up and over her head, where it then joined his wet towel on the floor. The bra came next. Her breasts tingled as they grazed his hard, bare chest; his mouth crashed onto hers once more. His kisses were hungry, demanding. She groaned low in her throat, feeling feverish all over.

Elijah's hand trailed down her hips, cupping her sex. He rubbed his thumb against her most sensitive spot, which flared white-hot at his experienced touch.

Her back arched, and she rocked her hips against his hand. "Elijah..."

He at last growled a curse. "Damn tights."

"They're leggings, actually," she started to say, when he gripped the pants and yanked so hard they ripped. The sound of tearing fabric—followed by shredded panties—only served to turn her on more. Which, considering her heightened state of arousal, she would have thought to be impossible.

"Finally," Elijah grumbled, lowering to his knees. Gripping each thigh with those hot, callused hands she loved so much, he spread her legs wide and raked his tongue over her. A cry of pleasure burst from her lips, which she promptly silenced with a clapped hand over her mouth. His tongue became hungry, insistent. She gripped the edge of the countertop, moaning as he brought her to climax.

Biting her lip to hold a scream at bay, she discreetly flicked her wrist. The soundproofing spell was nigh unnoticeable, at least to those who didn't know what that tingling on the back of the neck meant. And Elijah seemed so wrapped up in her—literally—that he couldn't care less about a simple spell.

Her heart leapt for joy. Progress. They were at last making some progress with his fears about magic.

She bucked her hips fervently, feeling the climax growing, climbing within her. Her nails dug into the granite. "Eli—"

Suddenly, cold air whooshed in as his tongue vanished, only to be replaced by the warmth of his cock seconds later.

Her head thrown back in a gasp of shock and pleasure, he groaned as he settled inside her and began to rock. His hands gripped her hips, holding her steady while he thrust. She clung to him, digging her nails into those thick, muscular arms of his, staring into his eyes as her pleasure built.

They held each other's gazes, hearts pounding in sync, one beautiful, synchronized unit thanks to the miracle of the mate-bond.

"Verika," he rasped.

The sound of his voice revealed the effect she had on this strong, seemingly invincible man...

Her core blazed and then at last erupted.

They came as one; wave after wave of liquid pleasure rolled through her. He didn't bother masking his groan as he came, throwing his head back and thrusting a few more times until they were both spent.

Verika's body felt like Jell-O, and in the best way possible. The warmth and glow of their love filled every muscle, and she relaxed against her mate, breathing hard onto his chest. In a busy world with a hectic life, the moments that pleased her most were those where it was just the two of them, their hearts beating as one, their breaths mingling as they simply held each other and at last found peace.

Elijah chuckled deeply. "I must have done a good job. You're speechless."

Verika lightly smacked his shoulder and sat up. "Don't let it go to your head."

"Me? Never." He grinned impishly, making the two dimples in his cheeks show.

Cupping his face, she smiled and kissed him before she hopped off the counter. He slapped her bare ass as she walked by, eliciting a giggle. "You should get ready." Verika still smiled as she retrieved her obliterated panties and leggings.

Elijah had turned to lean against the countertop, his big arms crossed over his chest. "And you should stay naked."

"We'll make a day of it—a glorious whole twenty-four hours of bare skin, silk sheets, Netflix, and meals in bed." She kissed the tip of his nose. "Someday soon, when this mess is all behind us."

His smile tightened. "Yeah. Someday soon."

She paused, studying him a beat before she nodded once and walked away.

Not right now. Now wasn't the time to ask why her mate's doubt had slipped through their bond just then.

She didn't even really need to ask, because she felt the same way.

Deep down, she, too, had started to think a day would never come where they could truly be together without fear they'd be torn apart.

CHAPTER FIVE

NIK WAS GOING TO KILL SOMETHING. OR, MORE LIKELY, someone.

Like a certain asshole brother named Elijah.

"Seriously," he said to Gage, who sat way too poised in front of him while he paced around his office like an agitated tiger. "How, exactly, after years of silence, did he all of a sudden get the gall to show up out of the blue like, 'Hey, by the way, guys, I'm alive and well.' Like, what the *fuck*?"

Gage eyed the tumbler of Scotch on the coffee table, which was centered in a trio of leather couches. So far he hadn't even taken a sip, but Nik sensed he wanted to. He was probably trying to be the responsible one and all that.

Saint Gage. As someone with a personal history of being an asshole by nature, Nik found it both endearing and annoying how perfect and nice Gage could be.

But he loved him anyway, because that's what brothers did.

"I don't know," Gage murmured, turning his eyes back to Nik. "Perhaps it's Verika. Love has a way of making you grow a pair."

Wasn't that the truth. Though it could be argued love could also scare the hell out of you and turn you into a dickless pansy. Most days, he still didn't feel worthy of Alara's affection. He was still afraid someday she'd recognize the ugliness in him, tuck tail, and run, but so far she hadn't.

And he prayed to God she never would.

A knock sounded at the door, quiet but not so much as to sound timid.

Nik's heart pounded. It felt as if he were about to go into battle, only this was one fight he wasn't looking forward to. Dread wrenched his gut, twisted his insides, and made him feel as though he were about to come unglued from anxiety.

Why are you so scared? Don't be a pussy.

Gage eyed his older brother curiously before at last speaking up, because it appeared Nik's voice had vanished. "Come in," Gage called.

Dammit. He sounded so together, while Nik felt as though the world were about to fall apart all over again. Just as it had done the night they'd been bitten.

Just as he had the moment Elijah walked out of their lives forever, leaving a crying Nik screaming his name into the night.

He remembered that night clear as day. Blisteringly cold wind had chapped his still-damp skin. He'd just gotten out of the shower and had run outside as soon as Gage told him Elijah was leaving. He didn't want to believe it. He'd looked up to Elijah too damn much. Had learned everything he knew about being a damn good big brother from Elijah.

Bursting through the screen door, he'd stumbled down the porch and into the newly fallen snow. His eyes had scanned the darkening horizon for a lone figure. The silhouette of a man—his brother—grew farther away. "Elijah!" he'd screamed.

His big brother had kept walking.

Overwhelming pain brought on by the agony of abandonment had wracked his body. He'd cried out, a howl of grief lancing the night as he dropped to his knees in the snow.

No. No, Elijah was supposed to keep them safe. He'd promised to always be there, to never let anything happen to them.

"Elijah! Don't leave me!"

"Nik?"

Nik startled. "What?" He blinked several times, pulling himself out of the memory and focusing on Gage, who now stood beside him. He looked at his older brother with worry.

"Er, Eli's here." Gage gestured to the door.

Everything slowed down as Nik turned to look at his older brother.

Elijah stood there, dressed in a black T-shirt that was a bit too tight for his muscular body, torn, faded jeans cinched at his waist by a black leather belt, and a pair of sneakers that were beat halfway to hell.

At first, all Nik could do was stare. In disbelief, in shock, in fear, in awe. He didn't know what to feel. It felt like seeing him for the first time in years all over again.

Elijah stared warily back. A multitude of emotions passed through his eyes.

Overwhelming relief crashed into Nik, making his knees shake. He wanted to hug Elijah so badly, to know he was real, that he was at last here to stay. But his arms wouldn't move. His body felt as if it were made of stone, tethering him to the spot.

Gage was the first to step forward after the most awkward, tense silence the earth had ever witnessed. "It's been too long, brother," Gage said in a shaky voice, embracing Elijah.

Elijah seemed stunned at first, not hugging him back initially. Then his big arms wrapped around Gage. Though Gage was muscular too, his body looked much leaner compared to Elijah's. Elijah was a tank, standing a bit taller than Gage.

The two brothers hugged each other tightly, clinging to each other as if afraid to let go.

Nik's hands balled into fists at his sides.

Gage and Elijah at last separated. Gage smiled warmly. Elijah gave him a tentative smile back and looked at Nik. The second he did, his smile vanished.

Anger rolled off Nik in waves, and his fists shook. "Where the hell have you been?" Nik asked in a quiet, stone-cold voice.

"Nik—" Gage stepped between them and held up his hands.

"No!" Nik shoved past Gage, getting in Elijah's face. He grabbed hold of Elijah's T-shirt collar and shook him hard enough to rattle his brain. "Where the *fuck* have you been all this time? Huh? Did you not think we'd worry? Did you not think we'd given you up for dead?"

Pain flickered in Elijah's eyes. "I was trying to protect you. I walked out because I couldn't stand being around our dad anymore, for bringing the curse on us, for ruining our childhoods. Then I fell into trouble and...I couldn't come back."

Nik searched his expression and tried to detect any whiff of bullshit. At last, he let him go. "Tch. Yeah, right. You were probably just too strung out to come find us. Or maybe you were too busy getting balls deep in Mistress Black, our mortal enemy."

Elijah's eyes flashed gold, and a warning growl rumbled in his chest. "I'm not going to pretend like I wasn't a horrible, rotten piece of shit, because I was. I was strung out. I was an adrenaline junkie. Hanging out with her gave me the best high of my life." He shuddered. "Until I got a brutal wake-up call."

"What happened?" Gage cut in as Nik opened his mouth. He shot Nik a warning look.

Get it together, Gage's demanding voice boomed in his head. *Don't let your anger take control of you. You're better than that.*

Dammit. Much as Nik would love to knock Elijah into next week, Gage was right. Elijah could help them. Hell, it was a blessing he'd bedded the enemy for however long. Whatever information he held could save their lives. For all their sakes, Nik had to cool it.

Elijah sighed hard and ran a hand through his dark hair. He glanced at the tumbler of Scotch on the table. "I hope you have more of that, because I'm gonna need it if we're talking about Mistress Black."

An hour later, Nik sat, stunned. And numb, but that could have been from the bottle of whiskey he'd knocked back on top of the Scotch.

Every shadowy secret of Elijah's past had tumbled out. Gage had a knack for coaxing people into spilling their deepest, darkest secrets. Nik…well, Nik had other methods. Usually ones involving knives and a helluva lot of blood.

Listening to Elijah spin his sad tale hadn't snapped a nerve in Nik like he thought it would. Even when Elijah had gotten to the part where he'd met Verika, Nik hadn't felt a damn bit jealous. How could he when he was mated to the perfect woman? And bit by bit, as Elijah talked, Nik found his anger fading away and changing into sympathy and sorrow. The collective weight of those heavy emotions made him feel as if the ocean of alcohol he'd just drunk had added an extra fifty pounds to his midsection.

The three brothers sat in heavy silence, staring at their empty glasses and bottles, of which there were many. A lot of booze was drunk this past hour.

"Damn," Gage said at last.

"Ditto." Nik shook his head. "I had no idea…"

"Yeah, well. I had preferred to keep it that way." Elijah

shifted his weight, not looking at either of his brothers. "I guess in addition to protecting you two, I was also protecting myself in a way. I didn't want you to be disappointed in me, but I guess that was inevitable since I never called."

"No. I can understand why you didn't." Gage leaned forward and squeezed Elijah's arm. "You'll always be our family. No matter what you've done."

Elijah stilled, staring first at Gage's hand and then lifting his eyes to his baby brother's face. "You mean that?" he asked quietly.

"Of course." Gage nodded and looked at Nik expectantly.

Nik's eyes flicked between his two brothers. The two people left on this earth who shared the same blood as him. God, he'd wanted this, had wanted his big brother back. It wasn't so much because he needed someone to look out for him as much as he'd just missed Eli so damned much. They were so much alike, in so many ways. The betrayal he'd felt at him walking out on them, abandoning them, remained and would take a long time to go away, if it ever did.

But this…this was a start.

Nik met Elijah's questioning, hopeful stare—and nodded once.

An enormous weight seemed to lift from Elijah's shoulders, and he gave Nik an unsure, but grateful, smile.

And for the first time since seeing him, Nik actually gave him a small, tight smile back.

It's a start.

And, really, that's all he'd ever wanted. A second

chance, an opportunity to lay old hurts to rest. Of course, letting go of his anger would take a long time.

But he was finally willing to try.

Alara had to admit—Nik was handling it better than she thought he would.

At least he hadn't "ripped that motherfucker a new one," or so he'd promised last night. There Nik and Alara were, locked away in their bedroom and having perfectly hot sex, when Nik had started to ramble. About how much he hated Elijah, about how he was going to storm up to his room and throw him out on the street to be collected with the rest of the trash, and so on. Alara had at last given up on a romantic, drama-free evening alone with her mate, and with a sigh of exasperation and resignation, had called their sexcapades quits.

Then she'd found out Gage wanted Nik to join him in a meeting with Elijah, to get his side of the story. Though part of her thought it was a good idea—and a much-needed discussion between the three brothers if they were to ever get past this drama—she'd also expected a bloodbath. At the very least she'd expected yelling, maybe even a few thrown punches. Which was why she hadn't batted a lash as the yelling began.

Danica and Verika hadn't fared so well. They'd both tensed as the three she-wolves listened outside the office door.

"He sounds really angry," Danica murmured, nibbling her lip—one of her unqueenly quirks.

Alara suppressed a smile. She could imagine her mother rolling in her grave, bemoaning what a travesty it was to have such a commoner for a queen. "They're just hashing it out the only way they know how. They need this. All of them."

"Let's just hope Nik leaves me enough of a mate to curl up with tonight," Verika muttered as she crossed her arms. She stared at the door so hard you'd think she had X-ray vision.

"He'll be fine," Alara assured her, masking her worry. Truth was, she wasn't so sure Nik wouldn't let Elijah walk out without a scratch or two.

Or maybe a busted lip. Or a broken nose. Or a blackened eye—

Stop it. Gage wouldn't let things get too out of hand. She'd sensed the king's nerves when he'd arrived, a mixture of apprehension and excitement. The ache of losing Izzy made her desperately wish the brothers would find it in their hearts to forgive one another before it was too late. Family was too precious to take for granted.

"Come," Alara said. "Let's leave them alone. The guards will step in if it gets too rough."

Verika gave the door one last doubtful look, but she finally followed Alara and Danica down the hall.

Danica and Alara chatted quietly as they walked toward one of Alara's private sitting rooms, while Verika trailed them, looking around and keeping to herself.

She's weird, Danica said telepathically.

Alara smiled softly. *She's just shy. And a bit socially awkward. I think I intimidate her.*

Can't imagine why, Your Royal Perfectness.

Not wanting to give away the fact they were having a private conversation, Alara refrained from nudging Danica with her elbow.

So is she seriously a Black Witch? Danica asked, sounding more curious than anything else.

Yes.

Danica's eyes flickered with worry. *Do you think she's sided with Mistress Black?*

Alara thought about it. *No, I don't think so. She seems to want her dead as much as we do, probably for what she did to Elijah.*

Danica's expression turned dark. *Yeah. Gage told me about that on the way here.*

Alara had a feeling the version of Elijah's past Elijah and Verika had relayed to them the other night was truncated. That there was a whole lot more to their stories than either of them was letting on.

Honestly, more power to them. They had just as much right to keep secrets as anybody else. God knew Alara and the rest of them had their fair share of secrets.

The sitting room was by far the girliest of the rooms in the manor. Alara had to fight with Nik to let her redecorate, saying the place sorely needed "a woman's touch." When he'd at last given in, she'd been ruthless in tearing down every drab, boring curtain, ripping off outdated wallpaper, and pulling up hideous shag carpet that belonged in the seventies—or in the fireplace.

The fresh, feminine look of the room now, with its sunny buttercream walls, white gauze curtains, turquoise rugs, and white couch and chairs, made it difficult to recognize the old room. The room finally felt like hers now, her own little sanctuary within the manor's imposing walls. She'd needed this when she'd moved here, to this strange place that didn't know her. Needed to make it hers, somehow.

After one of the maids brought them tea and cookies, they sat back and talked. Alara made sure to steer the conversation to safer topics, such as the weather, shopping, how impossible it was to live in a house full of male werewolves.

Verika replied only when spoken to, sipping her tea quietly while sitting straight up on the edge of the sofa.

Alara watched her carefully and with a hint of amusement. Verika could probably flick her wrist and kill everyone in this manor, and yet here she was, scared to death of a little girl talk. It was, admittedly, endearing.

Alara had heard witches and warlocks couldn't choose their powers. That they were handed down to them genetically. Verika could no more help being a Black Witch than Alara could a werewolf. It was just a part of who she was. It didn't make her evil.

Unless she chose to be.

"So, I'm dying to ask." Danica turned to Verika, looking like a kid who was about to sit on Santa's lap. Warning bells went off in Alara's head, but Danica spoke before Alara could stop her. "Can you really bring people back from the dead?"

Verika choked on her tea.

Danica! Alara snapped telepathically, knowing her

queen could hear her. As High Queen, Danica could communicate telepathically with any werewolf. To hell with the fact Danica outranked her in the werewolf world. She'd warned her to stay on safe topics because Verika was shy, and what did she do? Dive right into forbidden-topic territory.

What? Danica said telepathically, raising her brows at Alara. *It was bound to come up sooner or later. I don't think our witch here is as breakable and vulnerable as you're making her out to be. Just chill out.*

Verika coughed into a fist and set down her teacup with a clank. "Wow, you don't hold back, do you?"

Danica grinned. "What can I say? I'm not exactly known for tiptoeing around something I want to know. I've always been a fan of yanking the bandage off, so to speak."

"You don't say?" Verika murmured, sounding hoarse. She took a deep breath and let it out. "Well, no sense in tiptoeing around it, as you put it." She leaned back against the sofa, the first time Alara had seen her look halfway relaxed. "Yes, I can bring people back from the dead. Though I didn't know that until recently, with Nik."

Alara raised a brow. She'd assumed Verika had known exactly what she was doing when she'd brought Nik back. "You mean, you had no idea if your spell would work or not when you resurrected him?"

"No, I didn't. Though I've been getting these…'feelings' of what I should do. Call it a witch's intuition."

"Like, your magic is guiding you?" Danica asked.

Verika swallowed, going pale. "Something like that."

Alara stared at her, eyes narrowing slightly.

Danica, completely oblivious thanks to her curiosity, spoke up. "I think it's amazing."

Verika blinked in surprise. "You do?"

"Yeah! Totally. I wish I could use magic. I was a witch for Halloween almost every year while growing up. They're awesome in my book. Well, most of them. Mistress Black is kind of a first-class bitch, isn't she?"

Verika stared—and then snorted. "I never expected 'totally' or 'awesome' to come out of a queen's mouth."

"I get that a lot. There's a lot of misconceptions about how modern queens are supposed to act and how they are supposed to sound." She rolled her eyes. "I figured, hey, I'm a queen. I'll make up my own damn rules."

"You have a point."

"Right? That's what I've been saying all along. But some of us 'royals-by-birth' in here, not to point any fingers or anything, still chastise me from time to time."

"I've never chastised you," Alara said.

"Not out loud, anyway, but I've seen the eye rolls and the gaping mouths. Doesn't stop me from speaking my mind. You know, I figured the less bullshit there is in the higher courts, the better. I'm going to be myself regardless of how other people feel like I should act. And if that rubs someone the wrong way, then they don't deserve the time of day from me anyway. So no sweat."

Alara looked at Danica with something akin to pride. "Perhaps you're more queenly than I originally thought you to be. A queen needs to be sure of herself, to be able to stand on her own two feet."

Verika smiled in admiration at Danica. "I agree. You're very brave. A lot of people try to please others by pretending to be something they are not."

"Which is the problem with the world. If everybody just spoke their minds, I think there'd be a lot less drama."

Alara listened to the two of them chatter. Verika unwound, turning into a much more talkative person than she'd been in the garden earlier. It stung a little that Verika warmed more quickly to Danica than her, but then again, Alara had never expected them to become best friends. And Danica had a way of making even the most uptight people like and trust her.

A powerful gift for a queen to have.

"Verika? What's wrong? Are you okay?"

Alara's eyes snapped to the witch, who leaned forward with her hands clutching her belly as if she might be sick. Her pale skin had gone chalky white, shimmering with sweat.

Alara frowned and started to stand. "Veri—"

"Oh God," Verika gasped, right before her mouth flew open and out spewed a torrent of vomit.

CHAPTER SIX

GAGE STARED AT THE STRANGE MARKING ON HIS ELDEST brother's back with apprehension. "So this...*brand* ties you to Mistress Black's soul?" Despite learning about Elijah's sad, lonely life, nothing could have prepared Gage for this twist.

"Correct." Elijah nodded grimly. "To my understanding, so long as I bear this mark, if Mistress Black dies, I die with her."

Nik swore. "That fucking bitch did this on purpose. She knew we might prove troublesome once we learned Elijah was alive, so she slapped this blood brand on his back as a means of ensuring her own safety."

Gage's thoughts ran with similar theories. "But how did she know we wouldn't want to join her cause? She's definitely turned a fair share of our kind over to the dark side. No, I don't think that's the reason why she branded Eli. She has another motive, I'm sure of it."

Elijah's lips pressed together. Gage immediately

homed in on his eldest brother's discomfort. "You might as well spill it, because you know we'll needle you until you do."

"What?" Nik looked between them. "What are we needling him about? If you need someone to rough him up, I'm your man. I'm still pissed at you, Eli."

Gage's lips pulled into a small smile. The fact Nik had moved on from calling Elijah "motherfucker" and "asshole" to "Elijah" and now just "Eli" meant he was slowly forgiving him.

Good. Elijah's disappearance hurt Nik more than anyone else. Nik had always been closer to Elijah than Gage, thanks to their age difference. From the moment Elijah returned, Gage thought Nik's butt-hurt attitude showed how desperate he was to reunite with Elijah. But he had a lot of hurt to work through first before that happened.

"Can't say I don't deserve an ass-whooping." Elijah straightened. He sighed. "I had…a visitor the other night."

Nik stopped his relentless pacing to watch.

"Go on," Gage urged.

"Don't freak out—it was Mistress Black."

"Christ!" Nik groaned, running his hands over his face. "It's just like you to say something like that. Remember the time you broke your leg and were rushed to the ER in an ambulance? You called Dad and were like, 'Don't freak out, but I'm in the hospital.'"

"What did she want?" Gage pressed.

"She wanted me to come back, saying the longer I was away from her the sicker I would become. Thanks to this." He pointed to the brand.

"You're feeling sick?"

"Yeah." Elijah shrugged. "No big deal."

Nik went to open his mouth, but Gage cut him off. "Go on."

"She proposed a trade—she'd remove the brand if I gave her Verika."

"What?" Nik spat. "Why the hell does she want her?"

Every muscle in Elijah's body seemed to tense. "Because she claims Verika is her descendant."

Both men stared at him as if he'd suddenly said the world was flat.

"You've gotta be shitting me," Nik said.

"I wish I were," Elijah replied grimly. He coughed, swallowing hard.

Gage frowned as he watched him. "You feeling all right?"

"Yeah. Just had too much to drink, I think."

"Buuuullllllsssshhhhiiiitttt," Nik drawled. "A Johnson having too much to drink? There's never *enough* to drink for one of us."

Elijah clamped his lips together, his cheeks puffing as if he was trying to hold back bile. "Oh *hell*." He leapt off the couch and rushed toward the garbage can behind Nik's desk.

Nik ran after him. "No, no, no! That's a wire—"

The sounds of retching filled the air. Nik and Gage both winced as Elijah hurled his guts into the basket. Thanks to the wire frame, the vomit spattered all over the floor. Their noses wrinkled as the smell of barf hit them. It reeked so much of alcohol, they could probably get a buzz off sniffing it.

Gage silently went to the mini-fridge and retrieved a bottled water and a paper towel. He handed them to Elijah once he'd straightened. Elijah's skin was noticeably paler, and sweat had broken out on his brow. His eyes glimmered faintly with red sparks.

Gage's eyes narrowed. Was that Blood Magic? No other type of magic bore that color, save for Red Magic, but something told Gage it wasn't that.

"So," Nik said slowly, shoving his hands in his pant pockets. "That was pretty epic."

"Are you certain there's nothing to Mistress Black's warning? About the brand making you sick?" Gage asked quietly.

Elijah looked miserable. He wiped his mouth with the paper towel and shook his head. "I didn't want to believe it. I don't know. I just don't fucking know anymore."

Gage! cried Danica through their mate-bond. *Something's wrong with Verika.*

What is it? What's happened? Are you all right?

Yeah, yeah, I'm fine. She's really sick. We don't know what happened. One minute she was fine, and the next she was puking her guts up.

Where are you?

Sitting room, east wing.

Stay put. We'll fetch Heath and come find you.

"What is it?" Nik watched his brother's face carefully.

Gage glanced at Elijah. "Danica says Verika just got sick."

Holy crapmonkeys, that was a lot of puke. Verika couldn't remember heaving that much since having the stomach flu back in high school. It had been going around, and a lot of kids were out with it. Verika had thought she was going to get lucky and not come down with it, but nnnnn-nnnnooooooooo. She was never so lucky. Never.

The boys burst into the room within a minute of Alara directing Verika to lie down on the couch.

Elijah went instantly to her side, his face drawn with worry. He ran his hands all over her face, touching the back of her head, gently stroking damp strands of hair back that had gotten stuck to her sweat. "Love, look at me. Are you all right? Does it hurt anywhere?"

Her throat felt raw, but that was honestly about it. "No, I'm fine. Just…well, actually, I don't know what came over me."

Nik, who stood nearby with his arms crossed, cleared his throat loudly and cast a pointed look at Elijah, who glared at him.

Verika looked between them. "What is it?"

Elijah sighed. "Don't kill me."

"Always a great way to lead in to something you don't want to tell someone else."

When he'd finished explaining Mistress Black's warning, she definitely didn't feel like killing her mate—she felt like killing Mistress Black.

The brand she'd laid upon him was actually making him physically ill. Well, it was making both of them sick, she supposed. If that lying snake was to be believed, which Verika was inclined to say she wasn't.

And not only that, but the only way Mistress Black would remove it was if he surrendered to her.

Unbelievable!

She'd sensed there was more to the story than Elijah was letting on, but also knew he'd omitted whatever it was with good reason. No point in questioning him in front of everyone else. She'd do so later on when they were alone in their chambers.

A Blue Warlock named Heath, who looked more as if he belonged on some wilderness survival show on the Discovery Channel than in the medical field, had followed the boys in and looked her over as Elijah explained what was going on. "Actually, you both getting sick due to Elijah's brand is not so far-fetched." He inserted himself into the conversation. "From what I've seen and heard, Blood Magic can impact a wolf's mate via the mate-bond."

A colorful and creative string of curses ensued from both Nik and Elijah. It would be fun to watch them get into a curse-off. "So the sicker I get, the worse off Verika will be," Elijah said.

"Afraid so." Heath gave a sympathetic smile.

"Dammit!" Elijah stood with a snarl, balling his fists as he paced about like a pissed-off tiger. He eyed the wall, as if trying to decide whether or not it would be a good place to put his fist.

"Easy there, bro." Nik stepped in front of him, cutting him off. "Alara just had this room redecorated. I don't think 'angry-male-punching-holes-in-the-walls' is the type of look she's going for."

"Sorry," he muttered sheepishly and rubbed the back of his neck. "Do you have any experience with Blood Magic, like how to lift a brand?" he asked Heath.

"Sorry, man. All the stories I know of say a brand has to be removed by the one who did the branding."

"Which means, either way, I'm going to have to face Mistress Black."

Verika felt a trickle of fear through their bond as he thought of Mistress Black's magic, of the things she'd done to him and forced him to do.

Oh, Elijah.

She desperately wanted to go to her mate, but right now she didn't feel as if she could walk without toppling over. Instead, she seized his hand as he stalked by the couch. "We'll think of something. I'm not letting her anywhere near you if I can help it."

"We might not have a choice," he murmured, staring into empty space with that hard look he got when he was overthinking something. His spine stiffened, and he clapped a hand over his mouth. A second later, Verika's stomach churned.

"Crap!" she squeaked.

Alara, who had been watching both of them like a hawk—or, more appropriately, a wolf—was already prepared. She shoved a decorative bowl in front of Elijah, just in time for him to puke in it.

Verika grasped her hair and did the same in the wastebasket Danica had set beside the couch. Danica bent over her, gently holding her hair back with a grimace.

"That does not sound fun," she said as Verika straightened with a groan.

"It's not. It's absolutely wretched." She graciously accepted the wet towelette Alara handed her and wiped her mouth. "My body's starting to hurt, too. It kind of reminds me of when I had the flu."

"How do you feel?" Gage looked at a ghastly Elijah.

"Sorry, I couldn't hear her over all the vomiting. Did she say the flu? Sounds about right."

"I'll get you both something for the aches and nausea." Heath scurried from the room.

Verika settled back against the throw pillow. "Guess Advil and Pepto-Bismol are just as good for magic-induced flu-like symptoms."

"You can't remove the brand?" Nik asked her.

"No. I tried. I think it really can only be removed by Mistress Black herself. Blood Magic is particular like that. That's why so many people use it to secure top-secret information. Think of it like a magical thumbprint or voice recognition, like what you see in spy movies."

The room went silent. Everyone wore the same grave, stumped expression.

A moment later, Heath returned with tablets and Sprite. "To help settle your stomachs." He handed red and pink pills to both her and Elijah. "And good old acetaminophen for the pain."

"Thanks, man." Elijah took them both down in one gulp.

Verika would swallow a whole elephant if it would make her feel better. Knocking back the pills and the soda, she focused on taking deep breaths instead of fussing over her roiling stomach.

"Well, we're not going to get anywhere just standing here stewing over it," Gage said. "I say we let Verika and Elijah rest for now, and convene again at supper to discuss a plan of action." He looked at Elijah with a mixture of sympathy and understanding underscored by cold-hearted ruthlessness. "I know you're...troubled about confronting Mistress Black, but we ultimately need to face her. This is never going to end until we can get rid of her for good."

"I know," Elijah said quietly, swallowing hard. Verika swore he got paler.

With a curt nod, Gage clapped him on the arm. "Danica and I will stay until this is all sorted out. Um, get to feeling better."

Seemingly at a loss for words, the werewolf king walked out of the room, chatting with Heath along the way.

Verika got how he felt. Really, she did. If she'd had a long-lost sister all of a sudden pop up again in her life, she'd be unsure how to feel, too. On one hand, you'd be hurt they'd abandoned you and hadn't thought enough of you to call over the years. On the flip side, you'd remember all the happy memories you had as kids, and would want to return to those good times.

Though she'd never voiced it out loud, she doubted the brothers would ever be able to return to the level of trust they used to have. Or maybe she was projecting her own feelings onto the situation. Once her trust was broken, it took a long time for it to return.

If it ever did.

For them, at least, she hoped and prayed it did. Especially for Elijah's sake. She'd watched the guilt and self-loathing for abandoning his brothers eat away at him day by day, hour by hour, and had felt helpless to heal him like she so desperately wished. But someone else's love couldn't remove another person's scars. Sometimes you had to face your demons by yourself if you had any hope of conquering them. Sometimes, you had to let your loved ones fight their own battles, and keep standing by them so they'd know they were never alone.

Danica glanced at the door and back at them. "Uh," she said, awkwardly running a hand through her golden hair, "I'm going to see if Gage needs my help with anything. Being a queen never stops and all that."

After Danica left, Verika started to stand. When Elijah took a step toward her, Nik said, "Actually, could I have a moment with her, Eli?"

Alara went still.

Elijah glanced between Nik and Verika and gave a cautious nod. "Yeah. Okay."

He looked at Verika over his shoulder as he walked away. She gave him a reassuring smile, though her chest fluttered with butterflies.

Alara and Nik stared at each other; Verika assumed they must be having a private conversation.

At last, Alara nodded slightly. Casting Verika and her mate one last look, she wheeled about and followed Elijah out of the room.

Verika tensed as the silence in the room stretched. This might possibly be more awkward than her mother walking in on Elijah naked.

What could she say? Sorry? I'm happy for you? Nothing sounded right.

Damn her inability to start a conversation like a normal person!

Nik chuckled. His face lit up with that carefree smile Verika had so adored when they were together. It was still cute, but it didn't tug at her heartstrings as it once did.

"I never got a chance to thank you." Nik came to sit beside her on the couch.

Verika had thought about this moment, had felt it coming. There was much to say between them, and yet there wasn't. What was done was done. The past was in the past and all that. Still, she found her old guilt returning as she said quietly, "Yeah, well, it's the least I could do after I…"

Nik took her hand and turned her to face him. "Don't feel bad. I mean, yeah, I'm not gonna lie. You leaving me hurt like hell at the time. But I see now everything happens for a reason. Every hurt, every trial. They have purpose. You walking out the door and never looking back allowed both of us the opportunity to find our true mates."

She gave him an unsure smile. He smiled back, letting go of her hand.

Verika studied him from the corner of her eye. It would feel too weird to blatantly stare at him. It was hard trying not to. Here was the man she'd once thought she loved, whom she would have given up everything for at one point in her life, sitting here less than a foot away. A man whose heart she'd ripped out, along with her own, the day she'd decided to end things. A man she'd dreaded seeing since.

And yet she felt…content. At peace.

A long sigh broke her lips, and her shoulders eased as the burden of hurting him finally, at long last, lifted.

He'd forgiven her. Though he hadn't explicitly said as much, she knew that's what he meant. The reason he'd wanted to talk.

She was truly, deeply thankful for that. Freeing up her own hurts afforded her the clarity of mind to focus on healing her mate's emotional wounds. Though it may not be her place, she said anyway, "Are you still pissed at Elijah?" And immediately regretted it when a sour look came over his face.

She bit her lip. Of course he was. Duh!

Smooth, Verika.

"Yeah." A muscle ticked in his jaw. "I can't easily forget or forgive him for ditching us like that, not when we most needed him." He growled a sigh and rolled his massive shoulders and then his neck. Verika heard a few bones crack. She wondered how much rest he'd gotten since becoming Alpha, and then firmly reined in those feelings. He was no longer hers to fuss over. That was Alara's job.

Nik's expression saddened. "I missed him so damned much. Still can't believe he's back, like it's too good to be true. I'm afraid…I'm afraid that if I let him in again, if I let him get close, he'll leave."

"Well, he and I can't exactly live here," Verika said with a wry smile, nudging him. "I don't think Alara would go for that."

He snorted and nudged her back. "That wasn't an invitation to move in, love. You know what I mean."

"I don't think he's going to run. He wants to be a part of your lives. He wants it as badly as you do. And don't try denying it," she added as he began to protest.

Nik pressed his lips together and gave an imperceptible nod. With a glance at his watch and another heavy-hearted sigh, he stood. "I should get you upstairs where you can rest." He offered her his hand, and she let him pull her up. She'd forgotten how strong he was. How supportive he could be.

Alara was a lucky wolf, but then again, so was she.

A wolf.

Crap, that's right. Her first Change was coming up soon. How was she going to manage that on top of this illness?

Breathe.

Nik supported her with an arm around her shoulders as he led her out of the room and up the stairs.

"So," she said softly, leaning into him as her knees trembled. "Just to make sure we're on the same page—we're good?"

Nik smiled. "Yeah, doll. We're good."

Tears of gratitude stung her eyes. "Thank you," she said quietly.

At least if she died soon, she'd rest easy knowing one less person in the world hated her. Because once word got out she was a Black Witch, she had a feeling she'd shoot straight to the top of the Underworld's Most Wanted List…and become one of the Underworld's most feared—and loathed—witches.

CHAPTER SEVEN

LIJAH WAS WAITING FOR HER WHEN SHE GOT BACK TO the room. He'd been sitting on the bed, head hanging low, hands pressed on his knees, looking as though he had the weight of the world strapped to his shoulders.

She could relate. She was so going to need a good massage when this was all over.

If she wasn't dead.

A shiver rattled her bones.

"Hey," Elijah said with concern, rising and going to her. He rubbed his hands up and down her arms. "You okay?"

"Yeah," she answered in a shaky voice. "I'll be all right. Just feeling a bit queasy."

"Tell me about it." He pulled her to him.

She eagerly went, pressing her face against his warm, strong chest, and wrapped her arms around him. She closed her eyes and listened to his heartbeat, memorizing this moment so she'd always have it to hold on to when things got dark.

Which was inevitable, considering the way things were already going.

She wanted to curse. Wanted to scream. Mostly, she wanted to pull Mistress Black's hair out.

Or set her on fire.

Or torture her.

Her eyes flashed open with horror. Holy shit, since when had she become so bloodthirsty?

Her power snaked under her skin, whispering dark thoughts to her. She wanted to hurt her. Needed to make her pay for what she'd done to her mate.

Since discovering her magical affinity, she'd been conducting research on it nonstop, courtesy of a little magical hacking spell that covered up her trail on the World Wide Web. No need to alert the DPI's cybercrime department to her massive search queries on "Black Magic." It was undoubtedly one of the department's hot words by now, used to try to track her whereabouts.

At any rate, she'd compiled quite the Black Magic database inside her mind, though half the time she wished she could unlearn what she found. On the bright side, it was spooky. On a darker note…downright spine-chilling.

Elijah held her like that for a long while. Which was fine by her. Let the world stop, if only for a moment. It owed them at least that much in exchange for attempting to save it.

Verika felt her mate tense slightly before he spoke. His voice was so quiet, somewhere below a whisper, as if he was afraid to even speak. "There's one more thing I neglected to mention, about Mistress Black's visit."

Her heart stuttered. Immediately pulling back, she looked up into his eyes. "Tell me."

He told her. And her jaw nearly hit the floor. "Excuse me, I'm supposed to be descended from *her*? That monster?"

"She says as much. Or, at least, she's delusional enough to believe it's true, even though it might not be."

What. The. Hell?

Could she be? Sure, she supposed it was possible, anyway. She didn't exactly know much about her birth mother. Okay, she didn't know jack shit about her real parents because they had given her up, supposedly "for her own good."

Dammit, she was sick and tired of people telling her what was and wasn't good for her.

She was pretty sure being related to a psycho-witch wasn't a good thing.

"What else?" she demanded. "I know you're holding back information."

He bit his lip. "She also said she'd remove my brand if I gave her you."

"A trade," she said flatly.

"It would appear so."

Verika's brain stopped working. When it started up again, all it could muster was one word. "Fuck!" she shouted, pulling away.

Elijah's eyebrows rose into his hairline as though there were balloons attached to them. The F-bomb rarely tumbled out of her mouth. She liked to think she was a sophisticated curser.

But sometimes, the F-bomb was the only word to do a situation justice.

She needed to hit something, now.

Going to the wall, she formed a fist and punched.

"Ow! Mother—"

"Whoa, there! Take it easy!" Elijah grabbed her hand, which throbbed now as if she'd dunked it in lava, and kissed it.

She winced. Tears sprung to her eyes. "That hurt," she said miserably.

He chuckled, giving her an amused look as he gingerly rolled his thumbs over her sore knuckles, gradually massaging away the pain. "At least you formed the punch correctly and didn't break your thumb. Though your hand's going to be sore as hell, I'm afraid."

"I never understood the point of punching things until now. I just…grrr, God! I needed to release the anger somehow. Next time, I'm going to aim for a pillow."

"Wise choice, Muhammad Ali."

She lightly punched him with her free hand. "You're hopeless."

Elijah opened his mouth to say something, when he swayed. The color leached from his skin, and he stumbled toward a chair at the dinette set.

Verika went to him and sank into an adjacent chair, resting a hand on his arm. His skin was cold. He was never cold.

"Elijah?" she asked with worry.

"I'm all right," he rasped. His breaths sounded labored,

as though it took every ounce of strength he had to simply breathe. "Just letting it pass."

"Has this been happening for a while now?"

His silence confirmed just as much.

"When did it start?" It wasn't an angry, or even accusatory, question. Just a curious one.

"When we first hit the road. I'd been having 'little flus' here and there since I left Mistress Black's, but they were so mild and few and far between that I didn't pay them much mind."

They sat in silence for a while. "I wish you'd told me," she whispered.

"I didn't want to wor—"

"Sssh," she whispered, leaning forward and pressing her finger to his lips. She got up and hugged him. "You're my mate. I'm going to worry about you regardless. It actually helps me worry less if I know what we're up against." She cupped his face in her hands, forcing him to hold her gaze. "I'm not breakable. Don't hesitate to share your worries with me. I can take them." Her lips quirked up in a grin. "I'm actually kind of a mystical badass, if you haven't noticed."

"Yeah. I got that part."

Dropping a kiss on his forehead, she sighed and sank back down into her chair. "So what are we going to do?"

"What do you mean? Wait, you're not considering handing yourself over to Mistress Black."

She twiddled her thumbs and stared at her hands. "If it's the right thing to do."

He shot out of his chair. "Bull-fucking-shit it's the

right thing to do! Verika, she's insane! She'll kill you, or worse!"

She stood up too, her own voice rising in anger. "I can't sit around and watch you slowly die!"

"And I can't give up the only person who makes me want to live to the one who almost destroyed my life!"

Verika's thought process stumbled. "Elijah…"

Pinching the bridge of his nose, he cursed and sat down. His back stooped, and he kept his gaze hidden from her as he said, "I can't lose you. I can't. It would break me, Verika."

Speechless, she wet her lips and paced, nibbling at a fingernail. "We'll explore other options. I think we should do as your brothers suggested and rest. Our brains work on things subconsciously while we sleep. I know it works for me. When I have a problem I can't seem to solve, I sleep on it and usually wake with the answer."

"But what if *she* comes? In my dreams?"

"That won't happen." Her eyes went cold as her power crackled through her. "If she comes, I'll rip her apart."

Elijah stared at her hands, where green energy had gathered at her fingertips. He swallowed hard.

The glow immediately winked out. Crap. She needed to calm down before she freaked him out more. She had to get a rein on her power before it became unruly.

Elijah blinked and looked away. His gaze found the window, staring. "Maybe we should run away, keep my brothers out of this."

Her heart ached for the sorrow in his eyes.

She knelt before her mate and took his hands in hers.

"We came here to ask for your brothers' help. I'm so proud of you. I know that couldn't have been easy, facing them like you did." She kissed the back of his hands. "And I know it's tempting to return to old habits because they're comfortable. Diving into the unknown is scary. I should know. I was scared to death when I discovered what I truly was. At one point, I would have given anything to return to being an affinity-less witch because it's what I knew. But change happens for a reason. It helps us grow and makes us stronger. We need your brothers." She stood. "Running isn't the answer anymore, Eli. We can't run forever. The only way it's going to end is if we stand and fight."

She bent; her lips hovered over his. "I promise, through thick and thin, I'll be there fighting right along with you. Forever."

Then she kissed him.

A promise, filled with all the passion she possessed in her soul.

CHAPTER EIGHT

A S THE WAITRESS SET THE STEAMING, HOT-OFF-THE-grill steak in front of him, Elijah couldn't wait to dig in. Screw Mistress Black for the next ten minutes. He was eating some goddamned steak.

He grabbed a fork and knife and went to town. It took a few minutes for him to notice everyone was staring.

"What?" He looked around.

Verika, he, his brothers, and their mates were gathered around a long, rectangular dining table in the manor. The meal's theme was "soul food": fried chicken and okra, green beans bathed in bacon fat, mashed potatoes loaded with garlic, sour cream, and butter, bowls of white and brown gravy. Sweet tea with lemon, frothy, ice-cold beer, corn-on-the-freaking-cob glistening with butter, corn-bread—hell, yeah!—black-eyed peas. And he was pretty sure he could smell a pecan pie roasting in the oven.

This was by far the nicest meal he'd had in months. His stomach practically wept in happiness.

Pressing his lips together, he gently set down his fork and knife. No one else had touched their food.

Gage cleared his throat. "We, um, thought it might be good to give thanks first."

Elijah raised a brow. Their mother had been sort of religious: she believed in demons because she constantly prattled about the ones taking over their father—read: "addictions"—but their father sure as hell never much believed in a higher power. Their family had gone to church maybe five times a year, and that was only on potluck nights for the free meals.

But hey, Elijah wasn't judging. Prayer was fine by him, welcome even. They'd need all the help they could get, divine or otherwise.

Taking Verika's and Alara's hands, he bowed his head.

And suddenly felt ashamed.

Who the fuck did he think he was, asking God or the Creator or Allah or whoever they were praying to for help? He didn't deserve it, not after the things he'd done. He felt naked in the darkness of his subconscious, all his sins laid bare. He was filthy, disgusting.

Nothing more than an animal.

When Gage said, "Amen," Elijah jerked his hands back as if he'd been burned. Alara and Verika cast him curious looks, and then glanced at each other before picking up their silverware.

Elijah's chest rose and fell with more labored breaths than before.

You okay? came Verika's quiet, understanding voice inside his head.

He latched onto her presence, let it soothe him. *Yeah. I'm fine. Just wigging myself out.*

I didn't know anyone actually said that anymore. A small smile.

Yeah, well, I'm quirky like that. He smiled back.

Now, about that steak business…

Conversation didn't resume for another blissful fifteen minutes. And when it did, Elijah felt like throwing up everything he'd just eaten.

"Do you know where Mistress Black is?" Nik asked after a hefty swallow of beer.

Gage glared at Nik, giving him a "Really? Did you really just throw that out there?" look.

Verika reached for Elijah's hand beneath the table. He squeezed it and then backed off, not wanting to break her delicate fingers. He took a few deep breaths.

Just breathe. Breathe, dammit.

You can do this, Verika coaxed gently.

Talk to my brothers, or talk about Mistress Bitch?

Both.

He felt her warmth, her sunshine. Despite being a Black Witch, she was the kindest, brightest person he knew. Her whole soul radiated goodness, the likes of which he'd never known.

With mechanical effort, he forced air into his lungs, enough to give voice to his thoughts. "Sort of." The air felt thin, cold. Probably just him. "I have…these patches of memories. What the place looks like. General area. I don't remember exactly where it is."

"Why not?" Nik again.

Gage gave an eye roll of exasperation, wadded up his napkin, and threw it on his half-finished plate. "Would you back off?" he growled to Nik.

Nik merely raised his brows, as if to say, "What?"

"It's fine." Verika spoke up. Everyone had stopped eating. Talking about a mass-murdering psychopath was a sure way to kill conversation—and appetite. "We need to talk about this."

"Couldn't he have waited after I'd gotten done eating?" Elijah grumbled.

"My thoughts exactly," Gage murmured.

Alara cleared her throat. "So I'm assuming Mistress Black has blocked your memories somehow?"

They all turned to stare at him as they waited for an answer. It felt as though he were smothering under a pile of rocks.

He shrugged. Or he tried to. His shoulder felt as if it had locked in place. "I guess. Sounds like the kind of thing she'd do."

"Wise move on her part." Gage leaned back in his chair, arms crossed, with one hand massaging the light stubble around his chin. "I bet there are spells and wards not just on her base of operations but on everyone who's ever been near her."

"Can't we just break the spells preventing Elijah from remembering where she lives?" Danica prompted.

Elijah felt as if he'd swallowed ice. The cold settled in his gut, knotting it up.

Breathe. Breathe. In and out. There ya go.

"That might be a possibility." Verika smiled politely

at Danica, swooping in to save her mate, who felt as if he were drowning in the Arctic Ocean. "I thought of that, while we were on the road. But we never had a chance to test it out because we were always running."

Elijah inwardly smiled at the clever little lie. So innocent and believable coming from her. More like "yeah, my mate is scared shitless of magic, so we didn't go there."

"If we can't break the spells on Elijah's memory," Gage said, his voice calm and commanding, "then we should look into locating Mistress Black's hideout based on detecting a massive amount of wards. Can a tracker spell do that?"

"I suppose it's possible." Verika got that excited glimmer in her eye. She always got it when talking about magic. He could tell she really loved it, that despite possessing one of the most dangerous magics known to man, she felt more whole now knowing she wasn't broken. That she did possess a power, just like any other "normal" witch or warlock.

Too bad he fucking hated magic with every fiber of his being.

You promised. You made a promise you'd try, and you'd better fucking keep it.

He wasn't going to focus on being actively afraid of magic, not anymore. Part of his cognitive therapy he'd learned about at a bookstore they'd stopped by on their way here. He never was a fan of self-help books. Didn't believe in them. But when you had little cash to pay a therapist, sometimes yourself was all you had.

"You don't remember what state you were in, what

part of the country…if you were even in this country?" Nik asked.

Suppressing his dread at thinking a magical barrier was inside his head, Elijah replied, "No. Not really, anyway. I remember there being a forest outside her mansion. That's what it was, a mansion." Flashes of memory came back. His brows furrowed. "I remember the trees trying to kill me."

People blinked. Then blinked again.

"The fuck?"

"Nik!" Gage reprimanded.

"Apparently," Verika went on quickly, "Mistress Black bewitched the trees as a type of security. They literally came to life and went after Elijah, from what I understand?" She looked at him.

All he could manage was a nod. God, his neck felt stiff. His whole body felt stiff.

Fuck, he didn't want to be here.

Deep breaths. Deep breaths.

"Damn," Nik said. "I don't suppose they were like Treebeard and the Ents from *Lord of the Rings*?"

Danica stared. "You watched *Lord of the Rings*?"

"What's *Lord of the Rings*?" Alara's head swished back and forth as she looked from Danica to Nik.

"Are you kidding me?" Nik's eyes went wide. "Only the greatest fantasy epic ever."

"That's debatable," Gage muttered. "You obviously don't watch HBO."

"I'm surprised you find time, Your Highness." Nik grinned at Gage's pointed scowl. "Anyway, babe," he said, addressing Alara again, "we've seriously got to have a movie night. Plan on setting aside twelve hours or so for a *Lord of the Rings* marathon. Actually, better make that twenty-four hours. We'll need to watch *The Hobbit*, too, to complete your education."

"Good God, these films are twenty-four hours long?"

"Nah. About twenty, twenty-two hours, give or take a few. I was just planning for bathroom breaks and sexy time on the couch."

"All right," Danica said loudly, "let's get back to the topic at hand here. How are we going to find Mistress Black?"

Elijah's throat tightened.

Find Mistress Black.

He didn't want to talk about this, ever. He wanted her to just crawl into a hole and rot and die. Or jump off a cliff. Or run into rush-hour traffic.

He wanted her to disappear.

Verika glanced at him and then back at Danica. "I'll run a tracking spell after dinner. I should be able to mask its origin from anyone looking for us." She gestured between Elijah and herself.

"Speaking of which," Gage said, "why haven't the DPI showed up?"

"Yeah," Danica chimed in. "I mean, I know you covered your tracks well the last time they were here. With the disguising glamours and invisibility spells—super-cool, by the way. But once they realized who Elijah is kin to, you'd think they'd come banging on our doors. Again."

"My doors now, actually, love," Nik said. "Though *mi*

casa is *su casa*."

"They didn't know who Elijah was when he was booked," Verika said. "He was simply a John Smith." She nibbled her lip.

"What?" Gage asked, eyeing her carefully.

Verika inhaled a deep breath. Let it out. "You know I told you the DPI's been compromised? Well, one of my co-workers knew about Elijah. She was working for Mistress Black."

"Fuck me," Nik wailed.

"Nik," Alara snapped. "Not at the dinner table."

"I didn't mean literally, love."

"Neither did I." Her eyes narrowed. "Language."

"The world's going to shit, and you're worried about my table manners?"

"Can we please stop bickering and get this sorted out?" Danica said, exasperated. "I, for one, would like to prevent the Apocalypse or whatever Mistress Black has planned."

"Yeah, about that. Do you know the nitty-gritty on her plans?" Nik interjected, flinging the question at Elijah, who was on the verge of hyperventilating.

Thoughts kept spinning round and round his head: break the spell preventing him from remembering, find Mistress Black, tracking spells, magicmagicmagic.

"I can't do this," he said quietly.

Everyone looked at him.

"Eli," Verika said softly, squeezing his hand. It was hard for her to grip, he was sweating so.

"Say what?" Nik said.

"I can't do this," Elijah said louder, shaking his head

and closing his eyes. He saw the brand in his mind's eye, burning dark red with Blood Magic.

You'll always be mine, Elijah.

"You have to do this, Eli," Gage said quietly. A command from a king to a subordinate.

Nik's eyes had turned to stone, as well. As had Alara's.

Fuck, they were going to force him into compliance. Probably strap him down while he choked on the stench of magic, let it invade and violate his body. Tear his mind apart.

Elijah started to stand. He stumbled; his chair tipped backward.

"Where are you going?" Gage called as he went for the door.

Away. Anywhere but here.

Ican'tIcan'tIcan't—

Nik blocked his exit. "You're not going anywhere."

"Get out of my way," he growled, on the verge of Shifting. No one cornered a frightened animal, let alone a wolf, and hoped to get away unscratched.

Nik's anger leaked out. "Don't you want to help? Don't you give a damn about anybody but yourself?"

Alara started to stand. "Nik—"

"No, he needs to hear this. I'm fucking tired of you running away. When things get tough, you turn your back. Like a goddamn pussy."

"You don't know what she did to me, what she made me do."

"Yeah? That's because you never fucking tell us shit. You don't trust us. You've never fucking trusted us with the truth."

"That's not true." His voice sounded weak, even to him.

"Isn't it, though? Isn't that the reason you never called, emailed, or wrote? Why you refused to open up to us? You weren't trying to protect us. You never were. You were only trying to protect yourself." His eyes shone. The anger had faded, leaving disappointment. Which was ten times worse. Elijah would gladly take an angry Nik over a Nik who was disappointed in him.

The faint echo of a headache throbbed in his head. On a whim, he glanced at his mate. She still sat at the table, massaging her temples with her face scrunched up.

Gage appeared behind Nik, rested a hand on his shoulder. "That's enough. Calm down."

Nik didn't fight him. "It's fine. I'm fine." He started to walk away when his jaw ticked—and that's when Elijah knew he was in trouble.

The shine dried up, leaving raw fury in Nik's eyes. "Nah. On second thought, no I'm not."

He tackled Elijah.

The women shot from the table as the two men tumbled on top of it, tipping it over and scattering plates, food, and silverware everywhere.

"Oh my God!" Danica exclaimed, watching with a hand clapped over her mouth.

Verika backed away toward the wall, still clutching her head, as Alara and Gage dove for Nik and Elijah, who were a tangle of limbs.

Nik was a lot stronger than he looked. More so when

that strength was powered by anger. As Nik made to bite down, teeth sharpened to points and glinting like the fancy cutlery now strewn about the floor, Elijah brought his arm up. Fangs pierced skin and tore muscle. Fuck, that hurt.

The lights flickered in his peripheral vision. Or at least he thought they did. It was hard to tell from rolling and tumbling so much. And being bitten. That kind of sucked on a few different levels.

Bitten by his brother.

Bitten by his brother, who was also a werewolf. With fangs.

Bitten by his brother, who was also a werewolf, who decided he'd do more damage if he shook his head like a shark.

Damn.

Ow.

"Nik!" Danica screamed from the background.

Two sets of hands, one delicate and soft and the other scarred and callused, made a grab for them, trying to pry them apart. "Snap out of it!" yelled Alara, teeth gritted and muscles strained. "You don't want to do this, Nik. Pull back now before you do something you regret."

Nik let up on the bite long enough to say, "The only thing I regret is not doing this sooner."

His attack resumed. Gage got a foothold in, managing to dislodge his brother enough to start peeling him back.

Until Nik elbowed Gage in the mouth.

Gage's hands slipped as they flew to his busted lip. "Son of a bitch!"

"What the fuck, Nik?" Danica screamed.

"Stop it." A quiet, pleading voice—Verika's.

Verika.

God, how could Elijah have forgotten about her? Lousy didn't begin to cover how he felt. Sure, he was being assaulted by a land shark, but that was no excuse. Lesser wolves still protected their mates, still thought of their well-being twenty-four-seven.

Fuck, he didn't deserve her. Maybe he should turn himself in to Mistress Black, offer her his body and soul in exchange for Verika's safety.

What the hell was he thinking? That idea was completely irrational. For one, as if Mistress Black would ever leave Verika alone after finding out she was kin to her. Secondly, he knew it was his fear of magic talking, giving him the same old spiel wrapped up in the noble thought of "abandoning her for her own good."

He could never leave her, ever. He'd die first. Which, if Nik had his way, would apparently be sooner than he'd thought.

Dishes rattled in the background. He glanced over. And stopped breathing.

Were the dishes—were the dishes *levitating*?

"Stop it."

That same voice, more strained this time. Female.

His mate's.

"Verika," he breathed.

Alara and Gage's voices faded away to silence as he focused in on his mate. The bond felt tight, agitated.

Stressed.

Verika, he said, straight to her head.

I…can't…hold it.

Hold what?

"*Stop it!*"

The sound of exploding glass filled the room. Danica shrieked as Gage leapt in front of her. Nik dislodged himself from Elijah and dove for Alara, throwing her to the floor and shielding her body with his.

Elijah sat straight up. His eyes scanned the room, heart thrumming so fast he feared it might give out.

There was Verika, standing in a corner, shaking. The windows lay in shambles around them, and the carpet glittered with glass and porcelain fragments. All in a perfectly clean two-foot circle around Verika. Her fair skin didn't appear to have a scratch on it.

Verika's terrified green eyes locked on his, pleading, searching.

"I'm sorry," she mouthed.

The next second, she doubled over. Vomit spewed from her mouth, landing in a pile on the carpet.

No, not vomit.

Blood.

Verika swore she hadn't lain down this much even on her vacations. Not that she'd taken many.

Back in their room, Elijah sat by the bed, watching her carefully and stroking her skin. He felt so hot. Or maybe that was because she felt as if she'd turned into a human Popsicle. God, she was freezing.

Blankets had been brought in and piled high upon the comforter. The hearth had been restocked, and a fire burned bright, showering the room with its hot breath. Little good all of this did her. The cold wouldn't go away. It had seeped into her marrow, lingering there and making her feel absolutely wretched.

"I still don't understand why Elijah didn't get sick," Danica said. She and Gage were gathered around the bed, though at a healthy distance.

She couldn't blame them. Though Heath swore neither she nor Elijah was contagious, one couldn't be too careful.

"It might affect her differently." Heath dropped her wrist, checked his watch, and marked something down on his chart. "Perhaps the Blood Magic the brand stems from doesn't mix well with her Black Magic."

Elijah chewed on his lip. Verika reached up and lightly touched his face, skimming her thumb along his bottom lip.

You'll worry a hole in it if you're not careful, she chided lightly, smiling.

I know. He took her hand, kissed her palm. *I can't help myself.*

Heath took a few more vitals before he performed a healing spell. Elijah looked as though he might vomit, but he refused to leave his mate's side. After Heath left, the silence in the room was heavy.

"I don't like stating the obvious," Gage said quietly, "but I believe this leaves us no choice but to find Mistress Black. By any means necessary."

He looked directly at Elijah. Meaning, "scared of magic or not, you won't have a choice."

Elijah swallowed hard and nodded. "Agreed."

Verika's heart swelled. He was so, so scared. Glimpsing his dreams, she knew the nightmares of his past—the torture, the pain, the grief—lingered just below the surface of his consciousness at all times. But he was being brave for her.

Gage sighed and ran a hand through his hair. Verika had noticed, with amusement, that all the boys did that when they were frustrated, exasperated, or just plain at a loss for words. "I'm going to go check on Nik."

Danica smiled sweetly and gave a little wave, following him out and closing the door.

Elijah leaned forward, rested his head on her lap, and closed his eyes. "I fucked up."

"Hush." She stroked his hair in long, soothing movements. "Nik started it."

"But I instigated it, in a way. I tried running away again."

"And no one can blame you. It takes time to heal from trauma. Years."

"But we don't have years." He sat up and looked at her, looking haunted. "We have weeks. Days. Hours, even."

She did what her mother did in tough situations. It came naturally to her. She took his hand, squeezing it, and smiled. "Then we'll make the most of them."

The silence turned bittersweet, swollen with the thought they could both be dead very, very soon.

CHAPTER NINE

THE SILENCE OF THE UNDERGROUND CHAMBER WAS complete, but Mistress Black preferred it that way. Here, she could truly meditate. Not that she had trouble anywhere else, being as well-practiced as she was, but the silence helped calm her mind and erase her thoughts.

She needed her mind to be smooth. A blank canvas.

Breathe in, exhale. Repeat.

Not even the milky bathwater stirred around her naked body as she soaked in the tub. Though it was hard to remain still. The sweet and spicy smell of herbs, meant to be relaxing, only served to excite her.

She was finally going through with it, with the spell meant to restore her to her original form. The magic she'd been gathering from all those dead paranormals had swollen inside her to the point of combustion. Even in this dreamy state of mind, she could feel the undercurrent of power flowing through her veins.

It was divine, like liquid sunshine.

In less than an hour, she would undergo the ritual to transfer her soul from her borrowed body to her original. She focused on her breathing, on calming her tittering heart, the racing nerves.

She couldn't afford mistakes. If her borrowed body wasn't loosened up enough, the transfer would fail.

That couldn't happen, not when she was this close to being restored for good.

Once she was whole again, she would prepare the world for its transformation. Oh, yes, people would try to stop her. Would try to kill her, as they had all those years ago. People hated what they feared, what they could never understand, what warped their perception of reality. Magical powers? Witches? Devil's work, they'd said.

She'd show them devil's work, a hundred times over, for what they'd done to her kind. No witch or warlock deserved to be treated the way they had been over the years. Even in the paranormal world, they'd had to fight for their rights as equals. The oldest of the paranormals, the Fey, angels, and demons had fought to keep them suppressed because they'd feared their power. Rightfully so. It was vast. Unless their race was kept in check, the witches and warlocks stood to overrun the Underworld someday.

And if the aforementioned paranormals were to keep their crowns, they couldn't very well let that happen, now could they?

She had to concentrate, had to prepare. Had to be ready to lead her people into a brighter age.

Breathe in and out. Through the nose and out the mouth.

A ripple of pain broke her concentration. She gasped, spine arching, head thrown back, mouth wide open in a silent scream. Oh, it hurt. Hurt all over: in her toes, her brain, her bones.

It was gone as quickly as it came. She fell back in the tub, banging her head against the porcelain rim and cursing.

Anger boiled her blood. Her nails dug into the rim, threatening to split.

Damn.

Her body felt as though it had been hit by a car, dropped off a cliff, and ravaged by the most ungodly flu the world had ever seen.

In other words, in this condition, her transference ritual was fucked.

Tongue ablaze with every curse word in every language she knew, she pulled herself from the tub. Her knees shook; God, her body felt heavy. Her foot caught on the rim, nearly sending her toppling down the stone steps and onto the floor. Snatching a towel off the rack, she dried herself, wrapped her hair, and donned a violet silk bathrobe.

She was about two steps away from flinging open the door and giving the guard the beating of his life when cold realization hit her.

The pain hadn't come from some magical attack within the mansion—it had come from inside her.

But from where?

Sitting on her chaise, she leaned back, closed her eyes. Breathe.

She sent her magic searching, stretching, reaching its long fingers through her network of witches and warlocks. She was sure the pain had been magically induced, volatile even. Like it would gladly tear her apart.

There.

Her magic latched onto a writhing, pulsing thread of magic, slinking closer and closer to its source. The farther it went, the ache in her body turned into a throb and then into knives lancing down her side. This magic was sickened by something shimmering red wrapped around it, squeezing—Blood Magic. She'd worry about why there was Blood Magic involved later.

Just a bit farther.

Gritting her teeth, she endured, sought out the magic's source.

A flash of red hair and emerald-green eyes in her mind's eye had her ending the search. Her body sagged against the lush velvet cushion. Her breaths came hard and fast. Sweat had beaded on her brow.

Verika. The wheels in her head turned, working.

Elijah's brand was making Verika sick through their bond. But of course it would. Mistress Black had known that.

What she hadn't known was Verika's bond to her, through their shared lineage, would also make *her* sick.

"Fuck!"

Forcing herself into a sitting position, her head pounding and screaming at her for it, she rubbed her temples and formed a plan.

She either needed to remove the brand from Elijah

102

to stop the pain, or she needed him by her side, preferably with Verika. Now knowing she was magically linked to Verika turned the tables a bit. She couldn't afford to let something happen to Verika on the chance it could also affect her personal well-being. The girl needed to be brought here. And besides, she would never be able to complete the transference ritual as Verika's pain grew because her borrowed body had to be absolutely calm and in good health.

No, this wouldn't do at all. She'd have to think of something else, some other way of getting her soul back into her own body. But first, she needed the girl. Either way, she had to acquire Verika. If her power was so great as to affect her in this way, it meant her powers had grown immensely since the last time she'd glimpsed her via scrying. A power like that couldn't be left unchecked. The threat was too great.

And if there was one thing Mistress Black excelled at, it was eliminating threats.

Rising and stumbling to the door by sheer force of will, she opened it and looked at her guard. "Rick, you were a thief, a killer, and an all-around despicable person before you met me, correct?"

The shadow stepped closer. Red eyes glowed, highlighting the contours of fangs. "Yes, Mistress."

Apparently, he thought that was a compliment.

She smiled sweetly. "Good. Because we're about to break a whole slew of laws, and I need someone without a conscience."

CHAPTER TEN

ELIJAH COULDN'T GET THE IMAGE OUT OF HIS HEAD, OF the blood spewing from his Verika's mouth.

You failed her. He eyed his reflection in the bathroom mirror. The others waited outside, in their bedroom. Waiting for him to get it together, to finally face what he had run from for so long.

He could do this. He couldn't afford not to.

Verika's pained expression flashed through his head once more, and he growled.

This was Mistress Black's fault. She was the reason for all of Verika's pain and suffering.

So help him God, nothing and no one hurt his mate. Ever. And he would be damned if he let any further harm come to her because he was too much of a pussy to face his fears.

Magic be damned. He was going to save his woman.

He told himself that over and over again, using it as his strengthening mantra, as he inhaled a deep breath, let it out, squared his shoulders, and at last walked into the bedroom.

Everyone glanced up at once. Verika gave him a concerned, questioning look.

He smiled at her. The expression was a bit tight, though he'd meant for it to be comforting. "Let's start with trying to break the spell on my memories."

The choice to go through with this at all was his, Verika had insisted, despite what the others said. Though it made sense they would vote for this option over the other. Potentially alerting Mistress Black that they knew the location of her hideout was too risky. Breaking his memory sealant was the safer alternative, even if the thought of doing so made his knees shake and his pulse race.

You sure? Verika said through their mate-bond.

He nodded, determination turning his will to iron. *I'm sure.*

No, he still wasn't sure about magic. No, he wasn't sure whether he ever would be sure and secure around it.

But the one thing he was sure of sat right in front of him, gazing at him with more love than he thought he'd ever deserve.

And he wasn't about to let her down again.

Verika was officially an asshole. Her shaking hands and her wrenching gut told her so.

She sat on her legs next to Elijah, who lay before her on the floor of their bedroom. He was pale as the moon, and though he put on a brave face, his hands kept clenching and unclenching—an obvious effort at trying to conceal how badly they trembled.

Oh, Elijah. Please forgive me.

Well, as much as one person could forgive another for making them relive every horrible experience they'd ever been through. Which, she was pretty certain, would happen once she broke the seal of her mate's memories. Memory spells could be brutal. Once the seal was broken, *all* of his repressed memories would come back, including those blocked by his own mind to protect his sanity.

Like she said—asshole, with a capital A.

"Can we get this over with?" Elijah rasped. "I'd rather rip the Band-Aid off than prolong it, if you know what I mean."

She did, because she felt exactly the same way. "I'm sorry," she mouthed.

He took her hand, squeezed it. His grip was clammy and slick, and a reminder of how much he was sacrificing to save her from pain.

God, she couldn't screw this up. Messing with people's memories was a shaky business, at best. Sometimes they ended up forgetting who they were, or even had the most important times of their lives erased. She knew of one man who'd paid a witch to make him forget about his wife leaving him for another man, and she'd ended up erasing all of his memories after the age of two. While the mission had been accomplished, he'd had to move in with his parents because he'd mysteriously "gotten amnesia" and could only respond and think like a toddler.

She thought about what would happen if she

accidentally did that to Elijah. If she wiped out all the memories of their time together.

Her stomach, which had grown increasingly more upset the closer they drew to casting the spell, threatened to send back up everything she'd nibbled on at dinner. The words "I can't do this" almost rolled off her tongue, but she bit it, holding her fear back. She would not allow it to rule her. Though she'd insisted on trying to track down the wards used to hide Mistress Black's lair instead of performing a memory-retrieval spell, Elijah had refused, stating "the spell could backfire and alert her that someone had found her." Then she might uproot and hide out elsewhere, or go dark completely. If they lost her now, they might never be able to find her again.

So, here they were, sitting in their bedroom, about to perform one of the most dangerous spells known to witchery.

Don't. Screw. This. Up, she told herself for the millionth time.

"Close your eyes," she said. "And though it sounds useless, try to relax."

He chuckled dryly.

Yes, I know that seems next to impossible, given the circumstances, she said privately through their mate-bond. *But the magic will work better if your mind is relaxed. Try meditating, like I taught you.*

I don't think I can calm my thoughts.

Try. She almost rolled out a Yoda reference to when he was beating Luke's ass on that swamp planet, but she refrained. Now was not the time for jokes, though it was definitely one of those times where she felt if she didn't laugh, she might just cry. But there was no time, or use, for that either. She had to get serious.

If she didn't, things could go south quickly.

With one last lingering, loving glance at her, Elijah closed his eyes, inhaled slowly through his nose and out through his mouth. Verika waited a minute, until the jittering of his nerves settled a bit through their bond. Then she lifted her hands, letting them hover over his head, and began to silently chant.

The spell was in Old Gaelic, making it of Irish descent. It was always surprising to find out which country had come up with certain spells. Spells, of course, could be translated, but they held the most power when you used the original language they had been written in. In one of her nerdier moments, she'd made a "spell-ology tree" for her office back at DPI headquarters, similar to a genealogy tree in that it traced the roots of every spell she could find. The research had been fascinating, though she'd earned a few eye rolls and head shakes from her peers. To a lot of them, their gifts were boring, their day jobs something they had to do to live. For Verika, her gifts were precious, and she lived for her job. She'd been lucky, she knew. Most people went through life dreading the nine-to-five, waiting for retirement so they could begin to live. Satine and her parents had taught her to be herself and never settle. "Just because everyone else is content to live life like a zombie doesn't mean you have to."

She was thankful for that wisdom, that support, now. Without it, she might not have had the courage to pursue her dream of using her talents full-time. Her time at the DPI wasn't all sunshine and rainbows, but it had trained her well for the spell she was about to perform.

With shaking hands and a deep breath, she sent up a silent prayer and began to crack open the spell locked around Elijah's memories.

CHAPTER ELEVEN

Lijah felt a prick along his brain, deep in its recesses. It was the only warning he had before he was sucked into a living hell.

He was back at Mistress Black's mansion, where shadows seemed to cling to every surface of the small, dark room he stood in. A child whimpered in the darkness ahead of him. Even with his werewolf sight, he couldn't see the child.

Sinewy, feminine hands snaked across his shoulders and down his pecs. The warmth of female curves pressed against his backside as Mistress Black leaned in, resting her chin on his shoulder. "He's yours for the taking."

"Who is?" His mouth took awhile to move, and his tongue felt swollen. That's right—he'd been shooting up some magical cocktail with Mistress Black. A drug that hadn't seemed to faze her in the least.

"This." She pointed at the child. Not him—this. An object.

He tried to feel disgusted but couldn't. He couldn't feel anything. Couldn't think. All he could do was stare as light suddenly poured down from a bulb on the ceiling, shining on a large, box-like object as a black drape was yanked from it with unseen hands.

The little boy couldn't have been older than five. He scampered back from the front of the cage, where his pudgy hands had been gripping the bars. The cage rattled as his back slammed against the back of it. He stared at Elijah and Mistress Black with fearful eyes.

Eyes that burned red like hellfire.

Elijah felt a flickering of surprise, but that was all. He didn't mind the numbness, because it was comforting. It meant not feeling guilt, pain, or suffering. "What is he?" Elijah asked in a monotone voice.

"Take a whiff."

He did. A snarl bubbled up. The child cowered, and Elijah had enough sense of mind to clamp down on his tongue before he frightened him further. Vampire or not, he was still a kid. And scared out of his mind. His fear saturated the room like acid. The sharp tang of it burned Elijah's tongue and nostrils.

"What are we going to do with him?" Elijah's heart started to pound harder.

"Kill him, of course."

The child began to cry big, fat bloody tears.

The air vanished. Or Elijah forgot how to breathe. "Why?"

"What do you mean, 'why?' It's a vampire, vermin to your kind. I thought you'd be thrilled."

"He's just a child."

"It is an abomination! Honestly, would you want to be stuck at four years old forever?"

It did sound horrible. But killing him solely for that fact wasn't an option. Killing him wasn't an option. "So you think you're granting him a mercy by killing him," Elijah said flatly.

"I won't be—you will. End its life."

The child wailed, crying out for his mommy.

Elijah couldn't swallow. "I can't."

"Can't or won't?" A challenge.

He turned around and faced her. "Won't."

Her beautiful face gazed upon him with glacial thoughtfulness. She smiled. "We shall see." With a snap of her fingers, a portal appeared in the air. Through it, Elijah saw two young men in the woods, huddled together by a dimming fire.

Elijah's breath caught. His heart shot up to his throat, nearly choking him.

"Your brothers are safe for now," Mistress Black said. "But that can easily change. A sudden gust of wind to blow those embers into that dried grass about a foot away. A freak snowstorm to freeze them in their sleep. Wolves, bears, or other creatures more terrible and fantastic than you can imagine hunting them—"

"Enough," Elijah growled. "Stop it."

The image winked out. Mistress Black crossed her arms. "Does this mean you'll comply?"

"Do I have a choice?" He felt something at last—bitterness. Resentment. Both had been building for a while now. No wonder they were his strongest emotions and able to get through her drug's spell.

Mistress Black pointed. "Finish it. Show me you're loyal and can obey orders without question."

Or else you'll kill my family.

Every night, he saw his brothers' faces, younger than the image just showed to him because they'd been younger when he left, but they were his family all the same. And every night, he'd cry out for them in his sleep. Every day they passed through his thoughts several times, plaguing him with worries for their safety and guilt over abandoning them. The guilt had been piled high. It had had plenty of time to accumulate.

He'd thought about running from this mansion, from this house of endless horrors, but by then it was too late. He was in too deep. Once Mistress Black found something she liked, one of her lackeys in a similar position had told him, "She never lets it go without a fight."

Bitch.

He made a vow right then and there to destroy her someday. To slit her throat and watch her bleed. Or to deliver a cut for every crime she'd committed. He wasn't sure whether he'd enjoy getting her death over with or taking his time with killing her. He also wasn't sure with option two if there'd be anything much left once his repressed rage took over.

Another worry for another day. Right now he had to protect his brothers.

So he started forward—and the hatred for himself grew.

The spell cracked at a glacial pace.

Must be careful, must be careful, must be careful, replayed over and over in the back of Verika's mind—not enough to distract her but enough to remind her. *Must be careful, so as not to damage his memories.*

Must not do anything that could make him forget about her.

Her heart clenched. Her chest had felt tight this entire time—with guilt, fear, and a hope so bright it nearly crushed her sternum.

Please hold on, Elijah. We'll find Mistress Black, together.

His breath caught, his body jerked.

Her eyes narrowed on his face.

The color slowly leached from him. Beads of sweat had begun to form on his forehead, his chest.

She didn't see the claws start to protrude from his nails.

Elijah stopped before the cage, claws extended. He watched the child cringe and cry, his face wet with bloody tears. Tiny fangs protruded over his bottom lip.

He was trembling.

Elijah's claws retracted. "No."

Cold silence greeted him. "Do it," Mistress Black finally said, with quiet fury.

"I said no." Elijah turned around to face her, jaw set,

eyes narrowed. "You can't hurt my brothers. Your powers have grown, but they aren't that vast yet."

"I'll send someone to hurt them."

"If you were going to, you would have already done so." He took a step forward, stopped in front of her so he could look down at her and emphasize how much bigger he was than her. Drugged or not, he still dwarfed her by a foot and a half.

She was unfazed. Not a woman to be cowed, Mistress Black stared back up at him without batting a lash. Her eyes glimmered with the promise of violence. "You dare insult me? One of the greatest witches to have ever lived?"

"Not so great anymore without your powers."

He should have kept his mouth shut. Really, he should have. But when his anger took over, there was no reasoning with him.

Mistress Black's ruby lips pursed and popped. "Very well. This 'has-been' witch will show you exactly how terrible and vast her power still is."

Before he could blink, he flew back across the room and slammed into the cage. The child screamed. Elijah barely got a look at him before he was flung up into the air, his back rattling the ceiling, and tossed down again with lethal force. His jaw smashed into the concrete flooring. He heard a crunch, felt a pop—pain lit up his face. He made to move his jaw, but it flared up in protest.

"Bitch," he spat.

"Thank you," she said coldly before she flicked her wrist. He flew back and forth from the ceiling to the walls to the floor, like a damn doll. Each time he made contact with something hard, he heard something else crack—a rib, a hand, his knee. Even with accelerated healing, he'd be sore as fuck. It might even take him a few days to recover if she kept at it like this.

And it looked as if she wasn't done. In fact, it looked as though she was just getting started.

As he fought to Shift, to save himself and the child, he struggled against the invisible force holding him down. His heartbeat threatened to split his veins, it was so violently fast.

But he felt nothing when he saw the flash of a blade as she stepped forward.

"No one insults me," she seethed. The blade shone in the dense, white light of the bulb. She knelt by him on the cold, concrete floor. A bloodred fingernail ran thoughtfully down his bruised jaw. Pain sang in the roots of his teeth as she pressed harder.

She raised the knife—"No one," she repeated—and plunged it into his abdomen.

It wasn't until she started to carve up his insides that he screamed.

CHAPTER TWELVE

SOMEONE—NIK?—JERKED VERIKA OUT OF THE WAY AS Elijah roared and Shifted. The spell instantly snapped, the connection lost as the great black wolf snarled at them. Nik and Gage were in front of the girls instantly, fully Shifted and snarling back, hackles raised. The tension in the room shot through the roof as they waited.

The black wolf at last turned and leapt through the balcony doors. Glass and wood exploded as he burst through, jumping over the balcony and landing deftly on the lawn before racing toward the woods.

Alara growled in frustration, rubbing her temples. "I'm so sick of replacing balcony doors. How many werewolves have jumped through them now?"

I'm going after him, came Gage's voice inside their heads.

The brown wolf gave a bark. *I'm going with you.*

"No," Alara said, taking on her queen voice. She started forward. "I am."

Absolutely not, snarled Nik. *He's in full-on wolf mode. He could not recognize you and hurt you.*

"As if he could? I'm damn fast." Alara raised a brow. She rubbed her mate's head. "I have the best nose—you said so yourself not too long ago, if I recall. I can track him faster than either of you can."

He groaned, the wolf equivalent to grumbling. He whined as she went to stand beside Gage.

"I'll be fine." She bent down to kiss him on the head. "You stay here and guard the house in case he comes back."

With that, she Shifted into an elegant umber-colored wolf, and together, she and Gage went the route Elijah had taken. Gage's pure-white wolf looked like a phantom streaking through the night.

Nik watched them disappear into the woods before he turned his big wolfy head to glance at Danica and Verika. *Um, would someone mind getting me a change of pants or something?*

Danica blinked, tearing her eyes off the woods and on to Nik. "Uh, sure! Hold on!" She went to the wardrobe and pulled out a pair of jeans and a T-shirt.

Verika was grateful Danica had responded first, because she felt as though she couldn't think right now. Not when her body trembled and her mind kept repeating *What have I done? What have I done? What have I done?*

Nik padded into the bathroom. Danica set the clothes down on the countertop before she shut the door. There was a pop and some grunts, and then a minute later Nik opened the door, fully dressed. "Dammit." He glanced again at the direction his mate had gone, concern written on his face. "What happened?"

Danica gave Nik a warning look and made a motion with her hands, as if to say, "The topic is off-limits! Can't you see how shaken she is?"

Nik, in typical Nik fashion, apparently didn't give a damn. "He was fine one minute, and the next, he flipped out. What did you do?"

"Nik!" Danica hissed.

What did you do?

The words struck her like individual blows. "I don't know," she whispered. She stared at her trembling hands. "All I can think of is that I unearthed something he'd forgotten, something so traumatic maybe his brain had made him forget it in order to protect his psyche."

"Oh, Elijah." Danica's face saddened.

Nik chewed at his lip, a scowl on his face. He crossed his arms, shifted his weight, and at last settled with his hands on his hips, though he didn't stay still. He glanced again at the woods. The moon was rising.

Verika stared at it, unable to look away. It was as if it were calling to her, urging her to Shift and come run under its silvery light.

To hunt, to feed, to mate...

Her gut twisted. *Oh, please. Let Gage and Alara find him before he hurts himself.*

The black wolf ran, faster and harder than he'd ever pushed himself before. The forest was unfamiliar, but it didn't stop him. He leapt over brambles, crashed through bushes, felt the sting of barbs and bark as they cut his flesh and snagged his fur. It dawned on him that he was leaving behind too much evidence, making it easy to be tracked, but the thought was as far away as his human self. The fear, the terror of being tortured by that bitch, had surged the wolf to the surface. Like any loyal animal, the wolf could tell its master was ill at ease. It yearned to protect him, which it had done in the form of taking over completely.

And Elijah had gladly let it. The wolf was stronger. It didn't have the same nightmares or fears he did. Let it lead.

The memory of the knife plunging into his flesh, carving him up like a goddamned pumpkin, flashed through his mind.

The wolf sensed his fear and ran faster.

Must get away. Get far away, so she can't hurt us.

He heard the echo of her laughter inside his head, felt her nails trace their way over his bloodied, razed flesh. Relishing the carnage, craving more blood. A retribution for his insults.

The wind shifted, blowing two new scents his way. He tensed.

He wasn't alone.

Though the air was tainted with the alluring smells of prey, this was something—no, two somethings—much larger.

Wolves.

He was being hunted.

With a snarl, he darted away from his course as two shadows appeared in his peripheral vision, one on either side of him. He heard the hot swish of rapid breathing, smelled the rustic earth being kicked up by oversized paws. They were swift, especially the umber-colored wolf.

Elijah was faster.

His wolf snapped his teeth as a snow-white wolf bumped into him while they ran, trying to make him stumble. He quickly righted himself and kept running, this time darting alongside a river. The metallic smell of the water filled his nose. He hadn't realized how dry and raw his throat was until now. Dry from the terror of reliving the earlier memory, and raw now from running like crazy.

The wolf firmly shoved his human spirit down, insisting they were in danger and needed to focus.

He fought for control with his inner wolf, but it snarled at him. He snarled right back, baring his teeth, but it didn't care. It was too focused on getting them away from—

It felt as if a truck slammed into him. He yelped as his body was thrown into a tree, smashing into it and breaking at least one rib, he was sure, if the pain in his side was any indication.

Gage! snapped Alara's voice inside his head. *Was that really necessary?*

It is when he's gone wolf.

Him? Gone wolf? Nah. That phrase was only reserved for the weak-minded individuals who couldn't control their inner wolves.

His hackles raised. Was Gage implying he was weak?

I am not weak, his wolf growled.

Elijah's anger surged with his wolf's, multiplying as he bared his teeth and growled low in warning.

The umber-colored wolf glanced at the white one with her big, dark eyes. *You sure about this?*

Elijah swayed as a sudden wave of dizziness overtook him. God, he was tired. The earlier feeling of being scared out of his mind assaulted him.

His wolf sensed his fear—and attacked.

The white wolf barely had time to dart away. Elijah's jaws snapped the air where the white wolf had been standing. He immediately whirled, gathering his haunches and preparing to lunge again.

Threat. Threat. The wolf had taken over completely now, and he was too tired to stop it.

Brother, this isn't you! a male voice yelled inside his head.

His snarl answered. He leapt, missing the white wolf's throat by mere inches, but grasping a mouthful of fur.

The white and black wolves danced around, each trying to outmaneuver the other, while the umber-colored one barked and bayed. The black wolf barely paid her any attention; his focus was on killing the white wolf who posed such a threat to his master.

Must keep his master safe, at all times, at any cost.

The umber-colored wolf yipped frantically, right before the white wolf stumbled and fell into the river.

The black wolf plunged after it. An adept swimmer, he quickly caught up to his opponent, driving him under. They bit and clawed. Teeth and claws sank into flesh, shredding, tearing, mauling.

Something heavy splashed into the water behind them. A fresh set of teeth pulled at his ear, yanking backward. A harder bite, this time on his paw. The black wolf yowled, letting go of the white wolf's throat he'd been about to crush in his jaws.

Furious at his opponent getting away, he whirled and attacked the new threat. Water splayed in the air, shimmering in the moonlight like crystal. The umber wolf thrashed, trying to swim away.

No you don't. Not this time. My prey will not escape me this time.

The black wolf latched onto the female wolf's back leg and *twisted*.

There was the snap of bone, the sound of tendons ripping. The umber wolf screamed in pain.

NIK!

The female plea inside his head startled him out of the red haze that had eclipsed his vision. The taste of her blood, hot and wet on his tongue, made him gag once he realized whose it was.

Elijah instantly Shifted back, nearly inhaling the river in the process. "God!"

Gage had already Changed. He crashed into the river, rushing to meet the umber wolf, who awkwardly paddled with three paws to the shoreline. Elijah swam until his feet touched the embankment. Able to stand, he got his balance and went to help Gage pull a now human Alara from the river.

She wailed as they dragged her ashore, writhing and gasping for breath.

Elijah looked at her leg and paled.

It was mangled, damn near twisted off. Deep teeth

marks oozed blood. The fair skin was torn and shredded, as if it had been through a meat grinder. Moonlight glistened on blood and bone, turning Elijah's stomach.

He fell to his knees in the dirt, grabbed fistfuls of his hair, and stared at her leg. "What have I done?"

The frustration, anger, and guilt built past their boiling points, bubbling over into an agonized scream that ripped the night in half and made all manner of feathered creature startle and take flight.

CHAPTER THIRTEEN

OD BLESS DANICA AND HER BELIEF THAT HOT TEA WITH
lemon and honey cured all worries.

Verika gratefully sipped her steaming cup as the
women sat on the sofa in Verika and Elijah's suite while
Nik paced a short distance away. He hadn't stopped moving since Danica had the tea brought up. Every now and
then, Verika saw him glance outside, eyes lingering on the
woods.

"Feeling better?" Danica gazed at Verika over the rim
of her teacup as she took another sip.

Verika nodded. "Yes. Thank you. Whenever she was
stressed, my mother always chugged tea like they were going to quit making it."

Danica giggled. "Can't say I'm not the same way."

Though the silence that followed was more relaxed,
an undercurrent of tension remained. Verika looked again
outside.

Danica rested her hand on Verika's. "Don't worry.

They'll find him."

Verika's eyes glassed over, to the point the moonlight and woods became a white and indigo blur. "It's my fault. He's been through so much trauma, and I made him relive something awful. He hasn't even told me everything he's been through. But from what I do know, I'm certain it had to have been something awful."

"Awful or not," Nik crossed his arms but continued his relentless pacing, "we're going to have to try again when he gets back."

"No."

Nik stopped now, stared at Verika. "Come again?"

She shook her head. "Absolutely not."

"But we were making progress."

"Doesn't matter."

"It damn well does! This could be our chance at—"

"I said no!" Verika snapped. Energy crackled around her hair, lifting it on a phantom breeze as the furniture in the room rattled and the floor vibrated with power.

Nik swallowed but said nothing more. Even Danica's spine had stiffened; she was backed up into her side of the couch as much as she could be.

As far away from Verika as she could get.

Verika sighed wearily, and the power surge stopped. She set down her mostly emptied teacup on the coffee table and rubbed her temples. "We'll have to go the other route. We'll have to find Mistress Black based on locating the spells masking her hideout. There's also the matter of the DPI figuring out who Elijah is, if one of Mistress Black's rats hasn't told them already, and them coming here. If they figure out you've been hiding us, that you lied to them about our presence here once already, they'll take you all in. Elijah and I are a danger to you all. I think that much is clear," she added bitterly.

"It probably would be best if we took this show on the road, to evade them coming here. If they even do," Nik murmured. "I'll mention it to Gage when—" He stiffened and turned to the forest. "Something's happened."

Danica and Verika both stood and followed him to the balcony. He sniffed the air deeply.

There was the almost inaudible sound of his breath catching, his eyes widening to match.

The next instant, he was across the room and bounded down the stairs as fast as he could run.

The bloodcurdling scream that broke the night had Verika and Danica following swiftly behind him.

"Nik!" Danica cried out. "What is it?"

He didn't reply, keeping up his breakneck pace down to the foyer. Verika and Danica raced down the stairs, trying not to trip. "Nik!" Danica called again.

Nik was already at the front entrance by the time they caught up to him. Danica grabbed his wrist as he reached for the handles. "Tell us what's going on," commanded the queen.

"Blood," he breathed, face pale with worry. "I smell blood. Alara—she's been injured."

Verika's breath caught. Danica merely nodded. "Go. I'll send for our guards and follow close behind."

Nik didn't have to be told twice. Soon as he was outside, he Shifted into a large brown wolf. He knelt, giving a bark to Verika, who hovered nearby.

She raised a brow. "I'm not riding you."

A growl was his response.

"Fine, fine, we'll get there faster. Point taken." She got on Nik's back, grabbed fistfuls of fur, and they were off, tearing through the countryside and into the forest.

She sent a thought toward him: *Do you think anything's happened to Elijah?*

Don't know. We'll find out soon.

No sympathy, no words of comfort. He was just as black and white about things as Elijah.

It didn't take long to find them. Although Verika's nose couldn't quite detect the blood yet, Nik's could. He used it like a breadcrumb trail, following it to the source.

And when they found it, Verika wished they hadn't.

She nearly heaved at seeing Alara's mangled leg. Gage looked up from his spot beside Alara, who whimpered and writhed on the ground. Elijah stood nearby, looking shaken.

Verika instantly went to him and threw herself into his arms. He didn't move to hug her back at first, which made her step back and gaze up at him with puzzlement. "I was so worried…are you all right?"

His face was grim, his lips pressed together tightly. His eyes jerked uncertainly between Verika and Alara.

Nik instantly went to Alara's side the second he saw her. His face was pale, his features drawn with worry. "What the hell happened?"

Elijah and Gage looked at each other.

Nik glanced between them. "Did he do this?" He pointed an accusing finger at Elijah, who winced but tried to cover it up.

Too late.

Nik launched himself at his brother in a fit of rage the likes of which Verika had never seen. Even when he got wasted and picked fights easily, Nik had never been this angry. This bordered on rage, the type of animalistic instinct that could drive a person to kill someone.

Even their own family.

"Nik!" Gage came up behind Nik and grabbed him, narrowly holding him back from tearing Elijah a new asshole.

Elijah stood there, mutely staring at his brother with sorrow in his eyes. As if he almost wanted to be hit, clawed, marked.

Punished.

Crushing guilt jarred Verika's nerves through their mate-bond. Oh God. Had he really done this? Was he the one who had hurt Alara?

Nik kept snarling and snapping his fangs at the air, like a wild animal. Murder gleamed in his eyes.

"It was an accident," Gage growled, the muscles in his neck straining as he held Nik back. "Calm down before you do something you regret."

"The only thing I regret is not killing him the second I saw him!"

His words rang through the air. Each word seemed like a blow to Elijah.

"Nik," Alara rasped, shaking her head.

Grief-stricken, Nik glanced at his mate, and then his eyes flitted back to Elijah. His gaze became filled with hatred. "What did you do? What the fuck did you do?" he screamed. With every word, he fought harder against Gage's hold.

"Stop, brother!" Gage ground out through gritted teeth.

Nik kept screaming, "What did you do?" over and over, thrashing about.

Footsteps approached—Heath and a trio of guards.

Heath went straight to Alara's side, ascertaining her injuries before he worked his Blue Magic.

Alara screamed as the bone began to right itself.

That did it—Nik broke free.

Verika held her breath as he charged her mate, claws raised high, ready to slice him open.

She thought about intervening with her magic, had already summoned tendrils of flickering black flames to her fingertips.

Then Nik jerked to a halt. He growled and whirled on Gage. "You *command* me to stop, brother? After you vowed never to invoke the Alpha's Right on another wolf after all Malachite did?" He barked a bitter laugh. "This is low, even for you."

"You left me no choice." Gage's voice sounded strained. Sadness shone in his eyes.

Two of the guards, one on either side, grabbed Nik.

"Take him to the dungeons to cool down for an hour." Gage wearily rubbed his temples.

"Seriously, bro? You're taking his side? What the fuck? After everything we've been through? After everything I've done for you?"

Gage was silent, his face grim as the guards started to drag Nik off. Nik fought, eyes glued to Alara. "No fucking way am I leaving her out here, with him. The son of a bitch who did this to her."

Elijah's stoic expression never changed. Verika rested her hand on his arm and squeezed, studying him with worry.

He never even responded to her touch.

Her heart broke. He'd shut off the bond between them, too, masking his emotions from her. Or more likely to keep from overwhelming her with them. God, the guilt and shame he must be feeling right now...

"It's fine."

They all looked up as Alara spoke, her voice wispy from screaming. "Don't worry. Go."

Nik stopped struggling, his face incredibly sad. He stared at his mate a long while, no doubt warring it out with her in some telepathic mate-bond conversation the rest of them weren't privy to.

Evidently, Alara won. Nik's face set in a scowl.

With a huff and another snarl thrown at Elijah, he turned on his heel and stalked toward the manor, leaving his guards jogging to catch up with him.

CHAPTER FOURTEEN

ALF AN HOUR LATER, ELIJAH STILL COULDN'T BELIEVE what he'd done.

Alara had been patched up and given a sedative to knock her out while Heath's spell finished repairing her leg.

The image of her injury was burned into his mind. It flashed through his mind's eye, making him sick.

He squirmed on the sofa in Nik and Alara's bedroom.

Alara and Nik had taken over Gage's old rooms once they'd come back to Crescent Manor as the Alpha pair. Though the space was definitely bigger, the furnishings were no more opulent than those in his and Verika's chambers.

Would he ever own anything half as nice? The thought of fussing over a mortgage and credit card bills sounded blissfully mundane. Peaceful, even. He wanted that kind of life for him and Verika.

But if he didn't get his shit together, that was never

going to happen.

He'd lost control of his inner wolf again. The first time he had nearly killed Verika, a diverted disaster that still made it difficult to face himself in the mirror. Now, Alara had been the victim. He was hurting people he cared about, and felt powerless to do anything about it.

The guards Gage had posted inside the room watched Elijah like hawks, barely blinking. Elijah couldn't fault Gage for being careful. Hell, it made him feel better they were there. He didn't exactly trust himself right now.

They were big boys, too, and imperially trained. These guys could probably fuck him up six ways to Sunday without breaking a sweat. Not that he had any plans on testing his mettle.

Guilt and regret washed over him anew as he turned his attention back to Alara.

He had some apologizing to do…soon as she woke up.

But first, he needed to sort some stuff out on the inside.

There could be no more running from his trauma. It was finally time to face his nightmares—or risk letting them destroy his life and everyone in it.

Verika wandered the garden, trying to sort out her thoughts. And having absolutely no luck.

Elijah had insisted on waiting beside Alara's bed until she woke up. Sensing he needed some alone time to figure things out, she'd volunteered for some fresh air. Though it bothered her to leave her mate by himself when he was in such a wrecked mental state. She wished there was some way she could make it better, some magic she could perform to take away all his pain and suffering.

But that's precisely what had landed them in this mess in the first place.

Magic.

It had been a long while since she'd felt so helpless. Magic could fix damn near everything. That's one of the things she loved about it. But it was a double-edged blade that could also deal irreparable harm.

Elijah, and so many others like him, couldn't be healed from an outside source. They were going to have to heal themselves.

Elijah choosing to wait for Alara to wake up so he could beg her forgiveness was part of that healing process. And she suspected he didn't want Verika around right now because he was so ashamed over what happened. He didn't need to worry about her judging him; she assured him she loved him to the moon and back.

Which was why she didn't argue when he asked her to be alone, no matter how much it pained her to walk away.

Verika rounded the corner. She was back at the courtyard with the stone angel. She'd been aimlessly wandering around, lost in her own thoughts; she hadn't paid attention to where her feet took her.

She sat down on the bench and watched the koi swim about. Alara was right—it was peaceful. A good thinking place.

A chilled wind brushed her hair, smelling faintly like—

She startled, looked around.

That was magic she had detected, though faint. She was sure of it.

Her skin tingled with the sense that another paranormal creature was near, but the signature wasn't strong enough to detect exactly what it was.

Footsteps approached, sounding harried.

A second later, the sensation vanished, right before Gage walked into the courtyard.

Verika scrambled to her feet. "Your Majesty," she blurted. Should she do a curtsy? Did she even know how to do one?

Gage rolled his eyes and sighed in exasperation. "Please, not you, too. I get enough of that 'Your Majesty' business as is."

The tension drained out of her body, and she smiled. "I could see how that would be annoying."

"You have no idea," he mumbled as he ran a hand through his disheveled hair. He looked more haggard upon his arrival, much leaner and wearier than the passionate, soft-spoken man she remembered.

But he was no longer just a man—he was a king of wolves. Thousands of them, all the lives of which were on his shoulders. And from the looks of it, it wasn't a light load to bear. The job of High King had already taken a toll on him.

Her heart squeezed. Maybe after this was all over, she could find a way to help him with the stress. She hated seeing any of her friends suffer.

Gage paced a time or two, looking as though something

was on his mind. "I just came from the dungeons."

"Oh," Verika said quietly, twisting the hem of her shirt in her hands. "How is he?"

Gage inhaled a long breath, let it out. "He's calmed down, somewhat. So that's a relief." He pressed his lips together. "It's going to be awhile, I think, before we'll be able to bring the two of them together again."

Verika swallowed hard. She'd expected as much. Nik could hold a grudge.

Gage sighed and pointed at the bench. "That seat taken?"

"Not at all. Besides, you're a king. You can do whatever you want."

"Still polite to ask." His eyes sparkled with his smile. The mirth was gone as quickly as it came. They both stared out at the fountain, the running water the only sound as the minutes stretched on.

"I've never seen him like this," Gage murmured. "Eli was always so strong. Now he's… I don't recognize him."

Verika watched him in silence, waiting for him to continue.

Gage's nails dug into the bench. "Mistress Black changed him, just like Malachite changed most of the members of our pack before I became Alpha. They broke them inside. Some days I think we'll never put the pieces back together. Even I'm still trying to come to terms with what Malachite did to me, what he made us do to each other in those fighting pits. I…I know where Elijah is coming from. I get it. And I want you to know I don't blame him. It's not his fault, him being the way he is. It's

Mistress Black's."

Verika's throat grew tight. "I'm sorry we brought this on you guys. Eli didn't want to get you involved. He wanted to protect you for as long as possible."

"You didn't do anything wrong. There's nothing you could have done to protect us. It was coming regardless of your actions."

She supposed he was right. In hindsight, they weren't the only ones involved in this fight. The whole nation was, if the string of attacks the DPI had been called out to investigate were any indication.

"I guess this means we'll be going with plan B, for finding Mistress Black's lair," Verika said.

"We could try again—"

"No," she said firmly. "I won't risk subjecting Elijah to more buried memories. I can't do that to him. I won't, even if you are a king and command it."

He stared at her. Finally, he blinked and smiled. "You might not have been a werewolf for long, but you're as ferocious as any she-wolf I've ever met when it comes to protecting your mate. I'm glad Elijah has you."

Her lashes fluttered as her cheeks heated. It was the first time Gage had really said much of anything about her relationship to his brother. "Thanks," she mumbled, looking away.

Gage stilled. He tapped his head. "One of my guards just informed me Alara's woken up. Nik will want to see her. He made me promise to tell him the second she woke up." He stood and held out his arm. "Shall we go see her ourselves?"

Verika stood. "Let's take our time, so Elijah can have some one-on-one time with her. I think they both need it."

"Agreed."

They started to walk away. Verika's spine tingled, and she glanced behind her. The sensation of being watched was back.

"What is it?" Gage looked around.

The tingling dried up, and Verika shook her head. "It's nothing. Just my imagination."

Or, at least, that's what she kept telling herself as they walked back toward the manor.

CHAPTER FIFTEEN

At first, Alara saw only blurs when she opened her eyes. As the world focused, she realized she was staring up at the ceiling in her room. The moments leading up to this realization were hazy.

How had she gotten here? What happened?

She started to sit up, reaching out with her senses for her mate. And cried out as white-hot pain flared from her leg and up through her backside.

"Easy," a deep male voice said. Warm hands pressed her shoulders back down, urging her back against the pillows. "You're still probably sore from the spell."

Spell?

She looked up at the owner of the familiar voice she couldn't quite place. She blinked. "Elijah?"

He stared down at her with a mixture of worry and something else—regret?—in his eyes. He looked away, clenching his fists. "Do you remember what happened?" he asked quietly.

She searched her brain. Gage and she had been running through the woods, tracking Elijah right after he'd Shifted and ran for it. There had been a brawl, and he'd—

Her breath caught. Flipping off the covers, she surveyed her leg. The skin was smooth; only a thin scar remained of the ghastly wound.

"Heath healed you." Elijah gestured to her leg and shifted his weight again. He wrung his hands and wiped his palms on his pants, seemingly unable to keep still. He at last shoved his hands inside his pants pockets.

Alara studied him. He seemed nervous. And guilty as hell.

She recognized that kind of shame. It was exactly the same shame she'd harbored following those long, dark weeks after her family's murders. And in that moment, upon recognizing him as a kindred spirit, she instantly forgave him.

He took a deep breath, still not looking at her. "Alara, I'm so—"

"You don't have to say anything." She reached for his wrist and pulled his hand out of his pocket, squeezing it. "I'm all right. It's fine. Everything's fine."

"You're not fine. It's not fine," he said sternly. "I could have killed you."

"But you didn't," she insisted, smiling up at him. "And I know you would never intentionally hurt me."

"How? You don't know me."

She studied him. "It's…more a sense I get about your character. When I'm around you, when I look into your eyes. I saw how fiercely you fought when you first arrived.

Even though the room was swarming with DPI, you came in anyway and helped. That requires selflessness. And though you might have been fierce and frightening to behold that day, I've sensed no malice in you since. Though I have detected a great deal of suffering and self-loathing. Uncertainty. Doubt. Fear. Like your spirit's nearly broken."

He looked down at their joined hands, stared at them. At last he took a step back, letting go. He stood several feet away, as if not trusting that he wouldn't Shift right there and try to kill her.

Alara rested her hands on her lap, studying them. "You can't go on forever blaming yourself. That kind of guilt will destroy you," she said softly. She took a deep breath. "When my...when my family died, I thought it was my fault. I wasn't there to save them. I was the reason this happened to them. The reason they died the way they did. I held on to my guilt, punishing myself, for a long time. Eventually, that guilt gave way to anger. My anger turned into rage, and..." She shook her head, blocking out the horrid memories of what she'd done to those poor men in that chicken factory. "The point is that I nearly let my guilt and rage consume me. Those feelings hurt me more than anything else I'd ever done. They almost ruined not only my life, but the lives of the people around me. Elijah, you have to forgive yourself. If you don't, if you hold on to that self-loathing and hatred, it will kill you from the inside out. Trust me, you don't want to look in the mirror one day and not recognize who you've become. It's scary."

He was silent for a moment.

"It won't be easy." Alara smiled softly. "I'm still working

through my inner demons. Some days are good, and some are bad. I just take things one day, one breath, one moment, at a time, and hope for the best. Just keep moving forward. That's all you can do."

He looked at her for a long while and then tentatively smiled back.

A soft knock came at the door. One of the guards went to open the door when Nik burst through, followed by Gage, Danica, and Verika. Nik's haunted eyes roved over Alara, as if he were trying to assure himself she was still alive.

Elijah immediately stiffened as Nik's gaze landed on him and sharpened.

The room held its breath, waiting and prepping for a fight.

At last Nik turned away. "Just get out," he said halfheartedly.

Alara exhaled. She pressed her lips together but remained silent. They should count their blessings, really. It was a miracle Nik hadn't moved to immediately take Elijah's head off.

Elijah started to walk toward the door, when he paused and looked back over his shoulder at Alara. "Thank you."

She smiled and nodded.

Nik's hands clenched into fists, and his face got redder by the second.

Elijah must have sensed Nik's rising fury, too, because he swiftly walked out the door without a backward glance.

CHAPTER SIXTEEN

VERIKA CHEWED ON HER LIP AS SHE SILENTLY FOLLOWED her mate back to their room. He hadn't spoken to her, wouldn't look at her. She might as well be a shadow tracing his path.

Once inside their room, she decided she'd had enough of the silent treatment. It was time to end the pity party she knew was going on inside his brain. Placing her hands firmly on her hips and cocking her head, she said, "Talk to me."

Elijah went to go wash his face in the bathroom, splashed icy water on it. Still, he hadn't looked at her. "There's nothing to talk about."

"There's plenty to talk about." She followed him into the bathroom and leaned against the doorjamb. "You just don't want to talk about it."

"Is that so hard to believe?" he asked, an edge to his voice and a hard glint to his eyes.

She stared him down, unabated.

He sighed; his shoulders sagged slightly. "I can't stand the thought of you looking at me," he at last said on a ragged whisper. "I'm…trash. I'm…"

Her breath caught, and she swallowed hard. Something told her not to speak, to let him tell her how he was feeling as he figured it out, one emotion at a time.

There was the trembling of a fist, right before he drove it straight through the wall with an enraged cry.

She jumped, startled, and then dove to catch him as he sank to the floor with a defeated sob. His face looked red from holding back tears, which gathered in the rims of his eyes. He let her cradle him to her chest, rock him back and forth.

In those silent, sweet moments, she swore she could hear her heart breaking. Though she could tell Elijah was trying to control himself, she felt his pain through their bond as clearly as if it were her own. Heartache, rage, and guilt roiled together in a hot, messy soup of volatile emotions. She'd been there, done that. Played the blame game. She knew what was going on inside his head. Wanted to fix it. But she knew she couldn't unless he let her in.

"Easy," she murmured, pressing a kiss to his head. "You're all right. It's all right. I'm here."

Something about what she said, or maybe it was the softness in her voice, had him lifting his arms to clutch her so tightly it became a chore to breathe. Not that she minded. It was moments like this, the ones where they felt as if they had nothing else in the world to hold on to except each other, that seared themselves into Verika's head and drove out the dark memories.

These were the moments that kept her sane.

Verika let him hold her, and she, him, for as long as he needed. Their mate-bond calmed and unwound, the emotional tension draining from it like water down a drain. His breathing steadied, as did his voice when he spoke.

"I apologized to her, to Alara. And she forgave me."

"I knew she would."

"And I needed it, needed to hear her—*my victim*—say that she didn't blame or hate me. I thought it would make me feel better, but if anything, it makes me feel worse. She's a better person than I am. A far better person. If someone did to me what I did to her, I'm not sure I could forgive them."

"You can't go beating yourself up forever. You have to forgive yourself and let it go."

"I can't."

"Yes, you—"

"No!" He untangled himself from her arms and stood, looking down at her. "You don't understand. What if I lose control again? What if I kill someone? What if I kill…?" He reached for a strand of curly red hair dangling over her shoulder, as if to brush it aside or stroke it. At the last second, he changed his mind and let his hand drop.

Verika got to her feet. "You're not going to hurt me. We're going to conquer this, together."

"Tch. If you knew what was good for you, you'd stay the hell away from me."

Her anger flared. "Why? Because you're so big and bad? What about me? Have you seen my powers, what they're capable of?"

"You have more control than I do."

"Ha! That's hilarious, Elijah… Ah, screw it. You're going to find out eventually."

"Find out what?"

"My powers are growing, have been growing at an alarming rate, for the past few weeks. Every day, I lose a little bit more control over them. If they get much stronger, I won't be able to keep them in check."

"Jesus, Verika. Why didn't you tell me?"

"Because you had so many worries piled on your back, I didn't want to add to the burden!"

"You could never be a burden to me, do you hear me?" He grasped her shoulders, squeezed for good measure. "I love you too damn much to ever think of you as a burden."

She shuddered; her eyes blinked. "Say that again."

"You could never be a bur—"

"No, no, no—the other part."

"Huh?"

"Oh, just forget it," she breathed. Her eyes dropped to his mouth. "I love you, too, you big goof."

Seizing his face, she yanked his head forward and slanted her mouth over his.

Her emotions, her desire for him, flared brilliantly hot, consuming all rational thought.

Yes, they had an insane witch to track down.

Yes, they needed to deal with Elijah's emotional scarring before it cost them all something very dear.

But did they need to see to those things this instant? Hell no.

Right now, the only thing that mattered was him in

her arms, all of him, both their souls bared to each other.

There was the tearing of clothes, the moan of pleasure as hot flesh met, and then he was taking her on the carpet.

He pumped into her wildly, his mouth ravaging hers as surely as his body did. She felt the hot rigidness of his sex gliding in and out of her, the roughness of his palm as he pinned her wrists above her head with one massive hand.

He suckled a breast, fondled the other. Squeezed, licked, and prodded. Her back arched as she thrust her hips up, bucking them in time with his.

Sweat glistened along their flesh. There was a shudder, punctuated by their cries as first she came and then he.

Spent, they lay there, still sculpted together, breaths hot and melding as they stared into each other's eyes.

He tenderly brushed the damp hair back from her flushed face. "Some things words can't express," he said raggedly.

She smiled and kissed him, unable to agree more.

When one of the servants came to tell them dinner was ready, they asked whether it could be brought up. Too much had happened today for anyone to be able to make polite dinner conversation. And judging by how well the last family dinner went, neither of them was in a hurry to relive the experience.

As they sat in bed picking at plates piled with steamed vegetables slathered in butter, creamed potatoes rich in sour cream and garlic, and prime rib that was as spicy as it was juicy, Verika's mind turned over the events that came before this quiet moment of peace.

Elijah hadn't wanted to go through with the memory probe; she knew he hadn't. Could feel his fear screaming in protest through their mate-bond. Yet, at everyone else's insistence, she'd coaxed him into it. If anyone were responsible for Alara's injury and the cutthroat tension between Elijah and Nik, it was she.

At a complete loss of appetite, she set down her forkful of asparagus and stared glumly at her half-eaten dinner. "I'm sorry."

Elijah paused in conquering his mashed potato pile to stare at her. "For what?"

A half sigh, half sob rushed out of her. "For everything! It was my fault. It's all my fault."

"What is, darling?" He'd set down his fork and scooted closer to her, grabbed her shoulders. "You're not making any sense."

Tears stung her eyes. Dammit, she hated crying. Had used to cry all the time when she was a child, desperately wishing to fit in with other children her age who had already manifested powers. Back then her tears could fill a river—until she realized that didn't accomplish anything. Then she'd plain stopped caring about friends, acceptance, loneliness. Had made peace with the fact that she was different and there wasn't a damn thing to be done about it.

Suppressing her anger at herself and the situation, she said, "I shouldn't have pushed you into the probe. I should have tried harder to defend you, to do something other than just go along with whatever everybody else wanted.

To hell with everyone else!"

"Sssh," he soothed, taking her to his chest and holding her tight. "None of that was your fault. I chose this. Me. Not you. In case you forgot, I'm a two-hundred-and-ten-pound mass of muscle and stubbornness. Nobody can make me do anything."

She smiled a little. "The stubbornness part might be understated."

"There's my girl." He kissed her forehead and let her slide out of his arms.

She sat back with a hard sigh. The gears in her brain spun. "I just don't understand what went wrong. I was so careful…"

"Maybe nothing went wrong. Maybe you did everything perfectly. Wasn't it you who said magic was unpredictable, at best?"

That was true. Master magicians had floundered spells they'd mastered decades ago due to circumstances outside of their control. Magic had a mind of its own sometimes. Still…

She got up off the bed and went for the laptop nestled on a corner desk. Binding up her hair in a messy bun, she flipped the laptop open and pulled up a browser.

"Whatcha doing?" Elijah came up behind her.

"I'm not going to be able to stop thinking about it until I figure out what I did wrong—or what went wrong," she amended quickly at Elijah's raised brow. "Call it my inner spell nerd, but I don't like making mistakes this big. I have to ensure it won't happen again."

Elijah swallowed hard. For a moment, it looked as

though his dinner might come back up.

She squeezed his hand. "Not that we're attempting that spell again. I already forbade it when Gage broached the topic earlier."

He sighed and smiled. "Thank you."

She gave him a brief smile back, and then turned her full attention to the computer. The rapid firing of keys filled the room.

Eventually, Elijah wandered off, muttering something about going to bed. Verika whispered a drowsiness spell the second he closed his eyes to help him sleep nightmare-free. It took serious effort to keep her eyes open after several long hours of studying, reading, and working complex magical equations. And some serious willpower not to punch a hole through her computer. Or throw something. That seemed to be werewolves' favorite way of venting anger and frustration.

It was still odd, thinking of herself as a werewolf, but she might as well get used to the idea. Honestly, she didn't mind it. Unlike with witches, a werewolf was just a werewolf. Well, sure, there were Alphas, Betas, and Omegas, and the Omegas certainly got looked down upon. But the pack took care of its own. Everyone belonged, everyone was important because the pack was only as strong as its weakest link. No one was considered useless or worthless, so long as you pulled your own weight. Not doing so meant risking exile, which in itself didn't sound so bad. At least then you'd be your own boss, free to make your own choices.

With witches, there was a social class "superiority

ranking" based on what type of magic one manifested—
or, as had been the case for Verika's entire lonely childhood, what type of magic a witch did not manifest. Blue
and Gray Magic seemed to be at the bottom of the "Most
Coveted Powers" list. Green ranked somewhere in the
middle, with Red above it because fire was arguably the
most destructive element. Higher-paying jobs seemed to
favor Red Magic because the ability to cause mass destruction was a highly prized asset.

Then there were White and Black Magics, the most
prized of all magical gifts for various reasons. Namely, the
power to command life and death itself earned top dol-
lar in the magical arts industry. But since coming into her
powers, Verika had given very little thought to how she
could monetize her newfound, and terrifying, abilities.
Honestly, she knew she was really avoiding thinking about
it because the longer she didn't acknowledge this was her
new reality, the less real it seemed. As if her life could go
back to being the way it was before. When she was powerless, at least she knew who she was. She had an identity.
Now, she'd gone from being comfortably shunned—or, at
worst, ignored—to irrationally feared. Which frightened
her more than anything because every time she looked in
the mirror, she wondered whether people were right.

As if maybe there really was something inside her to
fear.

Shortly before dawn, she ran out of coffee. Which was
just as well, because she'd also run out of brain power and
patience. The night had produced nothing new. She was
no closer to figuring out why she'd failed in the probing

than when she'd started, though she was closer to a migraine than before.

Surrendering, she at last crawled into bed just as dawn's first rays broke the horizon. The crackling of an unfamiliar paranormal signature, the same eerie sense of being watched by something not quite human, tickled her senses as her eyes fluttered shut, but by then she was too tired to care. It was probably her imagination.

Probably.

CHAPTER SEVENTEEN

HE FIRST TRICKLE OF SUNLIGHT KISSED DANICA'S sleeping face, warming it. That was the problem with gauze curtains; although they looked pretty and feminine and all that, they didn't do much for actually blocking light or heat. Not that she minded. Though she'd never tell the moon for fear it would get jealous, she loved the sun. Sunrise and sunset were her favorite times of day because she was a sucker for all the pretty colors.

She lay there in bed, staring at the brightening light with a soft smile on her face. The manor was quiet, nothing at all like the noisy corridors of the palace that never seemed to sleep. The quiet used to bother her when she lived alone because it was a constant reminder she had no one special in her life, no one to come home to.

No family.

No doting husband or boyfriend.

Nada.

The house had felt empty and cold, mirroring the

growing depression eating a hole through her chest. It had taken every ounce of willpower in her to keep it at bay, to keep it from sucking all the joy out of her life. Onyx nearly killing her had just about been the tipping point. Though she'd never told anyone, she'd come dangerously close to letting him that night in the parking lot outside of Howl. To letting him squeeze the life from her, to drain away all her sorrow and worries. The bills were piling up, she wasn't getting any richer, and everyone she'd ever counted on had literally abandoned her.

Then she met Gage. Sweet, wonderful, thoughtful, strong Gage.

Her mate. Her king. The best damn thing to ever happen to her.

Until now.

She wasn't surprised when the nausea crept up her throat, as it had done for the past few weeks. First thinking it a cold, she now knew it was so much more than that.

Slinking out of bed, she padded to the bathroom and softly shut the door. A twist of the tap, and cold water splashed noisily into the sink, obscuring the sound of her heaving into the toilet.

Gage had been so preoccupied with court matters that he'd either been up and gone before she was, or he slept like the dead and didn't hear a peep of what happened in the room around him. Seriously, the wolf could sleep through a hurricane.

Wiping her mouth, Danica stood and flushed, and then washed her hands and splashed her face with cool water and rinsed her mouth with mouthwash. God, the chilly water felt good. With her hormones in an upheaval, she was either constantly burning up or frozen to the bone. Usually a little of each several times within the same hour.

Fun times.

Turning off the tap, she turned to the side, lifted her shirt, and admired the slight bulge just below her navel with a grin. It warmed her to see her child—*their* child. The tiny, precious life growing inside her, filling her with his or her love. Maybe *their* love.

When she'd first found out, it had been scary as hell, and there had definitely been an "Oh shit! I'm going to be a parent!" freak-out moment. This little person was going to depend on her. *Her*, who barely had her own shit together. Though her life had felt significantly more stable since meeting Gage, crazy witches and lovestruck ex-alphas excluded. But hey, everyone's life had to have a little weird, right?

Her palms slid over the smooth bump, as they so often did when she was alone. It still amazed her every time that she was carrying a baby—and made her happy beyond belief.

A warm glow grew inside her, the love of her new baby—her pup—spreading through her like liquid sunshine. A deliriously excited giggle bubbled from her.

"What are you laughing at?"

Shrieking, she nearly jumped out of her skin. She'd been so distracted by admiring her new baby bump that she hadn't heard Gage sneak up on her.

Her handsome husband leaned against the doorframe,

arms crossed, lips stretched in a yawn. "I thought I heard you throwing up. Is everything... o...kay?"

His entire body literally froze. Like really freaking froze. Blood drained from his face. His jaw went slack. Eyes turned the size of silver dollars.

Eyes that were very much glued to her stomach. In her shock, she'd turned halfway around, clearly exposing the bump for what it was.

The air itself seemed to suck in a breath as Danica stared at her mate, and he stared at her belly.

"I was going to tell you today," she breathed, stepping forward tentatively and quickly thrusting down her shirt. "You've just been so busy lately, and with Elijah, I didn't want to worry you more, or give you anything else to fuss over." She knew she was rambling but couldn't stop. It wasn't one of her finer traits, the spew of word vomit whenever she was nervous. Something every woman in her family inherited.

Gage's blue eyes looked up at hers. So many emotions passed through them, it was impossible to keep up.

Before she could blink, he stepped forward, swept her in his arms, and kissed her breathless.

Dazed, she fought to catch her breath when he at last released her, one hand still gripping her head. "You are wonderful," he rasped, kissing her hard again. "Amazing. Incredible. The most beautiful mate a wolf could ask for." He kissed her again, this time reaching deep with his tongue and eliciting a moan from her. Her inner wolf stirred, wanting to mate, but her very human—and very pregnant—body was so tired and queasy it immediately shut the idea down.

After he had kissed her senseless, he at last left her mouth alone long enough for her to speak. "Are you mad?" she whispered.

He blinked. "Why on earth would I be mad?"

"Because I didn't tell you right away."

"You're telling me now." He brushed some loose curls away from her face before he pressed his forehead to hers. "And that's the only thing that matters."

Alara's eyes bugged as she set down the cup of hot cocoa. "Well, how'd he take it?"

The majestic wolf had been Danica's go-to gal when she'd seen the pink plus on the pregnancy test. In other words, she'd flipped out and called Alara at, like, two a.m. because she was just that awesome.

In hindsight, she didn't even know why she'd thought to call Alara first. Probably because, in some bizarre way, she'd come to think of her as an older sister. Someone she could talk to and trust, without fear of being judged. Of course, she felt that way with Gage, too. It's just, well, sometimes a girl needed to talk to another girl.

Danica grinned. Her damn face hurt from grinning so much this past hour. "He was floored. And ecstatic."

"Congratulations." Alara smiled warmly. "That's wonderful. The two of you are going to make wonderful parents. And I suppose, in a way, this makes me a future aunt?"

"You bet." Danica reached out and squeezed Alara's

hand. "Trust me, there will be plenty of babysitting opportunities and loads of playtime with Auntie Alara."

Alara's eyes shone. "I'd like that very much," she said roughly.

Danica smiled back, forcing the cheer into it. She knew, thanks to her and Alara's growing friendship and "sisterhood," that she and Nik had been having trouble conceiving. Which broke her heart. If anyone would make awesome parents, it was those two. They would make that kid their world. Plus, because Alara's own sister had died, Danica and Gage having a baby would give her another chance to be an aunt. A bittersweet fact.

Alara blinked her tears away. "Thanks for visiting me, by the way. I know you've been feeling…under the weather yourself lately." She gestured with her eyes to Danica's baby bump, hidden beneath the flowing hem of a white blouse.

"Girl, of course! I could have the flu and still drag my ass out of bed to come visit you. Well, probably not. Since I wouldn't want to make you sick."

Alara grinned. "I get the picture."

"See? You sound 'hipper' already, thanks to hanging out with me."

"I have much to learn, apparently. Nik ran off downstairs to retrieve this *Lord of the Rings* and *Hoggle* trilogy he's determined for me to watch."

"Actually, it's Hobbit."

"What?"

"Hobbit. You said Hoggle."

Alara stared.

Danica twiddled her thumbs, staring down at her hands suddenly. "I, um, may or may not be a fan of Tolkien."

"And who is this…*Tolkien*?" She struggled with the name, stretching it out and making it sound harsh.

"Only one of the greatest fantasy writers to ever live!"

Alara stared distantly at her comforter. "My parents would never let me watch or read many fantasy books. They said I needed to live in the here and now. Funny, isn't it? Considering we're technically creatures out of a fairy tale…or a nightmare, depending on the circumstances." She shivered.

Wasn't that the truth? Danica winced, knowing without needing to ask that Alara was imagining being attacked by Elijah. God, that had to have been scary as hell.

What would she do if she were in that situation?

Yeah, so everyone talked about the upcoming war with Mistress Black. War typically implied violence. Under normal circumstances, Danica was very much against violence. Bloodshed, gore, pain… All things that were very non-Danica. Mostly the inflicting pain upon others part. That one upset her more so than the other aspects of battle. If she had to fight, she didn't think she'd be able to hurt a fly. Though, if her baby's life was at stake, she knew she'd choke a bitch if needed.

Danica sighed, getting her head out of that depressing topic, and back into the present. "You're going to love LotR. Just saying."

"LotR?"

"*Lord of the Rings*. Add that one to your 'cool people'

vocabulary."

"Okay." Another small smile.

Something fluttered past the window—the shadow of a bird or leaf, Danica couldn't tell. Her sixth sense tingled, alerting her to another paranormal's presence, but it was fleeting.

Huh. Must have been her imagination.

Her stomach gurgled. Uh-oh. That definitely wasn't a figment of her overactive imagination.

"Um, excuse me." Danica stood with a sheepish smile. "My stomach's about to bitch me out again. God, I hate hormones."

She made a dash to the bathroom, shutting the door and throwing open the toilet lid just in time to hurl. When she finished, she wiped her mouth with a piece of toilet paper and murmured, "I thought it was supposed to be 'morning sickness,' not 'puke any minute of the day sickness.'"

Climbing to her feet, she flushed and went to wash her mouth out. When she opened the bathroom door, the room was notably darker. Like, super dark.

An icy, tingling sensation crawled over her skin, and she froze, instantly on alert.

Something—or someone—was in the room with them; she could feel it. Just couldn't see them, damn it.

She paused a moment, listening.

Silence.

"Alara?" she whispered, searching the darkness. God, it was like ink, it was so thick. And it smelled, like sulfur.

Her heart pounded. "Alara?" she said, louder.

Something rustled, like fabric. Or clothing shifting.

Her inner wolf growled, its hackles raised, ready to come to the surface the moment she decided to Shift. Her nails extended to form claws. A warning growl rumbled in her throat. "Come out! Show yourself!"

Two red eyes glowed in the darkness, and a fanged mouth smiled, seeming to glow.

"As you wish."

She didn't even have time to scream before the darkness swept her away.

CHAPTER EIGHTEEN

Gage and Nik stood in Nik's office when it happened.

Gage felt the sudden absence of his mate in his soul, like a gaping black hole had hollowed out his chest, before he heard her cry out in his head.

GAGE!

He nearly dropped the tumbler of Scotch he was holding. The glass was partly raised, on its way to be clinked with Nik's, who had also gone still. And white. They were about to celebrate, as there was much to be thankful for. The baby. Alara's recovery.

But now…

Their eyes snapped to each other's. Fear swam in Nik's gaze, likely mirroring Gage's own. Chills crawled up his spine, slithering into that hollow place in his core and settling there.

Without a word, both men slung the glasses aside and took off at a dead run. Gage summoned guards, every damn guard within his command, to go to the Alpha pair's suite on the second floor.

"Brother," Nik breathed, "I can't feel her. Alara—"

"I know," he clipped. "I can't feel Danica."

Saying it aloud only made his fear coalesce, forming a spike and driving it straight through his heart. God, he couldn't breathe.

Please, please, please, he silently pleaded as he bounded up the stairs, taking a whole flight at once in one fierce leap.

He burst through the doors of the Alpha suite, Nik right on his heels, a fraction of a second before the first wave of guards arrived.

They both paused. The air felt...*wrong*. Too thick, and faintly tart smelling. Like death and sulfur.

"Gage."

Gage's eyes snapped to where Nik pointed. There, in the corner of the room, stood the guards Gage had posted inside and outside Alara's bedroom and balcony.

The brothers glanced at each other before slowly approaching them, one careful, silent step at a time. Nik lifted a hand, about to lay it on one man's shoulder when someone snarled, "Don't touch him!"

They both startled as Elijah stalked forward, eyes brilliant golden flames and fangs bared. "I saw all the guards running up here and decided to follow, figuring something had happened." He answered their unspoken question. "This room reeks of Black Magic."

From the doorway, Verika muttered an incantation; one hand rested against her chest while the other made smooth, circular motions in the air. The air glistened with faint white shimmers before she opened her palm. Shadows moved through the air like little rivers, flowing toward Verika's open palm and vanishing, as if being absorbed into her skin.

She was literally sucking the darkness out of the room; at least, what was unnatural. A few shadows remained; Gage hadn't realized how dark the room was at first because all he'd been focused on was finding Danica. Who clearly wasn't here.

Verika's hand snapped shut into a fist the moment the last swirl of darkness evaporated on her palm. With a sigh, she lowered her hands, clasped them in front of her. "I've cleansed the room of the remaining traces of Black Magic."

"It won't hurt you, will it?" Gage frowned.

Verika shook her head, those wild red waves tumbling about her face. "I don't think so. Actually, I know it won't." She bit her lip.

The universal sign for discussion closed. He got it. There were some things he hadn't told Nik over the years, secrets so dark that he'd barely told Danica had she not bared her soul to him first. God, what a coward he was at times.

Though he was a king, and one of the most powerful creatures in the Underworld, he felt absolutely useless at this time. Danica was gone, clearly taken by Mistress Black, as was his brother's mate.

All because he hadn't had enough foresight to see this kind of thing might happen. Hell, that it would happen, eventually. It was them they were talking about. They were

Johnsons. Something always happened. It was just a matter of time.

Sure, he'd posted guards. But he should have done more wards, strengthened those already on the place. Because, clearly, they hadn't been enough.

"Stop it," Verika chided quietly, stepping forward and studying him with those beautiful green eyes. Painfully, they reminded him of Danica's. Thinking of her, of the possibility of never feeling her verdant gaze upon him again, full of adoration and love, made him sick to his stomach.

"Stop what?"

"Stop beating yourself up." Verika smiled softly.

"How do you know I'm doing that?"

She stared at her mate a thoughtful moment, then looked back at Gage. "Because it's the same look Eli gets whenever he's being hard on himself."

Walking past him, she reached for the guards. Elijah caught her hand, worry gripping his expression.

"I'll be fine," she assured him. "Her magic can't hurt me."

Gage's eyes narrowed slightly. She'd hesitated before saying that. Just barely, but enough to be noticeable. She truly wasn't sure. But she cared about them enough to risk it.

Elijah reluctantly let go of her hand, which she then placed on one guard's shoulder and turned him. She gasped, eyes going wide, and took a step back.

Hell, everyone's eyes had widened, and a collective chill rolled through the room. Gage had the sense every wolf's hairs stood on end.

For the most part, the guard looked like himself—except the inky blackness that had spilled over his eyes, eclipsing his irises. His mouth was open wide in a silent scream.

"Jesus," Nik spat, followed by a few curses. He put his hands on his hips and turned away, wiping a hand over his face and eyeing the garbage can by Alara's bed as if he wanted to rush over to it and vomit.

Gage knew the feeling. Slowly, Verika turned each guard. They all looked the same, caught up in some unseen nightmare that was clearly an illusion but all too real to them.

Verika's face settled into grim pity. Then her eyes crackled with purple and green sparks as that pity morphed into anger. "Bitch."

She raised her hands and her voice. "*Domini vectura espri canta mestizo!*"

A gale ripped through the room, crackling with power, swirling around the guards and leaching the darkness from their eyes. One by one, the men stumbled and fell, shaking their heads and glancing about as if the room were spinning.

"What happened?" one of them asked.

"Someone bewitched you," Nik said darkly. "A nightmare enchantment, to make you believe you were living your own worst nightmare."

"Someone bewitched us?" another asked incredulously. "After all the wards and charms we put into place?"

"This was no ordinary witch or warlock we were

dealing with," Nik said. "This one possessed Black Magic."

"Are you sure?"

Nik glanced at Verika, who nodded. "Yeah." He sighed. "I'm sure."

"I wish it weren't true." Verika stepped forward. "And I'm so terribly sorry that you all had to endure that pain and suffering."

The guard, a tall, lean man with flaming-red hair, looked at Verika. His eyes widened, and his breath hitched. "It was you!" He stumbled backward so fast he nearly tripped over an upturned corner of a rug. He thrust an accusing finger at her. "I saw you with my own eyes! Monster! Demon!"

Elijah growled and started forward, but Gage cut him off. "Hey," Gage said sharply, "Verika is probably the purest soul in this house right now. I don't know what you saw, but it wasn't her."

"I know exactly what I saw! The hair, the eyes, that smooth skin…"

Elijah growled louder.

"Easy," Verika murmured, placing a reassuring hand on Elijah's arm. He glanced at his mate, and his expression softened. Gage knew they were talking telepathically to each other. Watching that private exchange sent a longing through him for his own mate. His heart rate doubled with fear, and every tendon in his body felt as though it were wrung so tightly it may snap at any sudden movements.

He took a deep breath, let it out. He'd been in so many stressful, dangerous situations throughout his lifetime, you'd think he'd be used to the stress by now. Handling foreign policies, entertaining important people, hell, even giving speeches were a walk in the park compared to this. Losing his mate was the kind of ice-cold terror that made his soul seize up, made him breathless and unable to think. Danica's sweet, beautiful face, with her kind, loving smile, dominated his mind's eye and made it impossible to think about anything else.

The guard, whom they'd dubbed "Red" back home due to his distinctive hair color, growled in frustration and shook his head. "Again, I know what I saw. It was her all right, down to that cute little mole on her right upper lip."

Verika's grip tightened as Elijah's eyes flashed gold, and a muscle in his jaw ticked.

Gage rolled his eyes. "Will you cut it out? Throwing compliments at another wolf's mate is like asking to have your tongue ripped out. Now, what do you remember? I want to know everything."

They used the bathroom as an interrogation room, pulling each guard in one by one and comparing their stories. Gage dismissed the guards once they were all finished recounting what had happened.

"They all said the same thing." Gage sighed and glanced at Verika with an apologetic look. "The guards at the door both said that you came up to them, wanting to see Alara. The guards stationed at the balcony and the three inside the room all said that the room turned pitch black the moment Verika stepped inside. They said..." A shudder rolled through him. "They said that's when the nightmares began. They were each transported back to their worst memory, and forced to relive it over and over again."

"Some people believe that's the definition of hell." Verika shivered. She rubbed her arms, as if trying to warm herself up. "There are spells that can do that, that can take control of a person's mind like that, but only advanced witches and warlocks can perform them. It makes for a huge drain on his or her magical resources. Only someone with a vast pool of magic could pull that kind of spell off."

"Do you think it was Mistress Black herself?" Nik asked.

Elijah paled. He shifted his weight, looked away—at the pearlescent flooring of the bathroom, at the decorative tiles on the ceiling, anywhere but at his mate's questioning and concerned gaze.

"I don't think so." Verika shook her head. "She wouldn't risk coming out of her hideout just to kidnap a couple of werewolves. I'm sorry," she said softly at both Nik's and Gage's sharp looks. "I didn't mean for it to sound the way it did, like your mates are insignificant. They mean a lot to you, as they do to me."

"We know you didn't mean to insult, Verika." Gage's shoulders heaved with a long sigh, and he reached up to rub his weary forehead. "The stress is taking a toll on our nerves, is all. We both might be a little quick to temper."

"Understandable," Verika said. "And no offense taken."

"Sire."

They all turned around as a stately man dressed in the gold-and-silver uniform of the High King of werewolves strode into the room. He was an older man, probably around his fifties, with a look of wisdom to his eyes accented by the sharpness of having endured many long, hard years.

Gage turned to address him. A fluttering of hope tickled his chest. "Captain Axel," he said by way of greeting as the man bowed and placed a hand over his heart. He raised a brow, waiting for his captain of the guard's report.

Axel straightened, a grim look on his face. "We searched the grounds, the house, everything. There is no trace of them—no scent, no footprints, no paranormal signatures. It's as if they just vanished. We even scanned the security footage, but it all cuts out around the time they disappeared."

"Dammit," Gage hissed.

"Whoever took them," Nik said, "they sure knew what the hell they were doing to cover their tracks like that."

"Can you track them?" Gage looked at Verika with renewed hope. Everyone had turned to look at her. Elijah looked uneasy; he shook his head slightly as she glanced at him.

"I could try," Verika said after a few seconds' pause. Her voice sounded shaky.

Gage's eyes narrowed slightly. Was she afraid? If so, why? What did she know that she wasn't telling them?

Elijah took her hands and squeezed them. He pulled her around so she faced him. "You don't have to do anything you don't want to do," he said quietly, rubbing his thumbs soothingly on the backs of her hands.

"I know." She took a deep breath and let it out in a whoosh. She smiled slightly and poked him in the chest. "Trying to turn my own advice back on me, are you?

Subtle."

"Look," Gage said, "Elijah's right. I can tell you're scared. Don't worry, I won't press you as to why," he added at her startled look. "But anything you can do to help us would be much appreciated right now."

Verika searched his eyes first and then Nik's. She steeled her gaze, raised her chin. "I will help you any way I can."

The group broke up briefly so Verika could change clothes. Due to all the commotion earlier, and worrying it was caused by an emergency, Verika and Elijah both had rushed out of their rooms in their pajamas. Well, Elijah had rushed out in his boxers, while Verika wore nothing more than a silk nightgown and matching robe. And that wouldn't do now, considering they would need to go outside for at least part of the spell.

Verika swapped the silk for jeans, boots, and a simple dark-green sweater that complemented her hair color. Elijah dressed much the same, donning some beat-up jeans, hiking boots, and a T-shirt. The T-shirt was nearly too small for him, his muscles were so big. Not that Verika was complaining or anything. The thin, light-blue cotton accented every hard ripple, every dip and valley on his sculpted chest.

She licked her lips, her inner wolf yearning to strip their clothes back off, but she firmly pushed those carnal desires down. Now was most certainly not the time for romance. Her sister-wolves were missing, and she may very well be the key to getting them back. If, that is, she didn't muck up the spell she was about to attempt.

It made the most sense to check the place where the girls had vanished, so that's where they started. Returning to Alara and Nik's bed chambers, Verika took a deep breath and steadied her nerves.

You can do this.

It hit her all over again what she was about to attempt, and her stomach roiled. The words "insane," "ludicrous," and "suicidal" came to mind. The words seemed to reverberate inside her head. The voice of her fears and doubts grew louder until she wasn't sure whether she wanted to crawl on the floor in the fetal position, or burst into giddy laughter at how crazy it all sounded. A few weeks ago, the words "insane," "ludicrous," and "suicidal" would never have been associated with Verika Tate. No, not sweet, perfect Verika. Who always obeyed the rules, always followed orders. Never attempted the next to impossible.

"You're insane," she muttered under her breath.

Elijah hadn't stopped frowning since he tried convincing her not to follow through with it back in their bedroom. "It's too dangerous," he'd said, pacing back and forth, shirtless.

Verika had almost been so distracted by all the rippling muscles that she nearly missed what he was saying. "Yes, it's dangerous," she said. "But I can't run and hide every time the going gets tough. They need me, need my powers."

Elijah came to stand in front of her, worry written all over his face. He rested those big, warm palms on her shoulders, searched her eyes. "This might make me sound like an ass," he said, "but are you sure you're not just doing this because you want your powers to feel useful? To feel respected and appreciated instead of feared? So you can prove to yourself, and everyone else, your powers can be used for good instead of evil?"

She stared back at him, lips pressed together in thought. "You're right," she said with a slight smile. "That does make you sound like an ass."

"Sorry."

"I'm used to it."

"Hey, now," he growled, pulling her in close and giving her ass a light slap. "Don't make me have to punish you."

She leaned into him, maintaining eye contact the entire time as she gave him a long, slow kiss. "Promise to do so later?"

His pupils widened with lust. "I won't forget. Wolves have long memories."

"Among other things." She cast a mischievous smile downward.

A low growl rumbled in his throat. "We could get on with that punishment now." He tugged her back against his chest as she tried to pull away.

"Sorry, love. You know we can't now. We have a job to do, both of us."

"It sounded to me like my brothers were just out to exploit your powers."

"Hey, I volunteered, remember? Besides, I can't sit by and do nothing while Alara and Danica are in the clutches of that madwoman. They've been so kind to me, even

Alara. I know if something happened to them, I'd never be able to live with myself. I'd always be asking, 'What if I could have done something to change their fates, to stop that awful thing from happening?' Because it will be awful, Elijah. It always is with Mistress Black."

"But if you use your powers to try to track her, it's like opening yourself up to her. You'll be vulnerable. Not just because you share the same magic type, but because you're...potentially related."

"I know. 'Like calls to like' and all that," she said bitterly. "But I have to try." She inhaled deeply and let it out slowly, thinking. "Besides, I think I know a way to block her. I won't let her get the best of me, I promise."

Elijah looked skeptical, but he'd been supportive.

As he was now in Alara and Nik's chambers as she raised her hands to begin the spell.

He'd stopped asking her whether she was "sure" when they'd set foot in the room, though it hadn't stopped him from trying to dissuade her on the way over here. He must have asked her at least ten times to not attempt to track them. It had been hard not to give in to her mate's requests at first, to say no to all of this. But she also knew if she let her fear hold her back, gave it permission to control her, then it would be the start of a lifelong habit. She'd never been more terrified in her life than she'd been these past few weeks. Not just because of Mistress Black, though the threat of death and suffering was daunting. She'd also been afraid of growing closer to Elijah simply because he was a werewolf. Her last relationship with a werewolf hadn't ended well. A werewolf had killed Satine, had ripped her

174

apart like she was nothing. Had nearly killed her parents. That was another thing. Because she had contacted her parents, she now had to fear for their safety as well.

But crowning that pile of fears was the greatest threat of all, the one that kept her up at night and lingered not too far from her every waking thought.

The fear of not being able to control her powers.

That fear, more than the others, had battered at her defenses every day. She'd be lying if she said it hadn't dented up her courage pretty good. But she knew if she gave in to it, then she'd lose the precious self-confidence she'd built up all these years. It started growing when she was a witchling, unable to specialize in any particular type of magic. She'd had to steel herself against her peers' relentless teasing and ridicule. Had to build up her resolve that she was a witch, dammit, and she was good enough and had the right to learn and practice magic, even if a special ability never manifested in her.

That resolve, that sense of bravery and self-worth, had started out small but now had grown strong over the years. It rose up to defend her now, beating away the worries that assailed her.

She would do this, could do this. And nothing—demon, witch, or otherwise—would stop her.

I'll be fine, she said telepathically to her mate. *Trust me.*

I do.

So strong, so sure.

His strength fed into her own, filling her up with confidence and chasing her nerves away.

He took a step back, as did Nik and Gage as she took a seat, Indian-style, on the floor. Closing her eyes, she reached out with her senses. Felt the floor beneath her, reached farther until she grasped the strength of the earth. She sensed the coolness of water flowing through the forest beyond the manor, breathed the crisp air into her lungs, heard the crackling of fire in the almost spent kindling within the fireplace. She took the elements into her, weaving them into the threads of Black Magic pouring out of her fingers.

It felt as though a river had awoken inside her; she gritted her teeth, forcing the magic into several different threads, weaving together air, earth, fire, water, and darkness until they were pure beams of raw power.

It was a chore to keep her breathing steady and her thoughts focused enough so the magic wouldn't split. Her own Black Magic was the hardest to control: a wild, living thing with a mind of its own. The second she'd unleashed it, it seemed to sense the presence of another witch or warlock's Black Magic in the room and went into a frenzy. It thrashed and bucked, but by sheer strength of will, she managed to wrangle it up and tame it enough to do her bidding.

Well, at least for now, but she had no idea how long her hold on it would last. She could feel her energy depleting the farther her magic stretched, searching, seeking, looking for the source of the foreign spell that had bewitched the guards and spirited away her friends.

I can almost feel them, the intruder, she thought. Her brain concentrated so hard she thought it might break. It was only an inkling, a blurry image that filled her mind. The fuzzy silhouette of the figure—no, a man. Eyes that burned like hellfire shone out of his dark form. Shadows bearing the faces of the damned swirled around him, their moans so heartbreaking and painful she thought she might cry. Something rotten, like decaying corpses, saturated the air. Her throat grew tight, her breathing labored as she struggled to breathe.

God, the stench! It was nearly unbearable.

Was this what it would have been like for the guards? The feeling of sheer terror, of hopelessness? The thought you were never going to escape from this place?

She sensed the warlock's amusement, saw him snatch a shadow out of the air and smile with wicked, jagged teeth as it writhed in his grasp.

Verika's revulsion nearly snapped her concentration. This man actually enjoyed inflicting suffering upon others. It strengthened his magic, as surely as pain and fear did.

One word rang loudly inside her head.

Monster.

And her magic had projected her astral form so close to this being that she could almost touch him.

Her heart hammered inside her chest, her breathing so shallow she was on the point of hyperventilating.

Too close. She was much too close to him.

This being was pure evil, his soul as twisted and dark as the magic he wielded.

Had he always been this way? Was he once a good man, with morals and integrity? Or had Black Magic inevitably corrupted his soul?

Was this the future she had to look forward to?

She imagined herself, just for a second, turning into this nightmare. Imagined herself inflicting pain and death and destruction upon the world.

The siren's call of supreme power was intoxicating. All her life, she'd been picked on and ridiculed for not fitting in. For being less than, a weaker witch with no affinity to her name. Some didn't believe such mundane witches and warlocks were even worthy of the privilege to practice magic.

But that was then, and this is now. She wasn't weak anymore; not that she ever had been. But now a deep well of power coursed through her veins, ready and willing to tear apart anyone or anything at her command.

It would be so easy to rip the world apart. To make those who had made her life a living hell suffer the way she had suffered. To destroy those who had taken away what was most precious to her.

The urge to hurt, to kill, to punish was strong in its seduction. It had won the day she'd faced down Gerard. Too bad he hadn't realized that his gloating about killing Satine had been the final nail in his coffin.

Did she regret killing him? Some days, yeah. But mostly she resented the fact she couldn't seem to feel more regret over taking someone's life. Did that make her no better than Gerard, or the creature in front of her?

A woman's voice whispered to her through the channel of magic she'd created, speaking in low, velvety tones.

I can feel your power… You are so strong, darling, but

you're afraid of your magic. Don't be. You are a queen living among insects.

Who are you? she called out with her mind. Her voice echoed down the long, dark tunnel.

The man froze, looked about.

Verika's breath caught as his red eyes wheeled about, landing on her face and then passing over her altogether.

He couldn't see her.

Good. Her cloaking ward was working. Distantly, she could feel the ward burning against her throat, where it dangled from a piece of yarn. She'd hastily thrown it together before attempting the tracking spell. She should have taken more time in prepping the ward, she realized too late. The man, and now this woman whose voice hummed with unfathomable power, possessed magic almost too strong for her wards and charms to protect her from.

The lovely, dark voice laughed. It was both terrible and beautiful at once. *You know who I am. Have known me for some time. We are of the same blood, you and I.*

A face flashed in her head, nearly disrupting her spell. Gritting her teeth, she clung to her magic, tightening the threads and urging them onward. She had to find the man at any cost, had to follow the breadcrumbs of his power until she found him.

But the woman's face was burned into her mind. She was beautiful, without a doubt. If she were honest, she'd admit she was probably the loveliest woman she'd ever seen: Long, dark hair. Big, blue eyes ringed in black lashes. Full, ruby-red lips. Skin so white it seemed to glow like moonlight. Crimson nails to match her lip color.

Although, something was off about her eyes. The pupils glowed with faint purple light. And her skin did glow, radiating that same soft, violet hue.

Black Magic.

Her breath caught. "Mistress Black."

The woman smiled. *It won't be long now. Soon, you will belong to me. And we'll finally be together again, my darling, after all this time.*

Verika could feel shadowy hands grabbing her, pulling her forward. *No!* she cried out. *Stop it! Leave me alone!*

Don't fight it, my love. You belong with me, your flesh and blood.

You disgust me! Leave me alone!

The voice became sterner, to the point of being harsh. *That's no way to speak to your ancestor.*

You're not my ancestor. That's impossible.

Who do you think you inherited your power from? Black Magic runs in families.

Verika's brain froze. It couldn't be true. Yeah, sure, magic tended to be hereditary, but that didn't mean she was a descendant of Mistress Black.

Like calls to like, murmured Mistress Black. *How do you think you were able to get this far in your little tracking attempt? My own wards and counterspells would have stopped anyone else who is not of my bloodline.*

No. Verika shook her head. *You're wrong. I'm nothing like you, or that monster of a man who took my friends. I suppose you're going to tell me he's related to me, too?*

Not at all. He is only a pawn borrowing my power. But

you…you have true power, the ability to control death. And I recognize my own power. It flows in your veins, as surely as it flows through mine.

You're wrong!

I am right, and you know it! We are just alike, you and I. Two sides of the same coin.

Her body trembled uncontrollably now. She shook her head, wide eyes staring at the bottomless pit of darkness. No. No, it couldn't be true. She was not related to Mistress Black. The thought that even a drop of that woman's blood flowed through her made her want to rip open her veins and bleed them dry.

I feel your fear, whispered the man, whose eyes still roved the bleak tunnel of dark magic. *Your shield is fading.*

He was right. Verika needed to get a grip, and fast. Distantly, she heard someone call her name, felt rough hands shake her body.

Focusing her thoughts on the task at hand, she reached out with—

The man's red eyes snapped on her, narrowing. He smiled; it looked as if half his face had split open to reveal rows of sharp fangs.

There you are, he purred. *Trying to find me, in hopes of finding my mistress or the two I took? Better luck next time.*

He lifted his hand and slashed out with sharp claws. Her spell shattered, and she screamed as her astral projection tumbled back into her body.

She thrashed, bit, and clawed as a pair of strong hands

tried to restrain her.

"Verika, it's me! Baby, open your eyes!"

Her eyes snapped open, her breath nothing more than desperate gulps of air as she stared into the face of her mate. He looked pale, much too pale, and his forehead had broken out into a sheen of sweat. Her palm lay flat against his chest, as if she'd been in the process of trying to push him away. His heart raced as quickly as her own, his breathing ragged.

"Jesus," he breathed, pulling her to him and holding her tight. "I was going insane with worry. Are you okay? What happened? You started screaming, but we couldn't seem to wake you up."

"Something else was in there with me while I was tracking him," she said raggedly.

"Him?" Gage prompted. He and Nik stood nearby, both of them looking worried.

"I'm fine." She waved away their worries and pulled away from her mate. She sat up, took a deep breath, and collected her thoughts while her mind and body calmed themselves. "I saw the person who took Danica and Alara. Well, sort of. He was more monster than man, but he was definitely a man."

"Are you sure he took them?" Nik asked.

"Ninety-nine percent sure. He mentioned 'the two I took,' so I assumed it was them he was referring to."

"Did you get a lock on his location?" Gage asked, the brothers taking turns peppering her with questions.

She gulped. "No," she admitted, hating how small her voice sounded. It matched how tall she felt, about an inch.

"Once he figured out what I was doing, he broke the tracking spell."

"Damn," Nik growled. "So what do we do now?" His voice was edgy. In fact, he looked as if he were on the verge of pulling his hair out. Not that Verika could blame him. If their roles were reversed, she would be a wreck.

Gage, ever the calming presence when shit hit the fan, rested a hand on his brother's shoulder. "We look for them the old-fashioned way."

The old-fashioned way proved to be a bust. Gage was convinced the search party had missed something, that the kidnapper had left behind some clue they had yet to come across. "There has to be something," he said. "There just *has* to be. No warlock, no spell, is so good as to leave literally no clues behind."

Verika wanted to argue that point but opted not to. She liked her head where it was.

Using the noses werewolves normally found so useful, Gage and Nik deployed every wolf at their disposal. They searched the manor, the woods, and even drove ten miles in either direction down the highway.

Nothing. Literally nothing turned up. No footprints, no traces of cast spells. Even the guards' memories had begun to fade. None of them could say now, exactly, what had happened to Danica and Alara.

"Another byproduct of the curse he cast on them, I'm sure," Verika said as they traipsed through the woods. Nik had insisted they search the woods one more time, considering they were so dense and the most likely place the kidnapper would have hidden away his hostages. If he was still nearby. Though no one said that, even though she knew, from the doubtful looks on her fellow searchers' faces, that everybody was thinking it.

Verika and Elijah walked side by side, at the end of the group, while Gage, Nik, and several others took to their wolf forms to prowl the woods. Elijah had wanted to Shift in order to better help out, but after what happened last time, nobody else was keen on the idea. He looked about glumly as wolves of every size and color ran through the thickets.

"You're helping out just by being here," Verika said lightly, nudging him as they walked. "You're fine. Don't beat yourself up."

"Maybe that should be my New Year's resolution," he said with a weary smile.

Well, she supposed the New Year was coming up soon. It was already cooling down, and winter would be here any day now. Good Lord, where had the time gone? Something about having your life be in mortal danger seemed to make the days fly by at warp-speed.

"Maybe my New Year's resolution should be 'stay out of trouble,'" she said.

"Nah, wouldn't work. You have to make one you can actually keep."

"Hardy-har-har."

She stifled a yawn. They had all been going since dawn, since discovering the High Queen of Wolves and their Alpha female were missing. They were all tired and in need of some rest. Although what Verika wanted wasn't rest.

She gazed up at the nearly full moon rising in the east, admired how it dusted the tips of the trees in pale silver light. It looked so bright up there. The manor was removed from the city. Perhaps the countryside, away from the artificial glow of the city lights, made the moon seem that much brighter.

The itch to Change worked itself into her skin, making it tingle.

Elijah grasped her hand, squeezed. "Soon."

Her heart fluttered at that. Out of fear, out of excitement. Changing into another creature was terrifying. Which was ironic. There were plenty of transmutation spells out there to aid a witch in switching forms completely, even enabling her to disguise herself as an inanimate object. Although she wouldn't recommend that. Changing into something that didn't have a brain did something to a person. Twisted their insides and made their souls rot. If they stayed in that form too long, they might cease being a person altogether. The archives back at DPI headquarters were full of artifacts that had once been people. Everyone gave them a sad look, shook their heads, and sighed, "The spell just went wrong."

Wrong. Like how her rather pathetic attempt, now that she thought about it, at tracking the kidnapper had gone.

Her hands balled into fists, and she suppressed a growl.

Failed spells were weird for her, both for their ability

to stir her curiosity—her "where did I go wrong?"—and for their penchant at pissing her off. Growing up, mistakes with working magic meant ridicule, fodder for the bullies. And they already had plenty, from her wild red hair to her big glasses (helllllllooooo, contacts!) to the dips and swells of her curvy body. Mistakes meant she'd have to work twice as hard to prove herself worthy of studying, and staying in, magic classes. And she had worked hard. Far too hard to let some freaking nameless warlock poke fun at her by kicking her out of her own spell.

She'd show him.

Nobody bested Verika Tate-Johnson in magic.

Shouts erupted from the woods ahead. Elijah's and Verika's gazes both snapped up, their ears pricked, listening. Without a word, they took off at dead runs, following the trail of guards scurrying into the woods.

They didn't pause to breathe, didn't distract themselves with communicating telepathically. They leaped over bramble and stone as the shouts grew louder.

The brush parted, giving way to a single white oak bathed in moonlight. It stood tall in the clearing by the stream, its pale branches stretching so tall Verika had to tip her head back all the way to see the top.

But that spectacular tree wasn't the most eye-catching feature of the glen.

It was the message scrawled in blood on the tree's trunk that took everyone's breath away.

CHAPTER NINETEEN

CONTACT ME WITHIN THREE HOURS, OR THEY DIE.
    Straight and to the point. Nothing cryptic about it, which, in some morbid way, Nik appreciated.

He already knew their lives were in danger before reading the message. In fact, it didn't really surprise him. It had been expected. After all, if he were an evil son of a bitch with no soul—and sometimes, he questioned whether or not he still had one after some of the things he'd done to survive—he would ransom his enemy's loved ones' lives, too. It was a smart move.

Only, when that message came delivered in your loved ones' blood...well, let's just say that made an entirely different impression.

Soon as he smelled Alara's blood, he nearly vomited. His body went still, all but his hands, which hung limply at his sides, trembling.

He couldn't look away. In another one of those surreal moments of his life, his sense of where he was, why he was

187

here, whom he was with, abruptly vanished, as if his mind had gone numb. Like the growing horror in his chest as he slowly comprehended what he read somehow hollowed him out, made him feel as though someone had shoved a block of ice down his throat.

His mouth filled with spit. His tongue twitched, urging him to swallow, but he couldn't even do that. It was only when his eyes began to water from being open for so long, when that first hot tear fell on his cheek and forced him to blink, that he felt "in the moment" again.

And the horrible sense of loss was so great, it nearly sent him to his knees. A sob started to escape, but he snapped his mouth shut, sealed his lips. He was an Alpha, dammit. No way in hell would he cower—not now, not fucking ever.

But he wanted to. He wanted to beg God for mercy, to scream at him for letting this happen, to claw at himself for being so reckless as to leave his mate's side when war was on the horizon.

He should have known she wouldn't be safe. None of them were while that snake lived.

And who had brought her to his doorstep?

The rational part of his brain said, *Now, Nik, you knew Mistress Black was most likely coming to kill you all, anyway. World domination kind of works that way.*

But the irrational, pissed-off part that needed something to punch said, *Hell, naw, motherfucker. That SOB, sorry sack-of-shit brother brought this plague upon us, and he deserves to PAY!*

Gritting his teeth, he closed his eyes. Saw Alara's kind,

steady gaze in his mind's eye, felt the memory of her hand upon his cheek. *"You're stronger than your anger."*

He growled a curse in frustration, his eyes stinging all over again. God, he missed her so damned much. His mind skipped forward to the future. Instead of picturing him and Alara sitting on a porch in a little farmhouse somewhere in the boonies, sipping sweet tea with cute little lemon slices because she loved that shit, their hair so gray it looked like smoke, he instead saw nothing but darkness, and that terrified him, and God, he needed to release all this hurt, this gnawing anger, this relentless demon inside him that just wanted to rip the world apart.

"I hate you," he said quietly, fists shaking at his sides. The urge to rip his elder brother's head off and punt it into that damnable message was intoxicating, to the point he was choking on his rage.

Elijah—and the whole damn clearing—had gone still.

The wind rustled through the trees, shaking loose a few more russet-colored leaves. They brushed Nik's face, raking their brittle claws down his cheek before settling on the ground. He stared at the red leaf. Flashes of the crimson message, of Alara screaming his name while Mistress Black smiled and poked holes in her with a knife, assaulted his mind.

"I hate you so damn much," Nik growled, louder than before.

Elijah didn't say a word. He stared at his brother with a hardened gaze, mouth pressed into a firm frown.

Nik fought to control his breathing, to rein in his anger. "You have no idea how hard it is to look at you, to breathe the same air as you. To not let this…this *rage* control me. And you want to know what the worst part of it is?" He laughed bitterly and shook his head. "I don't want to hate you. I was actually glad to have my brother back. Still want to be. But I can't. I can't celebrate your return if it means the loss of my mate. So I guess I'll just have to make do with hating you."

Verika looked as though she wanted to say something, but a quick shake of the head from Gage kept her mouth shut. She stared solemnly at the ground, looking as miserable as Nik felt.

Elijah never said anything. Which only made Nik feel more like a dick than he already did. Somebody should have jotted that down and framed it: "The day Nik Johnson regretted what he said."

"I'm sorry," formed on his tongue, but his voice dried up. The words tasted true, but he couldn't say them, not yet. Maybe not ever.

Gage's calculating gaze stared at the tree. "We should prepare for battle," he said quietly. "Taking an Alpha's mate is an act of war."

"Agreed," Nik said in a steely voice. He was itching to tear that bitch's head off even more than he was Elijah's.

"We need to leave here, before the DPI figures out where we are. If they haven't already," Verika said.

"Yeah, you'll be useless from a jail cell," Nik said darkly, eyeing Elijah as if he were a piece of garbage he couldn't wait to be rid of. The want and need for his brother, for the three of them to finally be a family again, warred with his desire to scream and kick at him for getting himself tangled up with Mistress Black.

"But what if this happened for a reason?" Alara had said when Elijah had first showed up and Nik had confessed his frustrations to his mate in private. "What if he was destined to fall in league with Mistress Black? What if his purpose was to bring her to us because we're the only ones who can stop her?"

Nik never believed in destiny. No one could convince him it had been God's plan to have his father die, his brother walk out, for him and Gage to endure hell on earth under Malachite's rule. For Verika to leave him, taking his heart with her.

Then he'd met Alara, and suddenly, "fate" took on a whole new meaning. The sense of rightness he felt with her was indescribable. Suddenly, he'd started to believe some things might be preordained. That maybe the bad was kind of good sometimes.

But what little faith had been growing inside him was blown to hell the moment he realized she had been taken.

His mate, the other half of his soul. The better part of him in every possible way.

And he'd do anything to get her back.

"We should trade him over to Mistress Black for Alara and Danica," Nik said, pointing.

"Nik," Verika snapped, stepping in front of her mate, "you can't be serious. You're just upset—"

"No, *upset* is when you get a flat tire on the way home from a hard day's work. Or when your cable goes out during the Super Bowl. We passed upset a long time ago. Try pissed off and desperate, sweetheart."

Verika drew herself up to her full height. "Nikolas Austin Johnson! This is your brother you're talking about."

"And Alara is my mate, my Marked! Just as Danica is Gage's! We can't take any risks, especially not with Danica being with child."

He might as well have dropped a bomb in the clearing, everyone looked so stunned.

Elijah took a step back; his eyes flashed to Gage. "Danica is pregnant?" Verika stopped too, gaping at Gage while waiting for him to answer.

Gage flashed Nik an irritated glance. "Yes. She told me this morning."

"And you told Nik but not me," Elijah said flatly.

"I was going to eventually tell you."

"Why doesn't that sound more convincing?"

"Now is not the time to sort out hurt feelings," Verika interrupted. "We need a plan, now. What are we going to do about this?" She gestured to the tree. "Mistress Black said we have three hours to contact her. Plus, we can't stay here much longer. We need to find Mistress Black, and we need to get going."

Nik blinked. Verika had always been kind of a nerdy, soft-spoken girl. Clearly, she'd come into more than her dazzling powers. She'd found herself, her true power as a person, since meeting Elijah.

That's when it hit him—he and Verika were never meant to be. He could never have given her what she needed to grow and prosper as a human being. Elijah could.

Huh. Maybe there was something to this fate thing after all, but he didn't want to give it too much credit. Not yet, not until they'd found Alara and Danica, and had brought them home safe and sound.

Gage nodded curtly and placed his hands on his hips. He stared at the ground, thinking. "I'll call in every favor owed me and to the crown, contact every pack, and rally every wolf willing to help."

"That's a good start, and you should do that." Elijah stepped forward. "But I have another idea."

CHAPTER TWENTY

HE WAS AN IDIOT. OR HE HAD A DEATH WISH.

As Elijah situated himself on the bed, lying flat on his back, hands pressed to his sides, legs stretched out straight, he couldn't help but wonder whether he were about to make a huge mistake. If maybe his "grand idea" wasn't so grand after all.

"You sure this will work?" Nik said tersely, standing with his arms crossed in front of the bed. Gage stood beside him, as did a handful of guards, and Heath, in case anything happened.

Elijah's eyes flicked to Heath. He really hoped he wouldn't be needing medical attention afterward, and not just because he didn't care for doctors. Mostly, he didn't want to think about the many different ways Mistress Black could fuck him up with her magic, even in a dream state. His stomach churned, and a wave of vertigo hit him.

Thank God he was lying down.

"It'll work," Elijah said curtly. In part because his ass

was still chapped Gage had told Nik about his nephew or niece and not him, and in part because his throat was so tight he was having trouble speaking. "I've done this before to contact her, when she'd send me away on some bullshit mission and I had to report back."

Nik muttered something under his breath, a stormy look on his face. Gage hissed at him, too quiet for Elijah to make out what he'd said. Apparently it had been a reprimand, because Nik pressed his lips together and silently glared at Elijah.

Verika cast a look at Nik and rolled her eyes as she lay down beside him.

"What are you doing?" His heart skipped a beat as she settled into the soft mattress in their suite.

"Going with you, of course."

"You can't do that! It's too—"

"Dangerous? I know. I'm mated to you, remember? We Johnsons eat danger for breakfast."

"This isn't funny, Verika. Mistress Black could seriously injure you."

"Do you think I don't know that? While you're meditating, you also run the risk of her injuring *you*, and there's no way in hell I'm about to let that happen. I won't leave you unprotected. We'll fight fire with fire, or rather, Black Magic with Black Magic. I'm going with you, and that's final."

He stared at her a moment. She was dead serious. And once his mate made up her mind to do something, you either damn well got out of her way or aided her.

He nodded, his heart beating faster than before and

his stomach fluttering with nerves as they both laid back and she took his hand. It didn't help the brand was making his stomach upset, a feeling which hadn't completely left since it'd started.

"Together." She turned her head on the pillow to look him in the eyes.

He smiled softly and squeezed her hand. "Together."

Elijah looked at his brothers, the guards, Heath. "Do not disturb us, no matter what happens. Our souls have to make it back to our bodies on our own. If we wake up without them…well, let's just say that could be very, very dangerous."

"Understood," Gage said quietly. He smiled grimly and eyed them both. "Good luck. Safe travels and Godspeed."

Elijah turned his attention again on his mate. She was so lovely, so brave. And just as reckless as he was, sometimes. That, or he was rubbing off on her. "You sure you want to do this?"

She nodded, her gaze unwavering. "I'm sure."

Nodding again, distracted by both the comfort her presence brought as well as the worry over her safety, Elijah turned his gaze toward the ceiling and closed his eyes. He heard the satin pillow rustle as Verika readjusted, doing the same. Their breathing evened out, their thoughts emptying as Elijah began the chant that would take them into a deep state of meditation—and lead them straight to Mistress Black.

Elijah's hand felt clammy as he and Verika strolled through

the murky fog.

No, not fog—magic. He could tell by the ozone stench in the air and the electric hum riding his skin, making it prickle. Plus, the light-blue glow coming off the fog kind of gave it away as magic.

Verika looked around, clutching his hand tight, alert green eyes searching the surrounding darkness. "I have to admit, I'm not very fond of these tunnels between planes of consciousness," she said.

"Yeah," he said dryly, his voice whispery like hers. "The 'creepy as hell' vibe isn't very welcoming. They really should fire their interior decorator."

She snorted. "Thanks for making me laugh. Takes my mind off how dangerous this all is."

"You mean we're not doing this for shits and giggles?"

"I wish."

He swallowed hard. Verika squeezed his hand. *It's all right,* she said through their bond. *I'm right here. I'm not going anywhere.*

He squeezed back and stared into her eyes. *Neither am I.*

"Am I interrupting something?"

They both jumped; Elijah choked on a curse, and Verika gave a little squeak. The scenery had abruptly shifted, morphing into a tropical rain forest stuffed with lush greenery and neon-colored blossoms the size of Elijah's hand. A light floral smell coated the air, rising from the steam covering the surface of the lagoon like fog. Lounging in its cerulean depths was a stunningly beautiful naked woman. Her dark hair hung damp down her back, her muscles rippling as she lifted a butter-yellow sponge and squeezed it. Water poured down her outstretched arm as she slowly scraped the sponge across it.

She looked over her shoulder, flashed a coy smile at Elijah. "Care to join me? I was beginning to think you two weren't going to show."

Elijah and Verika glanced at each other. *That's Mistress Black?* she asked.

In the flesh…sort of. He glared at his old flame and immediately felt sick. Her packaging was pretty, sure. But how on earth could he ever have fallen for that sick sociopath?

Stupid, stupid, stupid.

Mistress Black tsked her finger at them, as if scolding a couple of children. "It's not polite to have a telepathic conversation when I can hear what you're saying."

Verika's eyes shot up.

"That's right, dear," Mistress Black said. "When you're astral projecting, you're technically already inside your head. Only the strongest, and most practiced, witches and warlocks can manage to keep their thoughts secret when traveling between planes. It's a rather marvelous trick. I'll teach it to you sometime."

"The only thing you've taught me is how much of a monster you are."

"Monster? That's a bit dramatic, don't you think?"

"You prefer 'bitch'?"

Mistress Black laughed, flashing a proud smile—and a whole lot of everything else, good grief—as she turned to face them. "Your great-great-whatever grandfather—my husband—had a snarky sense of humor. Could be a brute on some days." Her eyes sparkled softly with distant memories. "I miss him every day. I see a little bit of him in you. And me. You have my cheekbones, my hair and eye color."

"I'm nothing like you."

"No?" Mistress Black glanced down. "Well, I guess it can't be discerned in this form." With a snap of her fingers, her figure shifted, turning fuzzy like an analog TV screen before changing shape entirely.

Verika gasped, and Elijah went still. His lungs had stopped working, as apparently had his ability to blink. It wasn't so much his fear of magic rearing up as it was pure and utter shock.

The woman who stood before him looked nothing like Mistress Black but resembled every bit of his Verika. From her long scarlet tresses to her ivory skin, he would have thought he was looking at Verika's doppelganger had he not seen the wrinkles around her eyes, forehead, and mouth. Age had begun to wither the woman's fine face, yet it only served to enhance her enchanting beauty. Startlingly green eyes, the exact same shade as Verika's, gazed back at them from a face that was barely smiling, as if holding some dear secret close.

She wore a dress of dark-green velvet, which contrasted nicely with her flame-colored hair, and made her look like an Irish lass of old.

Verika stared, going white. "What is this?" she whispered.

Mistress Black's voice was different when she spoke, more feathery and lilting with the ghost of an Irish accent.

"Me"—she gestured down at her new form—"as I once was. And will be again."

"This is impossible." Verika's eyes shone with tears. A miserable frown trembled on her delicate pink lips as she shook her head. "We can't be related. It's all a lie."

"Would it really be so terrible?" Mistress Black stepped, or rather, floated, out of the pool. She landed on the grass, barefooted and completely dry. She took a step toward Verika, lifting a pale hand as if to caress her cheek. Verika jerked back, nearly stumbling.

Mistress Black's hand froze. Those delicate fingers squeezed into a fist, trembling slightly, before she at last let her arm fall at her side. "I cannot blame you for your disbelief. But you can't deny our similarities. Not only in looks, but in power."

Verika remained mute, staring at Mistress Black with a mixture of awe and revulsion.

Elijah saw the longing in his mate's shining eyes. Saw how much she wanted to belong to a tribe, to find out about her true family. It broke his heart. His parents might have been pieces of shit in many ways, but at least he knew who they were. He couldn't imagine growing up without knowing where he came from. Knowing that the family he had, no matter how great, was a lie, and only there because someone else didn't want him.

The breeze shifted, rustling the vibrant greenery. Mistress Black's and Verika's messy red curls lifted; the wind circled around them and sparked with green and purple embers.

Elijah instantly tensed. The ozone stench burned his

nose as it grew stronger.

"What are you doing?" murmured Verika, looking around almost in wonder.

"I'm not doing anything," Mistress Black replied earnestly. "It's my magic simply responding to yours. Like calls to like. Your magic recognizes mine, and vice versa. They call to each other."

Verika lifted a hand. Shadows and wind coiled around her wrist, tangling down her arm.

"The weight of our power is great, is it not?" Mistress Black asked seductively, watching her war with the worry trying to creep onto her face. "Let me ease the burden. Allow me to show you how to harness your power properly."

The shadows whirling around Verika's arm turned into snakes made of smoky air. They hissed, baring their fangs and staring at her with glittering purple eyes. Verika simply waved the apparitions away, and they evaporated. She crossed her arms, raised her chin. Ice settled in her gaze. "I will never let you touch my power."

"Even if it would save your friends' lives?"

Elijah and Verika drew still. A string of curse words tumbled through Elijah's head as Mistress Black chuckled.

"Thought so." She smirked. "If you need to see proof they're alive before bargaining…" With a snap of her fingers, the air opened up to reveal a darkened bedroom. Candles burned all around a huge canopied bed oozing red silk—on which lay two familiar, sleeping figures.

Danica and Alara looked perfectly unharmed, each dozing peacefully, as if they were merely taking a nap.

With another snap, the portal vanished. Mistress Black crossed her arms, mirroring Verika's haughty gaze. Her eyes shimmered with triumph. The bitch had already thought she'd won. Elijah knew she had the moment Verika opened her mouth.

"I propose a trade," she said evenly.

Mistress Black raised a brow. "I'm listening."

"I'll join your coven if you lift the brand from Elijah and return Danica and Alara to their mates."

"Absolutely not!" roared Elijah. "I'll die first before handing you over to that psychopathic bitch!"

"Quite possible, if the brand's curse has its way with you. By the way, have either of you started vomiting blood yet?"

The thought of Verika enduring that kind of pain on his behalf was too much to bear. Paling, he glanced at her; horror gripped his chest and made it tight.

"Thought so," Mistress Black said smugly. "You haven't considered all the consequences, have you, my pet? So handsome but not very thorough, are we? And I thought wolves were supposed to look after their mate's well-beings above all else."

"We do," he said through gritted teeth.

"Well, I hate to tell you, but you and your delectable brothers are doing a piss-poor job of it."

"Shut up!" Elijah roared. "There will be no bargaining."

"Elijah," Verika said quietly, resting a hand on his. "Let me do this. Please." She widened her eyes slightly.

Trust me.

The voice was hers but barely audible, as if a ghost

were talking to him. He wasn't even sure he'd heard it. Part of him wanted to reach out to her with his mind, through their bond, but he didn't want Mistress Black to hear.

Before he could respond, Verika turned. "We are in agreement, yes?" She extended her hand.

Mistress Black stared at it for a moment and at last shook. "Agreed. I'll send you a time and place to meet me. Come alone and don't be late. Oh, and don't worry about your friends. They'll be fine for now—unless you decide not to show, of course. Or bring backup or try anything cute. Then I can't make any promises as to their well-being."

With that, she grabbed her skirt and twirled, vanishing in a whirlwind of shimmering green sparkles.

Her laugh echoed all around them as the dream plane cracked and shattered, and Verika and Elijah tumbled back to reality.

CHAPTER TWENTY-ONE

ELIJAH SLAMMED INTO HIS BODY, FEELING AS IF HE HAD just fallen a thousand feet and hit concrete. He jerked upright, his lungs burning as he gasped for air for a few terrifying seconds. Beside him, Verika did the same. Her lovely face was flushed, her eyes wide and frightened.

Asking "are you all right?" seemed like a stupid question at the moment. Instead, he settled for grasping her hand and holding it close. Letting her know he was there, that he was real and she was safe.

For the moment.

"So?" Nik's gaze bounced back and forth between them after giving them a moment to catch their breath. "Did you find out anything? Are Danica and Alara all right?"

Verika cast a sidelong glance at her mate. *We can't tell them about our bargain,* she said telepathically. *Otherwise, they'll never let us go through with it.*

I don't want you to go through with it as is, Elijah said.

But I assume that look you gave me in the dream world meant that you had some sort of plan up your sleeve.

A slight nod.

"Would you guys cut the telepathic bullshit and just give us some goddamned answers?" Nik said, exasperated. The guy looked as if he were on the verge of pulling his own hair out.

"We talked to Mistress Black," Verika said calmly. "Danica and Alara are safe."

"Why do I sense a 'but' in there somewhere?" Gage asked warily.

Verika took a deep breath, prepared herself. "She said she would exchange them…for me."

"Absolutely not," Nik growled.

"Finally, something we can agree on," Elijah muttered under his breath.

"What does she want with you?" Gage's eyes narrowed.

"I'm not sure," Verika said quickly, cutting Elijah off before he could answer. "I assume it's because we're both Black Witches. There aren't many of us in the world."

"So, she wants to, what, bond with you or something? You're telling me she's suddenly feeling lonely, like an outcast?" Nik snorted. "Yeah, right. Give me a break. She wants something else from you."

"It sounds like a trap," Gage said.

"Well, duh," Elijah said dryly.

"She seemed keenly interested in my heritage," Verika said. "My late mentor, Satine, knew my mother—my real mother. My mother…kept a journal, which I now have, about me, that's supposed to 'reveal everything about my past.'"

"And have you read it?" Nik asked with surprising gentleness. He gazed at her with concern.

A low, nearly inaudible growl rumbled in Elijah's throat. *Mine,* she heard his inner wolf speak into her mind.

Verika placed a hand over his to calm him, to reassure him Nik was not a threat. Elijah's hackles lowered, though the flint remained in his eyes as he stared at his brother.

"No." A shiver ran through her, and she hugged herself.

Elijah put a possessive arm around her. "Before you open your big mouth, Nik, I already know what you're going to say. We should start there, with the journal. Maybe it contains some clues that will help us figure out why Mistress Black is so keenly interested in *my mate.*"

Verika nearly rolled her eyes at how he emphasized "my mate." And she would have, had terror not slammed into her at the thought of opening that book, at smelling her mentor's scent on its worn leather cover. The scent of the incense she'd burned in her magic shop, where the journal had been stored for so long.

Verika looked up at him. *I don't want to, Elijah. I don't want to know.*

I know. But we might not have a choice. He nuzzled her neck with his nose, took in her scent. *I'll be there with you the entire time, if you need me.*

She took a deep breath; the room had gone silent as everyone awaited her answer.

"Okay," she breathed. "I'll check the journal."

She'd locked the book away long enough, hadn't even dared look at it. Because every time she did, she was both reminded of what and whom she'd lost and that her parents hadn't wanted her.

But her reservations seemed petty compared to what was at stake now. She knew she couldn't put it off any longer. Not if she was to help the ones she loved.

It was, finally, time to learn about her heritage.

CHAPTER TWENTY-TWO

VERIKA'S HANDS SHOOK AS SHE HELD THE JOURNAL. ITS spine was crinkled, the indigo leather worn light-blue in places. A single red ribbon bound it around the center. Words were scribbled across the edges of the cover—a protection spell. Her mother—or possibly even Satine or her father—obviously hadn't wanted just anyone to read it. She studied it, stroked the boundaries of the spell with her invisible magic fingers. Curiously, she couldn't tell whether the spell had been broken or not, it was that subtle. Which meant Gerard had either been lying to her when he'd told her the answers she sought were in this book, or he was advanced enough of a warlock to be able to break through the spell and it had snapped back into place on its own once he was done fishing through the journal.

Verika was betting on the latter. Gerard had been a powerful warlock.

But he wasn't strong enough in the end, was he? her conscience thought with dark satisfaction.

She still hadn't forgotten the cold malice in Alara's eyes, so at odds with the sunshine in the garden they'd sat in, when she'd asked, "And, exactly, why am I your favorite witch?"

"Because he killed my family," she'd said simply.

In that moment, Verika didn't feel so guilty, so vile, for killing him anymore.

Which made her wonder, again, whether these powers were turning her into a monster.

Thrusting that chilling thought aside, she focused on reading the spell, trying to figure out where it started. *Find the seams,* Satine had told her. *Find the seams and then rip them apart.*

Her eyes scanned the words once, twice, three times. It was a riddle; the words were all rearranged so that in order to break the spell, you had to put the riddle back in the right order and hope the damn thing didn't backfire on you when you broke it.

Elijah and Verika stood in their room alone, save for the guards posted outside the open door. Elijah had rolled his eyes when he saw them take their posts, citing how helpful they had been when Alara and Danica had been abducted. Verika calmed him, saying they could use all the help they could get. Magic could be unpredictable. You never knew what was going to happen. Besides, Verika appreciated Nik and Gage's attempt at privacy and protection all in one. It was thoughtful and sweet, and reminded her they still cared about her, even if things were dicey between them and Elijah.

Elijah studied the journal cover with her. "Can you

open it? I can't make any sense of the incantation."

"I can," Verika murmured, barely hearing him. Her mind was so wrapped around trying to break the spell, to piece it back together in the right order. She went over to the desk and retrieved a pen and a legal pad. Sitting down, she scribbled words in different arrangements, furiously crossing words out and writing them in a different order. Thirty silent minutes passed, filled with nothing but the slash of her pen, before she at last got it figured out. And when she did, she laughed.

"What is it?" Elijah got up off the bed, where he'd floated off to in order to give her space to think.

"Satine must have put this on here." Verika cleared her throat. "'The only one worthy of a pass is he or she who doesn't have their head up their ass.' It was in Pig Latin, which Satine was very fond of."

Soon as she finished speaking the silly incantation, the ribbon lazily uncoiled itself and the journal flipped open to the first page.

Elijah blinked. "Seriously? That's what the big, bad spell said?"

Verika smiled and nodded. "Yep. Whoever said magic had to be serious?"

He looked at the journal and shook his head. "I'm gonna go lay back down. All this magic's making my head hurt." He rested a hand on her shoulder. "I'm here if you need me."

"Thanks," she said softly, squeezing his hand. She ran her eyes over her mate. His face hadn't been as pale this time, she thought with a small sigh of relief.

Then it hit her—what she was about to read—and it felt as though a rock had dropped to the pit of her stomach. She turned to face the journal with a heavy heart as her mate padded over to the bed. Even after she heard the mattress crinkle and her mate's soft snores filled the room, she couldn't bring herself to start reading.

She stared at the dried ink, the date that had been so painstakingly written holding her gaze captive.

It was her birthday.

She held her breath—and started at the beginning.

Dear diary,

I can't believe I still write those words. "Dear diary." It sounds so juvenile. Some people name their journals, but I can't bring myself to do that. It doesn't feel right to me.

It's four a.m., and I can't sleep because our little girl was born six hours ago. Labor was a bitch, all eighteen hours of it, but I'm glad I went through it. I'd go through hell and back for that little angel. Soon as she looked at me with those bright-green eyes—my eyes—I knew I was taken and I would move heaven and earth for her.

Verika's eyes pricked with tears as confusion and longing tightened her chest. She blinked the tears away and kept reading.

She is so perfect. We couldn't decide on Erica or Veronica, so we combined the two into Verika. Pretty, isn't it? And unique, just like her.

Verika blinked. She'd always thought her foster parents had come up with the name. Maybe they'd lied, as a means of protecting her. After all, they'd kept the fact she was adopted from her until she was nearly eighteen.

Verika had so loved playing detective growing up. After she'd come across the adoption papers while snooping around for her Christmas presents, there wasn't much use in them denying the adoption anymore.

The penmanship warbled, as if her mother's hand had trembled.

I've been praying she doesn't inherit my gifts. All my life I've either been shunned or feared, except with Michael. He's so wonderfully normal, this human husband of mine.

Verika stared. Her father had been human?

He knows about my powers—it's what attracted him to me—but he doesn't judge me. He accepts me for who and what I am. For once in my life, I belong. I have a family, a purpose.

The journal entry ended there.

Her mother had sketched a picture of a baby on the opposite page. It was quite good, very realistic. She'd even shaded in the shadows on the blanket swaddling the baby with crosshatching. Nestled around her neck was a beautiful, oval-shaped pendant, a polished stone of some sort wrapped in wiring.

Verika stared at the portrait of herself, and her throat grew tight and dry.

Flipping the page, she continued through the entries. Despite years of training as a cop, it was hard to be detached about the whole thing. To keep her emotions at bay and only care about the clues she may ascertain.

Her heart swelled the more she read. One thing became painfully clear within five pages—her mother and father had both loved her very much.

212

Her father had died of a bee sting when she was one. They hadn't even known he'd been allergic. She vaguely remembered his smiling face, but her memories of that time were hazy. No surprise, considering how much time had passed. But it still depressed her. She wished she could remember her real father. Remember what he looked like, what cologne he wore, if any, the sound of his voice. All those little seemingly insignificant details she'd give her right arm for.

One entry caught her eye.

It was the night before her mother abandoned her.

Her powers are growing at an alarming rate. Dear God, she's just a toddler! A toddler with the ability to turn the sun black and make the moon vanish. The other night, she caused an eclipse—an eclipse—in the middle of the day. It was all over the news, the papers. I didn't know where the spell was coming from until I realized it was her. My sweet little angel always did favor the shadows. It was all I could do to break her spell. I feel terrible casting a sleeping spell on her, but it was the only way to get her to stop. Heavens, her magic is so strong. I can't contain her powers anymore on my own, and I refuse to use a coven's help. They'll want to exploit her, as they tried to do with me. Already, they're looking for me, hunting her because of those news stories and that stupid eclipse I let slip by.

Verika's heart rate kicked into high gear as she read, her eyes skimming the page quicker and quicker.

I have to give her up. I have no choice. I can't let them take her.

Verika's eyes narrowed. Who?

The penmanship became sloppier on the next page, as if it had been written more in a hurry. And on a different day.

Dear God, save my soul. I didn't mean to. I swear I didn't. But I couldn't help myself. He tried to take her, tried to take away my baby girl. So I had to kill him. My power wanted to. Oh God, Jesus, what have I done?

The ink blurred, the page darkened by splotchy stains—teardrops.

Dear God, forgive me. Oh, please forgive me. I swear I never meant to harm any living thing. But he was going to take her, take her and harvest her power, he said. I couldn't let that happen. My power reacted according to my emotions. I can't control it. Lord, Jesus, I fear myself, fear what I'm becoming. I enjoyed killing him. Dare I admit that?

There's something dark inside me, something I've felt growing stronger for a long time now. It waited for the right time and then lashed out at the first appropriate victim.

My mother was right—our line is cursed. Cursed to bring death and destruction to everyone around us. I can't bear to let that happen to Verika—I can't. It would destroy what's left of my soul. She's so pure, so good. My little angel. Besides, the coven will come after me now that I've killed their leader. Verika would be in constant danger. I have to surrender her, for her own safety.

Verika flipped the next page so fast, she nearly tore it. Instead of continuing where it had left off, there was a new entry.

I gave up my baby girl today. I'm sobbing as I write this, even though I know it was for the best. She can't ever know about me, can't ever know about her abilities. Satine has promised to bind her powers. On top of what I've already done. It should hold, for a time. Though, Satine is certain she can keep her powers suppressed by adding new layers to the bind as Verika matures. She'll pose as her mentor, ensure she gets adopted by a loving couple. And when the time is right, she'll teach my daughter about magic. It's the perfect opportunity for her to learn about her craft, as she will surely manifest some powers, and for Satine to patch up the bind as it wears with age.

Verika sat back, stunned. Satine had only posed as her mentor, her friend, so she could control her. Suppress her abilities, as her mother had said.

Her heart tore in half. She'd been betrayed by a lot of people in her life, but this felt like a knife in the back. Had Satine been pretending the whole time to be interested in her well-being? To love her?

There wasn't much left in the journal after that. Though the last page made her breath catch, gave her newfound hope.

I saw my daughter today, at Satine's shop. She's grown quite fond of my little angel. Says she feels like her own child, which warms my heart. I am so very fortunate to have such a great friend looking out for her. It broke my heart to not have my own daughter know me, but I know it's for the best. I am so very blessed to have such a devoted guardian in Verika's life.

Satine says she's an ace at her studies, but feels anxious she hasn't come into her powers yet. I hate to do that to her. I know how young witches and warlocks can be to those who don't manifest an affinity. But it is for her own protection, and for the safety of those around her. Her powers can never be unbound.

I wish I could be there for her. To watch her grow up and become a woman. But I fear my time on this earth is limited. The coven of the warlock I killed draws closer every day. They've hunted me across the States, Europe, and back again. My redirects and dead ends won't stave them off for long. Magic has grown more advanced. There are so many aids we can employ now to boost our powers, get us what we want, to help us find what doesn't want to be found.

At least my daughter has the amulet, the one Satine helped me fashion. Through my blood, sweat, and sacrifice, maybe she can be protected from

The line abruptly cut off; something dark, like coffee, had been spilled across the pages, splattering the remaining text and making it hard to decipher.

Verika squinted, angling the book differently against the light. The dried liquid was russet, almost like—

Her heart pitched to the bottom of her stomach.

Blood.

Oh God. Was this…had her mother been…

Had her mother been murdered while writing this last entry?

Her mother had scribbled something else beneath the dried blood. It took Verika several long seconds before she could make out the final text.

I love you.

Verika stared at the message for several long minutes. A half hour passed. She knew the message was meant for her. It had to be. Who else could her mother have written it to?

Somehow, some way, she had known her daughter would find this book and read it someday. And she'd wanted her...wanted her to know the truth. That she had loved her, had done everything she could to protect her.

Part of her she'd kept locked up, the part made of stone, broke inside her. She let herself cry. Over the mother she'd lost.

Over the mentor, the guardian, the friend, who'd protected her.

Over the family who had been taken from her because she possessed a gift—a goddamned affinity—that she'd prayed, prayed, prayed for as a child, which the woman she'd grown into abhorred and wished to be rid of.

When Elijah finally woke, roused by her sobs, he immediately went to her. "Ssshh," he cooed into her hair. "It's okay. It's all right. I'm here."

He rocked her, let her cry onto his shoulder until she had no more tears left. Only after her breathing had evened out and her heart had calmed did she tell him what she had learned.

"Someone killed her." Verika clutched the journal to her chest with one hand and her mate in the other. She needed his strength now, needed it not to fall apart.

Her mind wouldn't stop turning over theory after theory.

"We don't know that," Elijah said quietly.

"But someone was after her. She'd said she'd killed the leader of a coven because they wanted me in order to use my powers. They would want revenge. A lot of witches and warlocks in the Underworld still believe in 'an eye for an eye.'"

He rubbed her shoulders and hugged her. He stood behind her while she remained seated in the chair she'd been reading in. "We'll figure it out, I promise. We'll find out what happened to your mother."

"Swear it?" She looked up at him.

He kissed her. "On my life."

A long sigh left her. Elijah had a way of making her feel at ease, at least mentally. Her body was still wound up in knots.

"Do you have any idea about that amulet she mentioned?" he asked.

"No," she said with a hoarse sigh. "I wish I did. If it's meant to protect me, maybe we can use it against Mistress Black. I don't know exactly what it is, but I have an idea of where to look for it." Shaking her head, she stood. Stretched her arms, her back, her legs. "I thought we'd explore my parents' attic. My mom is a bit of a pack rat. She likes to keep everything, especially when it comes to me. A lot of my kids' clothes are still tucked away in boxes up there." She smiled softly. A small pinch formed in her chest any time she talked about her family. God, she missed them so much.

Elijah gulped. "Why do I have the feeling magic is going to be involved in getting us to your parents' house?"

She smiled ruefully. "Because wanted fugitives can't exactly fly coach, now can they?"

CHAPTER TWENTY-THREE

IT HAD TAKEN SOME CONVINCING ON HER PART TO GET Nik and Gage to go along with their plan. The plan being they would sneak into her parents' attic to look for this amulet that may or may not be of any use to them at all.

At this point, Verika would be willing to try a home remedy printed off Pinterest if it promised to get rid of Mistress Black—or cellulite. Both were the bane of her existence right now.

"Besides," she told Gage and Nik, "it would be best if Elijah and I vanish in case the DPI shows up. That way you can't be accused of harboring wanted criminals. It would only complicate the situation further, and neither one of you can do Alara or Danica much good from a jail cell."

That logic won the argument, as Verika knew it would. There was little a wolf wouldn't do for the protection and safety of his mate.

Elijah promptly puked the moment they dematerialized inside her parents' attic. Verika couldn't blame him, and almost threw up herself. Her stomach had never fully recovered from the sickness caused by the branding. Plus, spells that bent the fabric of space and time did something weird to a person, biologically speaking. It scrambled your brain and rearranged your molecules. The "putting it all back together" part was what had her nearly swallowing her stomach as Elijah wiped his mouth and straightened.

She cast him a coy smile after weaving a simple sound-proofing spell. "Green isn't a very good shade on you. You feeling all right? I've sound-proofed the room, by the way, so feel free to speak aloud."

"Figured as much, considering the lemon furniture polish smell suddenly turned into burnt ozone. But to answer your question, I've been better. Been worse too. You?"

"Fine."

"Liar."

"Yeah, well, that's something else I've picked up from you Johnsons. You don't like people to worry over you, especially your mates, so you're inclined to bend the truth when it suits you."

"Can't say we aren't noble."

"Oh, I wouldn't go that far."

He shoved her playfully, and she smiled. It still felt a bit tight, as the weight of knowing her mother had been murdered trying to protect her still pressed down on her shoulders. But holy crap, it felt *good* to be back home, even if it was only in her parents' attic.

The faint smell of citrus clung to the air. She could almost imagine Elijah thinking *Who the hell dusts their freaking attic?*

Her mother, that's who. Verika could imagine her lovingly running a cloth dampened with polish over the boxes, singing out of tune some song from the sixties. Not a box out of place, no mess to be found. Her mother loved this house—it showed in the polished wooden floors, in the little lace valance she'd hung over the tiny window across the room.

"So why'd you insist just the two of us go?" Elijah asked, making her blink. She'd almost forgotten whom she'd come with. "'More hands make for lighter work,' and all that?"

"Mistress Black said she'd contact us, and we had to come alone. I saw an excuse to get us out of the manor and took it."

"Nice. Sneaky but quick thinking."

She shrugged. "I hated deceiving Nik and Gage, but we don't exactly have another choice, not if we want to get Alara and Danica back safely."

Elijah grabbed her wrist, tugged her to a halt as she started to turn away. He grasped her shoulders and pivoted her to face him. "I'm not handing you over to her. I hope you know that."

"It won't come down to that." She swallowed hard. She hoped it wouldn't, anyway.

Turning away before he could see her worry, she started looking.

"Okay, going back to my earlier argument: say we let Mistress Black take us. What if something happens and we need backup?" Elijah asked.

"Don't worry. I have that all covered," she muttered absently, half listening and half thinking. She was missing something.

"Damn. I forgot it." She snapped her fingers. Her mother's journal appeared in her hand. The air smelled of cinnamon, an odd side effect of that particular transportation spell.

"It smells like snickerdoodles." Elijah wrinkled his nose.

"You don't like it?"

"No, it's not that." *It's just the fact it's magic,* he didn't need to say.

Verika ignored his discomfort. At least he was dealing with it better. That was progress, at least. "Curiously enough, I've found you can actually scent some spells the way people buy air freshener for their cars or homes. My personal favorites are cinnamon, sugar, and butter," she admitted rather bashfully, her cheeks warming at how personal it felt. "All those scents remind me of home because my mom always used to bake snickerdoodles, my favorite cookie."

Elijah smiled. "Sounds like an awesome mom."

"She was. Still is, if I'd let her be." Her face wrinkled up with pain. "I still feel bad shutting her and Dad out of my life. They've been so good to me."

"It won't be like this forever." Elijah took her hand.

"No, it won't. I'm going to make damn sure of that." Her power surged as she thought of Mistress Black, as if it sensed her intense loathing of the woman. She promptly pushed it back down, but not before a few green sparks shot out her fingers. Elijah abruptly jerked his hand back, stepping away about a foot.

She sighed. *One step forward, two steps back.*

Feeling the air thicken with tension, she said, "How about we get busy?"

They searched in silence for a little while, being careful to put everything back exactly the way it was. She kept quiet, giving Elijah the space he needed to sort out his feelings about her magic. A lump formed in her throat. Sometimes, she felt as if her magic would always be the cause of this invisible rift between them.

A rift, she feared, that would only grow with time, should he be unable to conquer his fears.

Her heart ached as she pried open a box and took out a little yellow jumper she'd worn when she was a toddler. The fabric was buttery soft and smelled faintly of dust and lavender fabric softener.

Her hands shook faintly as her face grew hot.

Just one night. All she wanted was to be able to spend one night with her family without worrying they might get hurt. Something else she feared would never happen.

Soon, she told herself firmly. *No more negative thoughts. Just keep thinking in terms of "soon."*

Elijah ransacked a garbage bag of stuffed animals. He pulled out a teddy bear that was missing an eye, as well as most of his fur. "Sentimental much?"

"You've met my mother. You tell me."

He stared at the bear sadly. "I wish someone would have cared enough about me and my brothers to keep all of our childhood things."

She couldn't help it; she rose, slowly went over to him, as if approaching a frightened doe, and pulled him into her arms. He hugged her back without hesitation, and she at last relaxed. When she let go, she looked into his eyes. "When this is all over, I'm going to buy a camera. Then we'll travel, settle down, start a family, whatever you want. We'll create our own memories. And we can hoard all the knickknacks, abused stuffed animals, and anything else our hearts desire from the family we create."

He smiled, his eyes getting a slight sheen to them. "That sounds wonderful."

She smiled back, reluctant to step away. "Good." She paused, studied her mate. Only love shone from his eyes.

Love and hope.

Perhaps the rift between them wasn't as big as she'd feared.

The creak of the squeaky board in the kitchen had her blinking, bringing her back to the moment. "Let's keep looking. There's no telling where this thing is buried, and we might not have much time to find it if Mistress Black comes knocking."

A whole half hour passed before Verika started to get frustrated. After another half hour, she started to get pissed.

After casting three locating spells, all of which produced nada, she nearly screamed.

"Where the hell is that damn necklace?" She sat up and flipped her hair over her shoulder in frustration. She inhaled. A tendril of hair got sucked into her mouth.

Spitting it out with a scowl, she stood and walked over to the journal. They had it flopped open to the drawing of her as a baby, the necklace sketched out in messy lines of charcoal around her tiny neck.

Elijah joined her, his brow dampened by a light sheen of sweat. With his unkempt hair, it was sexy as hell. She briefly imagined him wearing a construction hat, work boots, and rugged jeans—or nothing at all.

Elijah's eyes stopped examining the drawing. Slowly, he turned his head to look at her, one brow arched in amusement. "You know, I can fulfill that fantasy for you sometime, if you like?"

"What? Oh hell." Her face flamed, and she buried it in her hands. "I forgot I can inadvertently project my thoughts on you, if the feeling's strong enough."

"If the lust I'm smelling off you is any indication, then it certainly is," said Elijah in a low voice, a wicked smile upturning his lips. He leaned in, tacking on, "Mrs. Johnson, you scandalize me."

Her face nearly burst into flames. Flustered, and partly to reclaim her personal space, she poked him in the chest with a pointed index finger. "I'm not technically Mrs. Johnson, you know."

"Not yet."

She paused, studying him.

Elijah swallowed, shifting his weight about. "Ah hell," he said finally. "Now's as good a time as any."

Verika watched with bated breath as he knelt and reached into his pants pocket. He took her hand, gently clasping it in his own, those big, rough fingers warming her to the bone. He looked up earnestly into her eyes, which had begun to heat with unshed tears.

"I love you," he said roughly, smiling. He pulled out a plastic gold ring with a green, emerald-cut rhinestone. "And I know I don't have much to offer you—"

"Oh, hush." She seized his face in her hands and kissed him. "You're the world to me, and always will be. I love you too."

"So, is that a yes?"

"Of course it's a yes. Now put that gorgeous ring on me."

He had to pinch the plastic tongs of the band to make it tight enough around her slight ring finger, but it settled on her hand perfectly. She turned her hand this way and that, admiring the new proclamation of his love.

His cheeks flushed slightly. "I'll get you something nicer when I'm able, I promise."

"Don't be ridiculous. I love it." And she did. For her, it didn't matter whether the ring cost five grand or five cents. It was perfect.

This moment—he—was perfect.

And she wouldn't ever let him forget it.

Enough happiness radiated from Verika to rival the sun. She was so dazzled by what had just happened, how surreal it was, that she nearly missed the paranormal signature walking through the front door downstairs.

CHAPTER TWENTY-FOUR

EVERY DROP OF SUNSHINE DRIED UP IN VERIKA'S AURA. Hell, it seemed like all the color and light had been sucked out of the room as she homed in on the most decidedly unwelcome visitor.

Verika scuttled to the door, pressed her ear and palms to it. Elijah's body warmed her back as he came up behind her, listening.

"Hello!" chirped her mother. "Please come in. So good to see you again, Rick!"

"Likewise, Mrs. Tate," said the man coolly. "Watching a little football?"

Verika's eyes narrowed slightly. His voice tickled the back of her brain. Why did he sound so familiar? She scanned through her memories, searching for a "Rick," but couldn't put a face with the name.

"You bet," said Mr. Tate amiably. "The Dolphins are going to stomp the Seahawks. Care to join us? Can I get you a beer?"

Is he on crack? Elijah said. *He sounds way too accommodating, like he's ready to make this 'Rick' his son-in-law.*

Sssh!

"No, thank you," replied Rick. The wooden floors downstairs groaned as they walked around. "I won't be here long. I'm actually here for your daughter."

"She's not here," said Mrs. Tate. Glasses clinked, and the refrigerator door opened. She was probably going to pour him a glass of sweet tea. Verika's mouth watered thinking about it. Hailing from the South, she still drank sweet tea whenever she could. Though she usually had to make it herself to get it to taste right. When she was feeling lazy, she'd buy a jug from the store, but it was never the same as homemade tea. She almost always had to add more sugar. And don't even get her started on artificial sweeteners.

"Actually, she's upstairs right now," Rick said.

Verika and Elijah both froze.

Silence. "No, she's not." Mr. Tate laughed.

"Yes, she is," purred Rick. His voice had taken on a rougher, darker quality. "I can smell her."

"Don't be absurd." Mr. Tate paused a beat. "Hey! Who the hell are you? Get the hell out of my house!"

Verika didn't stop to think. She threw open the door before Elijah could stop her, and ran down the stairs. Her heel missed the last step, nearly pitching her forward into the couch, but she caught herself on the wall and kept running. Thundering footsteps came from behind her as Elijah followed her through the living room and into the kitchen.

Verika drew up short in the entryway. Elijah stopped beside her. He bared his fangs, snarling at the tall, strange man who stood before them. His eyes blazed gold.

"Vampire." He sniffed. "But not."

Whatever shields had been masking Rick's signature dropped, and Verika paled as she caught a heady whiff of him. "He's half-demon," she whispered, staring, paralyzed by fear.

Rick was maybe six foot five, with a lithe, muscular build and ruggedly handsome features. His head was shaved, and week-old stubble shadowed his strong jawline.

He had his fangs buried in her mother's neck. Two lines of blood dribbled down her father's shirt from the fresh bite marks on his own neck. Both her mother and father stared blankly ahead, staring right at Verika and Elijah without actually seeing them. Their eyes had glazed over, their mouths open slightly. Like zombies.

Verika watched, feeling helpless. Her knees began to shake, so she gripped the doorjamb to steady herself. "Let them go," she said hoarsely.

The vampire-demon cast her a lazy glance. His eyes were almost solid red, glowing around pupils black as oil.

Something flashed across her mind, of a shadowy monster staring at her in the dream plane. "It's you," Verika whispered, eyes widening with recognition. "You're the one who took Danica and Alara."

Rick at last straightened, wiped his mouth with the back of his hand. "Yep."

"But...that power, the Black Magic... I don't sense it now."

"You mean this power?"

It was as though a floodgate had been opened.

He unleashed the fury of his magic. Shadows radiated from him like black fire, the flames curling across the floor and stretching their black fingers toward Verika as if to claim her. Souls shrieked in the fire, crying out for help, screaming in pain or terror. Verika felt her own fear creeping up, like a cold trickle down her throat. The reek of sulfur was strong enough to make her gag. His magic knocked the breath from her, and she stepped back from the force of its might. Beside her, Elijah grunted, steeling himself against the magical onslaught.

She took his hand, squeezed it.

I'm here. Do not be afraid.

She raised a hand. "*Dimini!*"

The flames flickered and snuffed out, as if someone had doused invisible water on top of them.

Rick laughed and applauded with slow, deliberate claps. "Bravo! I sensed the scope of your power in the astral field, but I didn't think it would be…well, like *that*. Damn. And I thought I was strong in the Dark Arts. I can see why my mistress is so interested in you."

"How did you hide your signature from me? Back at the manor?"

"Wouldn't you like to know? No, seriously," he said at Verika's dour look, "it's a variation of a simple cloaking spell. My mistress can teach you when I take you to her."

"She's not going anywhere with you," Elijah growled, on the verge of transforming. Muscles in his neck and arms veined, and his fingers were curled. Black claws tipped each digit, and the skin was stretched tight across each knuckle. Verika sensed his bloodlust, his desire to rip this prick's head off.

It was nearly as strong as her own.

Almost on a whim, Rick licked his index finger and rubbed the saliva on her mother's oozing neck wounds. The puncture marks started to close, shrinking and vanishing altogether to reveal smooth, bloodstained flesh. He did the same with her father. Neither of them responded to his touch.

Rick examined both their necks and smiled in satisfaction. He rolled his eyes, that grin widening. "Almost forgot. Sometimes, I get a little caught up in the moment, if you know what I mean."

Verika's eyes flicked to the blood droplets that lay splattered against the kitchen floor. The metallic tang of blood soured the lemony freshness that permeated the air. "I know exactly what you mean. I got so caught up in killing Gerard in the most excruciating way possible that it didn't dawn on me what I was doing until after he was dead. And you know what? I don't regret it. I know I should, and perhaps that makes me a shitty person. But it brought me great joy to see him suffer after what he put my parents through. What he's put others through."

A flicker of fear flashed through Rick's eyes as he paled slightly. One hard swallow later, and he was back to his old, grinning self. "Hey, I didn't like Gerard either. Total douche."

"At least we agree on that."

Rick studied her, his head angled to the side as those

dark eyes swept over her. "You know, I see a lot of potential in you." He leaned in conspiratorially. "I bet you could even be more powerful than Mistress Black."

"Leave. Now. While I'm still feeling merciful."

He laughed. "You're a piece of work, you know that?"

"And you're about to be a pile of goo if you don't get the hell out of my home."

"Okay, okay!" He held up both hands. "Just take it easy. Calm down."

"Ten."

"Ah. We're going to do the counting down thing, are we? Make me feel more intimidated?"

"Nine."

"I see how it is."

"Actually, I don't think you do. Not yet. Seven."

"Wait, what happened to eight?"

"Six."

"Tch."

"Four."

He rolled his neck in exasperation. "All right, but just remember you didn't give me any choice." With a snap of his fingers, both her parents about-faced and marched to the counter. They each drew a butcher knife from the knife rack and held the blade to their throats.

The number two froze on Verika's lips. "Monster," she breathed, her eyes darting between them. "You glamoured them."

"And you're surprised? Come on," he drawled, leaning against the countertop. "You had to have seen this coming. Then again, maybe not, considering you epically failed to prevent it."

"Shut up!" Elijah barked. "I've had enough of your babbling." He started forward, all menace and muscle and pissed-off werewolf.

Rick quickly straightened and backed away. "Ah, ah, ah!"

The blades against her parents' throats began to move. Her mother cried out softly as the knife's teeth split her flesh open.

"Stop! Stop!" Verika shrieked, taking a step forward and then quickly pulling back for fear the vampire-demon would command her parents to finish what they'd started.

Elijah barely restrained himself. He stalked back and forth in front of her, a caged animal working itself up into a rage.

If he snapped like he had at the house... Oh God, what would become of her parents?

All the happy times spent in this kitchen flashed before her eyes. Baking cookies with her mother and chattering excitedly about what she had learned in magic lessons, chopping an onion with her father and laughing over the tears streaming from both their eyes. Fixing huge mugs of steaming cocoa and watching the snow drift past the kitchen window.

Her eyes stung with tears. She'd thought about those happy memories many times over the lonely years since she'd left home. And the only thing that kept all those memories from becoming painful was knowing her family was still alive, waiting right here for her. If this madman took Mom and Dad away, then all she'd have were the memories, reminders of happy times long past. There would never be the potential to make new memories, at least, not on this side of the grave.

The request was on her tongue, buried in her heart. And the guilt made her feel ten times heavier for it. She wanted to send Elijah away. Send him out the door, away from all of this, before he could get them all killed.

Her stomach roiled with nausea for thinking such a thing. He was her mate, dammit. The one person she was supposed to believe in the most, even when no one else did.

And here she was, doubting his capacity to control his deep-seated anger. At the world, at Mistress Black, at himself.

You should help him.

When she'd mated him, she'd made an oath to be there for her mate no matter what. Through thick and thin, the good times and the bad.

So what kind of mate was she going to be? The kind who went back on her word at the first sign of tough times? Or the kind who strengthened her mate when he didn't feel strong enough?

Take my hand, she said to him.

He kept pacing, golden eyes fixed on Rick's smug face.

Verika stepped forward, took Elijah's hands in hers, and forced him to face her. He reluctantly turned, craning his strong neck to eye his prey until Verika reached up and cupped his cheeks with both hands. Those terrible, golden eyes at last met hers.

Just breathe, she said, searching his eyes. *You can beat this. You're strong enough. You are in control.*

He stared back, his breathing slowly growing calmer, the gold leaking from his eyes to reveal brilliant-blue irises.

He let out a slow breath, which was both a sigh of relief and a prayer of thanks. At the same time, all the tension drained out of their mate-bond, and the crackling anger faded away.

He smiled gently. *You're incredible, you know that?* he said telepathically, reaching up to caress her cheek.

She closed her eyes and leaned into his touch. Yes, the world she knew and loved was on the verge of falling apart around her. But she would give herself this precious moment in time to just close her eyes and remind herself she was never alone. To feel the strength of the love pouring off her mate.

Her future husband.

Hearing those words, even if only in her head, made her heart flutter, her hope soar. She would move heaven and earth for him. Brave the pits of hell, face any hardship.

Do you trust me? she asked.

Absolutely, he said without hesitation, never breaking her steadfast gaze.

"Helllooooooo? Earth to the witch and werewolf!"

Her teeth gritted. Add "kicking Rick's ass" to her To Do list.

Elijah let his hand slip from her face, trailing it down her side and to her hand. "I'm right here," he said softly.

"And I'm never going anywhere but with you."

"Thank you," she mouthed, her eyes burning. God, her emotions were a mess today. His love for her poured through their mate-bond, steady and true. The rock she would now use to lean on if she felt weak or scared. The enormity of his love was overwhelming. Now to prove herself worthy of it.

The strength of her resolve, of her love for him, gave her the courage to turn around and face Rick—and not magically rip his smirking head off immediately. No, she needed him. He served a purpose, this monster in front of her, as obnoxious as he was. He was proud of his power. It showed in the overconfident sparkle in his eyes, the swagger in his step. Like a spoiled child who'd been loaned Mommy and Daddy's Lexus to parade around town. He probably had a drop of Black Magic of his own, to be sure, but it was nothing without Mistress Black's amplifications. She was sure that's what she'd meant by "he is only a pawn borrowing my power"—she'd amplified his innate powers, probably gifted him from his demon side, by infusing him with some of her own magic.

And amplification spells had limits. They always faded over time. Verika just had to be patient, wait for his power to dial down.

Then, as Elijah would say, poor old Rick here would be "shit out of luck."

That made her smile. She knew there was frost in her eyes as she said, without blinking, without flinching, "Let my parents go, and we'll go with you."

Rick blinked, straightened up. He looked between

them suspiciously. "You will?"

Verika nodded.

"Just like that?"

"Do you want us or not? Stop stalling."

He pursed his lips, smushed them around and sucked them in before popping them loudly. "Well, I suppose I shouldn't complain. I got a nice drink out of the deal"—he slapped her mother and father on the back—"albeit, I wasn't even that hungry. The original glamour was wearing off, and I had to strengthen it with a blood tie. I mean, being a vampire's awesome for that little ability alone, but come on! Guess if I was a royal, I wouldn't have to redo my glams all the damn time. *C'est la vie.*"

Verika's jaw ticked. Something about the way he talked made her want to punch him in the mouth. Her fingers flexed and then fisted.

Elijah gave her a curious look. *So he needed to drink from them to renew the bond?*

Because their blood inside him means he can control them, she said via their private link. *Vampires can glamour a person with their eyes and magic alone, but blood ties always enhance the spell. It 'seals them,' so to speak.*

Ah. A slight nod.

She cocked her head to the side. *Didn't come across many vampires while staying at Hell's Mansion, did you?*

Not really. Mistress Black was as creeped out by them as I was. Though clearly her tastes have changed, he added dryly.

Verika nodded at her parents. "Well? Do we have a deal?"

"Spoil my fun, will you? All right, all right, stop glaring at me. I'll let them go. Jeez, lighten up."

Simultaneously, her parents lowered the blades.

"Go sit on the couch, or go garden or something." Rick waved them off with a bored look.

They glanced at each other and then back at him, confused by the mixture of instructions.

He rolled his eyes and gave a groan of exasperation. "Good Lord, sit on the couch, sit on the couch! Go on!"

Her parents' shoulders relaxed. They smiled and obeyed, quietly walking out of the kitchen and into the living room. Verika watched them as they sat down, all of her weight placed on the balls of her feet. Desperation to be close to them clawed at her, urging her to sprint past the vamp and run to her parents. To hug them one last time, in case this all—

No. Don't think like that. Remember what Satine always said? 'Defeatist thinking leads to defeat.'

And this was one battle she refused to lose.

"Well, come on, then." Rick spun on his heel and strolled toward the back door off the kitchen. "Best not to keep Mistress Black waiting." He shuddered, stroking his jaw almost as an afterthought. Verika noticed a fading bruise there.

"At least that's one thing we can agree on," Elijah said quietly as they made to follow him.

Rick stopped and smacked his forehead with his hand. "Oh, and I almost forgot. Duh. It's been a long day, and I haven't had much sleep." He turned around, a sly smile on his lips. "You can't be conscious."

"What?" Verika barely managed to ask before Rick rushed forward. There was a sharp crack, like knuckles striking her temple. Pain bloomed in her forehead, so sharp it short-circuited her brain. Then all went dark.

CHAPTER TWENTY-FIVE

THE DARKNESS WAS WONDERFUL, ALMOST COMFORTING, in its all-consuming embrace. The false sense of safety, the bliss of not having to worry about a thing, lasted only a few short moments before everything went straight to hell.

Verika ran through darkened woods, dressed in a gown of flowing white. The trees were black as oil, their bark like slabs of glass that had been glued together. Beautiful but grotesque, they reflected her terrified face as she ran, slicing her arms, cheeks, any exposed piece of flesh they could latch their teeth onto.

"Damn," she hissed as one jutting piece of bark slit open her forearm.

A howl soared through the misty air behind her, sending chills skittering along her clammy skin. Snarls reverberated off the glassy trees, followed by the thunder of a hundred paws.

She paused just long enough to scan the inky darkness

beyond the mist. Dark forms drew closer, their white fangs and golden eyes seemingly glowing.

Wolves—hundreds of them, each big as a horse. An awful, low drone—a horn blast—sounded in the distance.

The terrible realization hit all at once, knocking her into a tree. She gripped it for strength; the bark cut her palms, but she barely felt the pain. Her heart thundered erratically; the air turned unbreathable—or maybe that was her throat closing up. Her thoughts all turned to mud as terror flooded her veins, making her feel slow and stupid.

"Oh God," she breathed, her voice a cracked, shaky whisper.

She was being hunted.

"Run," a wicked voice commanded.

Her body wouldn't work. It was as if someone had glued her feet to the forest floor—

"RUN!"

The furious roar startled her back to her senses. Lifting her skirts, she took off, tripping and tumbling down valleys and ravines. By the time she hit the hard bottom of the forest floor, she hurt all over. Her bones ached as she hauled herself to her feet; her throat was dry, her voice hoarse from the icy air clawing at it with every desperate breath.

Run, her mind urged her. *Must run, must get away.*

The snarls drew closer. The glow of their fangs reflected off the bark of the trees around her.

No.

The forest lit up around her as the wolves closed in. Their golden eyes surrounded her from all sides but one.

She lunged toward the quickly narrowing opening—and slammed up against what felt like a wall of cold, hard steel.

No, not steel—magic. She'd been boxed in by a wall of pure, dense magic.

"No!" she screamed, pounding against it. She smashed her bloodied palms on it, streaking its surface with red as she clawed and whimpered.

Then she felt strong jaws close around her neck, the fangs tearing into her throat before she could draw breath to scream.

Verika sat straight up with a deep, desperate gasp, as if she had surfaced from an ocean after nearly drowning. Her skin was covered in sweat, the pearly silk sheets she lay upon cold and wet.

Her hands flew over her throat, her face, her arms. Not a scratch on them. No teeth marks, no lacerations. She was fine.

She was fine.

Feeling her shoulders slump as the hysteria drained out of her, she let her head hang for a moment to catch her breath. She closed her eyes, inhaled deep.

One, two, three…

Feeling more in control, albeit exhausted, with that weird undercurrent of terror still tickling her senses, she opened her eyes, lifted her head, and looked about.

The bed was gargantuan, she noted, as was the room it sat in. Four posts of polished, ornately carved ebony with a canopy of silver silk entwined with lavender gauze. The mattress and pillows were the softest she'd ever lain upon. The bed sat upon a dais covered in plush, cottony carpet. A sea of polished dark-brown floors spread out before the dais; a vanity of pure white perched against one stone wall, but other than that there were no other pieces of furniture. No TV, no modern amenities other than the elaborate crystal-and-glass chandelier dangling above the bed. A mirror that was at least as tall as Verika, with a fat gold-and-crystal frame, hung on the wall adjacent to the bed. A fireplace as big as her apartment living room stretched against one wall. It was all so…flashy. Garishly so.

Crystals of all shapes and sizes lay strewn across the pit of the fireplace, aglow with rainbow-colored flames.

Verika watched the flames dance, picking up on the slight prickling sensation along her senses.

Magic. The fire wasn't real—it was given life by Red Magic.

Her spine straightened as her inner wolf growled.

There was a flash of memory—her parents' attic, butcher knives, blood, Rick.

She fought to control her breathing as her heartbeat galloped.

Mistress Black's home. Or headquarters, or whatever it was. That's where she sat now, among this fussy finery. She might as well have been sitting in a dragon's lair, for all the horror she felt.

She opened her mouth, about to start uttering any spell she could think of to get her out of this mess, when she felt the bite of two cold bands of metal around her wrists. A zing of power zipped through her, making her blood hum and scrambling her thoughts for a moment.

She lifted her hands, stared at the plain gold cuffs. They were so shiny she could see her perplexed—and frustrated—expression reflected back at her. So shiny she could see the terror, clear as day, in her eyes. Along with the bags under her lids, and the hollows in her cheeks, made more severe by the firelight.

Good Lord, did she really look that bad? That drained of life and energy? Had all this stress, this frustration, this fear, this worry, eaten away at her to the point she hadn't even noticed she'd been wasting away?

Her sense of self-preservation kicked in, and she shook her head. Now was not the time to be nitpicking her appearance. To hell with it for now.

She gladly let her brain take over, let it shove her fears down, down, down. Her mind worked as she examined the cuffs with a critical eye, searching for a mechanism to release the clasps. Only there wasn't one. It was as if someone had molded them to her wrists.

Once her thoughts had cleared from the hit Rick had walloped her with, and the fog of sleep had lifted, she knew exactly what the bands were. A sinking sensation all but nailed her to the bed.

They were insurance. Or rather, binding cuffs. A smart move, preventing her from using her powers. Couldn't say she blamed Mistress Black for being cautious.

So much for her backup plan. No way was she going to be able to use her magic to help her allies get into the mansion if things went south.

She swore, annoyed. Oddly, she felt more vulnerable and, strangely, alone being cut off from her magic. It was as much a part of her as breathing, a piece of herself she didn't know how sorely she'd miss until it wasn't there.

Speaking of missing pieces of her soul…

Her heart leapt to her throat. "Elijah," she breathed.

Her hand shot out to feel for him—and patted damp sheets instead.

Her head snapped to the side, and she stopped breathing for a moment. Where was her mate?

"He's quite safe," said a lovely voice from the doorway.

Icy fear inundated Verika's pores.

She already knew whom she would see, though she was taken aback by the woman's appearance. Her long hair was all elegant dark-chocolate curls, with no traces of the fiery coloring she'd worn in the astral plane.

Mistress Black wore a simple black silk robe. Her hair was damp on the ends, as if she'd just gotten out of the bath. And yet she still wore a face full of freshly applied makeup.

She stared at Verika a long while, almost with astonishment. Her eyes shone with pride and affection and…something else. Something slimy that didn't belong among the warmer emotions. "You are so beautiful," she whispered, clasping her hands together because she couldn't seem to keep them still. "You look so much like my Idrina."

"Who?" Verika asked through gritted teeth. God, it hurt just to talk! What the hell had Rick done to her?

"My daughter," Mistress Black replied solemnly, her

gaze shadowing as she lowered her head. "She was the light of my life."

"And where is she?"

"Dead," Mistress Black said flatly.

Verika could see the deadness in the woman's eyes that revelation brought. "I'm sorry," she said, because it was the decent thing to say. No one deserved to have their child taken from them.

Mistress Black shrugged, trying to play it off as if it didn't matter, but Verika could tell it bothered her deeply. "She died a long time ago...as I should have," she murmured, almost wistfully.

Verika blinked. "I beg your pardon?"

Mistress Black crept into the room, that glittering, black gaze poised on Verika like a snake eyeing a mouse. "Do you know how old I am, darling?"

Verika's skin crawled at the pet name. "Late twenties, early thirties maybe." Better to err on the side of flattery, especially with a woman as vain as Mistress Black.

And she was vain. Already she had paused to look over her appearance in the looking glass suspended on the wall. The fact the mirror was so ostentatiously huge spoke volumes about the woman's desire to admire herself. Verika was willing to bet every mirror in her lair was body-length or larger.

Mirror mirror, on the wall, who's the fairest of them all?

Mistress Black managed to pull her eyes off her reflection and laughed daintily. "My dear, you flatter me. I am over five hundred years old."

Verika's eyes nearly bugged out. She looked her over.

Not a wrinkle or gray hair was to be found. "How? With an immortality spell?" Such a thing was taboo in the magical arts, but the scholar in Verika was acutely curious.

"No, darling, nothing so outlandish as that. An ancient enemy wished to wipe me—and all Black Witches and Warlocks—from the face of the earth. She cursed me, yanking my soul from my real body so I could never again be whole. But what she didn't expect was I found a way not only to keep my body from aging, but to keep my soul alive as well—*drak nacana*."

Verika went still. Had the temperature in the room dropped? When she found her voice, it was whisper-soft. "You used the forbidden arts?"

Mistress Black pursed her lips, tapped her long, red nails against her hip. "Oh, quit being such a Mary Sue. Yes, *drak nacana* is part of the Dark Arts. I don't see why you're so surprised. I am a Black Witch, after all. Where did you think the Dark Arts came from? They stem from Black Magic, of course."

"Just because the Dark Arts hail from Black Magic doesn't give you free rein to practice them."

"Ha! Listen to you, Miss Suzie Sunshine. Are you always this insufferably noble?"

Verika tempered her glare; her mouth formed a straight, hard line.

Mistress Black's expression changed, her amusement vanishing and giving way to something akin to disgust. "Yes, I suppose you are," she muttered.

Verika, copying Mistress Black's earlier nonchalance, shrugged. "I suppose I'm as noble as you are evil."

"Evil," Mistress Black said blandly, barely able to restrain her eye roll. She wandered off to fuss with her hair some more in the mirror. "Is that what you think of me?"

"You tell me."

Mistress Black primed and fluffed her robe. Her eyes lifted to Verika's in the mirror. "There are few things on this earth more evil than man. Can you argue that?"

Verika sat on her answer. She really, *really* shouldn't. But the werewolf in her—the Johnsons' influence—reigned supreme. "I can't think of anything more evil than the bitch I'm looking at right now."

It felt good to say that—very good. But her triumph lasted only a few seconds before terror flooded her veins all over again. Oh God. What had she been thinking? One of the most dangerous witches in the world was less than twenty feet away, and she had just *mouthed off to her*?

Verika braced herself for the attack. She imagined her head rolling, or Mistress Black melting her bones. The thought, the possibilities, of torture and excruciating death made her sick to her stomach.

Her entire body locked up as she waited for her fate.

Mistress Black's hand had gone still, as had her gaze. She stared not at Verika but at herself, those eyes cold and unblinking. At last, she smiled and turned around. "Well, you got one thing right—I am a bitch."

The tension drained from Verika's shoulders so quickly she nearly slumped over in relief. With iron will, she held herself steady, straight, and proud, knowing that to show weakness in front of this predator meant she might as well offer herself up for slaughter. And she somehow suspected Mistress Black respected defiance. Saw it as a sign of strength.

Mistress Black studied her, pacing in front of the bed about three feet away. "You have great power within you, Verika. Much stronger than I was anticipating."

"Is that a problem?"

"No." Another slimy smile. "On the contrary, it's quite welcome."

Warning bells went off in Verika's head, but she swiftly dismissed them. For now.

Mistress Black stopped her pacing and crossed her arms. "How are you feeling?"

"I've been better."

"What are your symptoms?" she snapped impatiently. "Headache, nausea, dizziness?"

"All of the above, I suppose. My head hurts something fierce from your lackey clobbering me."

Mistress Black pursed her lips. "Rick has been dealt with accordingly for striking you. My instructions were to bring you to me unharmed. Clearly, he doesn't know how to follow protocol."

Verika felt she should argue, to tell her it wasn't right to hurt Rick. But she couldn't force the words out of her mouth. In truth, she wanted him to pay, dearly, for what he'd done to her parents.

Instead, she nodded curtly. She cracked her neck. Holy hell, she hurt all over, but none worse than her head. Gingerly, she touched the tender skin over her temple, hissing when it flared with needle pricks of pain.

"You're a glutton for punishment, aren't you?" drawled

Mistress Black. "Oh well. At least the test didn't damage you too badly. I suspect you're sore all over, yes?"

Verika paused. "How did…? What *test*?"

"I have to test everyone who comes here to make sure they aren't harboring any spells or weapons of any sort— magical or otherwise," she said, examining a nail.

Verika wondered whether Mistress Black had ADD. She couldn't seem to focus on any one thing for more than a few seconds at a time. She was restless, too. Her weight shifted, and she tapped a slippered foot against the cool wood flooring.

Verika processed what she had said. Was this magical pat-down test what had caused her wicked dream? "It gave me nightmares."

"Unpleasant side effect, I'm afraid." Mistress Black shrugged and gave an insincere smile of apology.

Verika nearly rolled her eyes. Yeah, right. That sadistic psychopath wasn't sorry. If anything, it had given her plea- sure to see Verika suffer. Probably got her off.

Sick.

"Where's my mate?" Verika said.

Mistress Black's eyebrows lifted. "So demanding. You definitely get that from me." Another smug smile. Maybe Rick had gleaned more from her than magic. They both had that self-satisfied look, as if they owned the world and everyone in it. Verika hated that, detested people who thought less of their peers based on the delusion they somehow thought they were better. Perhaps it was because she'd been looked down upon her whole life by her co- workers, her classmates, anyone who thought she was a lesser witch just because she hadn't manifested a talent.

Or maybe it was because she'd had years of practice in honing her Asshole Meter, and it was going crazy right now.

That odd, motherly look had returned to Mistress Black's face. On a whim, she sat on the edge of the bed and rested a hand on Verika's leg. Verika jerked back, scooting as close to the headboard, and as far away from Mistress Black, as she could.

Mistress Black's jaw ticked, her motherly warmth quickly fading to icy indifference. "He's fine. Alive and well, as it were. I have not harmed him."

"What about Rick? Did Rick harm him?" The thought made her blood boil, turned her vision to scarlet.

"As I said, Rick has been taken care of." Irritation colored her voice, making it crisper. As if she were offended at being questioned. "And as I said, your mate is fine."

"You'll pardon me if I don't take you at your word. Take me to him."

Mistress Black stared at her a long while, sizing her up. "I am in control here. You may be my blood relation, but make no mistake—I will afford you no special treatment if you keep crossing me."

In other words, Verika had better leash her quick tongue or face Mistress Black's wrath. And she'd already seen what that could do.

A beat of silence passed before Mistress Black smiled. "All good? Then we are at an understanding." She patted the bed and stood. "Come along." She snapped her fingers.

Verika grated her teeth. What was she, a damn dog?

"You kept up your end of the bargain, so now I shall keep up mine. I am a woman of my word after all, something I pride myself on. Let's go remove that nasty brand." She took a few steps toward the door—and careened right into the wall.

Verika shot off the bed, not out of concern but out of curiosity. "Are you all right?" she asked with caution.

Mistress Black quickly straightened and smoothed her robe. Her breath had quickened, and her color had paled. "I'm fine," she rasped, clearing her throat and flipping her hair over her shoulder. She marched out of the room without another word.

Verika, dressed in a simple black nightgown with a neckline that was much too low for her tastes and black slippers, followed behind her. It bothered her slightly that someone had changed her clothes, had seen everything she had to offer. But all things considered, she realized how ridiculous that worry was.

Here she was, in the clutches of a madwoman who would probably end up killing her and Elijah both by the end of the night.

Yeah, so not worrying about a clothing change. Especially when the gown was so pretty.

She glanced again at the door, eyes narrowing and mind spinning with excited thoughts.

All the shifting around, how she'd kept turning her back to Verika to look at herself in the mirror.

Had it not been an attention disorder but an attempt to cover up an illness?

Mistress Black had access to the best physicians in the

world, or at least, Verika assumed she did. The woman clearly had an abundance of wealth. Plus, she was a powerful witch. Even Verika had often cured herself of everything from the common cold to the flu.

So what kind of virus or condition was so strong so as to weaken this very dominant woman?

More importantly, how could Verika exploit this weakness?

Elijah felt the chains first, felt their cold metal teeth digging into his flesh. A memory trickled into his sleep-addled brain, a distant thought of lonely, dark nights, of blood dripping from his lacerated flesh onto the dirty prison floor, of rats skittering about in the shadows, chittering excitedly. A woman, shadow and sin and every wicked thing of the earth incarnate, stepped forward. An ancient blade glinted in her hand, flashing red from the fresh blood coating its teeth.

His blood.

Fear throttled his heart rate.

It hit him like a bucket of ice water to the face, jolting him out of the magic-induced stupor Rick had put him in.

Gasping, wide-eyed, Elijah looked about.

No one's there, he reassured himself. He was alone.

A second later, he realized how terribly wrong that statement was.

"Verika?" he called, his voice coarse.

He reached for her through their bond—only to find it muted.

His terror mounted. God, what had he done? What kind of a reckless mate was he, allowing his woman to gallivant headfirst into danger?

They never should have gone to the damn farmhouse. If he'd had an ounce of decency in him, he would have ignored her pleas to trust her, swept her up and taken her as far away from Mistress Black and magic and—and—

He growled, realizing how ridiculous that sounded. She never would have forgiven him, or trusted him ever again, if he'd done that. He wasn't sure which was worse: allowing his mate to throw herself into danger on his behalf, or not trusting her to take care of herself and keeping her locked up for her own protection. Either way, he would have failed his mate.

He didn't deserve her. If time had proved anything to him, it was that the people around him got hurt. He was a plague upon their happiness, a harbinger of death and destruction.

Gage, Alara, Nik, Danica…he'd been the reason his brothers had lost their mates. He had been the reason Mistress Black had become so keenly interested in them in the first place.

He'd practically shone a light on Verika, broadcasting, "Badass Black Witch here for the taking!"

Did he mention he was a shitty mate?

He had to get out of here, had to find Verika.

If she were still alive.

No, he firmly shut that fear down, trembling with barely contained rage and grief that vile thought brought. No, she was alive, dammit. She had to be; he surely would have felt her loss in the marrow of his soul. Or so the legends went. He'd never actually met anyone else who'd been mated before. And the whole bonding thing with his brothers so hadn't happened, so it wasn't as if he could find out from them in leisurely conversation. One mention of the word "mate," and Nik would probably run him through with something sharp and pointy.

As the sleeping spell slowly drained from his mind, Elijah's senses began to wake…sort of. His head throbbed and felt as if it were stuffed with cotton.

Damn that vampire-demon-whatever-the-hell-it-was.

He squeezed his eyes shut, gritting his teeth against the persistent pounding against his skull. *Quit being a little bitch. Look around. Get a bearing on your surroundings, you pansy.*

He did. Silver runes glinted off dank, stone walls alight with burning torches. Claw marks marred bars in front of him, as though a wild animal had attacked them. Two of the bars were bent outward slightly, directly in front of where he stood chained to the floor by big, medieval-looking manacles around his wrists and ankles.

He stared at those crooked bars, going still. His heartbeat seemed to reverberate in the icy silence. With knowing dread, he looked down at the manacle clamped around his right wrist.

Something was crudely scraped into the metal—EMJ. Elijah Marshal Johnson.

He sucked in a breath. "That *bitch*," he seethed.

Typical. Why not "welcome him home" by throwing him in the very cell she'd tortured him in so many times?

Why not remind him of every terrible thing she'd done?

"Once a bitch, always a bitch," he murmured.

He didn't even bother looking for his initials on the other manacles; he knew they'd be there. It was one of the many horrific images burned into his memories. Mistress Black had thought it'd be hilarious to lovingly engrave his name on the manacles he so often frequented. She'd even used the blade she sliced him up with to do it.

His stomach rolled, and his throat grew tight as a wave of sickness rushed up. Swallowing it back down stubbornly, he took a few long, deep breaths.

The air tasted stale, and much too cold. Or maybe that was the fear pumping into his veins.

Get. A. Grip. He should print a T-shirt with that across the front, backward so he could read it every time he had one of his "come off the ledge" pep talks with his reflection.

"It's going to be okay. It's going to be okay," he muttered over and over again.

The more he said it, and the deeper the realization of where he was sunk in, the faster his heart beat.

Way to go, champ. Freak yourself the hell out.

Shutting down that self-deprecating voice, he focused on his top priority—figuring out how to get the hell out of here. He fought to control his breathing as he moved his limbs. Pain lit up his wrists and ankles, as if metal barbs grated against his bones.

Well, that was something new. Apparently, Mistress Black had upgraded her hardware.

He almost welcomed the pain. It would keep him awake, keep him from second-guessing whether this was a dream or reality.

He wished he were dreaming. That this was one of the many nightmares he'd had starring Mistress Black. Because you could wake up from a dream. But reality... well, he'd almost prefer the nightmare.

Almost.

Footsteps approached. His head jerked up. A nerve pinched in his neck, causing his teeth to grit.

The hairs along the backs of his arms and neck stood on end a moment before the sharp tang of magic tainted the air.

His heart skipped a beat, thrumming faster and faster.

And nearly stopped when a woman with flaming-red hair stepped into the room.

"Verika," he breathed. The air in his lungs rushed out in one loose breath.

The second their eyes met, they both stopped. Both their eyes scanned over the other's body, searching for any sign of injury.

With a relieved sob, Verika ran forward, grabbed the bars. She pressed her face against the cold metal, and he met her for the kiss.

"I thought she'd done—I thought I'd never—" She hiccupped.

"Sssh." He pressed his forehead against hers, her wide, frightened eyes still frantically scanning his face, as if she were unable to believe he was real. "She can't kill me, re-member? Not while I wear her mark."

"A situation we're about to rectify," came a cool voice.

Elijah's whole body seized up. It was like reliving every

violent, awful thing that had ever been done to him. Her dark voice seemed to burrow under his skin, digging its claws into his fears and lacerating his courage in one vicious swipe.

Barely able to contain a tremble, he bit his lip.

A soft hand reached through the bars and grasped his arm.

He blinked. The warmth of his mate's surety, the strength of her presence, snapped him out of his fears. And in looking into her eyes, at the courageous, pure soul within, he found the will to be brave.

He finally had a purpose, a calling stronger than all his fears combined. Protecting Verika—his lady, his love— was the only thing that mattered now. It was the only thing that would ever matter.

Mistress Black neared the bars. The orange glow of the torchlight cast her face in shadows and made her look the more sinister for it. Or maybe she just always looked that way. Yeah, she was beautiful. But after the things she'd done… Let's just say Elijah had begun to see her in a new light, pun intended.

Mistress Black smiled. "Hello, my pet."

He gave her a stony glare. Verika never stepped away. She gripped his arm, not in warning but for comfort.

"Not even deigning to speak to me, your master?" Mistress Black said archly.

"You're not his master."

They both looked at Verika, whose eyes had begun to glow faint gold. Her Change was near. It both excited and frightened Elijah. Excited him because he'd be able to take her on his moonlit runs. She'd be able to run through the night, feel the wind on her fur, the earth beneath her paws. It was extraordinary.

The fear came from knowing the Change would hurt like hell the first time. There was nothing to be done for it because it was going to happen one way or another. But as a wolf sworn to shelter his mate from all pain, it made his chest ache knowing he was powerless to ease her suffering.

Mistress Black stepped back, appraised her fellow witch. It was slight, but Elijah swore he sniffed a whiff of fear—from Mistress Black.

That fear quickly morphed into barely suppressed fury. "You dare challenge me?"

Verika swallowed hard, stepped forward to shield Elijah from view. His heart leapt to his throat. He grappled for her arm, trying to pull her back, but she shrugged him off. "I'm telling you I'll do anything to protect my mate. And you'd do well to heed that."

Mistress Black considered her a long moment, sizing her up while power crackled at her fingertips.

Panic started to set in. Elijah's eyes flashed from woman to woman. He let out a protective snarl. "I swear, if you hurt her—"

"You'll do what? You're not exactly in a position to follow up on your threats." Mistress Black cocked her head and looked at him with boredom. Her power flickered out, and in a blink the tension in the room was almost gone.

Almost.

Verika never budged as Mistress Black stared down Elijah. "The brand," Verika said, drawing Mistress Black's attention back to her. "You said you'd remove it."

Those dark, soulless eyes stared at Elijah a moment longer before at last blinking and looking to Verika with— pride? Hunger? Either sent a chill down Elijah's spine, and a possessive growl rumbled in his throat.

A slow, tight smile spread on Mistress Black's lips. "So I did." She snapped her fingers.

There was no warning before the pain hit him, an all-consuming inferno that set his brain, his body, his soul on fire. His back arched as the brand glowed brilliant red, him gritting his teeth to contain his screams so as not to frighten Verika further.

Verika kept hold of his arm as he thrashed, her expression strong even as horror and pain bloomed behind her eyes. The color began to leach from her skin.

The murmuring of an incantation rode the air between his agonized groans. Mistress Black stood with her arms crossed, watching him writhe with a satisfied smile.

There was the flash of silver, and then something sharp embedded itself into his arm.

"What are you doing?" Verika shrieked, making to remove the knife.

"Don't!" Mistress Black snapped. "Unless you want to screw up the spell and have your mate branded to me for eternity!"

Verika promptly drew back, worrying her lip. Her eyes remained glued to the dagger.

The very same dagger Mistress Black had used to torture him with time and time again. The one she'd used to slice open his abdomen.

Elijah steeled his mind, closed his eyes, and fought against the trickle of fear that wriggled into his bloodstream.

He would not be afraid. He would not let this monster make him cower any longer.

He pictured Verika's face in his mind, of the sun lighting up her hair like fire or how her smile always made him feel lighter. He dreamed of her gazing up at him, of the pride and love shining in her eyes, and marveling at how he'd never felt so cherished, so loved before.

He held onto that love, grasped it and used it to shield himself from the pain.

Something glowing slid down his arm; the brand had broken apart and was being sucked into the knife.

A sheen of sweat had broken out on Verika's brow. Her knees started to cave, but she gripped the bars to keep herself upright.

That's when it hit Elijah—she could feel his pain, too, through their bond.

"Stop," Elijah rasped. "You're hurting her."

"I cannot stop," Mistress Black said, her breathing shallow as she watched the blade absorb the brand. "An only partially removed brand is worse than a full one because the magic is broken. There'd be no telling what it would do to you—to all of us."

Verika cried out and then bit her lip as her knees at last gave way, and she sank to the floor with a whimper. Her eyes squeezed shut, and a tremble wracked her body.

Elijah looked frantically between the blade and Verika. "Hurry up!" he barked through gritted teeth.

"Al…most… there… ah!" The knife absorbed the last of the brand, and the magical glow winked out in a blink. Mistress Black staggered away from the cell. She caught herself on the wall to keep from falling over.

Verika's eyes snapped open, and she gasped for air, as did Elijah. He reached for her, damning the cage and the manacles for not allowing him to go to her. "Verika! Verika, look at me! Are you all right?"

"I'm—fine, just—stunned," she said between coughs. "Are you okay?"

"Yeah," he breathed, chest heaving as the adrenaline faded away to exhaustion. He tried looking over his shoulder. "Is it gone?"

"Here, love." Verika stumbled to her feet, ran to the bars, and peered at his back as he shifted so she could see. Her face lit up. "It's gone! Elijah!"

She reached through the bars and grabbed his hands, squeezing hard.

You're free, she said through their bond. *We're free.*

Almost, he said back darkly. His eyes flicked to the woman lingering in the shadows.

Verika steeled her gaze and turned to face her. "Thank you. It means the world to us for you to do this."

"Oh, it wasn't a favor." Mistress Black chuckled.

"Why am I not surprised?" Elijah said.

"You're going to give me something I want in return." Mistress Black pointed at Verika.

Verika tensed, as did Elijah. "I don't know what you plan on doing with her," Elijah seethed, "but whatever it is, you can forget it."

Mistress Black smiled. The knife floated up and away from her hand before flying to Verika's throat. Verika's breath caught as the blade hovered over her flesh. All it would take to end her would be a flick of Mistress Black's wrist...

Elijah, terrified, looked from Mistress Black to his mate. "Please," he said. "Don't hurt her."

"I wasn't planning on it. She's too valuable to my cause."

"You've made your point," Verika said tensely, eyes straining downward, trying to see the knife. "You're in charge. We get it. What do you want?"

"I need your help," she said reluctantly, as if admitting she needed assistance with anything meant she was weaker somehow.

"With what?" Verika snapped.

Mistress Black smiled.

"You're going to help me perform the Grand Rite so I can return to my original body."

CHAPTER TWENTY-SIX

THE FIRST THING ALARA THOUGHT AS SHE CAME TO was, *My head really hurts.* Like *zOMG get me an Ibuprofen now, bitch* kind of hurt.

Her second realization was never in a million years would she have thought that if she hadn't been living with Nik Johnson. Which meant he had rubbed off on her more than she originally suspected. A fact she didn't yet know whether to be intrigued, impressed, or disturbed by.

And thirdly… Where the hell was she?

As she looked about the Gothic interior and red and black velvet and silk dripping from every curling wrought-iron rod and heavy Victorian piece of furniture, she immediately thought, "I've died and gone to Transylvania." Her nose wrinkled in faint disgust at the tacky damask bedspread, flashy mile-long rugs, and showy cast-iron vent covers and Victorian baseboards and crown molding. Seriously, did the designer throw together this room drunk? Clearly they were going for opulence, the "I have a lot of money and want to flaunt it" look. But instead of the bold elegance expected out of a true Victorian showroom, the décor was in-your-face loud. Obnoxiously so.

A groan from beside her had her jumping so badly her neck cramped. She cussed, reaching up to rub the stiffness out of it as stars popped before her eyes.

Danica stirred, lying almost shoulder to shoulder with her.

Alara immediately bent over her, shaking her. "Danica," she hissed in a whisper. "Danica, wake up!"

"Wha—? Oh, hey, Alara, what are you— Holy shit-monkeys! Where the hell are we?"

"Sssh!" Alara clamped a hand over Danica's screeching mouth and glanced around. Her heart pounded in her ears as she listened. Every muscle in her body went perfectly still, all senses heightened for new threats.

All was quiet. No one had apparently heard Danica's panicked outburst, or if they did, they didn't give a damn.

"Don't freak out again," Alara commanded, her tone soft but serious. "I'm going to remove my hand now. Okay?"

Danica nodded.

Slowly, Alara drew back her hand, keeping it hovering just over the comforter in case Danica couldn't keep her word.

Danica breathed heavily. Her green eyes looked around, taking in every detail. "You know," she said quietly, "I kind of want to say this is pretty, but at the same time it's the most hideously decorated room I've ever seen."

Alara's shoulders relaxed. Part of her wanted to laugh,

if she wasn't in full-on offensive mode. Here they were, clearly having been kidnapped and dropped off in a location neither of them recognized, and the first thing they did was complain about the furnishings.

Typical women.

Deep down, Alara suspected they both were trying to distract themselves in any way possible so the fear wouldn't take over. Because fear had a way of turning your legs to lead, your thoughts to mush. And they would need both if they had any prayer of escaping this place.

Alara sniffed, searching for smells, anything that would help them. Someone had been burning incense, a sharp, heady mixture of cinnamon and cloves that subtly burned her nose. But why would someone bother lighting incense in the first place? Anytime Alara lit a candle, it wasn't purely for show and to watch the pretty twinkling flames.

It was to cover up another smell.

She sniffed again, searching for—

A sudden, acute wave of drowsiness slammed into her, nearly knocking her backward onto the plush pillows.

Danica swayed too, nearly toppling on top of Alara. She grasped at her head, as if holding it still would keep the room from spinning. "What's…going on?" she asked through gritted teeth. "I got so sleepy all of a sudden."

A bolt of panic zinged straight through Alara's core. Oh dear God. How could she have forgotten?

"The baby," Alara breathed, feeling more panicked than when she'd first awoken. "How are you feeling? Do you feel any pain, anywhere at all?"

"I'm fine. I'm fine." Danica waved away her worries, though her voice sounded groggy as hell. "The baby and I are both fine. I can feel him or her in my soul. My little angel is still with me." She rubbed her belly reverently.

Alara relaxed a fraction. Thank God for that. She blinked slowly, her lids seemingly made of steel. It took every ounce of willpower she had to pry them open again.

Something tickled her nose, the same acidic smell that had invaded her senses when the monster came for them.

Magic.

Her eyes flicked around, her spine going straight.

Someone wasn't just burning incense—they were casting some sort of sleeping spell. The incense was merely there to hide it. Or perhaps it was the source of the magic. Either way, they had to stop it.

The thought of falling asleep again made her blood turn to ice. What would their captors do to them? Would they hurt Danica's baby, once they found out she was pregnant?

A growl rumbled in Alara's throat.

Over her dead body.

Rising, Alara stumbled forward, groping along the bed to maintain her balance.

"Alara?" Danica started to rise. "Where are you going?"

"Stay there," Alara said, perhaps a bit sharper than she meant to thanks to the fact her mouth could barely move. Good Lord, it was becoming harder and harder to talk the farther away she got from the bed.

Or rather, the closer she drew to the source of the

spell.

She took one staggering step forward, and then another. It felt as if someone had turned up the gravity in the room; tremendous pressure to lie down, anywhere, and surrender to sleep pressed down all over her body.

But she would not submit: not to this spell, not to any oppressor. Clearly they did not know whom they were dealing with.

She was a Crescent, daughter of kings. And she would bow to no one.

Her bare foot snagged on a corner of the rug, throwing her into the couch. She caught herself, narrowly keeping her chin from colliding with its glossy wooden frame.

Behind her, Danica gasped. Alara could imagine her hands flying to her mouth, those green eyes wide and frightened. "Are you okay?"

Alara couldn't summon the strength to reply. All her focus was pointed at the fireplace looming but ten feet from where she crouched. A fire burned within its hearth, and several decorative trinkets sat atop the mantel.

She was sure of it now—the scent came from there.

Gripping the couch and forcing herself upright, she continued on. She gasped, dropped to her knees, and pitched forward. Her nails dug into the thick, coarse fibers of the rug. The weight of the spell had doubled, making it nearly impossible to stand, let alone stay awake.

Sleep beckoned her with each painfully long blink. Her body was so unbearably *heavy*.

The allure of slumber nearly crushed her thoughts, almost made her forget why she'd gotten off the sweet bed in the first place.

The smell of incense was all around her now, thick and suffocating.

Baby... Danica... Nik...

Picturing Nik's face in her mind, she used it as an anchor to pull herself up and out of her exhaustion-induced stupor. Grunting, giving everything she had, she hauled herself to her feet, shuffled toward the mantel. A vase set atop it; two thin reeds poked above it, emitting thin, red smoke.

"Gah!" She covered her mouth and nose with the top of her shirt. The cinnamon was cloyingly sweet this close, the cloves almost tart in their sharpness. Seizing the vase in a vise-like grip, she pulled it from the shelf and paused.

It took an eternity to think, her thoughts slowing to a crawl. She couldn't throw the vase in the fire. That would burn the incense quicker, and she probably would actually fall asleep right then and there.

Turning about, her vertigo skewed, and she nearly fell. The walls spun, swimming in and out of her blurry vision, but she spied a window. It was just a bit to the left—or was it to the right?

Planting a hand on the wall, she used it to guide her. Each slow step brought her closer to their liberation.

She groped for the window's lever but kept missing because her vision tripled and she was unable to tell which one was the real thing.

Damn. This. Spell.

After the third attempt, another set of hands reached for the lever.

Danica, looking as drained of energy as Alara felt, was up and grasping for the lever. With a grunt, she pulled it and chilly wind rushed into the room.

"Drop it, Alara!" Danica hissed.

Alara did just that. The vase tumbled into the darkness, along with those abominable sticks. Alara and Danica both gasped for air, the suffocating sleepiness at last abating.

They both collapsed and leaned back against the wall, slumped by each other.

"That…was…intense," Danica breathed, one last stubborn yawn escaping.

"Tell me about it. I don't think I'll be able to fall asleep so easily anytime soon."

Danica was the first to her feet. She dusted off her jeans, looked around with her hands on her hips. "So now what? You think we're in Mistress Black's HQ?"

"Most likely." Alara rose as they continued to evaluate the situation in hushed tones. "She would be the only person I could think of who would gain anything out of kidnapping us. I'm going to try to reach out to Nik."

Closing her eyes, she grappled for her bond. Her heart fluttered. It felt so thin, but it was still there.

Nik? she called.

She felt a whispery tug, a movement along their bond so subtle and swift she wasn't sure whether she had only imagined it.

After a few more failed attempts at communicating with her mate, frustration set in. "I can't reach him." She shook her head with a growl. "We're too far apart."

Danica bit her lip. "Do you…do you think I could reach anyone, being the High Queen and all?"

Alara considered it. "You might be able to. I know my father and mother spoke of being able to communicate over great distances. But I'm sure Mistress Black has this place bewitched to dampen telepathic communication."

"Doesn't hurt to try." Danica's eyes fluttered closed. She took a deep breath, let it out slowly. Her jaw started to clench. Her eyes flew open with a growl of frustration. "I thought I had it! I could hear Gage, calling my name. But he sounded a lot farther away than he normally does."

"Most likely a combination of the distance and that communication disruptor spell I spoke of. Looks like we'll have to come up with a plan B."

There was the sound of a lock being rattled.

They both turned just in time to see plan B walk right through the door—a guard.

Everyone froze for a long moment, staring at one another.

Alara scanned the man's telepathic signature. There was magic in his blood.

She smiled a wolfy grin. Perfect.

He stared at them, eyes wide. His hands clenched at his T-shirt, his jeans, his long hair, as if unsure what to do with them. "But you're…you're supposed to be asleep! The spell—"

"Yeah, about that." Alara's knees bent, muscles prepped for battle. "We kind of woke up. Guess we're stronger than you originally thought?"

Alara leapt, not giving the guard time to call for

backup. She Changed midair into a magnificent umber-toned wolf who landed on him as he pivoted to run for the exit. Danica swiftly shut the door while Alara bent her great wolf head into the man's terrified face.

She growled low, snapped at the air in front of his nose for good measure. The stench of urine filled the air.

Danica wrinkled her nose and muttered, "Gross."

Tell him he's going to do something for us, Alara instructed her comrade.

Danica put her game face on and crouched so she could look directly in the man's eyes. "You're going to do something for us."

"If—if it's escaping, I can't help you! Mistress Black— if she finds out I aided in your escape—"

His face lit up as Alara's eyes blazed gold. She saw herself in his wide pupils—a monster, straight out of a nightmare, all teeth and fur and menace.

"I'd be more concerned about my friend eating you," Danica said.

A high-pitched squeak spurted from his lips. Alara quickly pressed her paw to his mouth, muffling his pleas of mercy.

Tell him to do exactly as you say and we'll let him live, Alara told Danica. *Starting with lifting this damn communication-dampening spell.*

CHAPTER TWENTY-SEVEN

ELIJAH ROARED AND THRASHED AGAINST HIS CHAINS. His throat had started to grow a lump, his voice raspy from overuse.

God, he hated the dungeon, hated the stink and the cold and the abysmal loneliness of it. He kinda thought that was the idea, to make it as dreary as possible. Wouldn't want anybody getting hopeful down here, thinking they might actually escape or something.

Wouldn't that be a crying shame?

But he had to escape. He had to get the hell out of here and go rescue his woman from that psychopath. Before she…before…

He nearly choked, his throat became so tight. *Damn it all, pull it together!*

He wondered if he Shifted how badly he'd injure himself while still chained up. Bones would be dislocated, maybe even broken. Both of which he could deal with just fine. God knows he'd done plenty of both to his bones over the years he'd been a professional asshole and drunk, get-ting into fights with whoever would swing a fist at him.

His accelerated healing should help in that depart-ment too. Then there was the matter of getting out of the cell itself. Would werewolf strength be enough to break the door down? To bend metal like a superhero?

Doubts flickered up. He was no hero. If anything, he was the villain. He deserved to be locked away in some dank, dark cell. Have someone throw away the key and let the world forget he'd ever existed.

Except Verika needed him.

For that one reason alone, he would keep fighting. And God help anyone dumb enough to get in his way.

His mind studied the chamber, the chains. He'd tried Shifting before to break free, long ago when Mistress Black had first gotten it in her mind to put him down here, to "chain him up like the dog he was." That hadn't gone well. The chains had been enchanted. Feeling like an idiot, he sniffed one of the manacles. It smelled faintly of blood, sweat...and something sharper, more acrid.

His bones, thoughts, senses locked up. His breath stuttered, and his heart skipped a beat in a markedly faint echo of fear.

Oh, there was magic still embedded in those mana-cles, all right. Probably in the damn bars of the cell, too.

Which should have scared him shitless, made him tuck tail, and whimper like a frightened pup.

Only his fear of magic was trumped by a new fear—the thought of losing Verika.

He couldn't survive in a world without his mate. She

was his guiding light, the flicker of hope in his darkness. She made him want to try harder, be better, to not give up on himself. He wasn't sure he'd have the strength to keep fighting on his own without her.

Time to man up.

Preparing to Shift, he gritted his teeth and summoned his inner wolf to the surface. Prepared to sacrifice every inch of his humanity to the beast, the monster within if it meant saving the woman he loved.

He felt the magic rush up, making his skin tingle and stretch. The pain would be next. The tearing and ripping of muscles, bones snapping and cracking as the ancient spell broke everything that made him Elijah and remade him into a creature out of a nightmare.

Tonight, he would be the nightmare, would become something straight out of hell.

He had a witch to kill.

And oh, justice had been a long time coming.

He growled, giving himself over to the rising onslaught of bittersweet agony—

And immediately froze. The Shift stopped in an abrupt blink, the pain vanishing as his ears pricked.

Several pairs of footsteps came down the steps toward the dungeons deep below the mansion. An orange glow grew brighter, illuminating the stone hallway walls the louder the footsteps became. As the sound and the light reached an apex, two brilliant burning orbs of fire floated into the room, hovering in the air on either side of the entrance.

Elijah's eyes flickered to them briefly and then

immediately fixated once more on the door. He allowed himself a moment of fear for the magical flames. But only a moment. Now was not a time to be ruled by his fear.

Never again would there be a good time for that bullshit. Never again would he allow it to nearly cost him his mate's life.

One by one, his visitors filed into the room. The witches came first, two women who were vastly different in height and appearance. Whereas one was short and slender as a pixie, with bright-pink spiked hair and what appeared to be an entire stick of eye liner smeared around her golden eyes, the other witch was tall and about a hundred pounds overweight. With her round face, big eyes, and full, huge mouth, she reminded him of a toad.

They wore robes black as midnight, a single sigil resembling a snake coiled around a blazing sun sewn in golden thread across the right breast. Five men, all hooded in the same fine black robes, stood behind them, fanning out around the room and standing stock-still.

Too still.

He caught a whiff of something rotten, like garbage that had been out in the sun for too long. Every hair on Elijah's body pricked upright. There was something not quite right about the men, for they were men. Broadshouldered and tall, all five of them giants in their own right. They had no hands or feet that he could see, just gaping maws of endless black fabric.

"They don't like it when you stare."

He startled, snapped his attention forward. The pixie grinned. "What are they?" He eyed the men warily.

"Something not of this world." She sauntered toward the cell, the fabric swaying seductively across her feet. Gripping the bars, she leaned inward, raked a hot-pink nail up his chest. "And if you want to keep that deliciously hot body of yours, I suggest you remember your manners. And not stare," she added, widening her eyes and grinning like an idiot.

As if anything about this abysmal situation was funny. Freaks.

The fire orbs were coming from her, judging by her paranormal signature. She might look harmless, but her signature packed a wallop. Great power flowed through her veins.

So Tinker Hell wasn't as harmless and daft as she looked. He'd wager the Toad wasn't either. Her power twisted and lurched around her, lifting her hair, swaying the robes of the people who accompanied her.

A Grey Witch, with the voice of the wind at her beck and call. Wind always seemed like such a lame power to him—at first. He'd seen wind witches level towns with freakishly huge tornadoes. Watched them suck the air out of a man's lungs just to watch him suffer.

Yeah, no way was he messing with any of that.

Or any of whatever the hell these men were. On his Creep-o-Meter, they scored a twelve out of ten.

Another shimmering—dear God, she'd used *glitter*, like some twelve-year-old schoolgirl—hot-pink nail skittered up his pecs. "Will you be a good wolf and promise you won't bite if I open your cell?"

"That all depends. The hell you planning on doing

with me, sweetheart?"

"Oh, there are a lot of things I'd love to do with you." She licked her lips. Probably thought it was sexy, and hey, maybe it was for some men. It only made him want to vomit. She couldn't have been older than sixteen.

"But, sadly, I am to bring you to my mistress." She pouted.

That revelation kind of made him want to pout too. "What for?"

"You'll find out soon enough." With a snap of her fingers, two of the men started forward.

Elijah couldn't take his eyes off their feet. They floated, gliding as effortlessly over the stone flooring as if they'd been riding hoverboards.

A robed arm lifted. Elijah never saw a hand emerge with a key, but he heard the bolt twist all the same. Chills scraped up his arms, skittered over his spine in a way that made him shudder as the door groaned open. Somehow, with those things standing—or rather, hovering—there, this dungeon seemed twice as spooky.

The smell of decay became stronger, making him want to gag. As they came into his cell, his gut reaction was to shrink back, to press his body against the wall in an effort to blend in with it. As if that would do him any good. He *felt* their eyes on him, felt the oppression of their cold, hard gazes.

"Come on, hot stuff," said Pixie. "Let's get you cleaned up."

"Why?"

"For the Grand Rite. Mistress Black wants you there."

Mistress Black donned the black ceremonial robe of luscious velvet and fur lining with a keen sense of triumph.

Even if she had spent days languishing over the details of some complex plan, she couldn't have come up with anything any better. It was days like today she started to believe in fate again.

Tucked away within the shadows and soft candlelight of her private chambers, she allowed herself to feel a bit of long-awaited joy.

That damnable brand, bitch as it was to remove, was finally gone. Over the past hour since removing it, her strength had finally started to return, the nausea a dull ache in her stomach. But her new and improved health wasn't even the best part about this deal.

Now it wouldn't matter when she killed the witch and her dark knight, for her life was no longer tied to theirs.

Elijah would provide the last soul she'd need to restore her fractured spirit, and Verika's magic, once siphoned out of her, would be the power boost she needed to unbind her soul from this wretched, alien body and supplant her back into her own once more.

At last, she would be free.

She would be home.

She smiled and stroked the bloodred blade of the dagger strapped at her hip.

Soon.

CHAPTER TWENTY-EIGHT

VERIKA TRIED TO IGNORE HER SWEATY PALMS AND trembling knees as she was marched outside into the open night air.

It was a beautiful night, by all accounts. The temperature had yet to turn frigid, and this far out into the country, the air still smelled clean and fresh. The sky stretched into the horizon, an endless indigo blanketed with hundreds of thousands of twinkling stars. The moon hung overhead, a full, white orb shining brilliant, clean light on the party below.

Her eyes latched onto the moon; she was mesmerized as her skin began to faintly itch.

Her heart sped up.

Crap. How could she have forgotten tonight was the night of her first Change?

Maybe because you've been locked up in psycho central and were preoccupied with, oh, I don't know, saving the world.

As the moonlight bathed her skin in porcelain light, Verika racked her mind for every kernel of knowledge she knew about a werewolf's first Change.

She wouldn't lose her powers, that much she was certain of. So no panic there.

Most werewolves didn't Change right away, although some did. It was controllable to some degree at first, though the longer the newfound werewolf was exposed to moonlight the harder it became to control the Change. Eventually, it would consume them whether they were ready or not.

Her heart thrummed frantically, and she glanced around. Did anyone else realize what was going on with her? Was anyone else aware of the Change about to take place?

A breeze brushed her hair, bringing with it the scent of the woods. The smell of freedom, of endless nights spent loping over branch and bramble, of roaming the darkened forest with her mate and—

She shook her head, breaking the spell of the siren call of the moon. She grappled for breath, steadied herself. Good grief, was this how all werewolves felt on their first Change? So out of control?

Focus. She needed to focus.

The entire coven—the Order of the Sun, Verika presumed—was gathered on the yard. About a hundred people total, Verika estimated upon looking around. All clad in matching black robes, like the one she now wore. All standing in a circle around an intricate symbol Verika didn't know the meaning of.

The symbol was gargantuan, spanning at least sixty feet across and sixty feet wide. She knew because it was about the size of her parents' fenced-in backyard when she was a kid, before her mother had the old wooden fence ripped down in favor of viewing the endless countryside.

The symbol, made up of swirling lines and knots, was drawn from thousands of tiny blue crystals. They glittered and pulsed with pale-blue light, throbbing as one—as if the symbol had a heartbeat.

Verika's inner scholar couldn't keep her mouth shut, couldn't shut her brain off. "Tuning crystals?" Verika asked Mistress Black, who strode directly in front of her.

"Almost correct," Mistress Black said without turning her head. She marched them down the expansive lawn of springy, deep-green grass behind the mansion. "They are amplifying crystals."

"There's a lot of them."

"That's the idea." She didn't say another word, and Verika knew the subject was done.

Sure, Verika had heard of amps before, knew what they did. Some witches and warlocks, in their old age, used them to resuscitate weakened magic, or to help boost their powers for a particularly complex spell.

But to use so many... Exactly what kind of ritual were they about to perform?

Though the oncoming winter chilled the air with its icy kiss, Verika's sixth sense picked up on something else that made gooseflesh spring up along her skin. With a wary eye, she glanced about, her hair whipping around her face from the wind.

Everyone had hoods drawn, faces partly obscured by shadows. All but about ten figures she counted so far. They stood tall, far taller than their witch and warlock companions, with a broad sweep of shoulders and mountainous frames. She could find no pattern, no rhyme or reason to their placement. It seemed a bit haphazard, though they were easy enough to spot considering they stood a head taller than just about everyone else.

But intimidating as their stature might be, what made her look twice—made her heart hitch, her breath catch, her flesh chill—was the fact that when you peered into their hoods, all you saw was darkness. A cavernous hole, waiting to swallow you whole. No face. No trace of hands or feet, now that she thought to look. And while all the normal men and women—for these...*creatures* could not be normal—swayed while chanting, these figures stood still as marble statues. Not even the wind ruffled their robes.

No, there was something quite unnatural about them.

Verika felt eyes upon her as she passed another of those things. Hot breath reeking of decaying flesh lifted her hair, making her nearly gag on a shriek.

Protocol be damned. She scurried to stand by Mistress Black, who merely raised a brow at her presence.

"What are those things?" Verika demanded, still trying to get the stench out of her throat, her mouth, her nose.

"Ever heard of flesh guardians?"

Verika stopped walking altogether. "You *raised the dead*?"

Mistress Black paused too when it became clear Verika

wasn't going to keep moving until she had some answers. "Please, darling. There's more to it than simply raising the dead," she said with a flourish of her hand, punctuated by an eye roll. "Flesh guardians have been imbued with the power of earth to make them nigh unstoppable."

Verika wasn't even going to begin to get into all the reasons why casting such spells was considered an abomination—not to mention illegal.

"Oh, don't look so surprised, dove." Mistress Black smiled. "We're Black Witches. Necromancy is part of our birthright."

It made Verika want to throw up. "And you felt it necessary to raise these flesh guardians because…?"

"Because they're the best protection magic can buy."

"Protection from what?"

"You'll see. I have a very good reason for needing them. This spell can be very temperamental. I will only have *a* shot at it"—she held up one finger in emphasis—"so I have to get it right the first time." She started to walk away.

"A shot at what?" Verika called, frustrated. "You expect me to believe all this"—she swept her hand over the expanse of blue crystals—"is just so you can jump back into your old body? I know about transference spells. They're tough, but not this tough. You're not telling me everything."

Mistress Black sighed and turned back around. "The better to keep you in the dark with, my dear. Trust me, the less you know, the better off you'll be. And the less chances you'll have at overthinking this and trying to muck up all my hard preparation. Now, come along. There is no time to waste."

Two figures appeared behind Verika—flesh guardians. She didn't need to fully look to know that's what stood behind her. The sense of otherworldliness crawled over her skin like worms. They didn't belong here, in this world. Every fiber of her magic screamed at her to send them back from where they'd come.

Her fingers curled and stretched, the restless magic in her digits making them itch.

Mistress Black had stopped walking again. Her eyes flicked to Verika's hands, lingering there. She went still, her eyes turning flinty. "I would be very careful, if I were you. Flesh guardians don't take kindly to threats of any kind."

As if sensing their master's tension, the two figures behind her growled. Or more like hissed, a sound as thin and reedy as wind blowing through reeds.

Verika tensed—and glared at Mistress Black. The power at her fingertips swelled. "My magic doesn't take kindly to threats either."

Mistress Black pursed her lips, her face going red with fury. She snapped her fingers. "You've tested my patience enough for one evening, puppet."

The flesh guardians lifted their arms, and the long sleeves fell back to reveal skin in varying stages of decay. Bony hands barely coated in putrid strips of flesh grasped her arms in surprisingly strong grips. The smell of death coated her tongue, her throat, invaded every pore of her olfactory glands. She gagged as they dragged her forward, toward the center of the circle, past flickering candles, pulsing crystals, and more chanting figures.

At the symbol's heart, a circle of people—Mistress Black's inner ring of confidantes, Verika presumed—was gathered, clutching hands, swaying to the rhythm of the chant with their eyes closed. At their center lay an altar of black velvet, upon which rested a woman with red hair—

Hair the same shade as Verika's.

Her eyes went wide; her breath lodged in her throat. Mistress Black's real body.

It felt strange to see it in waking life, outside the confines of her dreams. It sent a chill through her bones, as if seeing her in person made the nightmares seem real.

Which they were. She was living one, right here, right this second. And as her eyes swept over the cloaked figures, beyond the glowing, glittering circle, past the looming mansion and beyond the murky hills and trees, she feared she might never wake up. She was truly alone out here. If she screamed, who would hear her? Who would care?

When the flesh guardians didn't stop at the circle of people, Verika was briefly puzzled. Then her eyes landed on a pair of stakes protruding from the ground, and her heart stopped beating for a second.

Her heels dug in as the flesh guardians approached them. "No," she breathed, writhing in their grip, their splintered fingertips scraping her skin red. "No! What are you doing?"

Struggling did her about as much good as fighting a mountain. Or a pair of them. The flesh guardians pulled her up as if she were a doll and pressed her back against the rough wood while they bound her with coarse rope. One length across her arms, another about her legs.

Mistress Black stood back, calmly watching with her arms folded. "My dear, please know I never intended for it to end this way."

"So everything you spouted in my dream about wanting to be a family again was nothing more than a lie!"

"No. Never a lie. It still brought me great joy to see you." She stepped forward to cup Verika's face.

"Don't touch me!" Verika's power flared, sizzling about her skin in vibrant green sparks.

Mistress Black snatched back her hand with a barely contained wince. She rubbed her fingertips, appraised her descendant with a cool gaze. "It might not seem like it now," she said after a beat, "but I'm actually doing you a favor."

"A favor," Verika barked. "How?"

Mistress Black's gaze softened. Her tone grew more somber as she stared upon Verika's face with pity. "Being a witch in this world, this world full of prejudice and injustice and bloodshed, is hard enough. But being a Black Witch? You don't even belong with your kind. The other houses of magic fear and loathe you. To be a Black Witch is to be an outcast forever."

"Yeah, when you're a psychotic evil bitch, I could see why people would be wary of you."

Mistress Black's lips pressed into a thin, bloodless line. "You haven't been through what I have, haven't seen the horrors I've seen. You don't yet have the right to judge me. And you never will."

"What are you talking about?"

"You're too soft for this world. You don't have the stone heart it takes to bear the power of death and destruction. Believe me, my dear, relieving you of your powers will be the greatest kindness anyone will ever do for you."

Verika processed this as Mistress Black walked away. "Wait, you're taking away my powers? That's why you brought me here?"

Mistress Black kept walking.

"I knew it," Verika spat, her fury breaking through her shock and making her voice hard as steel. Her words cut the air like daggers. "I knew there was more you weren't telling me. That all this trouble was about more than you simply getting back into your original body. You lied to me."

"I didn't lie," Mistress Black said over her shoulder, not deigning to turn around. "I just didn't tell you the whole truth. There is a difference."

"Truth withheld is still a lie in my book."

Mistress Black stopped walking. She fisted her hands and whirled around. "I *did not* lie. You shall help me return to my true form—by giving me every drop of magic in your blood. With your power, I shouldn't have any problems performing this spell."

"And you'll have one less threat to worry about."

Silence.

Verika laughed bitterly. "I knew it, knew there was a catch. That our bargain was too good to be true. But you know, some part of me actually wanted to help you return to your true form. I felt sorry for you when I learned of your past, about your family. But it was the glimmer of hope in your eyes when you spoke of being whole again that made me think, possibly, you could be redeemed. Like in being made whole, you'd somehow be made into a better version of yourself. A better person. Now, I see you're nothing more than a power-hungry monster waiting to prey on the weak. You disgust me."

Something close to hurt flashed over Mistress Black's face. Her eyes shone; the firelight flickered in them as grief washed over her face. "I know what I am, what I allowed myself to become, and I made peace with that a long time ago. I had to, in order to survive, to keep carrying on. Know that I am sorry. I had truly hoped we could be family."

"No, you didn't. If you had, you wouldn't have had me tied to this stake. You would've protected me, not sought to do me harm. Family looks out for one another, but you only look out for yourself."

"A creature of habit, I suppose."

"Please…don't do this."

"It's already done."

Verika swore and struggled against her binds as Mistress Black walked toward her body without a backward glance.

Horrors raced through her head, made her heart race and a cold sweat chill her flesh. She couldn't lose her powers. Sure, they had terrified her before, when they were new and she was less certain of herself. Now, on the cusp of losing what she had coveted for so long, Verika found the thought of not having her Black Magic as terrifying as dying. And knowing Mistress Black, she planned to kill her shortly after she had stripped her of her powers.

Any number of ritualistic deaths floated through her mind, driving her heart rate up, making it harder to concentrate on escaping.

If she could escape. All circumstances considered, her chances of that looked grim.

"Do not look so alarmed, my dear," Mistress Black purred. "I have brought you company so you won't feel so alone in your final hours."

Final hours. Two words that held so much weight and seemed to thin the air, making it harder to breathe.

She truly was about to die, and it didn't appear she had a chance in hell of doing anything about it.

But the thought of dying didn't sound so bad when she looked up, and her worst fear came to life. "No," she breathed.

A pair of flesh guardians marched Elijah forward, chained in those damnable manacles. Pure malice and loathing pooled in his dark eyes as he passed the coven. Then his gaze landed on her, and she swore she could see his heart breaking.

"Verika," he rasped, stumbling forward. The flesh guardians were quick to snatch him up, hold him close.

The cold, wicked teeth of a blade pressed into Verika's throat, and she fought a wince. Her eyes locked on her mate's, who'd gone still.

"That's a good pup." Mistress Black dug the blade deeper into Verika's throat. Verika had been so transfixed by Elijah's presence she hadn't heard Mistress Black creep up behind her.

A cry escaped before she could press her lips together as her skin stung and split, and a warm trickle of blood dribbled down her throat.

Elijah went still. And white, much too white.

He didn't move to fight as the flesh guardians dragged him to the second stake and tied him up. He craned his neck to look at her sidelong, a look of apology and despair in his eyes.

She shook her head. *It's not your fault. It's mine. I got us into this.*

Don't be absurd, kitten. I bring nothing but trouble and chaos with me. If anyone's to blame, it's me.

Well, we can play the blame game all night, and it won't do us a damn bit of good. Any ideas for getting us out of here?

He stared gravely at Mistress Black, trailed by her flesh guardians, as she walked back to the inner circle surrounding her body. They shifted, made way for her.

I wish I did. Elijah looked defeated. *Even if they were bad ones. Hell, I used to be the king of bad ideas.*

If he was the king, that made her the queen. Verika racked her brain, scrambled to come up with a plan, a prayer—anything—but she didn't see how they'd be able to claw their way out of this mess.

She tried accessing her power one more time.

Nothing.

Mistress Black raised her hands to the sky, and her coven went silent all at once.

"My comrades, you will not have to lend me your

power to preserve my true body any longer. After tonight, I shall be restored to my original self, my powers made complete by the souls and magic I've absorbed these past few months. And once I take my descendant's power, I—we—will be unstoppable. We can create a world where we don't have to live in fear of being judged, tortured, or killed for being different. A world where we can be ourselves in broad daylight. My friends, it's time to come out of the shadows. It's time for the Order of the Sun to lead the Underworld into a new era. Let us step into the light together."

Verika frantically searched the coven's faces as Mistress Black approached her with a knife. "She's using you! Can't you see that? She's going to start a war!"

"You're damn right I will," Mistress Black said coldly. She stopped in front of Verika, eyed her with nothing but contempt and malice. "And it's one, with your magic, I'm now positive we will win. Any last words?"

"Go to hell!"

Mistress Black's mouth twitched. "Been there, done that about a gazillion years ago. You haven't been through hell until you've watched your family burn. Thank you for your sacrifice. Your magic is about to aid a lot of suffering creatures who've been kept in the dark for too long." She angled the blade, tilted the point upward toward Verika's chest.

And plunged.

Time slowed. Verika became vaguely aware of sucking in a breath as her eyes dropped to the approaching knife, knowing there was no way for her to stop it. Elijah screamed her name, though she barely heard him over the ringing in her ears.

This is it. I'm going to die.

There wasn't time to blink as the tip touched her chest, penetrated her shirt.

It was as if a bomb went off.

Blinding light exploded from her heart, making Mistress Black hiss and drop the knife. She shielded her gaze, stumbled back. "What is this?"

Verika had never felt anything like it before: a warm, rich glow enveloping her inside and out.

Pure, raw power, coming from a crystal that had materialized out of her chest.

She gasped.

It was her mother's amulet, the one she'd seen in the picture.

"To protect me from all harm," she murmured, staring in wonder. The light didn't hurt her eyes. If anything, it was soothing. Dear God, her mother had hidden away the amulet *inside* her. The expanse of power it would take to accomplish such a feat—and to keep it sealed away for so long—was breathtaking.

She remembered a time when she was sixteen. At first, she didn't know why she was remembering this, and then it all became clear as day.

She hadn't had her license long, and had opted to pick up some late-night groceries for her adoptive mom. Cousins were coming in from out of town to visit the next day, and her mom wouldn't have time to make a grocery run before they showed. Verika had been on her way home when a drunk driver crashed into her along the highway. It'd been winter, and the road had gleamed with ice. The car spun, twisted out of her control as she screamed, terrified. She'd hit a tree, had banged her head so badly on the side window that she'd been rendered unconscious. When she came to in the hospital later, the doctor said it was a miracle she was still alive. No one had ever been able to explain it, though her mom had been convinced it was a guardian angel.

Now, she knew. It was the amulet, forged by her mother's love, that had saved her life that day.

And today, as well.

The brilliant burst of light retracted into the crystal, which shimmered and sparkled like bottled sunlight.

Mistress Black growled, a look of pure hatred in her eyes. "You wore a protection amulet. Very impressive, and sly. But it won't work against me. I will break it." Snatching the dagger up, she came at Verika with an enraged cry.

Verika didn't even flinch, knew she had nothing to fear as the blade met the glassy surface of the crystal—and snapped in half.

"*What?*" Mistress Black shrieked, staring in disbelief at the broken dagger.

"Your hatred is overbearing, Diedre," Verika said as images of Mistress Black's past flooded her brain with each pulse of the crystal, as if it was siphoning them from her enemy.

Mistress Black's eyes snapped upward. "How do you know that name? What power is this?"

"The kind you've forgotten. Or maybe you didn't

understand it in the first place. It's the power of love and devotion, and it will trump whatever dark forces you throw at me anytime, anywhere."

"This is ridiculous. A child's attempt at thwarting me. Even a broken blade can be used to kill."

Distantly, she heard someone calling her name, from inside her mind. She ignored it, her gaze intently focused on Mistress Black as she pointed the jagged piece of metal at her mate's throat. "Surrender yourself to me, or your mate dies."

Verika!

She blinked. She'd definitely heard a voice that time, calling out to her. *Hello?*

We're… for you.

What? I can't understand you! Your voice is breaking up! There's some kind of magical interference. Either that, or the voice, which sounded so familiar, was too far away.

"Last chance!" Mistress Black gripped a handful of Elijah's hair, jerked his head back to expose his throat. "Think very carefully about your next move, you sneaky little bitch."

She only caught it for a second from the corner of her eye, but Verika swore the air over the field *rippled*. She blinked, stared.

There it was again, as if invisible fingers were trying to pry it apart.

A howl went up in the distance.

Mistress Black glanced at the woods, searched their darkness with wary eyes. "Go find out what that was," she snapped, and two flesh guardians, along with a trio of witches and warlocks, took off into the night, torches blazing.

A sudden itching sensation spread over Verika's skin.

Tilting her head back, she gazed up at the moon. Its light was so pure, so bright that it brought tears to her eyes.

"Keep running toward the light," she murmured, feeling the tingling sensation growing in her skin as her bones began to vibrate. The moon was calling to her, begging her to let it take her, transform her.

That's when she knew what she had to do—and the moment she figured out, truly understood, who she really was.

She was neither werewolf nor witch. She was Verika Elaine Tate-Johnson.

And she was going to kick this witch's ass.

A gale picked up from around her feet, twisting and spiraling up and out. Not from her—from the crystal. It shone bright, clear as a star.

And Verika utterly trusted it. She could feel her mother's love within her, and wept over the depth of her sacrifice.

Even knowing she'd face certain death by crafting this amulet, her mother hadn't been afraid. And neither would her daughter.

Closing her eyes as power swirled around her, she gave in to the moon's call. She didn't fight the Change but let it take control of and transform her body. It hurt— oh God, it hurt—but she trusted the process, had faith she would be all right. That she could walk through fire, through pain, through suffering, and come out stronger on the other side.

As she morphed, the bracelets about her wrists groaned and snapped free. Her power flooded her senses, intoxicating, ushering in the Change. The world burst into brilliant sound and color as a great red wolf, the amulet swinging from its chest, took over her human body completely.

Her crimson fur and glowing golden eyes shone in the night, as did her fangs, which she took delight in baring at the closest warlocks and witches. Their eyes widened, and she drank in their fear, let it fuel the barely contained anger simmering below the surface of her control.

They had tried to kill her mate. And for that, her inner wolf was very, very angry.

Mistress Black staggered back, gazed openly at the red wolf with shock. "Impossible," she breathed. "Those binds should've held you."

"Nothing can stop a werewolf's first Change, dumbass," Elijah said.

Mistress Black seethed, her knuckles turning white as she gripped the broken dagger. "I'm going to cut that insufferable smirk off your pretty face. Then perhaps I'll feed it to some of my monsters."

It happened in a few seconds that stretched for an eternity. Mistress Black started forward, murder in her eyes. Her army of minions rushed behind her, surrounding Verika.

I will not be afraid, not anymore.

Fearless, she tipped back her head and howled.

A chorus of howls, achingly familiar, answered from

the woods. She could hear them now, hear the paws running toward her. She'd heard them the second she'd Changed and the wind had carried the scent of their salvation toward her.

Everything smelled sharper. She could practically taste the earth, air, and sky on her tongue.

A pair of wolves emerged from the woods, charging across the moon-swept lawn. Gold and brown fur gleamed as they ran, fangs bared, magnificent in their ferocity.

Verika howled again, and Danica and Alara answered.

Then the sky split open.

As magic pried apart the fabric of time and space, a ripple went through the air, knocking the coven on their asses. Verika saw the ripple coming, felt its power, and threw up a shield of Black Magic without a second thought.

Her magic felt...*different* in this form. Not bad, just more pronounced, as if its wildness recognized the beast she'd become and had become one with it. She'd never felt more in command of herself, of her powers, than she did now.

Mistress Black hadn't been as quick to react to the shockwave of power. Her shield was flimsy, shattering upon impact. She hauled herself from the ground, looking the most disheveled Verika had ever seen her. Her eyes were pinned to the sky in horror as a veritable army of witches, warlocks, vampires, and more werewolves than Verika had ever seen in one place rained down from the sky through a massive sparkling hole.

It was total chaos. Battle ensued, a bloody flurry of

fang and claw. Above the cacophony of war, Mistress Black shrieked at her unorganized coven. They scrambled about, clearly not having a plan in place for this turn of events.

She truly hadn't thought things would go south, she was that arrogant.

And so her vanity would be her undoing. How appropriate.

Taking advantage of the distraction, Verika immediately ran toward Elijah, but Gage had already freed him. The two brothers swapped looks, clasped hands, and then Changed into wolves of night and day. The pure-white wolf howled by its solid-black brother, who looked right at Verika.

Are you all right? Elijah asked.

She sensed her mate's fear for her, his gnawing worry. He didn't need those now. There was a time and place for them, but they both needed to focus on the battle at hand if they were to survive. And they'd been through too much together not to.

I'm fine, she assured him. *You just worry about you, I'll worry about me, and maybe we'll come out of this alive.*

No maybes about it. We will. Now let's end this.

She barked her response and dove into the fray.

She'd never practiced fighting with magic growing up and had struggled to control her powers in the few scrapes she'd had since becoming a Black Witch. But in this body, her powers responded to her whims with barely any effort. Blood stained the ground quickly, saturating the air in a thick cloud that stung her nose and burned her throat. It was distracting at first, but the grisly images of torn flesh and the screams of the dying were even more so. They snapped her attention back to now, just in time to dodge an arrow made of ice.

The Blue Witch didn't hesitate to fling another and another, though Verika's nimble body dodged them all. Charging her attacker, Verika leapt and slammed her to the ground. She screamed, throwing her hands up as her face froze in terror. Verika raised a paw and did her best at bringing it down and across the girl's temple without marring her face too much. Claws scored her skin in thin red lines, but she'd accomplished what she'd set out to do— she'd knocked her out cold.

The hatred and anger she'd felt earlier, two volatile feelings that easily could have turned into bloodlust, were gone now, attuned into adrenaline and sharpening her focus on staying alive. There was no need for her to kill, though if someone gave her one, she'd grant their death wish.

The cost of winning didn't matter, not anymore. She had to walk out of this alive. She and Elijah both.

She didn't look for him as she fought with magic, fang, and claw, relying instead on the tightness of their mate-bond. If it began to weaken...then she'd worry. Worry more, that is, though she knew she was being silly. Elijah was perfectly capable of handling himself, and he had been a wolf far longer than she.

She bit some half-Fae woman and sent her screaming for the woods. She bared her fangs, prepared to give chase, when a familiar vampire stepped into her path.

Rick looked significantly worse than the last time she'd

seen him. His face was bruised, his jaw swollen on one side. His eyes held her with contempt. "My Mistress punished me because of you." He flipped open a knife. "But she'll revere me when I'm the one who takes down the—"

Oh, shut up! Verika thought, snarling. Her magic shot toward Rick, and he went still.

His eyes widened. "I…can't move! What's… happening?"

Verika reached deep inside, used the ancient magic flowing through her veins to push her thoughts into Rick's head. *Word to the wise—if you're undead, don't take on a Black Witch without expecting her to take control of you.*

His eyes nearly shot out of his sockets, and his lips flapped stupidly. "Please," he said, "have mercy!"

She was silent a moment, let him wallow in his panic. *No one messes with my family. Ever.*

Further pleas for mercy were silenced as she flung him high into the air and across the field with her magic, right into a throng of werewolves.

It took no effort to walk away without looking back, to turn her heart to ice at the sounds of his screaming.

More enemies approached, each stupider than the last. She sank so easily into her power, used it to twist, break, and bend.

Like snapping twigs, she thought with morbid fascination.

She could see, for a fraction of a moment, how Mistress Black could've succumbed to such seductive power. Blinking herself out of it, realizing her bloodlust hadn't been satiated but rather stoked by what she'd done to Rick, she pulled herself back from the abyss, from that point of no return between woman and monster.

She had to get a grip on her powers, on her animal instinct to hunt and kill. She'd become one with her inner wolf so quickly that she hadn't realized how much of an effect her spirit animal had an impact on her psyche. Had taken it for granted, it was so subtle, until it literally waved its dominance in her face with a trail of bodies littering the field behind her from where she'd passed and fought.

And conquered.

Some ran in fear now as she approached, as they had every right to. Still, more met her with eager, reckless anticipation.

An umber-colored wolf bumped into her as she struggled more than she would've liked with a pair of demon-human half breeds.

Verika! The umber-colored wolf—Alara—snapped at the arm of a warlock and made him drop the sword he'd been clutching.

Boy, do I have a million questions for you. Snap, jump.

So I expected. Growl, lunge, twist.

How? How did you escape? How did you find us? How did you break the protective wards protecting this space?

I'll explain how we escaped later. Long story short, we threatened to relieve our guard of his testicles should he not help us communicate with our mates.

Sounds like you put up a very persuasive argument.

Quite. Gage and Nik called in every favor ever owed them and then some. People we've never met answered the call. The leaders of the other races sent their bravest and

302

finest. Everyone in the Underworld wants Mistress Black gone. With that many witches and warlocks joining powers, they managed to weaken the wards enough to damage them and break through.

So united we'll stand.

Damn right. United, we'll destroy—

Alara yelped, her body tossed aside like a doll. The flesh guardian who'd dealt the blow floated over the ground, racing toward the umber-colored wolf as she struggled to get up.

Alara! Verika yelled and bolted forward without a second thought.

The flesh guardian met her head on, shrieking like a banshee as it rushed toward her in a blur of dark robes and snow-white bone. Verika dodged, felt its bony fingers scrape her skin, pry up fur. Painful but not unbearable. The wolf was tough, an efficient killing machine built by centuries of hard-won evolution.

She ducked, swiped, and danced about the flesh guardian. He bent his hooded head back and shrieked into the open night sky. More guardians answered his call.

Nearby, Alara was on her feet and growling, hackles raised, as two more guardians approached. Blood marred her fine coat.

Verika had to end this. Leaping back as the flesh guardian's rancid teeth snapped where her muzzle had been, she summoned every drop of power in her blood, stretched the spell as far and wide as she could, across the whole of the bloody battlefield. She didn't have to say anything, just do it, will her magic to obey. Every muscle quaked with the strain of holding the magic steady.

Within moments, every flesh guardian on the field froze. The hoods had fallen back on some, revealing dulled, broken skulls stripped of flesh, of anything that made them recognizable.

Shells. That's all these poor creatures were now. Empty shells awoken from the grave to perform a selfish woman's bidding.

And so, she would lay them to rest.

Gathering her power, she pulled.

The Black Magic giving the flesh guardians life was sucked right out of them, through their eyes, mouth, ears. They shrieked and writhed as green tendrils of magic coalesced in the air, forming a writhing, pulsing ball.

Verika pushed. The ball exploded.

The magic swiped through the field, a tidal wave of power, and the flesh guardians at last stilled, their eyes dark, no longer dimly burning with the dark magic that had given them life. One by one, they fell, motionless, truly dead.

Verika at last released the spell with an audible gasp. Her body hurt, ached all over. Necromancy was an abomination, a crime against what was intended. And though Black Witch she may be, with the power to command death if she so chose, her body rejected the notion of controlling the dead. It wasn't…right.

Her stomach heaved as Alara approached, limping. *Are you all right?*

I will be, just need to catch my breath.

The enemies around them had seemed to pause, as

well, to ponder that awesome display of power. And to wonder whether they should retreat. Their numbers had been significantly thinned out, she noted. As had their own, she realized with a wince.

You saved me, Alara said.

Yes.

Thank you.

No thanks needed. Come. Let us find our mates.

Elijah lost track of time as he and Gage fought through the heat of battle. The art of destruction came to him as easily as breathing. Werewolf, vampire, warlock: it didn't matter. None of them were a match for him. He let go of his fears of magic and surrendered to his wolf's innate sense of self-preservation. Gave in to the wildness gnawing at him.

Gage broke off shortly after helping him dispatch a rather ambitious witchling who, clearly, had been one of the coven's newest members. Probably hadn't been in control of her powers for long.

I have to find Danica, Gage had said, *and get her foolhardy ass out of here before she gets herself and our child killed.*

Go, Elijah had said, and Gage had taken off.

He later saw Danica racing toward the woods, not a spot on her golden fur, as Gage fought off those who would have chased her.

The distraction was too long, because the next thing he knew there was a flash of silver, and then he barely dodged having that damnable broken blade buried in his neck.

He knew who would face him before he'd even turned around.

Mistress Black stood there, covered in blood, her hair a mess. Her fine robe had been torn, as had the flesh beneath. Looked as though someone, at least, had gotten a good chunk of her. He hoped whichever creature responsible was still alive so he might buy them a brew after this was all done.

Mistress Black tossed her blood-and-dirt-matted hair out of her face as wolf and witch circled each other. "I should have killed you the moment the brand was lifted. Would've saved myself a world of heartache."

He Changed back into a man, not caring in the least that he didn't wear a scrap of clothing. She'd already seen every inch of him, had defiled him. He had words to say— needed to say—as a man. The man she'd scarred so deeply he doubted he'd ever be rid of the wounds.

"They would've come for you eventually," he said easily.

"But perhaps they wouldn't have."

"Oh, I think they would've, sweetheart. Everybody in the Underworld wants you dead."

"Not everyone. I have an army of followers."

"Yeah? How's that army doing now? Because it looks to me like we're kicking their asses."

She hissed, lunged. Elijah sidestepped and shoved her, using her own momentum to cause her to stumble and nearly fall onto the carcass of a witch of Mistress Black's coven. Or what was left of her.

Mistress Black blinked at the corpse of her fallen subordinate and turned back to Elijah.

He raised a brow. "No vengeful cry? No tears of remorse for your friend?"

"She was not my friend. I have no friends. They make you weak, vulnerable."

"That's not what our army of friends tells me. You're just too scared to let someone in because you're afraid they'll see how ugly you are inside and hate you as much as you hate yourself."

"That's not true," she snarled.

"Isn't it? I know you said a friend of your family's sold out you all as witches, was responsible for their deaths. And for that, I'm sorry. Nobody deserves that. But just as cruel or worse has happened to plenty of other people, and you don't see them becoming murderous psychopaths."

"I'm justified! I have my reasons!"

"As do we for stopping you! Look around! The battle's over. You've lost."

"No."

He clenched his jaw. "If you surrender now, I bet the High Council will even spare your life."

She laughed. "And lock me up for the next fifty years, or however long I last, in this wretched body? I think not. I'd rather be dead."

She charged, and he Changed.

One of the jagged points of metal caught him in the side, scoring his skin, but he didn't even flinch. Plenty of knives had pierced his flesh in his lifetime. You got used to it after a while, lost your fear.

He went straight for her throat, throwing both paws onto her shoulders and knocking her over backward. They hit the ground hard; the breath whooshed out of her mouth as her eyes flew wide with shock. Upon impact, she lost her grip on the knife, and it skittered off to the side.

His maw was about her glistening, blood-covered neck, the taste of those she'd killed on his tongue as he prepared to snap his jaws shut.

There was a gentle shift in the wind right before his lungs began to burn. He wheezed in agony as his body lifted into the air, as if by invisible strings. God, it felt as if his throat was being squeezed closed.

He stared wildly at the ground, where the Toad Girl who had retrieved him from the dungeon stood. The gale he'd felt in the dungeon made sense now.

"Thank you, Mira." Mistress Black was on her feet now. Her voice rasped, and she clutched at her chest as she staggered over to the Grey Witch. "Hold him tight." She kept walking, slowly, deliberately toward Elijah.

She stopped in front of him, watching him choke, watching death approach with cold satisfaction. "I want to say I loved you once. But we both know I'm incapable of loving. Good-bye, Elijah."

She flicked her wrist and walked away.

Mira smiled, closed her fingers into fists. Elijah thought his lungs would burst as every drop of air was squeezed out of them.

It was ironic, actually. So many times in his life, he'd felt like a man drowning. Drowning in debt, worries, fears. Only this went beyond a mere sensation. This was real, clawing death, come to claim him at last.

Only, he no longer welcomed it. Hadn't ever since he'd first laid eyes upon Verika. He didn't want to die, he realized, not one bit. He had so much to live for, someone to live for. He had a sense of purpose now, the flickering of fragile embers of hope that would soon be snuffed out.

He struggled against the invisible hands that gripped his throat, against the fingers squeezing tighter and tighter.

Shadows ringed his vision, wispy splotches that grew larger and larger as his eyes began to close, his head lag.

Get away from my mate!

The air suddenly returned to his lungs in one violent whoosh as he was released and dropped to the ground. His body screamed for oxygen. The cool night air chapped his throat as it went down. He couldn't drink it fast enough, having just enough presence of mind left to maintain his wolf shape.

A red muzzle nudged him gently, whined. *Are you all right?* Verika asked through their bond.

Yeah, he thought back tiredly. *I am now.*

He glanced up. The Grey Witch had been thrown clear across the field and now lay in an unmoving slump.

Did you…? he asked.

Yes, Verika said. *I couldn't very well let her choke the life out of you.*

Thank God for that.

A scream of fury interrupted their conversation. Mistress Black looked as if she were about to come unglued. With her face bright red, she pointed an accusing finger at Verika. "You are a disgrace to our kind! Helping a lowlife like him—"

Verika growled and stepped in front of her recovering mate. *I'd be very careful with my next words, if I were you,* she said to Mistress Black, who seemed unfazed a werewolf was talking inside of her head. *That is my mate you're dissing.*

Mistress Black cast the knife aside, jerked up her sleeves. "I should've ditched metal for magic a long time ago. Time to finish this."

Finally, something we can agree on.

Mistress Black didn't wait for her to finish talking before lashing out with an awesome display of power.

But Verika was ready. She met the onslaught head on, sending out a force of magic the likes of which the Underworld had never seen. Her power collided with Mistress Black's, making the older witch grit her teeth and causing her heels to slide back a bit in the dirt.

The battle around them stilled, the survivors looking on in awe. Flashes of deep green and bright violet lit up the clearing as the magic sizzled and sparked.

The two witches were evenly matched. When one would start to gain ground, the other would push them back.

Verika realized her mistake when her foe began to gain too much ground. The entire battle, she'd been using her magic to thwart enemy attacks—to deflect, to defend. She hadn't realized how quickly she'd depleted her magical stores until she tried summoning more and there was none.

Panic sent her heart to racing even faster.

What's wrong? Elijah noticed the subtle change in her adrenaline.

My magic…I'm running out of it. She'd heard of witches and warlocks reaching the bottom of their magical wells, as it were, though most experienced ones knew when to draw back and how to conserve so they never did. But although experienced in general magic she may be, she hadn't been a Black Witch long enough for the thought to even cross her mind. Which made her feel stupid and angry at her misjudgment. That one silly mistake might just cost them their victory. And if it did, then she truly would be the world's most despised witch.

So much rode on her shoulders now, so many precious lives counting on her to save them. She couldn't, wouldn't let them down.

Lend me your strength, Elijah, she said, her voice strained.

How, love? Tell me how.

Just send your love, your strength, to me through our bond. Channel it and focus.

He did as she asked, his body drawing still. At first it felt like a trickle, a little tickling of power so strong she hadn't felt the likes of it before. When that trickle soon gave way to a mighty flood, she nearly wept with joy.

She could feel him, feel the combined force of their love. So strong, so pure, so endless. Using it, she threaded that power into her own, weaving an attack surer and stronger than anything she could have conjured on her own.

Mistress Black's power began to wane, driven back by

the pure, raw magic flowing from Verika.

"No!" Mistress Black screamed, her features drawn from fatigue. "I cannot—will not—lose!" She glanced about. "Brothers and sisters of the Order, lend me your power!"

They looked at one another, shifting nervously, murmuring and shaking their heads.

All but one.

Toad Girl stepped forward, her face serious. "What do you require of me, Mistress?"

"Cut my arm. Hurry, you stupid girl!"

The woman grabbed the blade Mistress Black had dropped and drew a thin slice across Mistress Black's upper arm. She looked at her leader, waiting.

"Now drive that dagger into your neck."

Verika's heart leapt to her throat. Blood Magic. Mistress Black was calling upon Blood Magic. She knew what would happen next, what Mistress Black would require of the girl. And prayed to God she wasn't so foolish as to follow through.

The woman never even flinched. "As you wish, Mistress." She raised the blade and drove it straight into her neck. Blood burst around the wound, and her mouth flew open in shock as she shuddered and then collapsed. Her body continued to quiver as the life drained out of her, her eyes at last glazing over as she drew still.

A gale picked up, as if the wind itself were angry it had lost a Grey Witch. A storm crackled and growled overhead.

Mistress Black threw her head back and shouted into

the tempest. "God of the dead and all the horrors in between life and death, I call upon your power! Heed my sacrifice to you, oh great lord of shadows, and grant me the power which I so desperately need!"

There was a whip of lightning, a roar of thunder. Then Mistress Black began to glow faint red. Shimmering bloodred lines oozed out of her fingers, crawling toward Verika.

What is she doing? What's happening? Elijah demanded.

She's going to drain my magic, Verika whispered. She watched in horror as the red worm-like threads inched closer.

Let go of me, Elijah! Run away.

No.

You don't understand, love. When she takes my magic, it'll affect you too while you're lending me your strength. It's the gift and curse of our mating bond. The pain will be unimaginable. I couldn't bear to see you hurt, to know I was the cause of it.

And I'll never live with myself if I walk away.

Please, Elijah!

I'm not abandoning you!

The threads were almost to her, a mere few inches away from latching onto her like the parasites they were and draining her dry of what made her a witch.

With ferocity, she realized she couldn't let that happen, wouldn't let this selfish woman take away anything else that belonged to her. She'd stolen the tender, happy moments of a first love, had turned them into a waking nightmare. That was unforgiveable.

She had to fight, had to hold on and drive her back if she could.

If she could.

She would sure as hell try.

Throwing herself into her power, she pushed farther and deeper. A shield of sparkling purple magic formed in front of her, and the Blood Magic hissed and coiled, striking the shield with whip-like tentacles, trying to break through. Verika growled, straining to keep the shield from breaking.

Farther. Deeper. Must go deeper. Need more power.

A white speck of light grew in her vision, inside her mind's eye.

Verika! Verika, wait! Elijah cried, until his voice was no more than a dull echo inside her head.

Still she pushed herself, refusing to give Mistress Black another inch.

The white spot in her mind grew until there was nothing but blinding white light.

At first Verika didn't realize where she was. She stood in her human form, donning the amulet, which glittered and sparkled in the bright light, and clothed in a simple, sleeveless white dress that ended just above her knees. Not one of her favorite colors. White tended to wash her out, make her appear paler.

But now she didn't mind the color so much. It felt clean and pure, like the light she walked through. White all around. It started to dim—that, or her eyes had started to adjust to its brightness. Something spongy and soft tickled her bare feet. Grass, lots of it. Green as an emerald.

She looked up, and the endless sea of white had given way to a hill topped by a single tree with fiery red leaves. Its curling branches shimmied in the breeze blowing off the crystalline sea just beyond the hill, its waters so blue that it melted into the sky. Little puffs of clouds lazily rolled along overhead, past a big, bold sun.

She squinted, used a hand to shield her eyes.

"Hello, daughter."

Her breath caught.

She knew that voice, had heard it when she was a little girl. Still occasionally heard it in fragments of memories.

She looked around—and stilled.

A lone figure stood on top of the hill, turned toward her as if waiting. Her red hair rose and fell in the breeze; the long gown of cream-colored chiffon and silk billowed around her. She stood just under the tree, but no shade dappled her pale skin.

That's when Verika realized it. There were no shadows here. She looked down at her feet, all around where she stood. No shadow.

Huh.

"Darkness cannot exist here in any form."

She looked up.

The woman beckoned her forward, so forward she went on trembling legs.

Her eyes stung with tears as she crested the hill, took in a face that so closely resembled her own. "Hello, Mother."

"Call me Moira."

"I can barely remember you."

"Part of the spell used to seal away your powers." She held open her arms. "Hi, baby girl."

Suddenly, it didn't matter that she'd left when she was a kid, that Verika had resented her and loved her on and off ever since. All the burning anger and stinging betrayal melted away as she went to her mother and hugged her.

She felt solid, warm. Real.

"Is this happening?" Verika asked after a long while, pulling back. "Is it really you?"

"It is, darling."

"Where are we?"

"Where do you think?"

"Heaven, I'm guessing."

"Close. This is the in-between, a place between life and death where the living and the dead can meet."

"So I'm not dead?"

"No, dearest. Not for a long while. But you must stop her."

"Mistress Black."

"Yes." She lifted the amulet. "There is another reason I created this."

Moira touched her daughter's temple. An image popped into Verika's mind, a set of instructions that left her tongue-tied in wonder. "I see," Verika murmured. "Am I strong enough? Can I do that?"

"Yes, baby girl, and so much more. I always knew you were a gifted witch. And I couldn't be more proud of you. Me and your father both."

"My father?"

"Yes, baby. Know that we'll always be watching over you, and that we'll be waiting for you when it's your turn to cross."

Verika's eyes burned as she realized this was good-bye. "But I want to stay with you."

"Oh, dearheart." Her mother took her into her arms and hugged her fiercely. "Part of me wishes you could because we miss you so much. But I also know if you stay you'd miss out on a wondrous life. We can't take that away from you, even if it was our deepest wish."

"Tell Dad I love him."

"I will, baby. I promise."

They hugged for a long time, Verika trying to memorize the scent of flowers and earth. Her mother had loved working in the garden, had hummed pretty tunes as she tilled and dug and watered in her wide-brimmed floppy hat. It was one of the few things she could remember: playing in the grass while her mother tended to her beloved flowers.

"You must go now." Moira reluctantly pulled back.

"I don't know the way back. I don't even know how I got here."

"You were able to come here because your power is linked to this realm, in a way, as Black Magic is the power of death. Not darkness," she amended as a shadow passed over Verika's face. "Death is a very natural part of life. There is nothing destructive or evil about it. It just is."

"So how do I return?"

"Through here. With a leap of faith." She took her daughter to the hillside, where a bluff rose up out of the deep blue.

"I have to jump?"

"Yes."

"What if I drown?"

"You won't. Trust me."

Verika bit her lip, deliberated. Looked at her mother one last time. "All right." She squeezed her again, pressed a kiss to her cheek. "I love you, Momma."

"I love you too, sweetheart. And I couldn't be more proud of you, your father and me both."

Verika smiled as tears ran down her face. Swiping at them, she turned, forced herself not to look back for fear she'd lose her nerve and decide to stay.

She had a mate to get back to, a battle to win.

So she jumped.

Verika slammed back into the present, no longer a wolf but a human woman. The white dress she'd worn in the other realm had come with her, the billowy skirt whipping around her thighs, her hair a wild tangle of red about her fearsome face.

The tentacles of Blood Magic continued to beat against the magical barrier Verika had thrown up, its shimmering, translucent green surface cracking under the pressure like glass. The cracks spiderwebbed across the globe surrounding her and Elijah, spreading faster and faster.

Elijah Changed back into a man, his face paler from fear leaching the color from it. Questions were written all over his face, but he knew better than to distract his mate in a time like this.

She slowly turned her head to him, the look of a warrior on her face. "Do you trust me?" she asked, her voice strong and sure.

"Yes," he said without hesitation, grasping one of her hands. "With my life."

She nodded once and turned back to Mistress Black. "I'm taking the shield down. When I do, I want you to close your eyes."

"What?"

"One…two…three!"

The shield shattered with nary a flick of her finger, and the barbs of Blood Magic surged forward.

Then the night exploded with white light.

Elijah gritted his teeth, throwing up his free hand to shield his eyes from the blinding glow emanating from Verika's amulet. It blazed hot and bright as the sun, burning up the strands of Blood Magic and filling the entire clearing with white light.

The gathered crowd slinked back in fear. Mistress Black hissed and cursed as the light approached her. "What's happening? What sort of sorcery is this?"

"Ties that bind, ties of blood, return this ancient soul of old to the place she is meant to rest." Verika's voice boomed in the clearing, seeming to echo off the trees, the sky.

Storm clouds raged and lightning flashed as the light strengthened, enveloping Mistress Black. "What…?" Her high-pitched shriek was all that could be heard as she threw her head back, her spine bowing as her soul was literally pulled out of her. The human host she'd occupied collapsed first to her knees and then pitched face-first into the dirt as the light receded, dragging the screaming, clawing soul along with it.

Mistress Black's soul, a gray ghost of her human shell, cast spells and curses alike, trying to break free as the light dragged her backward across the ground. Faster and faster it went, until she was sucked up in the crystal. Then the light winked out entirely, enveloping the lawn in darkness once more.

The tempest broke, the storm clouds dissipating as quickly as they'd come. The gale steadied and stopped, and all that was left was heavy silence.

Verika felt the weight of two hundred pairs of eyes on her, but all she could do was stare at the crystal in her hand. It no longer sparkled with magic. Its faceted surface was dull as a rock, leaving no hint as to the immense power locked within.

Darkness spawned by exhaustion—physical, mental, and magical—danced along her vision, but she fought it. She had to be sure.

She glanced up, where Mistress Black's host lay unconscious upon the ground, and then back again at the crystal. A half laugh, half sob bubbled up, and her knees shook. "It's over. It is done."

"Verika?"

She looked up at Elijah, smiling and crying, her whole body shaking with the flood of emotions rolling through her. "We won. We won, Elijah."

She took a step forward, just in time to collapse into

his waiting arms and tumble into darkness.

The battle was over and done after that. The enemy forces that remained quickly surrendered, their leader gone, the spell to resurrect Mistress Black thwarted.

Verika hadn't gone under long. Fifteen minutes, tops, though she'd wanted to sleep far longer. It was as if a part of her knew she was still needed by her friends, and thus wouldn't allow her to rest just yet.

She lay on the field, under the open sky. Elijah had knelt beside her the entire time, stroking her hair, pressing kisses to her damp forehead. Someone had given him a jacket, pants. His feet remained bare and caked in blood and dirt.

He explained everything to her when she awoke, after ensuring she had water and was treated by a Blue Warlock for injuries, magical and physical.

"She's exhausted her magical well, as it were." The warlock stood. "But she'll be fine in a few days, with plenty of rest. And she's not to use her magic, not even for little things. You hear?"

"Yes, sir. I'll make sure she doesn't."

After the doctor left to tend to the injured, Elijah sat by Verika, waiting for an explanation.

She sat up slowly, massaged her temples as she gathered her thoughts. It felt as if someone had put her brain through a meat grinder and had stomped and pressed on every bone and muscle in her body. "I'm sorry for frightening you."

"That's an understatement."

Verika's hands shook in her lap as she recalled what happened, and she stared at the pendant in wonder, not touching it, not quite. "I heard her, Elijah."

"Who, baby?"

"My mother. She spoke to me, inside here." A hand pressed to her heart. "And here." The same hand reached up to touch her head. "She told me what the true purpose of the crystal was, of the vision she'd had before creating it. My mother was prophetic. She knew of a great evil that would overshadow the world—unless I stopped it. Unless we stopped it together." She squeezed his hand.

"I thought I'd lost you. It seemed like I did for a moment. I...I couldn't feel you inside our bond."

"I believe I crossed over to the other side briefly, at least, in astral form. Similar to dream walking, only my powers of death allowed me to cross over to the plane of the dead."

"You died?"

"No, no, don't freak out. My astral form, my soul if you will, simply left my body for a short while because my mother called to me through the power of the crystal."

"Your soul 'simply left your body,' my ass." He barked a laugh. "You say it so casually, as if it were nothing. And you expect me not to freak out?"

"I'm sorry. I know this is a lot to take in. It's a lot for me too. I didn't know Black Witches had this ability. I mean, I'd read about it, in old stories. Black Witches and Warlocks tend to stay out of the media due to the stigma tied to our magic, so not much is known about the extent of our powers."

"You should write a book."

She smiled. "Yes, maybe."

"So you were able to rip Mistress Black's soul out of that poor witch"—he shuddered—"and bind her soul inside that crystal?" He pointed doubtfully to it.

"Yes. It's a soul gem. It must have cost my mother a great deal to create it." She ran her thumb over the smooth surface thoughtfully. "Blood calls to blood…"

"What?"

"It's why I was able to trap her. We share the same blood."

"So you used Blood Magic?"

"No, not literally. A form of ancient magic rooted in blood ties. A purer branch of Blood Magic, before it was corrupted by years of witches bastardizing it for their personal gain."

Elijah shook his head in wonder. "There's clearly a lot I don't understand about magic."

"You did all right out there, by the way. Given all the magic that was flying around."

"For you, I have to be brave. I want to be." He took her hand. She flipped his hand palm-up, skidded her fingertips over his rough palm.

"I…I don't think I would have been able to come back to this world if your presence hadn't been in my mind to ground me. You saved me."

"We saved each other." He kissed her tenderly.

She leaned into him, closed her eyes, and relished his strength, the surety of his belief in her, in them. "Where are the others? Is everyone else all right?"

He pressed his lips together. "There were casualties. A lot of blood was spilled tonight. Even more were injured."

"I should help in any way I can." She started to rise, but Elijah pressed her back down.

"You good to move? Maybe you should take it—"

"Don't you dare tell me to take it easy, Elijah Marshal Johnson. I'm a grown woman, and I can handle a little pain. This war started partly because of me. I need to see it through to the very end."

He couldn't argue with her, knew doing so would only anger her more. She'd just do whatever she damn well pleased, anyway. So he helped her up, made sure to support her weight as he led her out to the bloodied field.

"How were you able to turn back, to a human that is, before dawn?" he asked. "Most wolves can't during their first Change."

"I don't know. I suppose the crystal did that when I came back from the other world. My human body was needed, not the wolf's."

They paused by a fire, where a figure burned at its heart. Verika's eyes skimmed over a proud nose, hair the color of flame.

Mistress Black's real body, she realized. Wise, she thought. Burn the vessel so there would never be a chance for the soul to return. That is, if it ever escaped. Which she suspected, if her mother had anything to do with it, would never happen.

Still, she closed her eyes and said a quick prayer for Mistress Black's soul. She had been good at one time,

Verika was sure. But she'd let hardship, oppression, and suffering eat away at that goodness until there was only bitterness and hatred. And it had destroyed her.

"What are you doing?" Elijah murmured.

"Nothing." Verika gazed pensively at the fire. "Just thinking."

Did she regret having to kill her? No. She had still done so many wicked things. The atrocities she'd done to her mate she would never forgive. For those evils alone, Mistress Black deserved her fate.

Karma always wins, she thought, as Satine had believed. She wasn't sure where she stood on that until now. That everything you reap comes back to you eventually in some form or another. Now, she thought her eccentric teacher might have been right.

Unable to stand the stench of burning flesh, they walked away, toward the huge, dark house. Gage stood nearby, Danica safe at his side and seemingly without a scratch save for a bruise on her forehead. Gage spoke with a vampire, who nodded and strode off as Elijah and Verika approached.

"There's the hero of the hour." Danica walked up to her and kissed both cheeks. "We owe you our lives, all of us."

Verika blushed, not used to the praise. Danica was the first person to say thank-you. Verika had noticed, upon walking through the field, that people for the most part stayed clear of her. Some gazed in awe, others in fear. She shouldered their stares with practiced ease, wondering whether maybe this was her fate for the rest of her life. She may be a hero, maybe was a savior even, but the Underworld still had a long way to go before the stigma associated with Black Magic was lifted. It had been taught to fear it for so long that it would take a hundred acts of goodness to lift the shroud of hatred over the dark house of magic.

Gage hugged Verika next, thanking her in kind, and then hugged his brother. "How's the baby?" Verika asked, looking with concern at Danica's stomach.

"Fine." Danica rubbed a hand over her slight bump. "I knew the Change wouldn't hurt it, as the child is a pure-bred werewolf, and Gage pulled me out of the battle before I could see much action."

Verika bit her lip. It probably wasn't her place to ask, but she was curious. "Why did you do it? Why join the fight at all in your…?" Her eyes ran over Danica's belly once more.

Danica flushed. Her hands balled into fists. "I was scared—terrified, even—for my baby. But while I may soon be a mother, right now I'm a queen of wolves. And a queen protects her pack, her citizens, at all costs."

Gage rested a hand on her back, gazing at her with understanding and adoration. "Spoken like a true queen." He kissed her forehead, and she winced.

"So what's the bruise from?" Elijah pointed.

Danica rolled her eyes. "Me being clumsy after Changing back into a human. I tripped and banged my head on a rock. How lame is that?"

Verika bit back a laugh. "You should make up some grand battle story as to how you got it."

"Right?"

Their banter was quiet, the humor in it subdued by the heavy atmosphere of death all around them. Too many lives had been needlessly lost tonight to warrant much cheer.

Some more talk was exchanged, about numbers lost, about what happened next. The DPI had been called and were on their way to apprehend those in association with the Order of the Sun, and the leaders of every race in the Underworld were on their way as well.

"In other words"—Elijah looked around—"this place is about to turn into a circus."

"We should leave," Verika said. "We're still some of the Underworld's most wanted to the DPI."

"She's right." Gage grimaced. "I have some legal details to work out before the warrants out for your arrest are lifted. You should leave before they get here, lay low until I send for you."

Elijah gazed thoughtfully at the house, his eyes full of pain, hate. Regret. "There's one more thing…" he murmured, looking at Gage. "The house clear?"

"Yes. We've searched every room, released any prisoners she'd been holding."

Verika shivered as images of the dungeon flashed through her head. She could only imagine what it was like being held captive by that madwoman.

"Good." Elijah walked forward, toward the bonfire, and retrieved a large stick. Flames licked its end as he marched right back to the house, punched a hole through one of the windows, and tossed the burning stick inside.

Curtains caught fire first, and then furniture, the fire crackling and eating its way through the room.

Water witches and warlocks rushed forward to extinguish the flames, but Gage held out a hand. "No," he commanded. "Bring more fire. Bring every Red Witch and Warlock we have at our disposal."

As the highest commanding officer there, no one disputed him. They respected his command, his personal guards there to support him should anyone try otherwise. Before long, the entire house was ablaze, its glow staining the sky orange.

Verika and Elijah stared, watching years of darkness and pain burn away.

"I had a promise to keep," Elijah said quietly. He never took his gaze off the house. "I think it's time to leave this all behind me, in the past where it belongs."

She went to him, and he opened his arms. "We should leave," she murmured.

"We will. One more minute, I promise."

They hugged each other, Verika resting her head against his chest so she could listen to his heartbeat. Elijah pressed a kiss to her head, took in her smell and the amber light of the new dawn lightening the sky on the horizon. Bloody and sweating, they held each other and watched the world burn until the sirens came, and they at last vanished into the woods.

CHAPTER TWENTY-NINE

THE NIGHT OF ASH AND BLOOD. THAT'S WHAT THE Underworld media had called the fight between the Order of the Sun and the wolves and their comrades.

The humans' media merely thought some drunken heiress had thrown a lavish party and burned down her home, tragically perishing in the fire herself.

If only it were that simple, Gage thought, straightening his black tie once more and glancing outside. Storm clouds, heavy and purple with unshed rain, loomed over Castle Crescent. The private company his secretary had hired to put on the memorial service had been prepared, throwing up a sturdy canopy as soon as the forecast had turned dour.

His stomach twisted into knots, and he swallowed hard to shove spit past the lump that had lodged itself in the pit of his throat. He hadn't felt this nervous to speak before a crowd since he'd given his first Alpha speech back in Moonstruck. Yet knowing he was about to face all the grieving families of those slain but a week ago made him want to crawl into a hole. He would have to look into the accusing eyes and know that he was the real reason they had lost someone they loved.

Why their father would never tuck them into bed again.

Why their spouse would never be there to warm their sheets.

Why their child would be missing during holiday gatherings.

Those were the harsh realities he'd struggled to come to terms with throughout the long, dreary week since so much blood had been spilled on Mistress Black's lawn.

So much violence, so much death. He kept racking his brain, trying to come up with some way it could all have been prevented. And yet he knew that final confrontation had been inevitable.

Danica, Alara, Verika, even Elijah, despite all his faults… They had been worth the price, hadn't they? Slaying an evil that would have likely enslaved the world had been worth so many lives.

Hadn't it?

A soft knock came at the door.

Gage looked up. His heart swelled with joy.

Danica stood there, her belly swollen, emphasized by the elegant, empire-waisted black gown she wore. Long sleeves of inky velvet coated her arms, and the simple diamond studs he'd given to her because he'd felt like spoiling her dotted her ears. Her long golden hair had been swept up into a regal coif. A delicate crown of nickel-plated moons accented by pearly stars rested atop her head.

Her green eyes shone, a knowing smile on her pink lips. Silently, she stepped inside and closed the door before she crossed the room to her husband and mate. Her lithe pale hands, the nails of which had been painted a faint coral color that complemented her creamy skin tone well, slipped through his arms, and she rested her head against his shoulder.

They both stared at their reflection in the mirror hanging in his private study.

"You are so beautiful," Gage murmured, taking her hand and kissing it. "How are you feeling?"

"Tired. And my feet hurt. And my boobs hate bras right now." She smiled softly. "But I'll manage."

He kissed her lightly on the lips, partly because he didn't want to spoil her makeup and in part holding himself back. If he didn't, he'd have her atop the desk, legs spread wide, pants down by his ankles. Though he knew she felt more self-conscious than ever about her appearance, the sight of her belly, heavy with his baby, made her all the more irresistible to him. He nuzzled her neck, inhaled her scent of roses. He loved that his sheets smelled like her now every time he lay down. "You're gorgeous."

"And you look troubled. Gonna tell me what's going on?"

Gage sighed, methodically running his fingertips up and down her spine as he thought. "I feel so guilty."

"Why?"

"Like all the death, all the loss…it's my fault. I am their king. I commanded them to come to my aid, and they did.

And many of them paid dearly for it."

"First of all, I know you never would have exercised the Alpha's Right on anyone. You'd never command someone to come and help. They made that choice of their own free will."

"I know, but—"

"But hear me out." She cupped his face with her hands, holding his gaze with hers. "You feel guilty because you like to take the world's hurt and pile it on your own shoulders, as if doing so will ease the burden of loss for other people. You are kind, Gage. Too kind at times, perhaps. It's both your greatest strength and your greatest fault. You cannot blame yourself for something you had no control over whatsoever. Those men and women, while I also feel and grieve their losses, came to your aid because they respected you as their leader and king. They thought enough of you to lay down their lives to help you. They believed in something—in someone, you—so strongly that they were willing to risk everything for it. So before you blame yourself, please give them more credit. They acted out of loyalty to their crown, and their kin. To treat their deaths as anything but a fierce act of bravery would dishonor their memories. Mourn them. Honor them. That is the only way."

Gage stood there, dumbstruck. The clock on the wall ticked away the silent seconds as his mate searched his gaze.

"Well, say something." She smiled slightly.

He blinked, shook his head, and kissed her. "You're incredible, you know that? The kind of queen every king wishes he had."

"Well, then it's a good thing you have me." She grinned.

"Damn straight." He leaned in for another kiss, when a knock came at the door.

"Sire," someone said from the other side, "it's almost time for the ceremony to start."

"Thank you," he called. With a heavy-hearted sigh and a stomach that was full of butterflies, he leaned his forehead against his mate's. His eyes fluttered closed, as did hers.

He swore in quiet moments like these their hearts beat as one. He could feel their collective pulse, hear the gentle swoosh of their breathing as it synchronized.

As one. Now and forever.

Taking her hand, he started toward the door. She held tight, not saying anything. She didn't need to. Her grasp alone was enough.

It assured him she was there for him, and he for her, however long their lives may be.

And, because of the bravery of those fallen souls, that appeared to be for a while longer yet.

The memorial was beautiful. Gage had deviated from his speech some once he got going, his voice thick and raw with emotion. The sounds of sniffling had filled the air, breaking up the din of the light rain showering the countryside.

Mist rose off the ground. Everything had a bluish tint thanks to the relentless cloud cover, which made the trees and hills look sleepy and somber.

As people started to file out of the tent and into the castle for the banquet prepared to honor the fallen heroes, Gage swung by his office to check his appearance and scan over his next speech.

A soft knock came at the open door. Verika stood there, dressed in a simple black dress. Elijah wasn't with her, though Gage could sense his presence lingering in the hallway.

"Eli," Gage called tiredly, "you can come in, too. Don't be afraid."

Gage heard the sharp intake of breath. A moment later, Elijah joined them, donning a black button-down and black slacks. His hair had been slicked back with a bit of gel, and he'd shaved. The hollows of his face still looked too steep, the blue under his eyes a bit too pronounced. But it had only been one week since they fought Mistress Black. It would take time for him to heal. It would take time for all of them to heal.

Gage smiled at them. "Glad you could make it today."

"We wouldn't miss it," Elijah said gruffly, slinging a protective arm around Verika's shoulders as she shivered and hugged herself.

Gage's eyes softened in sympathy. He knew that grave look, saw the deep slope of her shoulders—Eli's too.

They both felt guilty.

What broke his heart the most was the fact he knew he couldn't help them. That was something they would have to work out for themselves. Someday they would realize the Night of Blood and Ash was not because of them but because of one selfish woman's insatiable greed for power. Her quest—to create a world where paranormals could live free from fear of persecution—might have started out with a nobler purpose once upon a time. When Mistress Black still had a soul, if she ever had one. He wondered from time to time whether the spell she'd used to gain power, whether her leaching off the souls of the innocent, had somehow warped her mind and heart. Whether, perhaps, deep, deep down, there had been some pure part of her worth saving.

He shook his head. Useless thoughts that didn't hold any meaning other than making him question their choices. And if there was one thing he hated, it was negative what-ifs. As a king, he couldn't afford to let himself get down in the dumps with dark thoughts. There was simply too much to do. Sometimes he jokingly said he was married to every Alpha, queen, Beta, Omega, pup, and everyone in between within the werewolf nation. Only it wasn't a joke. He wasn't just an Alpha anymore—he was *the* Alpha, the leader they all looked up to.

For protection, for guidance. He had an example to set.

Starting with righting some very epic wrongs.

He swiped a manila folder off his desk, handed it to Verika. "Your official pardons."

"I could kiss you right now." Verika stared reverently at the folder. "Only, I won't. That would be awkward," she quickly amended, glancing between the two brothers.

Elijah suppressed a smile, though gold briefly flashed through his eyes.

They each carefully removed their documents. His signature had barely had time to dry before he'd stuffed them into the folders. "So the High Council wiped our slates clean? No treason, no obstructing evidence, not even a Class A misdemeanor for practicing illegal magic?" Verika asked, her voice a bit high pitched from nerves.

"Nope. In exchange for your services in helping bring down one of the most dangerous witches to have ever lived, and basically saving the Underworld in doing so, the Council has decided to drop everything against you."

"Everything?" Elijah held his brother's gaze in question.

Gage smiled. "Yes, Eli. Everything. You're officially free."

The air left Elijah's massive frame in such a whoosh that it made several of the papers on Gage's desk take flight. Much to his disgruntlement—sorting papers was one of his least favorite things to do, but another necessary evil of being king—but he wasn't angry for long.

Elijah swayed, stumbled, his face heavy with emotion. Tears slicked his eyes, and he desperately clung to Verika as she steadied him. "I'm free," Elijah breathed, as if still unable to believe it. "I'm free." His knees buckled, and down to the floor he went. Verika went with him, rubbing his back in soothing strokes as tears streamed silently down his face. The paper shook in his hand, and he couldn't seem to take his eyes off it.

Gage went over to him and knelt, placed a hand on his shoulder and squeezed. "Yes, brother. You're free. We all are. No more running, no more looking over your shoulder. The Council destroyed your criminal record. You can start over now."

"Thank you," he at last blubbered, the words barely intelligible because his voice was so raw.

"No thanks needed. I'm glad to help." Gage stood, offered his hand. "Speaking of starting over...how about we do too? Starting with you—and Verika, of course—staying for dinner tonight?"

Elijah tore his eyes off the paper to stare at Gage's hand. He grasped it. "Yeah, I'd like that."

CHAPTER THIRTY

Two months later on Thanksgiving Day

VERIKA DIDN'T REALIZE HOW QUIET THE TINY, SECLUDED graveyard was until Elijah killed the engine. The silence of the surrounding woods immediately enveloped them. Not even the wind stirred on this chilly November morning.

Verika sat in the passenger seat, watching her breath fog the glass. Her body felt heavy, and she wasn't entirely sure why. There was the sting of grief, the ache of longing, the stab of loss.

And yet, underneath it all, she felt truly, deeply thankful.

Thankful she now knew what had happened to her parents, where they were. It had taken awhile to track down their graves, but she'd wanted to come to Florida to visit them as soon as she'd found out where they were buried.

Finally, she could lay to rest all the hurt she'd carried all these years over them supposedly abandoning her. They had wanted her, had loved her with all their hearts. Her mother's journal had proved that much.

So why did she still feel so guilty? Why was it suddenly impossible to get out of the car?

Rough, callused fingers rubbed her arm through her sweater. "You okay?" Elijah murmured, brows stooped in concern.

Verika took a deep breath, let it out. Turned her head to face her mate. "Yeah." She nodded. "Let's do this. It's not going to get any easier just sitting here."

A gentle squeeze was his response before they both silently got out of the car. Verika never heard the car doors lock as they trekked up the hill. Out here, in the boondocks of the deep South, there wasn't a soul for miles. The last farmhouse she'd seen had been over five miles back. She was kind of surprised no one else was out here. Holidays tended to pull people to graveyards, to remind them of people loved and lost. People who they weren't able to enjoy the holidays with anymore. Even the grass looked gray, though a few green patches remained here and there. Stubbornly clinging to life despite winter's approach.

Some of the heaviness in Verika's footsteps faded the farther they climbed. She kept her hands clasped in front of her because she didn't know what else to do with them. They felt sweaty inside her leather gloves, but she didn't dare pull them off. It was far too cold out for that. She'd have to wait until they got back into the car.

Elijah kept a hand on the small of her back the whole

way. Not so much pushing her toward the large headstone beneath the barren, grand oak tree so much as to silently remind her he was there, ready to catch her should her knees give out.

Curiously, the closer they drew to the gravestone, the stronger, surer she felt.

Her eyes read over the names etched into the gunmetal gray marble as soon as she was close enough to read them.

Moira Elizabeth Stone
Loving Mother and Wife
Michael Jason Stone
Doting Husband and Father

She didn't remember stopping before the grave, only vaguely registered how her heart skipped a beat, how her breath caught.

Her eyes slowly raked over the names again.

Elijah had let go of her, standing but two feet behind her, hands stuffed in his pressed black pants pockets. She could feel his concern, his strength through their bond. But he also knew she needed to do this on her own. Needed space to process the gamut of emotions tumbling through her.

Verika reached out, reverently ran her palm over the crown of the cold headstone. Her parents' final resting place seemed so plain, so ordinary, considering the life they'd lived. Especially her mother.

Verika's hero. A woman who'd done everything she could, sacrificed everything she had, so that her daughter might grow up in a normal world.

Or, well, as normal as being a witch could get. If anything, her mother's binding spell had made life more difficult for Verika in the witching community. Affinity-less witches tended to stick out like sore thumbs. The binding had made her a freak anyway. She'd been shunned regardless of her mother's good intentions. And they had been good. That much Verika was certain of.

So, despite the flawed logic in her plan, her mother's heart had been in the right place. And for that, Verika couldn't fault her.

For that reason alone, Verika could forgive her for not being there. For missing every birthday, every heartache, every triumph. Because, in a way, deep, deep, deep down inside, Verika knew her mother was still with her. That she'd never left, that she'd simply bottled her love in the form of the crystal Verika wore around her neck now.

A symbol of everlasting love that death could never take away.

Verika knelt in the soft, dew-damp grass. The sun had broken the horizon only fifteen minutes ago, its golden rays streaking the lightening indigo sky and cascading over the graves, trees, and rolling grasses of the surrounding meadow.

The grass tickled her stockinged legs as she nestled a bouquet of white roses at the base of the gravestone.

Her voice shook when she spoke; her heart fluttered in her chest. "Hi, Mom, Dad," she whispered after a pause heavy with unspoken words. Though she'd been saying Mom and Dad to her foster family, she'd always known in the back of her mind that it was a lie. A good one, because it meant she was lucky enough to have found a family to call her own. But a lie all the same.

In a way, even a tiny bit, saying Mom and Dad to people she knew weren't really her birth parents stung. Because it reminded her she hadn't been good enough to warrant keeping, hadn't been worth fighting for.

But she had. Her mother had sacrificed so much to save her. She realized that now, and the peace and joy that brought her lit up her soul. But there were still things to be said, as close to her parents' faces as she would ever get in this lifetime.

It took her a moment to collect her thoughts, gather her courage. "I don't know what to say, not really." Her voice was barely audible, even to her own ears, though she felt her lips moving. An acute sense of shyness nearly rendered her mute. Were it not for Elijah's warm hand on her shoulder, followed by a comforting squeeze, she might not have found her voice again.

"I've always wanted to meet you. Always wondered when I was a child, in my dreams, my nightmares, my hopes, what you were like. Why you aba...why you left." She wet her lips. "I thought it was because you didn't love me or want me. You found out what I truly was and were so disgusted you sealed away my powers in the hope of protecting the interests of the Underworld and mankind alike. There are many more reasons than that, but those were the most predominant ones in my mind. A million reasons that, I see now, could not be farther from the truth. You did love me. Loved me so much you died trying to protect me. Not just from myself, but mostly from those who sought to do me harm. And you know what? It worked. I'm safe." Tears started to fall as her voice broke on a sob. "I'm safe, Momma. Daddy. My mate is safe. The whole damn world is safe because you, Momma, loved me enough to sacrifice your life to help me. I just wanted you to know that, both of you. To know that I am safe, and I am loved, and…and…I want you to know everything is going to be all right now. I'm going to be all right now. So don't worry about me. You've done enough. More than enough. Go rest in peace now. Your baby girl is going to be just fine."

She paused right as she was about to stand and, almost as an afterthought, placed two fingers to her lips, pressed a kiss there. She then touched those same fingertips first to her mother's name, and then slid them down over her father's. Her fingers lingered against the cool stone, not quite ready to release. She didn't want to walk away but knew she had to.

When at last she stood, Elijah had to help her up because her legs were too wobbly to hold her. He looped an arm around her back, let her stand there as long as she wanted. The sun had fully crested the horizon by the time she was ready to leave. Even then it took Elijah's gentle prodding to get her going.

"We should hit the road," he murmured, wrapping his arms around her shoulders and pulling her close. His warmth knocked away the early morning chill; his lips nuzzled her ear, her neck. Chills of a different sort skittered through her. "Our flight leaves in two hours. Being a holiday, I bet security will be a bitch."

"Yeah. Okay." She nodded, her voice thick. Linking hands and casting one last look over her shoulder, she let Elijah lead her back down the hill.

"You know," she said after a moment of comfortable silence, "I do actually feel better, but…" *It still hurts, to know I'll never get to know them.* She couldn't say it aloud and didn't know why. Maybe because she'd be admitting a weakness, and her past had schooled her it was dangerous to show weakness, even to those you loved.

Looks like Elijah isn't the only one with some emotional baggage to sort through, she thought wryly.

Elijah gave her a sympathetic look. "I know, baby. The hurt will fade over time, but it never truly leaves. You just learn to live with it."

Live with it. Something so simple, yet so hard to do.

But she was ready to. She was ready, at last, to move on.

CHAPTER THIRTY-ONE

ELIJAH'S THROAT TIGHTENED IN AN ATTEMPT TO KEEP him from spewing his guts all over Crescent Manor's immaculate marble steps. His toe caught the lip of a step, making him stumble forward.

Verika gripped his arm to keep him from kissing the marble. "You okay?"

"I blame the dress shoes. Not used to wearing them." At her disbelieving look, he reached up, loosened his tie a little. Damn thing was driving him nuts, like wearing a collar. A distant, haunting image drifted like a ghost through his mind's eye: him locked away in a dark cell, deep within the earth, away from sunshine and freedom, where the air tasted like urine and metal, and cold iron chafed the skin around his neck. But, thanks to weekly therapy sessions he'd grown strangely fond of, the memory didn't linger in his brain, didn't elicit the fear that had once ruled his life. No, for the first time in, well, forever, he was able to remember the past and not get sick from it.

He was free.

Well, almost. He was still a work in progress.

"No, I'm not okay," he admitted. "I feel like I'm thirteen again. Like I've been caught drinking my dad's beer and he's taking his belt off. Like something horrible is about to happen."

Verika gently took his hands in hers, turning him ever so slightly to face her head on. "Nothing bad is going to happen. Well, it's a werewolf Thanksgiving. Gage warned me when the pack gets together for holiday meals, it can be like World War III. But it won't be the whole pack. It will just be family."

World War III he could handle. Kind of already did, in a way, back in the woods when he'd torched the house. It had all been very cathartic, though the smell of charred flesh, of kindling, never left him. He dreamed about it. Thought about it, smelled smoke even in the middle of a perfume store. The therapist said that memory was burned into his mind due to the severity of the trauma it wreaked on him.

Like he said, he was a work in progress.

"But what if something bad does happen?" he asked in a low whisper. "What if I show up and things go to hell? What if I ruin Thanksgiving for everyone?"

Verika's eyes turned sympathetic. Her warm palm cupped his cheek, the silk of her thumb caressing the light stubble blanketing his jawline. "I know it's been a long time since you've celebrated a holiday with family. But there's nothing to be afraid of. Contrary to what you believe, your sheer presence doesn't bring on death and destruction. You're amazing, Elijah."

"I didn't mean it as a sympathy plea," he said with a wry smile. "Though you can keep up with the 'You're amazing, Elijah' stuff."

She rolled her eyes, tried suppressing a smile. "You're hopeless."

"At least some things never change." Nervous butterflies tickled his gut. He started pacing, which only made it worse. "God!" He stopped, ran his hand through his hair. Sweat had started to form on his brow. "I mean, I don't know, baby. Thanksgiving, Christmas, Easter. They weren't happy times at my house growing up. They were usually just another day for Dad to get drunk, for him to take out his anger and frustration on Mom if she burned dinner. Besides." He sighed and shook his head. "I'm not sure I want to face them."

"Face them, or face Nik?" Verika said quietly.

Damn it all, she was right. That's exactly what this was about, his unresolved tension with Nik. Nik hadn't spoken to him at the memorial, hadn't called or answered his emails or texts throughout this past long, hard year while they rebuilt their lives. Gage and he had started speaking again, at least a few times a week. But Nik…Nik had remained silent.

Elijah supposed he should count the fact Nik hadn't blocked his number as a blessing.

A soothing hand rubbed his back through his thick black wool coat. "You'll be fine. You're making this out to be a bigger deal than it is."

"It's a big deal to me."

Verika sighed, let her hand drop away. Her head hung. "I'm sorry, Elijah. I didn't mean it like that, to say it like it doesn't matter."

"I know you didn't, love." He took her hand, squeezed it, kissed the back of her knuckles. "God, your hand is freezing. We need to get you thicker gloves."

She smiled wistfully. "Maybe Santa will bring me some, along with a few other presents when he sweeps down the chimney." She lightly pinched his butt, making him burst into deep, hearty laughter.

"Sounds to me like I need to block the chimney. This Santa Claus character sounds kind of unscrupulous."

Her brows rose. "Look at you, using fancy words. His Royal Gage-ness is rubbing off on you, after all."

He snorted. "He wishes. Although he has started to sound more posh since becoming High King. Must be all the wealth going to his head."

"Jealous?"

"Nah. Wouldn't want the title, or the responsibility. Besides, real estate taxes on that castle must be a bitch. Not to mention the insurance."

"Tell me about it. I'm content with our little country home, far removed from the city. And its sky-high real estate."

"I'm with you there, love."

It still made him proud to say it aloud, made his chest puff out, his shoulders pull back, his chin raise an inch— all with a genuine smile on his face.

Holy shit, *he* owned a house. *He* had a respectable job as a security advisor to the DPI. *He* lived in the beautiful

Southern state of Florida, close to in-laws and a scant thirty minutes from the ocean. *He* was married to a beautiful woman, who was the most incredible person he knew. If someone had told him his life would be this perfect a year ago, he would have laughed.

Elijah the Fuck Up, get his act together? Bitch, please. Never in this lifetime. He was a damned soul, destined for an early grave.

But Lady Karma could suck it because he just showed that bitch up. He was done with the haters, with the people and thoughts who told him he'd never be good enough. Because he was, dammit. And he would show them—show the entire damn world, if he had to.

Newsflash, Universe—Elijah Johnson had turned over a new leaf.

And he was willing to fight every damn day for it.

He shook his head. "You're right. As usual."

"You can keep saying that, if you like."

"Look at you, being all cheeky and sexy as hell. I like it." He kissed his wife dearly, his mouth lingering over her lips. "And I plan on showing you just how much I like it when we get to the hotel." Not wanting to crowd Alara and Nik, Verika and Elijah had opted to stay at a Holiday Inn in the next town about thirty minutes away. Moonstruck had a motel, but it was questionable at best. Maybe if a horde of roaches, stale coffee, and stained sheets were your thing.

Really, the idea of "crowding" Alara and Nik in this mansion was laughable. But Verika had insisted. Elijah secretly knew why, though they'd never spoken of it. Neither of them knew how tonight would turn out. Elijah could very well be leaving here with blood on his burnt-orange, pressed button-down and slacks, but neither he nor Verika was willing to say it aloud. Doing so might jinx them.

He offered Verika his arm. "Shall we?"

She took it, smiling warmly. "We shall. Lead the way, Mr. Johnson."

"As you wish, Mrs. Johnson."

She leaned in to kiss him sweetly on the lips. "I'll never get tired of hearing that."

"And I'll never get tired of saying it."

They started to kiss again, when the door opened.

Nik stood there, stone-faced, unreadable. And…and was that a *tie* he had on? Verika searched her brain. She didn't think she'd ever seen him wear one before, didn't think he owned one among his wardrobe of greasy hoodies and beat-up T-shirts. She scanned the rest of him. Khakis, dress shoes, a button-down—she nearly gasped—and it was *tucked in with a belt to match his shoes*. She nearly fainted from shock. Probably would have had she not felt her husband's tension crackling through their mate-bond.

Her eyes snapped back up to Nik's face.

Both Verika and Elijah froze, like two horny teens who'd been caught making out on Mommy and Daddy's porch.

Nik stared at Elijah.

Elijah stared back.

Verika just held her breath and prayed this wasn't

about to turn into a fistfight.

Nik finally smirked, as if relishing the fact Elijah was about to shit a brick. He rolled his eyes in exaggeration. "Oh, come on. They're making out on the front steps. No wonder it was taking so long for them to come inside."

Gage appeared in the doorway behind his older brother. Dressed much the same as the other two brothers, only he didn't look nearly so out of place in the more formal attire. In his hand, he clutched a wine glass partly filled with white wine. "What the hell are y'all doing out there? Get your asses in here. Danica and Alara just about have dinner ready."

Verika clutched the pecan pie they'd picked up at a diner on the way in town, feeling suddenly insecure about her choice of dessert. It was a homemade pie and probably delicious. But Danica and Alara were both rich. Which was a stupid reason for thinking they'd be able to cook well solely because of their money, but it was the first thing to pop into her head. Should she have brought something fancier, something more sophisticated?

They're going to love it, Elijah said, as if reading her thoughts. *And if they don't, I'll sure as hell eat the shit out of that pie.*

Thanks, baby, she said with a warm smile.

Both of them took a deep breath as they ascended the rest of the steps and walked into the house. Warm air from the roaring fire in the parlor immediately blasted them. The fire and fall decorations—glittering leaves, glistening pumpkins, and Happy Thanksgiving signs—gave the manor a homier feel.

One of the butlers took their coats and scurried off out of view. Verika felt herself start to relax. Elijah, on the other hand, looked more wound up than ever standing in the presence of both his brothers. For the most part they seemed welcoming, affectionate even. Well, Gage was. He pulled Elijah into a hug soon as he stepped through the door.

Nik shook his hand in a grip that might have been a bit tighter than required. There was a hardness that lingered behind his eyes, a sense of distrust as he stared at his older brother. That didn't surprise Verika. She expected the distrust, knew it would take years to mend Nik's faith in his brother. She was just thankful no blood had been spilled.

Yet. The night was early.

She shifted her weight while the brothers chatted, looking around, not wanting to butt in.

Nik spotted her discomfort. "You can take the pie and put it in the dining room. They have a dessert table set up. Here, I'll show you." He pulled her away. She cast a smile over her shoulder at Elijah before disappearing around the corner.

The smells wafting out of the dining room were amazing, and her mouth immediately began to water. "Hmmm…smells divine."

"Tastes even better. I've been dipping a spoon or fork into every dish they bring in. You know, to make sure it's up to the Johnson quality standards."

Verika snorted. "You haven't changed one bit."

Nik's eyes softened. He seemed to have more wrinkles, now that she noticed, and several silver hairs streaked the dark brown. "I've changed a lot," he said quietly. "Some for the better…"

He didn't need to say the rest. "Yeah," she said. "I know what you mean." They'd all been changed since that night. A night when the moon had ridden high in the sky, gazing down at a field awash in blood and death.

She shivered, shook her head, and shoved the thought far away. Not tonight. This was not a night to dwell on darkness. It was a night to be thankful for what one had. And she had so much to be thankful for.

They dropped off the pie, nestled it between a tri-layer carrot cake, a chocolate cream pie with girlish chocolate curls on its frosting, and red velvet brownies with cream cheese icing. She couldn't wait, in particular, to dig into those.

Nik ushered her into the massive state-of-the-art kitchen, a culinary kingdom of gleaming black appliances, glittering orange- and dark-red-flecked quartz countertops, and shining black tile flooring. An assortment of messy cooking aids—wooden spoons, measuring cups, timers, brushes, and mixing bowls—sat along the countertops. It smelled amazing; the warm aromas of roasting turkey, green bean casserole, and apple pie mingled in the air and reminded Verika of her own holidays back at home. Her parents hadn't minded one bit that she was going to spend Thanksgiving away from home, considering she'd already promised they'd spend Christmas there. Her father still wasn't too happy about her marrying Elijah, but he was warming up to the idea. It was hard to stay mad at a man who'd risked everything to save his daughter's life.

Danica and Alara scampered about in a cooking frenzy, checking this and that, all dolled up, hair and makeup perfect, aprons on to protect their dresses of silk and taffeta. The aprons were black, with *I heart werewolves* sewn across the front in swirling cursive script.

Danica wore gold, which looked fantastic on her. Really set off the paler yellow of her hair, which had been swept up into a messy yet elegant updo at the nape of her neck. Diamonds sparkled at her ears, and a gold-and-silver bracelet glittered about her wrist. Though she'd given birth about six months ago, her belly still held a bit of baby weight. The generous silk of the A-line gown rippled like water as she moved. She looked beautiful and elegant. Her face looked rounder, her arms plumper.

Verika smiled. Secretly, she wished that would be her someday. Elijah and she had talked about kids, had both decided they wanted them. They had already started trying, though nothing had come of it yet.

Yet.

A secret, hopeful wish, one she would pray for tonight at dinner.

But she wasn't bitter or jealous. After all that had happened, after every trial and tribulation they'd endured, she was thankful for everyone around her. For the jewels in her life, for they were many.

Her heart swelled with gratitude.

Alara wore her hair down, though tied halfway back at the base of her neck. She wore rose-colored taffeta and sequins that stopped right above her knees, and silver, sparkly pumps. A bit flashier than Verika had seen the werewolf princess wear, but she still looked no less poised for it. She had the feeling Alara could wear a bath towel and make it look glamorous.

And despite that revelation, she didn't feel the teensiest bit jealous. It seemed petty to be. After one had faced down death, had stared its bottomless, empty pits down, not much else seemed to rival it in severity.

No dark thoughts tonight. Only joy.

Alara and Danica looked up as Nik went to the fridge to snag another beer. Verika didn't even ask why he wasn't drinking wine, knew he preferred beer over "those fancy-smancy drinks" any day. She also had enough sense not to say that knowledge aloud lest it be too intimate an admission. Despite their relationship feeling less strained, Alara might not take too kindly to Verika saying something like that. It could be viewed as waving a neon flag in front of the other wolf's face, like shouting, "Hey, I used to be in a relationship with your mate, and we were close." And Verika had no desire to trigger Alara's innate territorial instincts.

Yeah, she'd better keep her mouth shut on that one.

Alara swatted Nik's bottom as he popped the cap and took a swig of his fresh beer. "Don't chug too much of that stuff. You're going to be full before we've even started dinner."

"Me, full? Do you remember you're married to a walking, breathing garbage disposal?" He grinned and kissed her.

Alara's eyes shimmered as she smiled back. "You're the sexiest garbage disposal I've ever seen."

"Speaking of sexy," Danica turned her gaze on Verika and smiled broadly, "that dress looks amazing on you! Really brings out your hair color!"

Verika's dress was crushed forest-green velvet that sat right at her knees. The stretchy material hugged her curvy body, the long sleeves coating her arms, and the V-neckline just low enough to be sexy but not trashy. She'd worn a black lace bra that doubled as a camisole, peeking above the dip of the neckline where the medallion her mother gave her rested. Black velvet pumps, black stockings, and simple black earrings completed the ensemble. She'd even taken the time to apply dark-red lipstick and smoky eye shadow. Her long hair was just as polished, with long loose curls dripping over her shoulders, her back. She looked pretty damn good, she had to admit. And the entire ensemble had cost her only fifty bucks, thanks to catching some pre–Black Friday sales and the right combination of coupons.

Verika blushed faintly. "Thank you."

Danica scurried over in her gold kitten heels and wrapped Verika up in a warm hug. It was hard to remember she was one of the most powerful women, politically speaking, in the Underworld because she was so...well, human. "You're welcome! I am *so* glad you could make it. Hope the airport wasn't too much of a nightmare."

"Thank you. It actually wasn't too bad. We didn't have a layover, and security ran things pretty smoothly in Florida. They even had our luggage ready to go soon as we got to the luggage belt in Little Rock, so all in all it was a surprisingly smooth trip considering what time of year it is."

"That is a smooth trip." Alara came over and hugged Verika, though not quite as tightly as Danica had. Verika suspected that was mostly because Alara was a more reserved person, or perhaps she wasn't the hugging type. "I'm envious. A black cloud seems to follow me around whenever I set foot inside an airport. You do look beautiful, by the way."

Verika didn't sense any hostility or bitterness in the other woman's voice, and her eyes lit up with her smile. Verika smiled back. "Thank you. So do both of you. How's the baby?"

"Spoiled rotten," Danica said. "I was actually just about to grab him. Come on. I'll introduce you." She peeled off the apron and tossed it on a dinette table. "You okay without me?" she asked Alara.

Alara waved a hand. "Yeah, dinner's pretty much done. I just need to candy the yams, butter the rolls, then we'll be ready. If I need any help, I'll draft Chef Nikolas."

"I'll butter your roll," he growled, pinching Alara's butt.

She yelped and swatted him on the arm with a spatula. "Do you ever behave?"

"Now where's the fun in that?"

Danica rolled her eyes and grinned as she turned back to Verika. "Let's get out of here before they decide to heat up the kitchen in more ways than one."

Danica led her away, down a hallway with more extravagant furnishings, things that probably cost as much as Verika made at her personal-assistant day job back in

Florida.

"How are things going with the new job?" Danica asked. "Working for the Hexes must feel like a dream."

It was, in many ways. It was certainly a position many a witch and warlock coveted. As thanks for her service to the Underworld in stopping Mistress Black, Sebastian Hex had aided Gage in convincing the High Council to pardon her crimes in aiding and abetting a known criminal (now, ironically, her husband) and as a reward had given her a job in the new company Hex Inc., which had opened up in the Southeast. It was about a half-hour commute from their little countryside home, but Verika didn't mind. Truly, she was thankful to be able to walk freely in a city without fear of someone recognizing her and turning her in to the DPI. The newfound freedom was intoxicating.

Was it her dream job? Yes and no. She got to work with magic every day. Despite being a glorified secretary to Sebastian Hex, she got to learn from him. He'd picked up on the fact she was a quick study and a talented and resourceful witch, and as such had taken to teaching her about business and magic whenever he could. Though she was intimidated by such a powerful family name at first, she'd grown to think of Sebastian as more of an older-brother figure. Warm, patient, and protective.

"I've learned a lot from Mr. Hex," she said carefully, "though I would love to someday open and run my own magic shop. Maybe even make it online only, and pay a warehouse to keep my potions and ship them when orders come in. That way I could work from home."

"Oh, that sounds amazing! I bet you'd be really good

at it too. You're so smart. Do you know what you'd call it, your business?"

Verika smiled wistfully. "Satine's."

Danica gave her a sympathetic smile and a gentle squeeze of the hand. "I think it sounds lovely. You'll do it someday. Just keep dreaming, keep praying, keep wishing. If you never give up, your dreams will come true."

"Thanks, Danica," Verika said quietly, her eyes growing hot.

Danica smiled and nodded. "Ah, we're here. We had to make an impromptu nursery, since none of the Moonstruck Pack members have pups young enough to appreciate a play room."

Verika felt incredibly awkward for asking the next question. Maybe it wasn't her place, but she was curious. "Are...Nik and Alara still trying?"

Danica sighed, crossed her arms outside a pretty baby-blue door. A baby's coos could be heard on the other side. "They are. They're not giving up hope for a baby of their own, though even with fertility treatments, the doctor thinks their chances of conceiving are slim to none."

"That's too bad." She knew Nik wanted kids, had really been looking forward to it. He'd never admitted it to anyone else when she'd dated him, though he'd confessed it to her deep in the night, when they lay tangled in each other's arms after fabulous—

Okay, that was definitely something she didn't need to be thinking about. The idea of having sex with anyone else but her husband made her cringe.

"They're sure Nik's the one who's infertile?" Verika

asked in a whisper.

Danica glanced around, leaned closer. "Positive. There's nothing wrong with Alara, so far as they can tell."

"A talented Blue Witch or Warlock should be able to repair that."

"Except Nik refuses all magical treatment. Something about not wanting magic to mess with his body again."

"Again?"

Danica's eyes widened a fraction, as if she had spouted off something she wasn't supposed to. "He's…been going to a therapist."

"Why?"

"For trauma. You know, when he died?"

Ah. That made more sense. She'd never known Nik to be afraid of magic, but perhaps he was now after Alara, being possessed by the doppelganger, had sacrificed him in an attempt to stop Mistress Black. Verika had been able to bring him back from the grave, but that didn't mean it hadn't left a mark on his psyche. He was so stubborn, so good at wearing masks and showing the world what he wanted it to see, that it had completely slipped her mind he might be suffering on the inside as well.

She felt sorry for him. "I can give him the name of the therapist Elijah has been working with. Eli's come a long way."

"Actually, I think Nik might not take it very well if he finds out we've been discussing his personal life. He'll fig-ure out a way to deal with it. I think part of the reason he hasn't is because he's still in denial that he's afraid. He's afraid it will make him seem like a weak Alpha."

"As if. Reckless maybe. And impulsive. But never weak."

"My thoughts exactly. Look, please don't say anything, even to Elijah. I don't want word getting around I've been blabbing about him behind his back. I just don't need the drama right now, not with taking care of my son."

"Understood."

Danica smiled, took a deep breath, let it out. "Good. Now that that's out in the open, ready to meet my baby boy?"

The dinner was perfect. Absolutely perfect.

Elijah still couldn't believe the direction his life had taken. Couldn't believe he was sitting around a table with his brothers and their mates, that the love of his life sat beside him. The smell of apple pie and all manner of sugary confections hung in the air as they dug into dessert. Elijah was so stuffed he thought he didn't have any room left for pie or cake. Then someone had plopped a slab of carrot cake, his absolute favorite, in front of him, and that's all the convincing it had taken.

Oh, how very lucky he was.

The baby, Max, giggled as Danica, clutching him with one hand, swirled a tiny spoon crowned in sweet potatoes through the air while making airplane noises. She popped the spoon into the pup's smiling mouth, kissed his forehead while he happily munched.

As if sensing him watching, the pup's eyes—green as a spring day—landed on him, and he grinned. Elijah couldn't help but to smile back. Those bright eyes were so full of joy and innocence, so untouched by the darkness of the world, that it struck him with wonder.

Verika slightly nudged him with her elbow, and cocked her head in an inquiring look. "Everything okay?"

He smiled softly, his gaze lingering on the pup. "Yeah," he murmured wistfully. "Everything's good."

After dinner, everyone helped clean up, men included. More wine and treats were passed around, and Elijah could honestly say it was the lightest he'd felt in a while. Nik had spoken to him some, though not as much as Gage. Even Alara, despite everything that had passed between them, had treated him with nothing but warmth and kindness. Given how he'd expected to be treated pretty much like a leper, he was ecstatic things were going this well.

Until Gage had the brilliant idea of inviting Elijah out "for a smoke" on the main balcony.

Naively, he walked outside with Gage, wineglass in hand while Gage carted out a box of cigars that probably cost more than Elijah made in a month. Gage set the box down on the wide marble railing and frowned. "Hang on, I forgot something. Be right back."

Elijah gazed out over the view of the darkened forest below, watched the tips of the distant oaks and pines sway in the cool breeze coming out of the north. Soon, there would be snow capping those tall points.

His expression turned somber. Winter always brought with it a sense of inner coldness, an acute prickling of regret, after he became a man. It had taken the fancy-smancy therapist, courtesy of Visa and MasterCard, to figure out why.

It had been snowing when he'd left home. When he'd turned his back on his family. The snow, the cold…they were "triggers," his shrink had called them.

Triggers was a soft term for the depression spiral the biting cold and glittering snowflakes plunged Elijah into every winter.

He shook his head. No more regrets, his therapist said. He couldn't change the past. All he could do was forgive, forget, and forge forward.

Don't delay progress.

The balcony door clicked open, and someone inhaled sharply.

Elijah turned—and froze.

There stood Nik again, one hand still frozen on the door handle as if undecided whether or not he wanted to come outside.

Elijah's heart pounded, nerves tickling his stomach. He could hear Nik's heart rate, racing along as fast as his own. He realized Gage's trick, that he had planned this all along, and silently cursed him.

Too late to back out now. Don't be a pussy.

"Hey," Elijah said gruffly, clearing his throat as his voice rasped from the cold-air exposure. He hated winter for more reasons than one. It also tended to bring on sinus infections.

Nik surveyed him for a long moment before at last closing the door and joining Elijah on the balcony. He stood a good three feet away, not looking at him as he leaned forward and placed his elbows on the railing. He gazed out at the sleeping forest, the sound of scraping branches and the light whistle of the wind the only sounds to be heard for what seemed like hours.

Well, this was awkward. Elijah ran his hand through his hair, fidgeted. Should he say something? Would it drive Nik away if he did? Should he wait until Nik was ready?

"What took you so long?"

Elijah blinked, snapped his gaze around. "What?"

Nik turned his body so he faced Elijah head on, a stern look of disapproval on his face. "I'm asking, why you just now coming around?"

Elijah stared. Was this a trick question? "I—uh—wait, what? What are you talking about?"

Nik rolled his eyes, looked away. That scowl was back. "You sent emails and texts. But you never called me."

"I thought it might be too much too soon. I thought I'd ease into things with texts and emails first. I didn't know you wanted me to call."

"Of course I wanted you to," Nik said tiredly after a moment. "I'm stubborn, and an asshole sometimes. All right, most of the time. But…" He growled a sigh and a curse. "Dammit, man, you're still my big brother, and I still missed the hell out of you."

Elijah's heart swelled, and he nearly took flight right off the balcony he was so overcome by hope. "You mean it?"

"Hell yeah, I mean it. Wouldn't be spouting off all this mushy bullshit if I didn't."

Elijah was so flabbergasted, he couldn't string together a coherent sentence. "I…wow. Wow."

Nik smiled wryly, one corner of his mouth lifting up. "Yeah. That about sums it up."

"So…do you want to, uh, what, hang out sometime?"

Nik snorted. "Nah, we're not in grade school, man. But we can grab a beer sometime and catch up." His gaze sobered. "I'm ready to listen now."

Elijah stopped breathing. He'd been praying for this, had been wishing every night since he left that his brothers would someday find it in their hearts to forgive him.

Elijah started to spread his arms, to approach his brother for a hug. Nik immediately tensed, and Elijah stopped. "Too much too soon?"

"Yeeeeeaaaaaaaaahhhhh."

"Noted."

Nik didn't linger long after. After giving Elijah what was probably the most awkward brotherly slap-on-the-shoulder in the history of the world, he went back inside. Verika pattered out a short while later, a freshly opened bottle of chilled merlot in her hand.

"Figured you could use this." She filled his glass halfway.

He smiled wryly. "Thanks." The cold wine tasted bittersweet going down.

Setting the bottle down on the floor, she wrapped her long arms around his waist. He draped an arm over her back, relishing the warmth her presence brought him.

"Everything go well?" she murmured against his chest.

He rested his head against hers, staring up at the

night sky. The moon was partly obscured by a smattering of clouds. The wind shifted them slowly, drawing out the pale, silvery light.

Elijah smiled. "Yeah. It did, actually. Surprisingly so."

"That's good to hear."

In a flurry of words, Elijah went over what Nik and he had talked about. "And he wants me to call him sometime so we can go for beers," he finished.

Verika chuckled. "Someone sounds happy."

"Yeah. Yeah, I really am, Vee."

She hugged him tighter. "I'm glad, because that makes two of us."

The two of them held each other in thoughtful silence. It was the lightest Elijah had felt in years, maybe since his early childhood, when the world was still fresh and wondrous.

Nik and Elijah's relationship still wasn't there yet, but he was hopeful it would be someday, if he didn't give up and kept working at it. Which made him deliriously happy. For the first time in a long while, he had hope.

For a better tomorrow. For a better future.

And, with his mate in his arms, for a better forever.

THE END

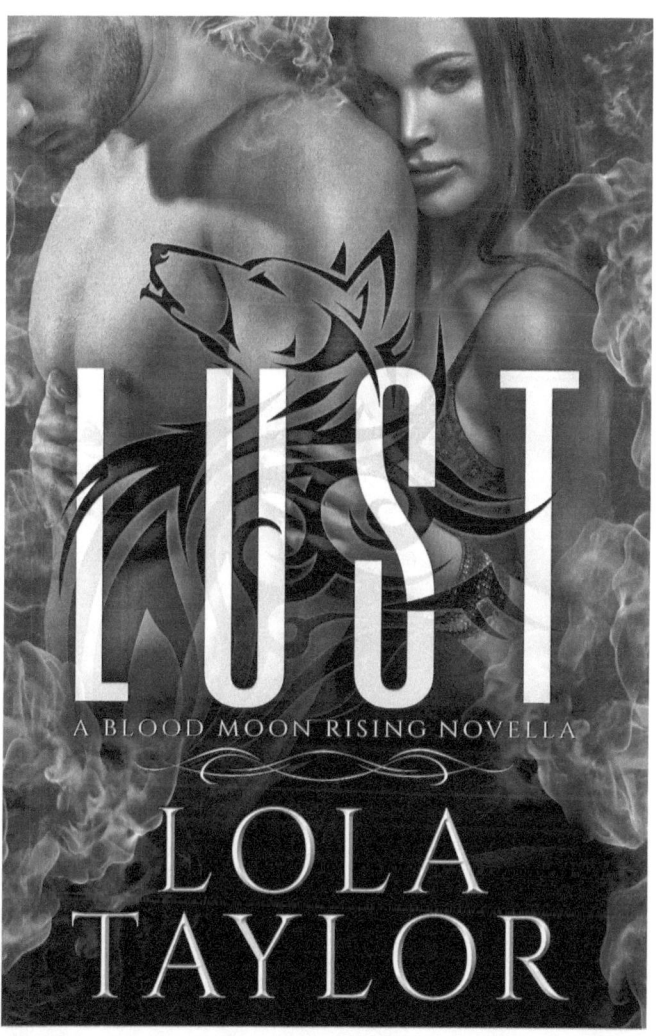

LUST

A BLOOD MOON RISING NOVELLA

LOLA TAYLOR

Looking for your next hot read? Try *Lust*, now available.

OTHER BOOKS BY
LOLA TAYLOR

The Her Dark Desires Trilogy
Carnal (free for a limited time!)
Sinful
Soulful (coming soon!)

Blood Moon Rising
Fever (free for a limited time!)
Protector
Betrayal
Captured
Sacrifice
Ritual

Blood Moon Rising companion novels
Lust
Forever (coming soon!)

Standalone novels
Shatter

For a full list of titles, please visit
www.lolataylorbooks.com.

For more information, please visit
www.lolataylorbooks.com

Your opinion matters—please leave a review!

Thank you for reading my book! If you have a moment, I'd really appreciate an honest rating and review. They help authors stand out in a busy marketplace, plus they give browsing readers the nitty-gritty on books they're shopping. Everyone wins when you rate and review, so please do! Your opinion counts!

ABOUT THE AUTHOR

"Lola Taylor" is a pen name created for the romances I can't show my grandma without blushing. My favorite genre to write is romantic suspense, usually involving hot werewolves, warlocks, or any other type of paranormal creature. Keep the action hot and the romance hotter— that's my motto! I'm a horror film junkie, I still love Halloween as an adult (seriously, I think I get more excited for it than some kids do), and what precious spare time I have is spent with my family, reading (everything from sci fi to middle grade), playing the flute, painting pretty pictures, or screwing around on Pinterest or Etsy. Hailing from the South, I currently live in the Midwest with five fur babies and my hubby.

You can connect with me on Facebook (www.facebook.com/lolataylorbooks) or my email (lolawritespnr@gmail.com). Learn more about me and my books at www.lolataylorbooks.com.

www.ingramcontent.com/pod-product-compliance
Lightning Source LLC
Chambersburg PA
CBHW020238200626
46816CB00001BA/28